PRAISE FOR GR ||||||||| T0059113

THE LAST THING SHE EVER DID

"Gregg Olsen pens brilliant, creepy, page-turning, heart-pounding novels of suspense that always keep me up at night. In *The Last Thing She Ever Did*, he topped himself."

—Allison Brennan, *New York Times* bestselling author

"Beguiling, wicked, and taut with suspense and paranoia, *The Last Thing She Ever Did* delivers scenes as devastating as any I've ever read with a startling, pitch-perfect finale. A reminder that evil may reside in one's actions, but tragedy often spawns from one's inaction."

—Eric Rickstad, *New York Times* bestselling author of *The Silent Girls*

"Olsen's latest examines how a terrible, split-second decision has lingering effects, and the past echoes the present. Full of unexpected twists, *The Last Thing She Ever Did* will keep you guessing to the last line."

—J. T. Ellison, *New York Times* bestselling author of *Lie to Me*

"Master storyteller Gregg Olsen continues to take readers hostage with another spellbinding tale of relentless, pulse-pounding suspense."

—Rick Mofina, international bestselling author of *Last Seen*

"Tense. Well-crafted. Gripping."

—Mary Burton, *New York Times* bestselling author

"With *The Last Thing She Ever Did*, Gregg Olsen delivers an edgy, tension-filled, roller-coaster ride of a novel that will thrill and devastate in equal measure."

—Linda Castillo, *New York Times* bestselling author

THE
WEIGHT
OF
SILENCE

THE WEIGHT OF SILENCE

A NICOLE FOSTER THRILLER

GREGG OLSEN

THOMAS & MERCER

Text copyright © 2018 by Gregg Olsen
All rights reserved.

Published by Thomas & Mercer, Seattle

www.apub.com

Amazon, the Amazon logo, and Thomas & Mercer are trademarks of Amazon.com, Inc., or its affiliates.

ISBN-13: 9781503901353
ISBN-10: 1503901351

Cover design by Damon Freeman

Printed in the United States of America

For Lindsay Jackman, who proves every single day that
her superpower is her smile

PROLOGUE

We are the bats.

We hang upside down like the undulating colony of flying rodents we observed as kids when our parents took us to Carlsbad Caverns. It was the summer the year before our mom left us for Hollywood. Stacy and I wore Hypercolor T-shirts that turned from pink to purple with the heat of the New Mexican day.

That was a long time ago. A lifetime ago. And yet a happy memory crosses my mind in the space of a tragedy. Or something even darker.

Right now my sister's blouse is no longer white but red. I twist as much as possible, suspended by the shoulder harness of my seat belt. I can't see Stacy's face. I can't really hear her. My breathing is shallow, and I feel every rib as my battered chest contracts. It is the only thing I can feel. My legs are immobile, and a spike of fear goes through my numbness: *Am I paralyzed? Am I dead?* The car's engine grinds as it struggles to keep running, though I know the wheels are spinning in the night air that now hangs over our feet. I manage to turn off the engine, and as it finally dies, I hear the Pacific Ocean striking the coastline like a mallet somewhere below where my Accord skidded to a stop.

"Stacy?" I ask.

No response.

"Are you all right?"

Again no answer.

I still can't see her, but something tells me that she's alive. The space is small, compacted by the crash, and I can feel my little sister's presence. Stacy has an aura that is thick and impenetrable, a force field that neither I nor anyone who knows her can deny. Some call it charisma. What Stacy has, I think, is more like the disposition of a vicious pet. It would come at you, sometimes unexpectedly, when she wanted to turn it on. It filled the room and forced out all the air. No one could be a match for that. As this goes through my mind, I think of my mother and how she wanted to be a star. How she'd ladled the love on her favorite daughter, only to turn on her later in life. Mom was jealous of Stacy. Stacy had that thing that celebrities, CEOs, and politicians have. It's an intrinsic power that can never be manufactured. It just is.

"Stacy," I repeat. "We'll get out of this. Hold on. It will be okay."

Even in that flash, I know that I've offered comfort to the devil. And yet I cannot help myself. No matter what Stacy is or what she's done, I love her. She's a virus. A disease. I've prayed to God all of my adult life that I'd be able to push aside our frayed but tragically elastic bond and just say goodbye to her once and for all. I'd never see her again. I'd lie to myself that there were more good times with her than bad and that I missed her every single day. In time, I might even be able to believe my own deceits. I could tell her daughter that she was a wonderful sister and mother. Emma would live the rest of her life thinking that Stacy Sonntag Chase was as beautiful on the inside as she had been on the outside. Not a hideous orange cream from the second layer of a Whitman's Sampler but a silky chocolate truffle from Godiva.

I have to get out of here. Emma needs me. My dad needs me. Carter will miss me.

I push against the ceiling with a bloody hand. It's littered with glass, rhinestones come to mind for some reason. I feel my feet, and a sigh of relief pours over me. I am not paralyzed. My legs could be broken, but I am not going to end up in a wheelchair. I amend my thoughts. I am going to live. I'm going to get both of us out of here.

"Stacy?" I ask again. My voice is froggy, and saying her name hurts. "Damn it, Stacy, you need to answer me!"

Finally her Staciness comes at me. I feel her presence. A gasp comes forth, then her favorite and most meaningless phrase. "I'm sorry, Nicole. I'm really sorry. I am. You have to believe me."

She's such a liar.

"I know," I say. "I know."

My breathing halts as I see her. She's battered from the accident. The skin on her face is lacerated to such a degree that I cannot mask my own horror.

"It's bad," she tells me, looking over with those beautiful eyes of hers.

Her eyes are red, white, and blue. *Patriotic,* I think. *Go USA! America the beautiful.*

"It will be all right," I say.

She touches her cheek, and a rivulet of blood winds down her arm. She gasps again. I'm not sure if it's because of the blood or the realization that she's never going to be the same. No surgeon will be able to fix what's become of her undeniable perfection. Her beauty has been eclipsed by a rollover accident.

"I'm going to be all right," she tells me. It's a hope. A prayer.

"You will be fine," I tell her.

My free hand finds my seat belt, and I undo the buckle, and suddenly I'm on the ceiling, bunched up like a bloody spitball. I can't remember if the driver's-side window was rolled down before the crash or if it is the source of some of the rhinestones. It's gone. As I slither out of my car, I feel every inch of my body. Every nerve is on fire. I think I'm crying, but I'm not sure about that. Glass falls out of my hair, and blood rains down everywhere. My blood. My red.

My sister is calling out. She's telling me to get her out. I right myself on the gravel of the narrow shoulder of the highway. A warm wind blows over me, but it's a silent breeze. All around me spruce and fir trees cower from the often-turbulent Pacific. *So peaceful now,* I think. I stand above the wreckage and look over the ocean. Off in the distance is a ship loaded with containers carrying cars, TVs, clothing from Asia. It's a wall across the vast horizon, spotlighted by the moon.

Stacy and I have a wall between us too. It's my car. She's on the other side. She's crying and begging for me to come.

I just stay still, frozen.

THIRTEEN DAYS EARLIER

CHAPTER ONE

Tuesday, August 15

It's a little after 4:00 p.m. on the hottest day of the summer—in striking distance of triple digits. A Subaru Forester stops hard in the parking lot adjacent to the Starbucks. The driver, a young man in his twenties, gets out, yanks at the rear passenger door handle, and swings it open with an abruptness that nearly unhinges the door from the midsize SUV's frame.

He struggles to pull a baby from a rear-facing car seat and yells so loudly that a woman coming out of the coffee store drops her Frappuccino. The cold and creamy drink splashes upward and covers her bare legs. She lets out a scream.

"What have I done?" the man calls out, lowering himself to the sticky-hot asphalt.

The woman, heading home after her shift at the Wendy's next door, forgets her drink disaster and runs over to the Subaru.

"Oh my God!" she says. "Call 911!"

"What have I done?" he yells again as he bends over the child.

The woman, Jordan Conway, asks the man if he knows CPR.

He shakes his head.

She's rattled, but she pushes him aside and unbuckles the child from the car seat. The little girl is wearing pink shorts and a white top with the appliqué of an elephant. On her feet are tiny white saltwater sandals. But she is still, her skin pallid, with areas of blue and pink. Her blue eyes are fixed.

Jordan took CPR for her job at her father's Wendy's but never used it on anyone but a practice dummy. The certificate she earned was tucked inside a memory album that she planned on assembling one day. As she hovers over the baby, she recalls how she'd been taught to blow into both the nose and mouth of an infant.

That afternoon, when duty calls, Jordan leans in and gasps. She is nearly overcome by the stench coming from inside the car. It is an odor she's never smelled in her life.

It is the hottest day of the year. In minutes the Frappuccino she dropped transforms itself from liquid to sticky goo.

"Save her!" the man yells as a growing circle of onlookers converges around the car. "This is fucking all my fault!"

Seconds later, the sound of sirens cuts through the drama, and the crowd parts. Jordan, feeling a combination of nausea, fear, and an emotion she can't pinpoint, gives up. Tears flooding her eyes, she steps aside so paramedics can save the little girl.

"I forgot she was in the car," the man says. "I fucking forgot. Now look what I've done. I've lost her. Goddammit!"

More sirens scream. More people arrive at the scene, the saddest Jordan Conway and the others gathered there have ever witnessed.

Chapter Two

Tuesday, August 15

My father's eyes are blue like my sister's. I know that he can hear every word I say, but it is late in the afternoon, and lucidity fades with the heat and duration of the day. He sits in a wheelchair facing the window that looks out over a courtyard planted with wilted red and yellow roses, a gift from a woman's family after she passed. Next to him are two men playing checkers without the benefit of a game board. Just plastic disks that they move around without any real rhyme or reason.

"Are you hungry, Dad?" I ask.

He doesn't respond.

I put my hand on his shoulder, feeling knobs of bone under his paper skin.

"Supper smells good," I say, though it is a lie. Nothing at Ocean View really smells good. That's not to say that it isn't clean. It is. The staff appears to care, though I cannot be sure if their alertness and regard for my father and the other patients is the result of compassion or excellent corporate training.

It is probably worth what we pay to ensure that he's in a better place than Medicaid would put him. It crosses my mind just then that my dad may outlive my resources. Alzheimer's is not only the cruelest of diseases; it is also one that lingers longest after its diagnosis. It steals the memories of those afflicted while creating hideous, painful, and depressive new ones for those left out of the fog.

"You're a good girl, Stacy," he says, finally looking at me with those storm cloud–blue eyes of his.

"I'm Nicole," I say.

I'm the good one, I think. *Stacy's not only a bitch, but she's worse than you can imagine.*

If you could imagine.

"You always were my favorite," he says.

I give up. We've done this a thousand times. I want to remind him that I'm the one who brought him to Ocean View. I'm the one who stops in on my way home whenever I'm not in the midst of a homicide investigation. I'm the one who tells the staff that the errant whiskers on his Adam's apple would drive my father to drink. If he noticed them, that is.

Which he doesn't.

I do.

Dad stirs a little. He's wearing gray sweatpants and a clean white T-shirt. I made a face when I saw him that morning. I want my father dressed as though he's still living a life. I don't want to see him looking as if he's ready for bed every beat of the day.

Even when I know he is.

"Dad," I say, "I'm going to take you to the bistro now." I'm using the euphuism that Ocean View employees use, the vernacular of the upscale. Rooms are called *suites.* The dayroom is called the *lounge.* The cafeteria is the *bistro.* The clientele that fall for the naming convention are those like my father. The more alert and with-it residents—those who might have physical challenges and not mental ones—recognize that it's merely a marketing technique. Most of those live in the north wing and dread the day that, like my dad, they are required to move south.

One of his feet has slipped from the stirrups of his wheelchair, and I kneel down to put it back. His nails are yellow and cracked, and his feet are a road map of broken blood vessels and capillaries that have exploded under his tissue-thin skin. I feel his knotted hand roll over the top of my head. It's a gentle swipe. I know it's meant in recognition for my help, not to shoo me away.

"You're a good girl, Stacy," he says once more. His hand drops, and I set it in his lap. When I was a girl, I wanted nothing more than to have my father think of me as his favorite. I wanted nothing more than his love, his approval. When our mother left us, it was me who did everything I could think of to hold us together. I cleaned the house. Mowed the lawn. I threw away the empty gin bottles by his bedside without even saying that I'd found them. When Stacy needed something for school, a hobby, or even a date, I was the one who made sure she had it. Layaway at the Aberdeen Penney's and a part-time job at Burger King after school fueled my sense of duty. I did all of it with an open heart too. Seriously. I just knew that my sister and my dad needed me—more than I needed anything for myself. The funny thing I learned about giving is that sometimes the more you give, the more recipients demand. It's like carbo-loading for a marathon. You eat for a purpose, but you find that you want it even more after the race is over.

I take in a deep breath and then slowly exhale.

"I love you too, Dad."

His eyes flicker.

As I push his chair toward the hallway to the bistro, I wonder if, by doing the right thing, I've done something very wrong.

I need a moment to decompress every time I see my father. It isn't just him, and I know it. It's everything. Me. My sister. My niece, Emma. It's everything that brought me back to Hoquiam, an often-dismal mill town on the edge of the Pacific. I can't think of a worse place to call home. And yet, sometimes I can't think of a better one. It's the town that made me who I am. For what it's worth, Hoquiam taught me that only with hard work and extreme fortitude could one escape the road map created by where they are born, whom they are born to.

I've boomeranged for sure. At least I'd gotten out and lived in the world. I tell myself that when I see the faces of the women and men I knew when we were young. Danielle works at the Stop 'n' Go. She'd been a cheerleader. Her boyfriend, Ricky, was captain of the football team and now works as a maintenance man for a resort development up the coast near Moclips. Many of those who stayed in my town look older than their years. A few proved that there was something better beyond the Hoquiam, Wishkah, and Chehalis Rivers that wriggle through my hometown and Aberdeen, the town next door. Some now live in the same houses their parents had owned.

Like me.

High-paying mill jobs have evaporated as technology has replaced workers and resources have dwindled. Cashiering is an inescapable and soul-crushing fallback for some. A few have turned to drugs. Even more have just given up. I can never give up. I have my seven-year-old niece, Emma, to think about. I have a job to do.

My silver Honda Accord's AC pours over me, a river of cool. I sit in the parking lot of Ocean View and lament that there is no view of the ocean there. Not by a long shot. Maybe from the roof someone could see the vast horizon over the Pacific, but that person would require a telescope and a very clear day.

My phone buzzes.

It's my partner at the Aberdeen Police Department, Carter Hanson.

"Still with your dad?" he says, his husky voice filling my ear.

"No, leaving now."

"Got a situation at the mall. Can you meet me there?"

"I'm five minutes away," I say. "What's going on?"

"Unresponsive kid. Left in the car."

My heart drops. "Oh, no. Not on a day like today."

"Not on any day," he says. "But, yeah, this heat wave is no joke."

"Where at the mall?"

"By the Starbucks."

"All right," I say, putting the car into gear and starting across the parking lot to the exit. "Be there in a few."

The last ten days have been sticky, egg-on-asphalt searing. Grays Harbor County hasn't seen temperatures in the mid- to upper nineties like that for more than a decade. The marine layer shrouding the area most of the season keeps late-summer temperatures in the eighties on the warmest of days. But in the week approaching the Grays Harbor County Kite Festival, the mercury has risen to the unbearable. Most residents in Hoquiam and Aberdeen don't have AC in their homes, so they sleep on sheets with fans blowing and windows open. The *Daily World* and the local radio have admonished locals to stay hydrated, to make sure their pets have water. No one has reminded anyone that leaving children in a hot car is not only dangerous but also illegal.

I think of Carter as I drive to the scene. I trust him. He trusts me. I know he's one of the good ones and has been through a lot. He is the divorced father of three. His ex-wife and children live in Kent, Washington, where she is a schoolteacher. Carter is a big guy with an even bigger heart. We met at the police academy when I was a new officer and he was back for training. After my fall—plummet, really—from grace, it was Carter who helped me get back into police work. He convinced his captain that I was worth a second chance.

I know it couldn't have been easy. I was on the periphery of a police scandal in Bellevue brought on by bad choices in men and a gambling addiction. Both are under control.

I'd vowed that I'd never date again. I'd never gamble.

In a way, both things were the same.

Carter didn't push. I know that he wanted more, but over time we developed a close personal relationship, an even stronger work dynamic. Not that he didn't try to ask me out. Which is all kinds of wrong, considering my record in the relationship department.

One time, not long after I was hired on, he suggested a dinner date.

"Carter, I owe you everything right now," I said. "Emma does too. You've given me a chance to do what I'm good at—and what I'm compelled to do. I can't mess that up again."

My tone was final, and I could see the disappointment in his eyes.

"Not everyone is a bad choice, Nic," he said.

"You're right," I answered. "But my experience tells me that when I'm doing the picking, the chances are that something terrible will happen. I'm a good judge of some things. Clueless about matters of the heart."

He left it there, and when he did, I knew that he wouldn't have been a wrong pick. If I could pick, that is.

◆ ◆ ◆

The parking lot of the Wishkah Mall is packed. Out-of-towners circle in shiny late-model cars for an empty spot near the entrance. It is easy to spot them. Their cars are newer, rust free, and packed to the gills with beach supplies. Flip-flops stick to the freshly tarred surface of the asphalt as people hurry for air-conditioning and the beer, burgers, and snack chips that will ensure their Kite Festival adventure will be Instagram and Facebook perfect.

I ease my Accord toward the Starbucks. An aid car and two patrol cars strobe the area with competing blue and red lights. I park next to Carter and get out. Over by what appears to be the victim's car, a red Subaru Forester, stand my partner and a young man. The man, I assume, is the child's father. He wears dark slacks, a white long-sleeved shirt, and lace-up shoes. His sandy hair is straight and appears to be recently cut. He has no facial hair. While he is young, his less-than-ideal posture reveals a slight potbelly. Silver wire-frame glasses with clip-on shades perch on his stub of a nose. He shifts his weight from foot to foot.

Spinning. Rocking. Barely staying on balance.

A woman clutching her sack of groceries stands next to one of the responding officers. Tears track through her makeup. A younger woman is talking with another officer. She's wearing a uniform from Wendy's.

Carter nods at me as I approach. He leans in.

"Girl DOA at the hospital."

"Oh, no," I say. "How old?"

"One," he says.

"Baby," I say, scanning the crowd that's traded the cool of their cars or the stores to watch something that will fill conversations over the next few hours as people judge and lament what happened.

"Says he forgot he had the girl in the car."

I don't say it. I think it. Carter says it, leaning into my ear. "Who forgets a kid in the backseat?"

He turns to the young man, whom he's identified as Luke Tomlinson. "This is Detective Foster," he says. "She's here to help with the investigation."

"It was an accident," Luke says right away. "Oh my God. Someone has to get my wife. She's at work."

I notice he's holding his phone.

"Have you tried to reach her?" I ask.

Luke looks around at the crowd, his eyes landing on the young woman from Wendy's for a second.

"Yeah," he says. "But she works at the hospital. She can't have her phone with her except at break time. She needs to know that something happened to Ally."

"Ally's your little girl?" I ask.

Luke wipes away sweat from his forehead with the back of his hand. His white shirt is soaked, and the outline of a full-sleeve tattoo ghosts a shadow through the fabric.

"I'm very sorry about your daughter," I say.

Luke doesn't respond. He just looks around, his eyes ping-ponging from the crowd to his car and back at Carter and me.

"Are you all right?" Carter asks.

Luke snaps. "No! My fucking kid just died."

I glance at Carter. Temperature and tragedy have converged. "We need to take this inside. Can't have a heatstroke victim out here."

Carter nods. "Let's go down to the department and take your statement, all right? An officer will go to the hospital and get your wife."

"*I* need to get her," he says, his voice louder than it needs to be. "I have to tell her it was an accident."

His words hang in the hot, thick air.

What else could it be?

"I have to tell her," Luke says. "I have to be the one. I've called. She's not answering."

Carter takes a step closer, and out of the blue, Luke takes a swing at him. "You fucking moron! My kid's dead. I need to get out of here."

Luke's fist doesn't connect with Carter, but he shouldn't have done that, of course. No one would have thought it was possible, but he's just made a dire situation far worse.

"I'm going to need to put you under arrest," Carter says, bulldozing the younger man, who now blinks back a mix of fear and annoyance. "Should keep your cool. Assaulting an officer is a serious offense."

A second later a patrol officer cuffs him. Luke is red-faced, and it's clear by the look behind his steamed-up lenses that he knows he made a very big mistake.

"I didn't mean that," he says.

It's too late. He's in the backseat of a patrol car. Carter and I talk with the crime scene techs who have taped off the scene. A reporter from the *Daily World* is hustling other officers, trying to get someone in authority to tell her something, but there's nothing we can say. It is tragic. It is horrific.

But is it negligent or a criminal act?

"After you process the scene," I tell an officer, "impound the car and get it to the lot."

"Car stinks like holy hell," the officer says.

I know the odor. All homicide detectives do.

"Yeah," I say. "Nothing worse on the planet."

Carter gives a quick nod. "You got that right, Nic."

I call Emma's day care on my way back to the police department and say that I'll be late.

"Carrie Anne, I hate to do it to you," I say, meaning every word. "I have a hot case right now." I cringe at my unintended pun. "Can you watch Emma until seven or so?"

She indicates without hesitation there's no problem.

"I heard about the baby on Facebook," she says.

Nothing escapes social media. It's omnipresent. It's like air. It's almost as if there is live coverage for every single crime these days. It used to annoy me to see a phone held up to capture everything I was doing, but now I barely notice it.

"Right," I say.

"Awful. No worries with Emma. We're having a great day in the pool. Made snow cones too. She made one for you that's turned into a purple patch of stickiness. See you at seven or so."

"Tell her I love her," I say before hanging up and dialing Carter to talk about what he knows as we drive separately to the office. He tells me that the hothead—again, I hate the pun—works at the grocery chain WinCo, in the office.

"That's less than a mile from Starbucks," I say.

"Yeah. He says he got off work a little early and was going to catch a movie. Said that he didn't know his daughter was in the car. He was supposed to drop her at day care this morning but forgot."

"Unbelievable," I say. "Forgot his little girl and left her in the car all day? In this heat?"

Carter doesn't answer right away. He's drawing on a cigarette. When we get to the office, he'll have consumed a couple of breath mints. "Yeah," he says, exhaling. "I know. 'Unbelievable' is right. Says that he looked in the rearview mirror and saw the top of her head and pulled over right away. He freaked out. You saw him. Freaked out big-time."

"So he says he went to work, forgetting his child," I repeat.

"Yeah. Worked seven hours."

"Where did he park?"

"He said WinCo's lot was full, so he parked in back, along the Chehalis River."

"Not his normal parking place?"

"No," Carter says after another puff. "With the festival and all, says that the place was jammed."

"At nine in the morning?"

"Kind of doubtful."

"Or maybe something worse."

We arrive at the same time as the patrol officer who brought in Luke Tomlinson.

"He wants to talk," the officer says. "He says he's sorry for his out-burst, Detectives."

I imagine he is.

"All right. He's waiving his rights, then?" I ask as I peer into the back of the patrol car and see the young father of the dead baby give a quick nod.

The officer speaks up. "Wife is on her way."

"Book him and we'll have a little chat," Carter says.

"Hey, I said I was sorry," Luke says through the glass, leaning in my direction and blinking his eyes as if there were tears to fall. But there aren't.

"'Sorry' doesn't cut it right now," I say. "Maybe after our interview, but not at the moment. Understood?"

Luke nods. The look on his face is proof positive. He knows that his bad, bad day is going to be even worse.

Later, when Jordan Conway attempts to tell her roommate, Charlotte, what had happened in the Starbucks parking lot, she finds she can't really talk about it. Not at first. It's as if the words are stuck in her throat.

"And after you did CPR, what happened?" Charlotte pushes.

"Nothing."

"Are you in shock or something? What's the matter with you?"

Jordan reaches for a peach wine cooler inside the refrigerator door.

"I guess I am," she says.

"Well, it's high drama, that's for sure," Charlotte says. "A kid dying in your arms."

Jordan opens the bottle and guzzles. "It wasn't that. I mean, of course the little girl not making it is the worst thing ever, but it wasn't the weirdest thing about what just happened."

Charlotte seems knee-deep in curiosity.

"What was the weirdest thing?" she asks.

Jordan slumps into a chair at the kitchen table. She runs her fingers over the surface, sending a drift of crumbs to the floor. "I feel like an idiot for saying anything."

"Say it," her roommate asks. "What?"

Jordan puts down the half-empty wine cooler. "While the dad was yelling about how it was all his fault—I mean, really yelling about it—he never once looked at his little girl. He kept his eyes . . ." Her words trail off and she decides she needs another good drink. The bottle is at her lips again.

Charlotte continues. "Where? What?"

Jordan looks at roommate, her eyes now wet. "I feel like an idiot even thinking this. But when I was trying to save his little girl, I swear to God all he did was look at my tits."

The other young woman's eyes pop. "No," she says.

Jordan nods. "Seriously. I know the look. I know when guys do that. I swear it. He was taking a peek for sure."

"While his kid was dying?"

"Yeah. Like that."

"Whoa," says Charlotte.

Jordan realizes then what the weird feeling she experienced was when she was trying to perform CPR in the backseat of that Subaru. She felt uncomfortable. The man was leering at her.

"The dad was a total creeper," Jordan finally says, wiping a tear that had zigzagged down her face. In doing so, she catches a whiff of the dead baby on her hands. The odor sends her rushing to the bathroom to turn on the shower. Her work clothes are shed in record time. She doesn't even pause for the water to warm. As the cold water pours over her face, she can't breathe. She lets the tears fall. What happened in that parking lot was the most traumatic thing that has ever happened to her.

And the baby. The baby couldn't be saved.

CHAPTER THREE

Tuesday, August 15

As we wait for booking, Luke seesaws in his desire to talk to us.

"Let's move this along while we wait," I say. "Car's in impound."

The lot is next door to the police department.

"All right," Carter says. "Have a quick call to make. See you there."

It's at the start of the case, and his distraction is a little annoying, but I know it's a call to his divorce lawyer. It's about his children. That's who he is.

Carter arrives at the lot shortly after I do. He's carrying two Dutch Bros. coffees. The weather has cooled by more than thirty degrees. He's wearing dark gray slacks, a tan sport coat, and a blue shirt. He needs Bombfell in the worst way.

"Starbucks parking lot is full of lookie-loos," he says, handing me a white cup with a blue windmill. "I guess around here a dead kid in a parking lot passes for a new tourist attraction."

I make a face, and he backtracks right away.

"No offense," he says.

I nod. He knows I made the connection to the Kelsey Chase case that had started in a Target parking lot, though it was not his intention.

"No problem," I say.

The guard lets us into the impound yard. Most of the cars there are drug-money cars, but this being Grays Harbor, they aren't luxury makes, like Mercedes, BMW, or Lexus. While we have our drug trade along the Washington coast, we're decidedly much lower-rent than where I'd worked as a detective in Bellevue, Seattle's moneyed neighbor to the east. Here the vehicles are mostly pickups and Toyotas, with one lone Escalade.

Carter cuts the evidence tape, and we go to work examining Luke Tomlinson's 2014 Subaru Forester. I mention the color and Carter informs me that it isn't just any red.

"It's Venetian red," he says.

Classy, I think.

We don gloves and get to work. The stench of what took place in the vehicle has not abated. Or if it has, my olfactory senses must be acute. Carter doesn't mention it.

We go about the business of identifying and documenting everything we can find in Luke's car. After we cover every inch, techs will do it again with the help of a vacuum. Being thorough is necessary. A recent case was tossed because the child was asthmatic, and the mother had loaded her car with lavender plants from a garden store before going into a bar for a couple of beers. The defense argued that the child's medical condition was a factor in the toddler's death.

After we're done, a mechanic will check the engine to see if everything is in working order.

"The last thing we need is for some court-appointed lawyer to hand us our asses because the AC was pouring carbon monoxide from the exhaust," Carter says.

"Right," I say as I focus on logging everything I find. Each item is numbered and secured in a bundle marked with the case number.

Two travel mugs.

French fries cut in the way that tells me they're from McDonald's.

A small Cookie Monster plush toy.

A box of baby wipes.

A child's picture book about ladybugs.

All of it is mundane. All of it makes up a three-dimensional still life of parenthood.

"How's it going there?" I call over to Carter, who has opened the hatch and is examining its contents.

"Skateboard and beach blanket," he says.

"I wonder who the skateboard belongs to, mom or dad," I say.

"I'd say Luke," Carter says.

I don't tell him that's sexist.

And then I find them under the front seat on the driver's side.

"Lookie here," I say, holding up a cache of Trojans in a gold-and-black box.

"Magnums." Carter pops his head up and rolls his eyes. "Impressive."

He's being sarcastic, of course.

"Who drives around with a box of these?" I ask, putting them in a plastic evidence bag.

"Someone having sex in his car," Carter says.

Carter can be so literal. That's one of his good qualities. There's never any guessing with him. "I get that," I say. "But, honestly, what do you think? Is this guy some kind of player or what?"

Carter takes a swallow from his Dutch Bros. and sets down the empty cup.

"For around here," he says, repeating a now-familiar refrain, "I guess he's what passes for a player."

I want to remind him that I'm from around here. And reminding me about how low the bar is gets on my nerves. But I don't.

The car seat is next.

It's a Graco. Appears to be brand-new. I can see where body fluids stained the blue-and-red fabric. I can imagine Ally trying to get out of that seat in the way that a person is held captive by a monster. The very straps that the manufacturer put there to ensure that she was safe paralyzed her. She was too young to figure out how to extricate herself. I wonder if she was awake. I hope she wasn't. I hope that there were no last terrifying moments when she called for her mommy and daddy to help her. My hope is that in the heat she just passed out, slipped away.

Carter helps me to remove the car seat and put it in a black garbage bag. It's going to the lab. Just to be sure.

I continue to photograph the car from every angle. It's unremarkable in the way that most newer cars are. The sole exception is the Nirvana sticker in the back window. I take a photo of that.

"He's too young for Nirvana," Carter says, over my shoulder. "He probably was under ten when Cobain died."

CHAPTER FOUR

Tuesday, August 15

The seesaw lands where we hoped it would. Luke Tomlinson sits in an interview room at the Aberdeen Police Department, where late afternoon coffee has turned, as it always does, to burnt mud. It smells terrible, but I suck the scent in through my nose, hoping the odor will take away the stench of the car we just examined.

It doesn't.

I let myself inside and take a seat next to my partner. We face Ally's father from the opposite side of the table, the doorway to his back. The ventilation is poor in the space, and all I can smell is Luke's body odor mixed with some minty chewing gum that he moves from one side of his mouth to the other. He's sweaty, and his glasses ride down the bridge of his nose. Every minute, or even less, he pushes the bridge between the lenses upward with his index finger.

"I don't know why I have to go over this again," Luke says. "I told the officers what happened. I need to be with my wife right now. She needs me."

"You can see her as soon as we are done here."

"Oh, man," he says. "I've got to be with her. She'll need me."

"We'll make that happen. After we talk," Carter says.

Luke kneads his hands together and rocks in his chair. He looks at both of us across the table. His eyes are hooded, either from weariness or by heredity. Hard to say.

"It was a fucking accident," he says, emotion charging his words. "I forgot. I'm such an idiot! I forgot that Ally was in the car."

"Right," Carter tells the father of the dead girl. "Let's start at the beginning."

◆ ◆ ◆

Luke continues to rock back and forth as he recounts the morning. Mia gets up early for a ten-hour shift at the hospital. On the days that she works, he says he's charged with dressing, feeding, and getting their one-year-old to the Little Pal's Day Care on Spruce, a few miles from their apartment building. He drops in some biographical detail too. He and Mia have been married for three years. She's studying for a nursing degree on the weekends and in the evenings. He's working his way into management at WinCo.

"I'm the assistant manager's assistant," he says, with some obvious pride that feels at odds in the milieu of a police interview room.

He goes on. The morning was typical, "just like every other day." He changed Ally's diaper, dressed her, ran a washcloth over her face, and packed her up in the car.

He stops to weigh the facial expressions of his audience.

Only then does he begin to sob. It's rapid. Staccato. It's a teakettle that's whistled to the boiling point. And then it stops.

"Ally's my girl. We have a good time. She's only one," he says, "but she's still a little buddy to me."

They leave the house at some time before nine.

"We stopped at McDonald's and I gave her some pancakes to eat. She's a good eater. Like me. She's been on solid food since she turned ten months. I prefer that. I mean, those bottles all the time were a hassle. Mia made me wash them by hand. God, we have a dishwasher. But no. She said they needed to be boiled."

Luke continues with his story. Every now and then, however, he takes a detour. He lets us know that he's a very involved father. Loves being a dad. Never wanted anything more than being a father. He admits that a little boy might have been preferable in the beginning.

"But now I see things differently. I'm her daddy," Luke says, between sobs. "That's an awesome position to be in."

I can't help but notice that he continues to refer to Ally in the present tense, as though she were still alive. I wonder if he is in denial. Even though he knows Ally died in his car, it is possible that a defense mechanism is at work. He just can't allow himself to speak of her in the past tense.

After McDonald's, he drove to work—not to Little Pal's Day Care.

"Here's the thing," he says, halting his story once more. "I just . . . I just don't know. I have no idea how I forgot her. She fell asleep, I guess. She was quiet. The radio was on. I was thinking about what I had to get done at the office. We were going to reconfigure a section of the store, and it was my job to manage a portion of that project. You know, start to finish. I have a big role in it."

He's hung up on showing how important he is.

"You just forgot her," Carter says, as though he couldn't care less about how important Luke was. What was important was Ally.

Luke looks up at the ceiling. "Yeah. I can't explain it better than I already have. I just forgot she was in the backseat. I got all the way to WinCo. I parked. I got out. I locked the doors and went inside. I just forgot. I know it sounds lame, but that's what happened. If I could do things differently, I would."

"You parked in back, isn't that right?" I ask.

He locks his eyes on mine. He knows what I'm getting at.

"Yeah," he says, almost dismissively. "With the festival this weekend, everyone was supposed to park away from the prime parking spots. You know, to leave room for customers. 'Customer first' is our motto."

I'd seen the ads on TV.

"Was the back lot suggested by management?" I ask.

He gives a quick nod. "I think so. I can't exactly remember. I work back there sometimes when suppliers bring in merch. Customers never park there."

"And when you parked there, you just forgot about Ally?" Carter says.

Luke's face tightens. "I told you that already," he says. "You need to hear it again for some reason?"

Defiance creeps into the room just then.

"We do," Carter says.

Luke shrugs like he's being inconvenienced now. "Yes. Ally slipped my mind. In my mind I thought she was at day care the whole time. Honestly, I really did. It was only after I left for the movies that I noticed she was in the car."

I'm surprised.

"In the middle of the day?" I ask. "The movies?"

"Yeah," Luke says. "I like horror shows and Mia hates them. I told her that I was going to see *The Conjuring 2* and then head home."

Luke stops and I push a little. "So then what? What happened next, Luke? After you left WinCo for the movies?"

Just like that, his pudgy hands are back on the surface of the table. He glances up once more. I find myself looking upward to see what he's staring at. Of course, other than a fluorescent tube light fixture, there's nothing there. Not even a crack in the ceiling. He's thinking. Maybe imagining? Maybe recalling? Hard to know. Then I see it. I watch a growing bead of perspiration on his upper lip. It nearly drips. He sees what I'm looking at and does a rapid-fire wipe on the sleeve of his sodden white dress shirt. As he does so, I detect the presence of that hideous scent that had permeated the car.

The odor of his dead daughter.

I know now that the sweat pouring from his chubby frame is the result of nervousness. *Good*, I think. It has nothing to do with the nearly one-hundred-degree heat outside. The Aberdeen Police Department's air-conditioning system works just fine. Some days, actually, a little too fine. In fact, hooked on the back of my desk is one of my mother's old sweaters. I wear it most of the summer when I work in the office. It keeps me warm, which is ironic in that Mom was anything but warm. When she left us, she stuck a note on the fridge:

Casserole. 350 for twenty mins. I'll call you from Cali.

That was it. Ten words.

No "Love, Mom." No "Goodbye." Just baking instructions for a casserole that my father and I would be too upset to eat. Not Stacy. She gobbled some up and went to watch TV in her room.

"You left WinCo and you drove across the bridge, heading toward the theaters," I say. "Is that what happened? Is that what you're telling us?"

"Yeah," Luke says. "I started driving. I was going to send a text to Mia to remind her about the movie. I know you guys don't want us texting, but that's what I was about to do, when for some reason I looked up and saw the top of Ally's head in the rearview mirror."

He stops cold. Carter and I stay mute. We want him to fill the space between us with what happened.

Luke puts his fingertips on his damp forehead and rubs away the wetness.

"I fucking freaked out," he says. "I pulled over as soon as I could. The whole time I was calling out to Ally. I was telling her that everything would be okay and that I was really sorry."

Luke stops. It's as if he thinks that's the end of the story. We wait a beat. Finally, Carter steps in to move things along.

"You remembered just then that you'd forgotten to drop her off that morning?" he asks.

"I don't know if I even thought of that," Luke says.

Again silence.

"What was your first thought?" I ask.

Luke shakes a little. "It was weird," he says, no longer rubbing his forehead. "It was like seeing a ghost or something. There she was. In the car seat."

"A ghost?" I ask. "So you knew she was dead?"

Luke snaps a little. "No," he says, right away. "Like a shock. Like out of a horror movie, I guess. I just never thought she was there. I never thought about not dropping her off. I just put it out of my mind. I tried to turn around a little as I drove, but I couldn't see her face even if I'd wanted to, because, you know, they make you face the kid backward."

I think back to a time when my sister let me take baby Emma for the afternoon. God knows what she was doing and whom she was doing it with. She gave me a diaper bag and some premade bottles of formula. She'd only breastfed Emma for a month.

"My uterus has shrunk, and that's all breastfeeding is good for," she told me one time. "I'm not about to have my tits look like water wings. Gross."

As I recalled, the car seat *did* face backward. It would be hard to miss a child sitting across from you as you got into the driver's side.

"Didn't you see her when you opened the car door to get in?" I ask.

Luke shakes his head.

"You passed the passenger door to get to the driver's door," Carter adds, pushing a little more.

Yet Luke doesn't flinch. Through his sweaty lenses, he looks right at my partner and answers.

"I know," he says. "But, no, I didn't see her."

"When you got in, didn't you smell anything?" I ask, referring to the grotesque stench of the one-year-old's decomposing body.

"I didn't finish my third Sausage McMuffin," Luke says. "I thought maybe that the heat rotted it a little. But really it wasn't that bad. I've smelled worse, you know."

I don't. I don't know anybody who has.

CHAPTER FIVE

Tuesday, August 15

My eyes take her in. Moments like this feel a little invasive, but they are part of a detective's job. We watch. We study. We dissect. Mia Tomlinson, twenty-two, arrives with a patrol officer within an hour after her husband is transported here. Her long auburn hair is up in a loose, messy bun. Freckles adorn pale features that have been ravaged by sudden and inconceivable grief. Her attire announces to the world who and what she's all about. A Sylvester and Tweety Bird smock covers her postbaby frame. She's a nurse's aide in the pediatric ward. She looks the part.

"I want my baby," she says, looking at me with red and puffy eyes.

"I'm so sorry, Mia," I say, using her first name because she's young and in a circumstance like this it just feels right.

"She might still be alive," Mia says with false hope cradling her words. "Maybe she passed out?"

I shake my head. I hate this part of my job more than I can say.

"No," I tell her. "She's gone."

"I'm practically a nurse," the young mother says, a little edge of authority in her shattered voice. "I know what I'm talking about."

Mia starts crying harder than anyone has ever cried. Ever. In the history of the world. Her body contorts. She shakes. She squeezes. She shudders. A second later Mia has found her way into my arms. Her eye makeup smears my blouse. She repeats over and over that Ally, her precious baby, can't be gone.

Words erupt one at a time from between her guttural sobs. "There. Has. To. Be. A. Mistake."

"I'm so sorry," I repeat as if saying it once more can emphasize my real understanding of the magnitude of her pain, the grief that I share with her. The grief is already beyond measure. "Ally's gone."

Silence. A shudder. More tears.

Finally, Mia pulls away, releasing a crablike grip from my wincing shoulders. I have never witnessed such anguish in my life. I have worked the cases of dead children before. I've seen extreme anguish in all kinds of circumstances related to my job in law enforcement. I have filed away the faces and pain into a catalog of reactions that I almost never revisit. This pain. This utterly stinging agony. It is something beyond anything I've ever seen.

"I want my daughter," Mia says. "I have a right to see her. She's my little girl. She's mine. She's everything to me."

"We'll take you to her," I offer. I wait a beat. I wonder why she hasn't asked about Luke or even why they're at the police department. Then she does.

"What's happening?" she asks, fighting with everything she has for some semblance of composure. "Where's Luke? Where's my husband?"

She looks genuinely concerned.

"He's out of booking by now," I tell her. "We'll need to take a statement from you."

Mia pulls back from me. "Booking him? But why? This had to be an accident."

33

"I'm sorry," I repeat. "But there are some legal implications here."

"What kind?" she asks. Tears continue to puddle in her eyes.

Only a jerk would say this, but I say it because it is my duty to do so. "It's against the law to strike a police officer. It's also against the law to leave your child in the car unattended."

Her eyes flutter. She's starting to cry again.

"Yes, I know," she says. "Why was she in the car at WinCo? The officer told me that's where it happened. Why wasn't she at day care? Luke was supposed to drop her off at Little Pal's. I start work early. He always takes her. What happened?"

"We're figuring that out right now," I say. I look over in the direction of victim advocate Nora Harper, who's just arrived. Nora is a tall woman with a calm and gentle presence that is entirely suited to her role. No one has ever complained about Nora. She's never been crossly Yelped or rated in an unkind manner by anyone. Ever. In her office at the end of the hall is a large bulletin board with pictures, drawings, and letters from those she's helped, attesting to her genuine goodness.

"We've charged Mia's husband," I say. "Assault. Leaving a child unattended."

Nora's eyes meet mine. "All right, then." She introduces herself to Mia and gently nudges her as the two of them walk slowly down the hall. Mia's rubber-soled shoes squeak against our freshly waxed linoleum floor.

"Ally's only one," I hear her say. "Just two weeks ago. We had a big party. Luke got her a special pink-frosted cake from work. The biggest cake they make at WinCo that's not for a wedding. Ally was so happy. She really was."

She stops and faces Nora.

"This isn't really happening, is it?" she asks.

I see Nora press her hand against Mia's heaving shoulders as she guides her past the other offices. The victim advocate doesn't say anything to the young mother.

Nora has been in moments of undeniable tragedy more times than she cares to revisit. She knows that no words matter right now. The only thing she can do is listen, acknowledge, and do her best to follow Mia's lead. The victim, or in this case the mother of the victim, always lets her know how best to help them through a nightmare.

"Telling someone that they'll be all right," Nora told me over coffee one time, "is the last thing anyone wants to hear. Sure, things will get better. Time will diminish the pain. But things will never be all right."

The officer who had notified Mia about her daughter in the hospital parking lot leans in and whispers in my ear. I step back and look into his eyes.

"Seriously?" I ask.

Mia Tomlinson is human tissue wadded up and sodden with the tears of a mother who has lost everything that matters. While Carter confers with the prosecutor's office and Luke is sulking in a jail cell, the young mother in the nurse's smock dissolves into tears in the interview room. She sits in the same chair that her husband occupied moments before. I wonder if she catches a whiff of the scent of her dead baby or her husband's nervous sweat.

Mia's messy bun is now undone, and her hair tumbles past her shoulders. With her eye makeup now on my blouse, she looks incredibly young—a teenager. I offer her water, and when she takes it, I notice she wears a Celtic-knot gold band on her ring finger. She pulls at the ring now and then. A nervous habit for a devastatingly stressful time.

"I still don't understand why Luke's been arrested," she finally says. Her blue eyes are soaked. Full of sadness. Heartbreaking. Mia's words are on a hamster wheel, and she keeps repeating the same phrase over and over. "I don't understand."

This is Nora's area. Though I want to comfort Mia, I can't at the moment. I need to know what she can tell me about that day.

More than anything, I need to know why she said what she'd said to the patrol officer.

"I left at six," she tells me, reaching for a Kleenex that I've scooted in her direction. Just in case. "Ally and Luke were asleep. I kissed them both goodbye. Soft, like. I didn't want to wake them. We'd had a rough night. Ally cried for almost an hour. Kept all of us up before she went down around 1:00 a.m."

"Was that unusual?" I ask.

"Lately, no," Mia says, fidgeting with her ring once more. "We don't have air-conditioning. We've opened all the windows and set up a couple of fans. We're on the second floor. Heat rises."

"It has been very hot this week," I say, stating the obvious, but doing so just to keep things moving. Just to keep her feeling supported enough to continue.

"Terrible," she says, sipping some water. "I wish we had AC. The people next door have one of those portable units that fits into the window. It costs them an extra hundred a month to run it. Luke says the expense would be worth it. I say we don't have the money."

"What else did you do this morning?" I ask.

"Packed Ally's diaper bag," she says. "Some snacks too. Also packed Luke's lunch. He brown-bags it most days. We're saving money where we can, because I'm taking classes to get my nursing degree. Like I said, money is really tight. I have another year to go."

"That's great," I tell her, though I'm thinking of the diaper bag. The evidence report indicated that besides diapers, the diaper bag contained spit-up rags; a change of clothes; and a peanut butter sandwich, an apple, and some chips—a lunch that he left in the car with Ally. It's odd, I think, that he didn't go out to the car to get his lunch.

"It isn't easy working full-time and being a mom too," Mia says.

I know and I nod. "Then what?" I ask. "What happened next?"

She wrinkles her nose and takes another tissue. "Nothing, really," she says. "I went to work. Luke texted me good morning around eight or so."

"Did he say anything about Ally?" I ask.

Mia stops to think, recalling the morning. "No," she says. "Just that she was happy. They were heading to McDonald's for breakfast, then to day care and to work after that."

I state the obvious, not because she needs reminding, but because I'm looking for a reaction.

"But Ally never got there."

Mia blinks back more tears, sniffs, and takes a second Kleenex from the box. "I guess not."

I think of what the patrol officer whispered in my ear before the interview, but for the time being I hold that peculiar detail inside.

"Didn't the day care inquire about Ally?" I ask.

Mia takes her eyes off me and reaches for her phone. "No," she says, scrolling through her messages. "They did send a note about a beach walk that had been canceled." She finds the message. "Nothing else."

"Was that a group message?" I ask.

"Yeah," she says. "Everyone got it."

I ask her what time it was sent.

She looks at the screen on her phone. "Ten twenty-three."

"Did Luke get it?"

She nods. "Yes, sure. Debbie's good at keeping everyone informed."

As with the lunch still in the diaper bag, I wonder why that message hadn't jogged her husband's memory that morning. When it came through, Ally was probably still alive. Didn't Luke see that and recall that he hadn't dropped his daughter off?

Mia is looking at photos on her phone. She seems a little lost right now. I can see that she's playing out the morning in her mind.

"This is Ally yesterday," she finally says, her voice growing stronger. "Just yesterday! It's the last picture I took of her."

She holds the phone so I can see the image. It's poignant and beautiful. Ally's red hair and blue eyes fill the screen with the most beautiful colors. She's smiling at someone as she sits in her high chair. A bowl of cereal with some loose Cheerios that resemble tiny wheels that have fallen off an axle sits before her on the plastic tray. A cat calendar with a Siamese next to a goldfish bowl adorns the wall behind her. A half-dead jade plant, its leaves shrunken and falling, sits on the cluttered kitchen counter.

"Her dad was making faces at her," Mia tells me.

"She's beautiful," I say.

All of a sudden Mia looks at me with renewed intensity. It's as if she's suddenly snapping out of a fugue and beginning to consider the circumstances that are swirling around her. The cyclone that is catching her. The whirlpool that nudges her inside.

"This isn't really happening, is it?" she asks.

I wish it weren't. "I'm so sorry," I tell her. My words come at her as softly as possible. "I'm afraid it is."

She puts down her phone but continues to gaze at the photograph.

Now is the time to bring it up. "You said some things to the police officer that I've been wondering about."

That propels her back into the moment. "What?" she asks, now meeting my direct gaze.

"Before the officer told you what happened to Ally, you mentioned two things," I say, weighing her reaction. "About researching hot-car deaths and about the possibility that Luke might have forgotten Ally in the car."

She barely flinches at what I've said.

"Yeah," she says. "He and I talked about the dangers of a hot car. He looked it up online and told me that a car can turn into an oven in a matter of minutes."

"When did Luke do that?"

Mia doesn't hesitate. "This week," she says. "A few days ago. That's what's so terrible and ironic about this. Luke and I *discussed* it. We'd seen that story about that mom in Texas who left her twins in the parking lot at Walmart and, you know, basically cooked them alive."

She doesn't draw a connection to Ally being cooked alive too.

"How did you research it?" I ask.

"I didn't," she says. "Luke did. Online. He even printed out an article about that Texas case. I think he was worried about it. He loved Ally so much. Told me every day that being a daddy was the best thing that ever happened to him."

"He was concerned that it might happen to her?"

She nods emphatically. "Yeah. Very. Told me that he was afraid that he'd forget her in the car. That he'd get to thinking about work or something and then just, you know, leave her by mistake."

"And that's what happened, isn't it, Mia?"

She takes a breath. "That's what I told the officer. It was almost like Luke predicted it."

Saying his name brings a new wave of tears.

"I need to see him," she says.

"You can't at the moment. He's been processed. Arrested. His next visit is with a lawyer."

Mia pushes back from the table and stands. "But this was an *accident*," she says, her voice rising in volume. "Luke can't be in trouble for an *accident*. That doesn't seem fair. That girl in Texas didn't get arrested. The police said that she'd been punished enough for her mistake."

◆　◆　◆

I catch Carter in his office after the interview with Mia. It's after seven, and I need to get Emma. I need to hold her in my arms and read her a book with a happy ending. I need to tell her that I'm sorry that work kept me away from her. It doesn't happen often. And when it does, it crushes me because I don't ever want to be that parent figure that doesn't put the child first. She'll know about Ally's death because Carrie Anne has the news on 24-7. I'll tell her that occasionally bad things happen to good people.

At seven, she already knows that, of course. From my job and from her own life too.

"Mom's in denial," I tell Carter.

"Dad's a strange bird, for sure," he says.

"I don't believe his story, one whit. Mom dropped a bomb. Says that Luke researched hot-car deaths."

"Yeah, Davis told me," he says.

Todd Davis is the reporting officer.

"Planned this, didn't he?" I ask, already feeling that I know the answer.

Carter nods. The sun is out, and I know that if I didn't have Emma to go home to that he'd ask me out for a drink.

"Just a beer," he'd say.

I'd decline, like I always do.

"I want to learn more about you," he'd offer, as though that's something I'd want to share with anyone.

"You know everything there is," I'd say, though I know that he doesn't. My fall from grace was well documented on the Internet. How my gambling addiction was fodder for the blogs. How my investigative partner and boyfriend, Danny Ford, botched the Kelsey Chase murder investigation. How my sister survived the propane explosion that killed her husband. All of it was there with a click of a mouse.

Well, not all of it. There were some things I'd somehow managed to keep to myself.

"Let's hit up his work colleagues tomorrow first thing," Carter says. "Then work our way back to witnesses at the scene."

"Day care too," I say. "I wonder what they know."

Carter shuts down his computer, and we head toward the back door of the police department.

The air hovering over the parking lot is hair-dryer hot. It blows in my face as Carter and I make our way to our cars, slotted next to each other. There's no awkward lingering. That's by design. We both have things to do. He's going to stop at the Long Shot Tavern on Columbia for a beer or two and then go home to his sparsely furnished apartment. I'm going to get Emma and bring her to the red-shingled house that has been part of my life since I was born.

The house where my sister, Stacy, and I learned to love and hate each other.

With Emma nearly finished with her recitation of what happened during her day, I twist the knob, and we go inside. Shelby greets us at the door, trying to jump up. I bend down and give her a little love. It's too hot to pick up my dog just then. Emma's been a chatterbox all the way from Carrie Anne's. Although I'm not really counting, she tells me that she hates hot dogs for the third time.

"That's what I had for dinner," she says.

"I'm sorry about that. We'll have pizza tomorrow night."

"I like pizza."

"I know you do," I say.

This is a girl who has no compunction when it comes to telling me what she likes or doesn't like. She's confident. Assured. She's a blond like her mother, but she thinks like a brunette, as my father would say. I know that's silly, but that's how I feel. When I pick her up, set her on the counter, and fish through the refrigerator for something decent to eat, she carries on, telling me like it is.

"Carrie Anne says hot dogs are good for you. Can you believe that? I didn't tell her that they are made up of guts and stuff."

"Not all hot dogs," I say. "Maybe Carrie Anne buys the good kind."

Emma looks absolutely certain. "There *is* no good kind," she says.

I give up on finding something good to eat for now and bend down to retrieve a Popsicle from the freezer.

Emma sees what I'm doing, but she doesn't judge.

"As far as Popsicles go," I say, "this is the good kind."

She smiles and takes it.

"Yes," she says. "Cherry. Real fruit juice. No artificial sweeteners."

Who is this kid? I ask myself as I take a piece of cold chicken and set it on a paper towel. (No need to wash a dish if I don't have to.) *Where did this mini-adult come from?* I know the answers to the questions running through my mind, but still they come. Her father is dead. Her mother is out of the picture. Emma no longer asks about them as she first did when we left the suburbs of Seattle for Hoquiam. My heart skipped a beat when her class did a family tree assignment at the end of first grade. It was just the two of us on her hand-drawn tree.

"You're my auntie mommy," she said.

I felt sad about that. I didn't intend to rewrite the history of her life, but I knew then that I'd been avoiding mentioning my sister, Stacy, and her husband, Cy. I decided to correct that then, because it was the right thing to do. "What about your daddy and your mommy?" I asked.

Emma got out a green crayon. "They are here," she said, pointing to a clump of grass above the tree's roots.

I didn't press it. I let myself believe that Emma had kind of buried her parents. That was fine. That was, I thought at the time, the way it should be.

"What about Grandpa?" I asked, partly because I was curious about what she thought of my father, but also because I wanted to change the subject. "You didn't include him in the family tree."

Emma made a face. "Oh, yes," she said, hastily drawing a figure of an old man sitting in a wheelchair. She thoughtfully coiled some hair on his head and gave him an alert look that didn't reflect reality at all. Finished, she looked up and smiled. "Here he is."

Now, as she sucks on her Popsicle, her tongue and lips are turning bright red. I eat my chicken and pour a glass of chilled white wine. Emma does most of the talking. Seven-year-olds have a way of uncorking the entire day. There are no boring parts. Everything is worthy of a recounting. I listen to her every word, nodding, looking interested. And while I am, I cannot stop thoughts of Ally Tomlinson from coming into the kitchen with us. What happened to her has hit a nerve, and there's no denying it. I think back to the case that led to my personal and professional demise. Kelsey Chase, a three-year-old, abducted from her mother's car in a Target parking lot.

The case was my unraveling. It took me to places that I never could have imagined. It transformed me in every way. I questioned my judgment. I passively stood by while everything I believed in was upended. My sister, Stacy, and the man that I thought I loved had been caught up in the ugliest endeavors, and I had been used to facilitate the cover-up of a murder. Or two. For the longest time I contemplated suicide. I thought only a kind of permanent darkness—a lights-out, I called it—would end my shame. Stop my self-inflicted suffering.

Not so. The little girl with the red tongue and lips was the answer. As Emma sits on the counter telling me about Carrie Anne's cat, Rex, using a potted plant as a litter box, I silently thank God for her. I love her with every fiber of my being. My salvation was in ensuring that she made it through life unscathed. Loved. Challenged in the right ways. Strong.

Everything that I wanted to be.

Even though she is not mine by birth, I know that inside of me is that agape love all mothers have.

All except Stacy.

I toss the paper towel and take the wooden stick from Emma's tiny hand. The upstairs windows have been open all day, fans doing double duty, but the space is still sweltering.

"Carrie Anne says that rich people have air-conditioning," she says.

I think about the house near Lake Washington that had been her home before everything happened. It had a pool. A butler's pantry. A media room. And, yes, central air-conditioning.

"Rich people only eat the best hot dogs too," I say.

She grins at me.

It's after eight, and though it's still light outside, with Shelby trailing us we go upstairs, feeling every creaking floorboard as we get to the top. Emma's bedroom is her mother's old room. Some remnants of Stacy's life before she escaped Hoquiam still remain. The walls are still Pepto-Bismol pink. The curtains are the same white lace. A bulletin board that Stacy once filled with photographs to help her visualize her future—a Mercedes, palm trees, a bottle of Dior perfume, Tori Spelling's house—have been replaced by images Emma cut from magazines and coloring books. All are from *Frozen*, Emma's favorite movie.

It's so warm, I tell her to sleep in a T-shirt and underwear.

"That's weird," she tells me.

"You'll be cooler," I say.

She makes a face and gets undressed.

"Carrie Anne says that the little girl's dad should never have left her in the car."

Carrie Anne says a lot. Not only that, Emma has very good hearing. I sit on the edge of her bed while Emma climbs under the top sheet.

"She's right," I say. "He shouldn't have."

Emma adjusts her pillow. "You're not supposed to leave a dog in the car without the window rolled all the way down," she says.

Frozen is the opposite of how the room feels.

"Even that's not a good idea," I say.

She snuggles deeper under the sheets. "Is she in heaven now?"

She thinks that heaven is a place that someone can go to and visit. She wonders about her father and if she can see him in heaven.

"Of course," I say.

I lie next to her and read a few pages from *The Wind in the Willows*. Before I finish, the love of my life is fast asleep. Shelby, who has planted herself on the cool wooden floor, whines a little. She wants up. I scoop up my dog and hold her. She's a hot-water bottle on a day when no one wants one. Yet at that moment I don't mind. Not in the least. I look around at these two. With Emma and Shelby, this place isn't so terrible after all.

The night ends with a surprise call from a supervisor at Ocean View. I've received late-night calls from my dad's care center in the past, and each time one lights up my phone, I wonder if he has passed away during the night. I look at the time. It's 11:00 p.m. This has to be bad. I brace myself for terrible, yet welcome news. I hate myself for thinking it. But he suffers in a fog that will never lift.

"Is he all right?" I ask, sliding my feet to the floor and standing.

"He fell out of bed this evening," the caller says. "He's going to be okay, but I'm afraid your father broke his wrist."

"How did that happen? I thought he was"—and I hated this more than just about any of the routine indignities my father endures— "restrained at bedtime."

The caller sighs. "I'm sorry. We have a new nurse, and she was unfamiliar with that part of our nighttime protocol."

I am angry, though not overly so. The nighttime protocol at Ocean View included cleaning his teeth, changing his diaper, getting him his meds, and turning on Beach Boys music very softly. Before I had the money, he suffered in a hellhole room next to the mill. The staff at Light of Day knew my routine and put on a show whenever I came from Kirkland to check on Dad.

That all changed when a woman I went to school with, but didn't know all that well, followed me out to the parking lot after a visit with my father.

"Look," Donna Totten had said, "I know you care about your dad. Most of the people here have no visitors. You come real regular. Here, no one does. Government checks come in. They cash 'em and do the minimum. I know you're a cop and all. I don't want to get in any trouble, but between you and me, your dad deserves better. I guess they all do. But no one else seems to give a rat's ass about the other patients. If I had the money, I'd get him out."

I didn't have the money. I'd lost every bit I'd had gambling. Sure, I won some. I lost even more. But a year after Donna told me to get Dad out, I found a source better than a casino.

Stacy.

My sister didn't give a crap about Dad. But she did have the cash. The last time I saw her, I twisted the knife and she wired me $50,000. It was blackmail. I knew it. I just didn't care. Everything about Stacy made me sick. I took her money. I never used one dime on myself. Everything was to help care for our father and Emma.

The funny thing was Stacy could have done it all along. She just didn't care. I want to laugh about it now. I thought I'd really done a number on her. I thought Dad would die in less than a year. Better care at Ocean View had changed everything, but he still didn't know who I was. Didn't know Emma.

The only person he knew was Stacy.

Emma was Stacy as a little girl.

I was Stacy as an adult.

That he could even think that about me was crushing. I'd done everything I could to be the good daughter. Everything. And in the end, I could just stand there and wonder: Why had I bothered? What was it about my family that made me into the person who was always covering for others?

No matter the cost to me.

CHAPTER SIX

Wednesday, August 16

With Emma at Carrie Anne's, and a coffee from the drive-through in hand, I meet Carter at Little Pal's Day Care on Spruce Avenue just after 9:00 a.m. It's a far cry from the tidy and homey appearance of Carrie Anne's home day care. At first blush it gives me the vibe of one of those places that give in-home day care centers a black eye in the media from time to time. Rundown. A little unloved. It's a pale blue house with white shutters and a chain-link fence that encircles the perimeter like a snake's skeletal remains. Stuck between dozens of the holes in the chain link are cones gathered from an enormous Sitka spruce that likely was planted when the house was new, seventy years ago. Carter and I stand at the front door and look inside. Too many kids. Not enough staff. Kids crawling everywhere.

"Hello?" I say as we stand at the glass door mottled with fingerprints.

Carter knocks again, and the glass rattles.

Finally, a little girl comes out. She's about Emma's age. She's wearing blue shorts and a strawberry-jam-stained white tank top. Her hair is fashioned into floppy pigtails, and if her brown eyes were any larger, she'd be a ringer for a Margaret Keane painting.

"Ms. Debbie is in the backyard," she says.

"Thanks, honey," I say as we turn to go out back.

"Glad my kids didn't have to go to day care," Carter says.

I bristle a little. I am only me. I have no one to help raise my niece. No family. It was my best—my only—choice.

"Emma's in day care," I say. "Sometimes that's what you have to do."

"Right. Sorry." He looks embarrassed. A little wounded even. Probably more than he should. Carter's like that. He wants to be closer to me, and every now and then I find an innocuous way to push him away. Just enough.

A sprinkler spins a spray of cooling water over a brittle brown lawn as a group of children work hard at turning the hardpan soil into a mudhole.

Ms. Debbie is sitting in a lawn chair under an umbrella, talking to a teenage girl. She holds a stained mug of coffee in one hand.

She looks familiar, and I hope that she's not another girl that I knew in high school.

Turns out she is.

"God," she says, meeting my eyes, "Nikki, is that you?"

No one calls me that. Or hasn't for the longest time.

I smile. "Debbie Manning?" I ask, though I pretend to be a little hazy in my recollection. But I'm not. Debbie was completely memorable. She and I got into it one time, and she slammed a locker door in my face. It wasn't over boys or anything important. It was over Starbursts, of all things. I'd eaten the last strawberry one from a bag that a bunch of us were sharing.

"I wondered when our paths would cross," she says, as though we are in the Denny's bar after the class reunion. "Not that I wanted to all that much," she adds, with a stilted laugh. "You being a cop and all."

I wonder if she's going to say something about my past misfortune. I'd made it out of Hoquiam, but I'd been forced to come back.

She doesn't. Mostly because I don't let her.

"Debbie," I say, "we're here about what happened to Ally Tomlinson."

She sets down her mug. It isn't coffee inside. It could be water. It could be vodka.

"Oh God, what happened is just awful. Horrible. It breaks my heart into a thousand pieces just thinking about that poor little girl. And her parents. Oh God! It must be just awful for them. I can't even imagine what they're going through right now. Just terrible."

"It is," I say, just to stop her from going on and on.

Debbie informs me that she's divorced. "SOB cheated on me and now look what I have to do."

The SOB was Justin Lancaster, a backup quarterback. Come to think of it, most of the guys claimed they were backup quarterbacks.

"Sorry," I say.

Carter looks at me. I know he enjoys my mini-reunions more than I do.

"Brooklyn, can you make the boys get along?" Debbie asks the teenager, who appears entranced by her phone. Her tone indicates that she is not making a request but a very firm demand. She was the demanding type in high school. When the yearbook came out at the end of our junior year, Debbie had a fit because Monica Alexander was featured in one more photo than she was. I was in the yearbook office when she stormed into the room to demand that we go back to press to correct the grievous oversight.

I remember everything about that encounter. Debbie's slight was marginal at best. Her reaction, not so much.

Debbie's lips *and* eyes were Max Factor red. "Monica wasn't even a princess for the junior prom. I was."

"You're in the group shot," the yearbook adviser—an overly sweet and patient woman who just wanted to get to retirement—told her as she pointed to a photograph of Hoquiam High's junior elite.

Debbie fumed. "Group shots don't count," she said.

I remember now that I couldn't stand her.

The day care helper, who probably can't stand Debbie either, puts her phone away and goes over to where two little boys have pinned down a third and are blasting water into his nostrils with a hose with a broken nozzle. The kid is laughing, but it's the kind of out-of-control laughter that comes just before screams for mercy.

While we look on for a moment, Brooklyn untangles the hose from the boys and placates them with the offer of a Popsicle.

"My twins have as much sense as their father," Debbie says.

There's a lull in the summer air. The boys are gone. Brooklyn is gone. The sprinkler is silent. Debbie leans forward in her lawn chair and sips some more from that coffee cup. She looks up at me and Carter, her eyes now wet.

"I just can't get over it," she says. "That poor child. That sweet little thing."

"I know," I say, suddenly remembering how Debbie convincingly played Emily in *Our Town*.

"You really don't think it wasn't an accident?" she asks.

Carter speaks up. "We need to investigate every angle."

"Right," she says. Sip. Sip. Sip.

"Did you expect Ally in the morning the day she died?" I ask.

Debbie has finished her cup of whatever it was. I can smell the alcohol now. I tell myself over and over that I'm the last person to judge anyone. I lied. I manipulated. I begged. I cried. I promised. I was addicted to gambling, and I know that alcoholism is a disease of equal magnitude.

"She misses a day or so a week. Her mom's a nurse's aide and her shifts vary. Most of the time she keeps Ally on days when she's able to. Mia's one of the good ones. She's on time. Pays on time. That's important."

"Yesterday, Luke was expected with Ally, right?" I ask.

Debbie stares into her empty cup as if it were a deepwater well and there has to be some liquid down there. *Somewhere.*

"Right," she finally says.

"Did you phone the Tomlinsons when she didn't arrive?" I ask.

"You mean like a Sandy's Law rule?" she asks. "Like schools are supposed to?"

"Yes," I say. "I know that day care providers aren't bound by that. But did you?"

"No," she says. "No, I didn't. Not because I don't care. I do. I care about my kids. My clients' kids," she quickly adds, amending her circle of caring.

"I can see that," I say, thinking back to her out-of-control twins and the poor little victim of their taunting with the garden hose.

Her eyes stay on mine while she reaches for her phone.

"You know," she says, "come to think of it, I did send an email blast to all the parents. I have fourteen kids here, you know. Five are mine. Nine others. I let them all know that the beach walk had been canceled. I couldn't get the church van. Not that I tried so hard."

She holds up her phone. "Right there," she says, tapping on her cracked iPhone screen. "That's Luke's email and that's Mia's."

I look at the time.

The email went out at 10:23 a.m.

Carter switches gears.

"Tell us about Luke," he says.

"Typical young punk," Debbie says. "Thinks he's hot shit and the rest of the world should get out of his way. How he ended up with a sweetheart like Mia is a mystery to me. Of course, I'm living the same story. Justin's just an older version of Luke. Better looking, smarter. But basically the same."

"That's not much of an endorsement," I say.

"Not meant to be," she says. "I'm nothing if I'm not truthful."

That's not the Debbie Manning I remember. She once took all the money from the PTA bake sale cashbox and said that she'd seen a stranger with shaggy hair and a dark complexion hovering by the red-velvet cupcakes who must have stolen the money.

"I know," I say.

She nods.

"How was he with Ally?" Carter asks, righting the sinking ship of the interview. I'm grateful. All I can think of is Ally, and every time Debbie speaks, I feel like she's more concerned with proving something about herself than telling us what she knows about the Tomlinsons.

"Surprisingly, he doted on her," she says. "Some dads come in here stressed out because they feel like they've been forced into a *Mr. Mom* scenario, and they can't tell a sippy cup from a teething ring. Luke was annoying in his puffed-up self-importance, but he was a calm presence around here. Got along with me. Probably no surprise there. I get along with everyone."

"The natives are restless, Debbie," Brooklyn says, as she emerges from inside and glides over the sun-scorched lawn.

"Did you give Jack and Mack a Popsicle?"

Brooklyn nods. "Yes. The others too."

Debbie makes an irritated face. "What's the problem, then?"

"It's hot, Debbie. The kids are hot. It's, like, a thousand degrees inside."

"Okay, fine," Debbie says. "I'll be right in." She gets up and taps on her cup. "Need a refill too."

Now I know it wasn't coffee for sure. Even though it's practically one hundred degrees, I gave Debbie the benefit of the doubt.

Debbie turns back to me. "This is Brooklyn Marinucci. She's my superstar helper."

I smile. It must be wonderful to be a superstar anything.

"Did you know the Tomlinsons?" I ask Brooklyn.

She pulls her hair to one side, holding it away from her sweating neck.

"Kind of, sort of," she says.

"Any insight into the family?" Carter asks.

"Mia's one of those moms who thinks she's better than the rest of us because she's got a nursing degree." She looks at Debbie. "Community college. Big deal."

Debbie nods and disappears inside. I can hear the freezer open and close.

"Did she put you down?" I ask. "Is that what you mean?"

"No," she says. "No. Not me. *Debbie*. She thought Debbie had made a big mistake having those five kids. Mia said she was getting her tubes tied. Twins ran in her family too. She had other things to do. I get it. We all do."

Brooklyn makes a face as we all hear Debbie call out to the kids to settle down. "So Debbie's coping skills aren't the best. She copes. And I'm here all the time."

It isn't easy, but I hold my tongue about Debbie's drinking during the day. If she'd been driving, I'd have gladly pulled her over. I can tell by Brooklyn's response that she knows Debbie's choices are far from desirable.

I focus on the reason we are there. "What about Luke?" I ask. "What's your take on Ally's dad?"

"Brooklyn!" Debbie calls out from the kitchen. "I need you."

She sighs. "He's, like, totally fine," she says.

"Fine?" I ask. "Like how?"

"Some dads are total creepers here," she says looking sideways. "Like Debbie's ex, for sure."

"Not Luke," Carter says.

"Brooklyn, get your skinny butt in here! I'm paying you above minimum wage for a reason."

Brooklyn mouths *What a bitch* and then heads toward the door. I'm thirty-seven, but I remember what it's like to be a teenager, so I smile at Carter. I also agree with her about Debbie.

"Luke is fine," Brooklyn adds over her shoulder. "Boring but nice enough." Her hair, now in a ponytail off her neck, sways as she walks away. I wonder if she understands that boring can also be cunning. Cunning and evil.

◆ ◆ ◆

Carter and I stand there a second before heading to our cars.

"Piece of work," he tells me.

No argument from me on that. "She's been that way since high school," I say.

"Not her," he says. "Brooklyn. She's, what, sixteen? Seventeen? Got everything figured out."

"Didn't you?" I ask.

Carter stands there and smiles. Despite the whisper of cigarette smoke that clings to him, he's attractive in that way that is hard to describe. Nothing about his face is spectacular. His eyes. His smile. His nose. All of it is average. Symmetrical but ordinary. And yet, taken as a whole, his averageness adds up to very good-looking. A little wear and tear on his face, lines etching into his skin, makes him handsome.

I give him a smile back. "We need a warrant for the Tomlinsons' phones and computers."

"Already in the works."

I smile again.

"Now that we know what we're looking for," I say, "I want to see if that email blast to Luke was received."

"And opened," he says.

"Yep. If he got it Tuesday morning, don't you think it would jog his memory on whether or not he left his daughter in the car?" I ask.

"You think?" Carter says.

"There's no doubt."

CHAPTER SEVEN

Wednesday, August 16

It is late morning and time to circle back to the scene of the crime. We're a small department, so I cover this without Carter, who returns to his office to work the case from there. The initial reports from responding officers indicated that Jordan Conway had been among the first to converge on Luke Tomlinson's Subaru when he stopped and called for help. I find her behind the counter at the Wendy's adjacent to the Starbucks.

Jordan is in her midtwenties, with alert green eyes and silver-streaked blond hair that she wears neatly clipped back, away from the burgers and fries that she bags up for customers, though her name tag says she's the manager in training. Her pleasant face immediately shows concern when I tell her who I am and why I'm here.

"We need to talk," I say.

"Oh," she says, shoving a tray toward an awaiting customer. "I don't know if I can. I'm off soon then I have to get home."

"Just a follow-up," I tell her. "You're not in trouble."

Her eyes land on mine. "I get off in five minutes," she says.

"Fine," I tell her. "I'll wait in the dining room."

She gives me a quick nod, and I order a coffee and take it to a table in the back of the restaurant. The place is busy with moms doing their best to contain children who swarm the space, dropping fries and spilling drinks. Laughing. Crying. Whining. I know being a detective is very hard work, but I don't think there is anything more difficult than dealing with customers at a fast-food franchise on a busy street. People come in, order, mess up the place, and leave without so much as busing a tray back to the front of the restaurant next to the big "Thank You" sign over the trash receptacles.

The coffee is terrible, but I drink it anyway.

Jordan comes over right away. She's no longer wearing her Wendy's uniform but is dressed in jeans and a lightweight pink sweater. She's transformed herself from a counter person to a more sophisticated-appearing woman. It seems to me that she could find a better paying job than Wendy's, but I have no idea what led her to this vocation.

Jordan tells me when she notices my surprise.

"My dad owns this place," she explains as she slides into the seat across from me. "We have one in Olympia and Long Beach too. I'm taking business classes." She looks over at a particularly unruly little boy and gives me a shrug. "Someday this will be mine. Lucky me, right?"

I smile. I like her right away.

"Jordan," I say, pretending to enjoy the coffee, "you were there when Ally Tomlinson was found."

"Right," she says. "I mean, I never thought I'd ever see anything like that in my life. Working here, you see a lot, let me tell you that. Probably the only weirder place to work is the public library. My roommate, Charlotte, works there. People are very strange."

I didn't know that about the library. I tell myself that the next time I'm there with Emma I'll be more wary.

"Tell me what happened in front of the Starbucks," I say as I half turn my head in the direction of the parking lot.

She thinks a minute. "Right. Okay. I was coming out of Starbucks and I heard this yelling. It was Luke Tomlinson. I mean, I didn't know his name at the time but I do now. Anyway, I saw him pull in off the road, into the lot, and brake suddenly. Like something big was happening inside the car. He opened the door and started yelling about his little girl."

"What were his words?" I ask.

She takes a breath to think. "Exact words? Not sure. It happened so fast. He was yelling that he needed help. You know, 'Help me! Somebody, help me! My little girl can't breathe!'"

"What was his demeanor like, Jordan?" I ask.

"At first, totally freaked out," she says, her confidence building. "He was yelling at the top of his lungs. You couldn't not hear him. That loud. It sent chills down my spine. I dropped my Frappuccino and hurried right over to see if I could help. I knew something terrible had happened. He was panicking. I mean, literally panicking. He said he didn't know how to do CPR. I told him I did, and we struggled to get her out of the car seat. It was weird, because he was struggling so much. Like he was so scared and out of it that he couldn't undo the straps. I took over. I have a nephew. It's tricky but not that tricky."

"You did CPR?" I ask. "Because he didn't know how?"

Jordan's mouth is a straight line, her eyes fixed on mine. She takes another deep breath and starts firing more of her story at me. "Right. We have to take CPR training because of the restaurant. Kind of required in case someone chokes or whatever. Anyway, I'm certified."

"That's good," I say, mostly because I believe it, but also because the young woman needs to take a breath. She's that intense.

"Right," she says, sucking in some much-needed air. "It's very important."

A mother starts to move her children to another table.

"Then what happened?" I ask.

Jordan waits a moment for the woman to get settled. "All hell broke loose," she says, dropping her voice a little. "People came from all over the strip mall, trying to help. One lady was screaming that the baby was dead, but I kept going until the paramedics came. I was taught that you keep going because you might be doing some good, but with a baby, well . . . it's kind of hard to tell."

I know that Jordan Conway gave it her all on that hot, sticky black-top. She was not a quitter.

"What was Luke doing?" I ask.

Jordan hesitates. She studies my eyes to measure what I'm thinking as if she's about to say something that warrants a little introspection. Finally she goes for it.

"I've seen enough TV to know that it's very important to remember that not everyone handles a stressful moment in the same way," she says. "Not everyone acts the way you'd want them to."

She's right about that, of course. She's thoughtful. She's the kind of witness that can help either side of a case.

"I'm interested in what you saw," I say. "Tell me."

Jordan takes a napkin from the dispenser and works on coagulated ketchup spatter that's found its way into the seam between the wall and the slightly worn tabletop.

Someday all of this will be hers.

"I told my roommate about it," Jordan says. "I didn't even think I would mention it to anyone ever again, but it just seemed kind of strange. Kind of inappropriate."

My heartbeat speeds up. "Inappropriate how? In what way?"

She stops cleaning and wads up the now-bloody-looking napkin. "Feels inappropriate for me to talk about his inappropriateness."

This is the world we live in, I think.

"It's fine," I say. "I need to know, Jordan. What happened? It could be important or it could be completely nothing. Don't worry about it. You're reporting your observation. You're not making a judgment."

And, yes, I understand: everything is a judgment.

She'd been so confident a moment ago, but I see her sink a little in her chair.

"Go on," I encourage her.

Jordan runs her hand over the clean table. "It makes me feel a little stupid," she says, looking away. "Like you think that I think that I'm all that, but, really, I know I'm not."

"What?" I press her. "What happened?"

"He kept staring at me," she finally says.

"At you?" I ask.

She looks at me. "At my top," she finally says. "I swear to God, that's what I thought at the time. I thought it was so weird, because his kid was basically dying, but he was checking me out. Really. I'm not even joking."

"No," I say. "I expect you're not."

She keeps her gaze directly on me. "You know what it's like," she tells me, as if I do. "Guys come up to the counter to order, and I feel like telling them, 'The menu is above me, not here.'"

She points to her breasts. They are substantial, but not in the way that should invite that kind of intrusive scrutiny. The truth is I really don't know what it's like. I never had much of a chest. Stacy, on the other hand, is better endowed—and yet she had implants too.

I suddenly flash to the time when Stacy told me that I was lucky to be average, because no one was jealous of average people.

"I envy you so much, Nicole," she told me after she married Cy. "You will always be you. I have to be the ideal."

It was a dig. Stacy was always a good digger.

"I see," I say to Jordan. "So that's what he did? When you were trying to resuscitate Ally?"

"Right," she continues. "And after. Like, every time that I looked at him I swear to God his eyes were there and not on anything else. It was really messed up. I know I'm right. Even though I've told myself a thousand times since that I must have been mistaken, because, you know, the adrenaline was really flowing."

Jordan stops and takes another napkin from the stainless steel dispenser. I think she's going to start cleaning again; instead, she catches a tear just as it forms at the corner of her eye.

"Sorry," she says. "But I really wanted to save that baby. I didn't know her but she was just so little. She smelled terrible. I thought it was a dirty diaper at first, but now I know better. I don't know what you think, Detective Foster, but if you ask me, I don't think that for one minute he cared about her. Not really. His kid was dying and all he was thinking about was playing with some strange chick's tits. Sorry. That's how I feel."

Jordan Conway gets up and says she needs to get back to work. I watch her depart. I know that her shift is over, but I don't say anything. Inside, I feel so sorry for her. She was traumatized by what Luke did that afternoon. For the rest of her life, she'll think of Ally.

Just like me.

Just as I'm about to stand, Jordan returns.

"I want you to put that fucker away for the rest of his life," she says, her eyes no longer sad but glowering in a kind of controlled rage that I wouldn't have expected from her. "No punishment is too good. Put him in a sauna and turn up the heat. He should feel what Ally felt. That's what you should do. That's exactly what I'd do."

She doesn't wait for a response.

"Thanks, Jordan," I say, not really knowing how to respond to that. I'm all about due process. Sure, I have fantasies about what could—or should—be done to a child molester, for instance. Everyone does. But true justice is built on facts, not a vengeful and misguided social media beatdown. Or a fantasy in which a perpetrator is put in his or her place with methods that mimic what they'd done to the child.

As I get in my car, I immediately crack the window and turn on the AC. I should have parked in the shade and risked the oozing pitch of the spruce tree that shaded the space two car lengths away. My phone pings, and it's a text from Carter.

```
Let's see how things were yesterday with
Luke at work. Meet me at the office.
```

I put my car in gear and drive in the direction of the Aberdeen Police Department. As the heat escapes, I think of Ally.

CHAPTER EIGHT

Wednesday, August 16

On the way to WinCo, Carter and I discuss the latest on the case. Luke Tomlinson's arraignment was scheduled for the afternoon, and we now knew that the prosecutor's office was looking at multiple charges, including second-degree murder, child endangerment, child abuse, and assaulting a police officer. A search warrant had been issued for Ally's father's laptop, work computer, phone, and any other electronics he owned or used on a regular basis.

"Mia's phone too?" I ask Carter, as we pull into the grocery store's busy parking lot.

"Yep. Hers too."

"Good."

"Autopsy tomorrow morning too."

"Lots going on," I say.

◆ ◆ ◆

The offices at WinCo are on the second floor in the back of the building. I've shopped there before, but I had no idea that it was a regional hub for the grocery chain. Luke's assistant district manager, Darren Huff, leads us to an employee conference room. Huff has little to add, even though Luke had boasted that he was the "assistant" to the assistant.

"Nice kid," he says. "Good worker. Sometimes a little distracted, but that's par for the course around here with this age group. Always on their phones. Watching Netflix at their desks. God knows what else they do when I'm not around. In any case, I'm in shock. I can't imagine how the hell Luke could forget that his kid was in the car. These kids today just aren't wired right. It has to be that. Internet's ruining an entire generation."

He stops and looks at Carter and me.

"Sorry about the soapbox," he says somewhat sheepishly. He points through the conference-room window. "These two guys are Luke's buddies here at work. Gavin is in purchasing and Al works in distribution. I told them they aren't in trouble."

As Carter and I go into the conference room, I notice Luke's portrait in the employee-of-the-month lineups that cover the wall. In fact, he is in three of them, for three different months. Apparently, he *is* good at his job.

Gavin Wilcox and Al Black are sitting at a large oak table, both doing exactly what their manager said they do whenever they can: looking at their phones. Gavin has a shaved head. Al wears his hair slicked back, retro style. Both in their midtwenties. The instant we step into the conference room to introduce ourselves, they set down their phones.

Gavin reveals himself almost right away as the more effusive of the pair. Al, it seems, is as laid-back as his hairstyle.

"Luke's our bro," Gavin says. "What they are saying on Facebook isn't true. He's solid."

I look at Al.

"Solid, yeah," he replies.

"I know he's your buddy," Carter says. "We're trying to piece together what happened yesterday."

"I don't know anything," Al says.

"That might be entirely true," I tell them. "But it is also possible that you know something but aren't aware of its importance."

"This was an accident," Gavin says. "Plain and simple. You're not gunning for the dude, are you?"

I shake my head. "Of course not. Even though it's very difficult— and I get how close you are—we have to figure things out."

The room is silent, and Carter takes the lead.

"Tell us about yesterday," he asks. "How did the day begin?"

The young men look at each other, and I wonder for a second if they've orchestrated some grand story to tell. Gavin speaks first. He tells us that there was nothing unusual about the day. They talked about preseason football and whether the Seahawks would make it to the Super Bowl or if their glory days were over.

"I'm a Broncos fan myself," Al interjects.

"The three of us went to lunch at Jersey Mike's at eleven forty-five," Gavin says. He stops and looks over at Al.

Again silence.

"What is it?" I ask.

"It's nothing," Al says, looking at his friend.

Discord replaces silence. The air becomes heavy. Whatever it is that Gavin wants to tell us, Al wants no part of it.

"A baby is dead," I remind them.

"Yeah, I get that," Al says.

"It might not be anything," Gavin says, shifting uncomfortably in his chair. He glances at his friend and coworker.

Al glowers and looks away.

"What?" Carter asks. "What is it?"

Gavin takes in a big gulp of air. He suddenly looks pale.

"Okay," he says, exhaling. "Fine. I know it isn't anything. It's just kind of weird. After lunch we stopped in at the office supply place next door to the sub shop. Luke needed printer ink cartridges."

"All right," I say. "Did something happen there?"

Gavin shakes his head. "No." He looks at his friend, but Al is still fixated on the tabletop. He refuses to look upward. "After. When we got back here, Luke went to his car to put the cartridges away."

Al has been silent up to now. I shift my gaze to him, and it prods him to speak up. "We aren't supposed to bring other retailers' merchandise into the store. Policy."

"What time was that?" Carter asks.

"About twelve thirty," Gavin says.

"Did you see him go to his car?" I ask.

Gavin shakes his head. "No. Not specifically. I just know he did. That day he parked out back by the river."

"Is that where he always parked?" I ask.

Gavin is mute for a second, but he finally speaks. It's clear he's very uncomfortable. His face is red, and a bead of sweat has collected around his temple. He kneads his fingers like putty. "No," he says. "Never."

"Lot was super full," Al says, once more playing defender.

The second hand on the big office clock behind them sweeps halfway around its face as both young men sit in silence. They know now that Ally was in the car. She had to be. They don't know if she was already dead or not. They know that their friend went to put something inside the sweltering vehicle. They know that any reasonable person would have noticed something.

"It doesn't mean anything, you know," Al says.

I am without words.

Carter picks up the interview. "Did Luke like being a dad?"

His tone is neutral. Not accusing. Just matter-of-fact. It doesn't sit well with Al, who knows that their friend is in big trouble. He gets up.

"I'm done here," he says. "You got it all wrong." He glances at his friend, his eyes urging him to make a break too. Gavin springs to his feet.

"Yeah," Gavin says. "He loved his kid. Kept a picture of her at his desk."

On the way out, we catch up with the manager, Darren.

"Gavin and Al tell us that Luke parked out back, by the river. Do you have cameras back there?"

Darren answers right away.

"You bet your ass we do," he says. "We have cameras all over this place. Got no choice about that. Shrinkage is our number one problem."

We walk toward the exit as shoppers push overloaded grocery carts past us.

"Can we get the recordings from yesterday?" I ask.

"You'll need a warrant," Darren says. "But yeah. Of course. I'll have everything ready."

We're outside in the oven air. I can feel the sweat start to collect on my brow as Carter and I walk around the perimeter of the building to the back lot along the Chehalis River. It's empty except for a pair of enormous dumpsters and a couple of seagulls. I spot a trio of cameras mounted in a configuration that allots maximum coverage over the parking space.

I feel sick inside. "Are you thinking what I'm thinking?" I ask my partner.

Carter studies the mostly empty expanse of the sticky blacktopped parking lot. The seagulls screech as they fight over a fast-food wrapper.

"If you are thinking that he went out here to see if his daughter was dead yet, then, yes, that's what I'm thinking," he says.

I swallow hard. My throat feels constricted, and it takes some effort.

"He planned this," I say.

Our eyes meet. "Researched it," Carter says, pulling a cigarette pack from the breast pocket of his hopelessly dated jacket.

"Yeah," I say, "that too. I wonder if Ally was still alive when he came out here. You know, like if he'd had a change of heart."

I still want to see some good in everyone. I've done that my whole life. It's gotten me into trouble in the past, no doubt, but seeing the good is the part of me that lets me know that there is a reason for my struggles. That there is a bright side to every dire situation.

At least, I think there's good in almost everyone.

"People who cook their kids in a car don't have a heart," Carter says. "So there's no change of heart. There doesn't have to be a real reason for it, either. He might have been pissed off that she cried all night. He might have decided that it was too much of a hassle juggling her, day care, and going to see a movie."

We start walking back around the WinCo to Carter's car.

"As long as I've done this job, as much as I've read about the criminal mind," he says, "I've come to believe that we are the ones looking for a reason. We are the ones who want to know why. Killers like Luke? They don't even go that deep into it. Killing your little girl? Could be something he just decided to do spur of the moment."

Carter is right about some killers. However, not this one.

"He searched on the Internet to learn more about hot-car deaths a few days prior to Ally's death," I remind him as we get inside the car and he turns on the air-conditioning.

"Yeah," he says. "I know. I just don't know why he had to take the car from WinCo to Starbucks."

"We might never know. Part of me thinks he just wasn't ready to make the big scene at work—or maybe since he parked in back there was no one to see him? You know, react?"

I tilt the AC vent away from my face. The air coming at me feels like November.

Carter puts the car in gear.

"Seems like he should have thought about that ahead of time," he says.

Chapter Nine

Wednesday, August 16

The day has been long. Interviews. Database searches. Warrants to seek. I'm beat. I say goodbye to Carter in the parking lot and pick up Emma. She is as chatty as ever, and I relish just listening for a change, as we go home to the house that had been my childhood home. We open the door, and, for the first time, Shelby doesn't come running. She's been slowing down a little lately, and the heat has been hard on her, zapping her energy. Dachshund owners sometimes joke that the breed sleeps twenty-three hours a day. With Shelby, I was sure it was only twenty-two.

"Go wake up that silly dog of ours," I tell Emma, who immediately takes up the cause while I fish through the refrigerator for the evening meal. I turn on the kitchen TV and listen to a reporter on a Seattle news station going on about the plight of the homeless. I think of the women I met in the shelter when I was homeless and wonder what became of them. I hope that the young girl who was abused by her boyfriend has moved on, that the woman who had a job interview the next day landed the position. I hope that and more. For a brief time we were bound together in a circumstance that seemed at once hopeless and punitive.

"Critics say that homeless camps draw more people to a lifestyle . . ."

The words of the reporter are a knife in my heart. Being homeless is not a lifestyle. It is a harsh reality, a last resort.

I find the hamburger and check the pull date. It's today. *Good*, I think. *Just in time.*

The meat goes into a hot skillet with a little olive oil, a chopped onion, and a clove of garlic.

Emma likes garlic.

Tonight, we're having her favorite: sauceless spaghetti.

I take out a juice box for Emma and a bottle of wine for myself. Not the whole bottle, of course. I pour a generous glass while the old hood over the stove does its best to suck in the steam from the browning meat. The moment reminds me of my mother just then. It was her recipe. She didn't like tomatoes because red sauce stained the fabric of Dad's T-shirts. Mom didn't like anything but perfection.

She must have hated me and Dad so much.

Stacy was her number one.

"Emma?" I call out. "Want some juice? It's strawberry kiwi."

I stir the meat with an old wooden spoon and think more of my sister and how I'm going to tell Emma that her mother is alive. I don't even allow myself to think just what it is that Stacy wants when she sends missives to Dad. There's a reason for that. Stacy's motives are always hidden. I know whatever she is planning on doing is for her benefit. I just never know the truth of what drives her.

The wine tastes wonderful. If I were single and didn't have a child to care for, I wonder if I'd become an alcoholic. Several people in my support group traded one addiction for another. Noreen A. attends GA, NA, and AA, the trifecta of addiction groups.

She told me one time that she had a host of food allergies that prevented her from overeating. "Otherwise, I'd likely be able to add OA to my weekly spate of meetings. Lucky me."

Emma calls to me from the living room. "Auntie Mommy!"

"Juice box is in here," I say.

"Something's wrong with Shelby!"

Emma's voice is charged with so much fear, I nearly drop my wine glass. I slide the meat from the burner. In a second I'm in the living room. Emma is on the floor next to Shelby.

"Honey," I say, joining her. "What's wrong?"

"I don't know," Emma says, her eyes huge with fear. "She won't wake up."

I scoop Shelby into my arms. She's limp, an expanded accordion. I feel her chest contract as she breathes. White spittle collects on one side of her mouth.

"Shelby, wake up!" I say.

Emma echoes my words. "Wake up!"

She looks at me. "What's wrong? What's wrong with her?"

"I don't know," I say, opening Shelby's eyes to find them rolled backward. "She was fine this morning."

With Emma trailing, I carry Shelby to the kitchen. I turn off the stove and grab my car keys. We rush outside.

The sidewalk rolls under my feet. I can barely stand. She's dying. My dog is dying. This can't be.

I put Shelby in Emma's lap and get into the driver's seat and start the car.

That dog has been through everything with me. She knows all my secrets, because she's the only one I could ever really trust. She listens. She loves me unconditionally. I would do anything for Shelby.

In five minutes we're at Dr. Kohl's office. I breathe a sigh of relief. The vet's lights are still on.

◆　◆　◆

Emma and I sit in the waiting room next to the giant scale used to weigh pets. We're quiet. The poster of dog breeds from around the world would have consumed our attention in another more routine visit. We barely glance at it.

I pray that everything will be all right. I promise God that I will spend the rest of my life doing good things for others. I will never fail again. If only Shelby can live. Before Emma, she was all I had.

Dr. Kohl emerges from the back room. His face is full of concern, and I think I'm going to let loose the tears that I have tried to banish from my eyes.

"How's Shelby?" I ask.

"We need to keep her overnight," he says. "You got here just in time."

I am so lost in my own thoughts that I don't even catch the significance of his words.

"What happened to her?"

Dr. Kohl looks at both of us.

"Poison," he says. "Maybe antifreeze? Rat poison? Hard to say without some blood work. I think she'll be okay. Not sure about any long-term damage, though."

Those tears flood anyway. Emma hugs me.

I'm shaking. "She's an inside dog," I say. "We don't have any rat poison. There's no antifreeze."

"She got into something," he says. "Or maybe someone gave her something."

His disclosure causes a jolt so strong that it stops my cascading tears. I pull myself together.

"Is she a barker?" he asks. "Not long ago I had a poisoning case. Seems like a neighbor who worked the night shift couldn't take the dog's barking during the day when he was trying to sleep. Fed the dog antifreeze to shut him up."

"Shelby is quiet," I say. "Everyone loves her."

"She got into something," he says. "We're lucky. She'll make it. Take a look around the house and see if you can find what it was that made her sick."

I take Emma's hand. "Can we see her now?"

"Sure," Dr. Kohl says. "She's sleeping. Come on back."

Shelby is curled into a tight ball on a dark blue cushion on a table in the back room. Emma and I stroke her as softly as we can. She stirs and whimpers a little, and my heart lifts. I thank God right then and there. I lean close and nuzzle her. She smells like Shelby, and that calms me. She is my family.

She and Emma.

"You're going to be all right," I say. "We're coming back to get you tomorrow." I look up at Dr. Kohl.

"Yes, tomorrow," he says. "Be sure to check around the house. No repeat of this, okay?"

Back home, Emma and I turn the house upside down as we search for the culprit. I put Shelby's ceramic water and food bowls into the kitchen sink and run hot water over them. In a complete frenzy I scrub them with a steel wool pad until my fingers bleed. How did this happen? I check the backyard for a sign that Shelby found a stash of weed killer or something. Nothing. There isn't a single clue as to what might have poisoned her.

CHAPTER TEN

Thursday, August 17

Though it is morning, a stack of mail on the passenger seat next to me is like the afternoon sun: I know I shouldn't look directly at it. Doing so will only have dire consequences. Make me blind, for instance. And yet it's there, and I have no choice. I don't even have to see all of it to know that the sliver of blue showing between the power and cable bills is another postcard from my sister to our father. I've received more than a half dozen over the past few months. All from Mexico, where my sister is enjoying the *Lifestyles of the Rich and Infamous* or some approximation of living high without a conscience.

I think of the last one. It comes at me vividly. Hard. Like a bullet. The card portrayed a Mexican sugar beach with slender, tanned figures laid out like hot dogs on that rolling grill at 7-Eleven. My decidedly much lower-rent frame of reference in the years since I returned home to Hoquiam.

Like a magician's assistant, I flipped over the card with an abruptness that startled me.

There, in her trademark purple ink, was my sister's handwriting, with heart-shaped dots atop the *i*'s:

> *Daddy,*
> *Having fun, I hope? I am. I have a problem, though.*
> *I'm a little miffed at Nicole. She's being a real b-i-t-c-h.*
> *She won't let me know how Emma is doing. Should I be*
> *worried? Has she gotten herself into that gambling mess*
> *again? Don't tell her that I said that. She's always been*
> *unstable. I don't want to rock the boat and send her off*
> *the deep end.*
> *Love,*
> *Stacy*

My blood was on a slow simmer when I read that particular missive. No rapid boil needed. When it comes to my sister, I'm a slow cooker. Stacy knows that our father has Alzheimer's and could scarcely understand the slip of paper in a fortune cookie. At least, on most days, that is. She knows that I'm going to read it. That's why she sends a postcard and not a letter inside a peek-proof envelope. She barely mentions Emma to our father because she is focused on me. It's a game. She's reminding me that she's out there, and that despite everything she has done, she has something over me. Sociopaths like my sister—there, I said it—might not be able to understand emotion or to empathize with others, but they do know love when they see it. She knows that Emma means everything to me. I wonder how she processes that. Like I'm a curiosity? Like I'm some kind of caged animal and she's in a perfectly pressed lab coat, pen poised and ready to jot down whatever it is I do—the manifestations of what love for someone looks like?

I tug at the postcard sandwiched between other pieces of mail. It's not another Mexican sky. It's a vintage image of a dachshund with his muzzle deep into a beer stein. Underneath the dog are the words "AT

HIS MASTER'S BIER." It's a cute drawing, though I know that even thinking so would get me in trouble with the ASPCA.

Dogs shouldn't drink beer.

I know. I know. I'm sorry I smiled.

When I turn over the card, I confirm it's definitely not from Stacy. It's postmarked Bellevue, Washington. She's thousands of miles south of there. Although the distance between me and where I used to live is a little over a hundred miles, it is a world away and might as well be Mexico.

Five words fill the message space. And, very oddly for a postcard, they are typed.

I know who you are.

My relief ebbs. My heart sinks. I almost wish that it were another of my sister's poison-pen postcards. I can never laugh those off, but I know who my tormentor is. This is faceless. Others out there know that I fell from grace. It isn't that I can hide my failures. It is the idea that someone feels a compulsion to remind me of them. To remind someone of their darkest moment is to show teeth in a smile, to insert a knife into a heart and spin it like a drill. Stacy is a game player, and she likes to remind me of her status in our family and in the world. Certainly she likes to hurt and inflict pain, but at least she is direct about it. This other person, not so much.

I take the postcard and turn it into confetti and stick it in the little plastic AAA trash bag that hangs over the console of my car. I try to put the postcard out of my mind. My anonymous hater is downshifted to a blip in my list of concerns at the moment. Right now, as I start to drive, all I really want to think about is Ally Tomlinson and how she ended up in that hot car in the back of WinCo. I see her little face so clearly, and when I do, I'm relieved that the image that comes to mind shows her happy, alive. That is a gift, and I'm grateful for it.

I head to the coroner's office with the knowledge that whatever he has to tell me will supplant that picture.

It always does.

CHAPTER ELEVEN

Thursday, August 17

Grays Harbor Community Hospital plays double duty in the Ally Tomlinson investigation. Not only does the deceased child's mother, Mia, work there as a nurse's aide on the pediatrics floor, but two floors below are the morgue and offices of Dr. Nigel Beakman, the longtime county coroner. His office is basement cool. A fan with a pale pink ribbon showing its jet engine–like velocity roars from the other side of the room.

Dr. Beakman is in his early sixties and by his own count has conducted more than two thousand autopsies. Though he works in a veritable backwater county, the doctor's reputation for being thorough and compassionate is widely known.

His most famous case involved the death of three men over a twenty-year period. Candace Derringer had gotten away with the murders of her first two husbands in Idaho, where medical examiners in Boise and Pocatello missed heavy metals—the marker left by arsenic—in their tox screens. When husband number three, a dentist from Montesano, succumbed after a long, debilitating, and painful illness, it was Dr. Beakman who figured out not only what Candace had done to him, but what she'd done to the other two men. She'd done what so many do. She'd spent all the insurance money and needed more. Since she hadn't been stopped in Idaho, there was no reason for her to think someone in Grays Harbor County would catch her.

Candace didn't know how methodical a coroner could be until her path crossed with Nigel Beakman's.

The coroner took it in folksy stride.

"Stopping a serial killer," he told *People* magazine, "is about the best thing a fella could do on a slow Monday afternoon."

When he sees me, Dr. Beakman nods through the window of the autopsy suite. He holds up a finger to indicate he'll be right out. Behind him, I can see the small figure of a child draped with a pale green sheet. Through the fabric covering, I can see the shape of Ally's little head, the slight bulge of her stomach and her feet. Tools of his grisly but completely necessary trade—Stryker saw, rib spreader—glisten next to her. He's done with Ally. She's been examined in every way possible. Her tiny body had become a puzzle that had been reassembled and stitched back together.

"Heart failure," Dr. Beakman says, coming through the door, "brought on by hyperthermia." A Mötley Crüe song comes from inside the autopsy suite, muting to a faint reverb as the big glass door shuts. His scrubs removed and his street clothes on, Dr. Beakman is as fit as a thirty-year-old. I don't doubt for a moment that he could outrun Al and Gavin from Luke's office. And most definitely he could best that Pillsbury Doughboy Luke Tomlinson. I wonder if seeing all that this man sees—bodies of all shapes and sizes over his long career—is the source of his ceaseless quest for physical fitness. At least once a week I catch a glimpse of him running along the river.

"Probably died around noon, give or take," he says, running his hand over his wiry hair to release it from the shape of the cap he's just removed.

He thinks that's what I've come for. It is, but only partially. There's something else I need to know.

"Doctor," I say, drawing myself deeper into the fan's cooling breeze, "the dad says that when he got in the car after work he didn't notice her right away. Not until he started driving. Witnesses at the scene say the stench was overwhelming."

"Putrefaction," he says. "Yes. It would be on a level that no one with olfactory senses could miss. Stronger than strong."

I recall Luke's excuse.

"Could, say, a rotten egg or sausage from a breakfast sandwich be mistaken for the smell of the dead body?" I ask.

Dr. Beakman lowers himself into his chair. A plaque presented to him by the local Rotary for community service is mounted on the wall next to his diploma from the University of Washington School of Medicine. A small plush Husky, UW's mascot, sits on the credenza behind him. He leans back and shakes his head.

"Detective," he finally says, "you know the answer."

He's right about that. I do. "I need to hear it from you. I'm not a physician."

"The smell of that little putrefying body, volatile gases being released into a sealed-up car with temperatures spiking on one of the hottest days of the year? It would be intolerable. I don't even know how he could open the door without succumbing to the odor. Let alone drive down the street."

"How warm do you think it became in the car?" I ask.

"Hard to be precise," he says. "Let's see, it was ninety-four on Tuesday. After about a half hour I would say about one hundred twenty-five. Give or take two or three degrees."

Seems pretty precise to me.

"He parked the car a little after nine," I say. "Ally was in her car seat. Coworkers say he went to his car around noon to put away something he'd purchased during lunch. What do you think the temperature was then?"

He thinks a second. "Maybe somewhere in the area of one hundred fifty degrees."

I want to stop the picture in my mind. "She was gone by then, right?" I ask.

He takes in my gaze and nods. "Yes. Likely so. And by then her body would have started emitting gases. She was wearing a soiled diaper. There was no way that the car didn't stink to high heaven."

For some reason I hang on the word *heaven*. That's where I told Emma that Ally had gone.

"The girl suffered," he says. "She clawed at the straps holding her in the seat."

I feel tears well up in my eyes, and I turn away.

"It's all right, Detective," he tells me. "I've been doing this a very long time and whenever I get a little one on my table, it's all I can do but remind myself that this is only evidence that the little boy or the little girl is gone."

Our eyes meet. "Thank you, Dr. Beakman. I appreciate that."

"We don't do this for the money," he says. "We do this work because we're on the right side of things."

I start to work my way to the door to leave.

He stands up. "Report will be ready later this afternoon," he says. "I'll send it over as soon as it's done."

"Thanks for that," I say, my words absorbed by the whir of the fan. "Appreciate it."

"Nicole," he says, using my name for maybe the first time ever, "we each do our part. Let's make sure this guy goes away for good. As her body temperature went up and up, the little girl cried her eyes out until there were no tears in her body. I've been around a long time. There is no crueler murder than one perpetrated by a parent on a child."

Because I'm close by and because I can't stop myself from loving him, I stop at Ocean View to see my father. He's in his bed, a cast on his right arm. "God Only Knows" is playing softly on the CD player on his bedside table. He looks at me with what used to be gin-soaked eyes, but which now seem vacant and cloudy.

"Stacy," he says, a smile coming to his thinning lips. "There's my beautiful girl. My good girl."

I don't respond right away. I've grown weary of the stalemate I've forced between us—the one in which I made the decision not to correct my father because it confuses him and there's no point in it.

I lean over and kiss him on the forehead.

"Where's your mother?" he asks. "She hasn't been here in a long, long time."

I glance at a nurse as she walks past the open doorway. I don't know why I do it, but I lean in toward my dad's ear, where there is a porcupine of hair erupting from the ear canal.

"Mom dumped you, Dad," I whisper. "She was fucking the county commissioner before she split for California to find fame. Instead she got cancer. She's dead. Stacy killed her husband, Cy. She's disappeared, Dad, and I'm raising your granddaughter, Emma. Do you understand? Can you understand anything at all? I'm Nicole, your oldest daughter. I'm all you have now and you still treat me like shit. See you tomorrow."

I pull away just as the overdubbed vocals on the Beach Boys song coming from the CD player fade to their conclusion.

God only knows is about right.

"How's he doing?" an aide asks as I walk past the nurses' station.

I don't stop. "About the same," I answer.

My Accord revs as the air-conditioning moves from furnacelike to cool. It's on the maximum setting, but it does little to cool me. It's easy for me to say things to my father when I know he doesn't understand any of it. I know that whatever he plays on that continuous loop in his brain is an amalgamation of memory and fantasy, a mean-spirited blend of selected bits and pieces from my years growing up in Hoquiam. Somehow he's been able to pick the joy from the pain and create some kind of scenario that made his wife and daughter out to be something they never could be. I'm petty. I confess. I should be happy for him, but as if I were some dog that's peed on a new carpet, my father rubs my face in it every time I see him. The doctors tell me his Alzheimer's has made his mind into a Jenga game. The pieces of his memory tumble into nonsensical and inaccurate order. I know this. And yet every time I see him, he makes me feel worse instead of better. It's like when Mom left and I cleaned the house to win him over, and he was angry because he said he couldn't find anything.

"Your coffee mug is in the cupboard," I told him one time.

"Don't you sass me, girl," he said, reaching over with an open hand.

Target hit.

My hand jumped to my hot, stinging cheek, and without so much as a peep from my lips, I ran up to my room, skipping risers to get there as fast as I could. Seconds later, Stacy appeared in the doorway on the pretense of being there to comfort me. Stacy was three years younger than I was but a know-it-all from the day she came home from the hospital.

"Dad's drunk," she said, as though it was some kind of breaking news flash. "He didn't mean it. You know that. He loves you, Nic."

I nodded at her. To engage any further was an invitation for Stacy to poke at my humiliation, my awkward embarrassment that my dad had slapped me. I sat there on the bed, clutching the soft frayed edges of the chenille coverlet that reminded me of when Mom still lived with us. *When we were a family.* I didn't cry. I never cried much at all.

A few seconds later I heard Stacy downstairs telling Dad that she didn't know why I was such a bitch. I heard him agreeing with her.

It's funny how things eluded me for so many years. Stacy was always a double agent. Ten minutes later the front door opened and closed. A car pulled up in the driveway, music blaring.

My sister found a way to turn my misfortune into something wonderful just for herself. She wasn't supposed to go out on a school night, but because I'd purportedly been so awful, she was given a free pass.

◆ ◆ ◆

I put the car in gear and merge into summer beach traffic to meet Carter at the Tomlinsons' apartment unit. We're about to execute a search warrant. I know then that whatever problems I had growing up, whatever complications I have right at that moment, are nothing compared to what happened to Ally.

I survived my childhood.

I was lucky.

Ally got into her dad's car to go to McDonald's and then on to Little Pal's Day Care. The one-year-old with big blue eyes and a sprout of red hair who'd celebrated her first birthday with a big pink-frosted cake just days ago never made it that far. Instead, she was abandoned in her car seat, trapped in a hot, airless vehicle. She'd become a victim of her father's negligence or something far worse. And when I thought of her, all I could see was how she was covered in a pale green sheet, face up in a cooler in the basement of the same hospital where her mother works just a couple of floors above.

Chapter Twelve

The Clark Terrace Apartments' buildings are nice, as Aberdeen rentals go. Painted in a creamy white with a bland, timbered facade, they are newish. Clean. They lack curb appeal, but Aberdeen was never a town concerned much with that. Like Hoquiam, Aberdeen was built with economy in mind. An unkind person—or someone who's never lived in a mill town—might turn up their nose at such a place where face value is always front and center. People who weren't raised here, a place where billowing ocean fog adds the only designer touch to the landscape, don't get it.

I think of my father just then. How he would come home from the Harbor Paper mill smelling of vanillin, the synthetic vanilla extracted from pulp. He'd grab a beer and start pounding nails on the addition that he was building. No permit. No plans. The end result showed. The windows to our den leaked from day one. He had an endless supply of caulk that he would squirt into the cracks every season. It was a patch job, to be sure.

I park next to Carter's car and get out. On the way there, I'd filled him in on what I'd learned from Dr. Beakman. Carter said little during the call. I know that he's thinking of his own kids. Cases like this one always bring a father or a mother back to their own children. It's just the way it works.

A couple of kids in board shorts and tank tops watch us from a driftwood log that was probably brought in by landscapers. The apartment manager, a beefy man with a soul patch and massive forearms that instantly make me think of Popeye, stands by the door with a master key ready. A patrol officer and his partner have cordoned off the space between the parking lot and the front door of the unit.

Carter sees the look on my face, a lingering layer of sickness that marks me as having come from a toddler's autopsy.

"You okay?" he asks.

"I'm fine," I say.

He gives me a quick nod and turns to Popeye.

"No need to wreck the door," the manager says, letting us inside. "Security deposits don't cover what they used to."

It hits me hard. Right away. I wonder if Carter feels it too.

Immediately, the apartment comes across as a tableau of a little girl's lost life. By the front door is a basket of little shoes; over it is a pegboard decorated with a row of hand-painted daisies. An impossibly tiny denim jacket hangs next to a larger one—*Daddy and Me,* I think.

Our warrant is specific. We're looking for laptops, personal computers, phones, tablets—anything that might provide an electronic chain of evidence to prove that Ally's father had deliberately left her in the car to die. Even as I process those words through my brain, I have an arduous time believing anyone could be so cruel, so utterly callous, that they would torture their own child to death.

I think of different ways people have murdered their children. Beatings come to mind. Shaken baby syndrome. Smothering with a pillow. Those scenarios are hideous, of course. Yet I know from cases that I've worked that often there is alcohol or drugs involved. That didn't appear to be the case with Luke Tomlinson. He was sober enough to go to work. Most infanticides are fueled by rage. A mother or father is pushed beyond the brink of their ability to cope by a child who can't stop crying, a baby who refuses to sleep. Even rarer are those who kill their children because a mental illness pushes them into doing the unthinkable. Andrea Yates, the Texas mom who drowned her children one by one, did so because voices inside her head insisted that by doing so she was sparing them from evil on earth and sending them straight to heaven.

The only parallel I can conjure as I survey the Tomlinsons' apartment is the case of a man who set fire to his house to kill his children for insurance money. It is similar because he turned on the gas, lit a candle, and waited for the house to blow up.

Like Ally's dad, that killer was absent from the scene of the crime.

It is, I'm sure, the most cowardly way to kill.

Just as we are about to start our search, Mia Tomlinson shows up. The hair she carefully put up in the morning for work has come undone, and her makeup is smeared. She, as my father used to say, "looks like she's been dragged through a knothole."

Sweat rolls from her temples and down her cheeks.

"Luke's lawyer said you would be here," she says in her mint-green and white nurse's aide uniform. She sets her purse on the table next to the entryway and instantaneously wedges her way between Carter, me, and the living room. "All you had to do was ask."

"We could have asked," I say, "but in the end, we're working a case. We have a lot of procedures to follow."

Mia's mouth is a straight red line.

"You know about procedures as a nurse," Carter says, hoping to defuse what might turn ugly.

"Right," Mia says. "Of course. I just wanted you to know that neither Luke nor I have a thing to hide. Open books. That's what we are, and you are making us feel as though we're bad people. You're really making things a lot worse by sneaking around and going through our stuff. You know, without asking."

"Look," I say, "we know that no other time in your life will be worse than what you're going through now. We get that, Mia. We also owe it to Ally to make sure that we know what happened to her."

Mia is tough, unwavering. "I know that you already think my husband did something wrong, but you are wrong about that, Detectives. And, yes, you are making this worse than I could have ever imagined. My baby is dead! Do you know how that makes me feel?"

I don't, and I can't deny Ally's mom that one bit of truth.

"No one can," I tell her. "I'm sorry."

There was nothing more to say about that.

"Mia, you are welcome to observe," Carter says. He hands her a copy of the warrant. "While we are here looking for specific items, we are able to examine anything that's in plain view."

Ally's mother sits in one of those white molded-plastic Ikea chairs that look cool but couldn't possibly be comfortable.

"Fine," she says. "Just get it done. I have to go back to work when you are finished."

We let her sit as we move as a pair from room to room. The living room is first. It's a bit of Ikea and a bit of Goodwill. An enormous TV hangs on a wall. It is so obnoxiously large, I find myself looking up at it very often. A black behemoth looming over the space. A PlayStation and an Xbox sit on top of a small white laminate stand beneath the TV.

Luke, with his roly-poly middle, looks like a gamer, not a runner. That's for sure. Also beneath the TV is a basket of toys, dolls, stuffed animals, and the like. I wonder which of them had been Ally's favorites.

A Care Bear stares out at me, bringing back memories of my own child-hood. Our parents bought me and Stacy a bunch of Care Bears for Christmas one year. Stacy coveted the pair that I'd been given. She begged for them, and as much as I loved them, I gave them to her.

A few months later I found them in the far reaches of the base-ment, next to the canning jars that our mother had sent me after. Stacy hadn't wanted those Care Bears at all. She merely hadn't wanted me to possess them. That scenario would play out over and over in our adult lives too. So much so, that at times I was afraid to tell her that I wanted something that I didn't yet have. Whenever I slipped, I'd find Stacy with the blouse I'd admired at Nordstrom, the dog that I'd wanted, the dream car.

The Tomlinsons' living room is tidy, and the toys make the scene so sad.

"Luke wouldn't have done this on purpose," Mia says. "He and I talked about it. We did. We knew that a hot car was dangerous to children. We aren't stupid."

Not stupid, I think, *but oddly clairvoyant.*

Carter wants to hear more.

"When did you talk about it?" he asks.

"The beginning of the heat wave," she says. "We saw something on the news about dogs being left in a car and then we remembered how that lady in Centralia left her baby in the car when she went into a tavern. It was an accident. Sad. And we felt for her at the time."

"It was tragic," I say, remembering the case, but also remembering Luke's Texas Walmart mom.

Mia is scrolling through her phone, looking at pictures of her baby.

"Mia," I say, "I know everything we say and ask you feels hurtful, but you have to remember it's for a good reason."

She looks up and sees my outstretched hand.

"What?"

"Your phone, Mia. I need to take your phone."

"My phone? You can't be serious!" Her eyes puddle. "You can't take my phone. I need it. It's my lifeline to Luke. It has all my pictures. You can't take it."

"This paper says we can," Carter says.

Mia grips her phone like it's the rocky ledge of El Capitan and she's about to plunge to her death.

"I need my phone," she says.

"Our techs will copy the phone and return it to you. All right? I'll tell them to do it first thing in the morning and I'll make sure you get it back right away," Carter says.

She looks at him, then at me. Her eyes are wet, and she's angry. Defeated. I'd seen delayed grief more than a time or two. I know that a person's response to grief varies. Some cry. Some stay mute. Some punctuate their words with tears and screams.

"Luke and I each have a laptop," she says, pulling herself together and giving up her phone. "I have a MacBook and we also have a Dell that's on life support. They're in the baby's room. That was our office before Ally."

Carter stays with Mia, and I retreat down the hall, going past some bland artwork that reminds me of a motel in the middle of nowhere.

Ally's room is a complete surprise as far as little girls' rooms go. Not in a good way. With the exception of a crib that's been converted to a toddler bed, it is mostly an office by design. A long white Formica desk runs under the window. On its cluttered surface are two laptops, a docking station, and a monitor. On the wall above Ally's bed is a poster of local hero and Nirvana front man Kurt Cobain. It's a strange choice for a nursery. Not so strange for a twentysomething's office. It hits all three marks: retro, ironic, and very Aberdeen.

I call for Carter, and he's there in a flash.

"Taking in these two laptops," I say.

He nods. "Okay. Anything else catch your eye?"

I indicate the poster with an askew glance.

"Weird," he says.

I'm grateful that he doesn't quip that it smells like Teen Spirit.

The door to the master bedroom is open, and I go inside. Carter follows. It's neat, like the other rooms in the house. Organized. The spread is a deep royal purple, and the shams are black, making the space look as though Elvira and not that winsome—and toothy—Texas couple from HGTV had decorated it. I can tell which is Mia's side of the bed because the time she's set her alarm for is for her shift at the hospital. Luke's side of the bed has no clock. On his bedside table, however, is a Neil Gaiman novel. And while my reality both professionally and personally is so very brutal, I never gravitate toward fantasy as a means to escape. I amend that thought right away. Gambling was all about fantasy. Winning was always the unicorn.

As I turn to leave, I notice the headboard and the outside posts supporting it from the floor. The posts are worn on both sides as if something—or someone—might have been tied up in bed. Into some rough stuff, those two.

Maybe not Elvira after all, I think.

More like the Marquis de Sade.

Chapter Thirteen

Thursday, August 17

I know that some other addiction often replaces a vanquished one. It's like there's a foundation of vices that exist separately but create a whole. Like bricks in a building. I don't want to be an alcoholic, but I do like a good glass of wine. This evening I sit alone in the living room while Emma sleeps upstairs. The sauvignon blanc was on sale. It's a good bottle: ninety-four points, New Zealand's Marlborough region. It's better than I normally buy. I drink only a glass each night. Sometimes two.

I feel the presence of my dad in this house more than my mother's or my sister's. The indentation that his head has left on the old green recliner is a reminder of the hours he spent in front of the old pecan console TV and record player that ceased functioning twenty years ago and now serves only to hold the flat-screen that Stacy and Cy bought him on one of their guilt trips to Hoquiam.

The spot on the headrest of the recliner is slightly discolored by the oil of Dad's scalp. Above the chair is an oil painting—*no*, I think, *acrylic*. It's a seascape with a pair of surfers fighting the waves at Washaway Beach, not far from here. The palette is gray blue with a slash of red on one of the boards. The artwork is only a notch above Art-Mart quality, yet I love how it reminds me of Dad. He used to take me to Washaway when Stacy was too little to go. I'd sit on the driftwood and watch him for hours as he and his friends played Washington's version of the Beach Boys. It was cold. Gray. Yet he seemed so happy.

I wonder if he remembers that.

I sip my wine, letting the citrusy and grassy notes coat my tongue before swallowing. Under the coffee table is a shelf brimming with old magazines that portray my father's interests: diving, motorcycles, and the one that brings a smile to my face, carpentry.

He was so terrible at that.

As I sift through the magazines, another item catches my eye for the first time. It's a cream-colored photo album that I immediately recognize. My mother started it before she left us. Its leather cover is scuffed. Embossed on it in a fancy script that makes it look as though the people whose images are inside are as regal as the Windsors or the Kennedys: *Our Family*.

The first few pages are blank except for the gummy residue indicating where photographs had once been affixed. I run my fingers over the cellophane covering. In my mind's eye I can picture what was there: photographs of my parents' wedding. My mom was the most beautiful woman I'd ever seen. In those images, now gone, she appeared like a movie star or an angel. Or maybe it was a combination of both.

I turn the page, and there is a photo of my parents standing in front of the Tokeland Hotel on Willapa Bay, south of Grays Harbor County, where I know they spent their wedding night. My dad stands tall and handsome; his arm is around my mother's perfect waist. I cannot tell anything about how she was feeling at that moment.

Someone—my father, I think—has excised her face from the photo.

As I look through the pages, I see the recurring theme. Mom, who left us all alone in pursuit of her dreams, has been eliminated from "Our Family." I can't blame Dad. She hurt him to the core. Mom was a cyanide-laced apple. Outside—gleaming, flawless. Inside—something so vile and so selfish that she was unable to possess a shred of empathy. I've known that my whole adult life, but it isn't until this moment that I know there is another word for *mother*: sociopath. We were never anything more than something she could manipulate. Everything was a game to her.

I turn the page, and I see the proof that has eluded scientists for a hundred years. Stacy. She looks at the camera with the face of an angel. She stands next to that pony she insisted Dad buy her. Her face is lit up. Her smile is a bright crescent moon in a night sky. I remember how she tired of that pony. I remember how Dad told her that a pet is a commitment that lasts a lifetime. Candy was a Shetland, light brown with a dark, toffee-colored mane. She was gentle and unafraid of children or dogs. We kept her in the backyard.

I drink some more wine and look at the bottle. More than a glassful of wine, less than two. I fill my glass to the rim.

I remember when I came home from school one afternoon. I was worried about Stacy because she'd been ill that morning and had stayed home. When I got inside, I dropped my backpack by the door. Mom and Stacy were on the couch watching *The Sound of Music* on TV. It was the old console then, flickering through a fading picture tube.

"Don't go in the backyard," Mom said.

Stacy looked up, a frown on her face.

"Why?" I asked.

"It's Candy, honey. Candy's gone."

My mother always used the word *gone* as a euphemism for *dead*. It was casual. Dismissive. When our grandmother went "gone," I thought she'd driven to the store.

I started to cry. I wanted to know what happened to Candy.

Before turning back to the movie, she said, "Poisoned. Someone poisoned the poor thing."

Stacy looked at me.

"She died real fast, Nicole," she said. "She didn't suffer."

I never forgot that exchange. It came back to me time and again. I never had the guts to ask Stacy, but in my bones I felt like Stacy—or maybe our mother—had done something to that pony. How was it that Stacy knew that Candy didn't suffer? Or how long it had taken for her to die?

I flip through the pages of the album. I know that I'm the oldest. I know that in most families the number of photographs of the oldest versus the youngest is nearly two to one. In my family things didn't work out that way at all. In fact, it is the reverse. When I flip though the remaining pages, I also notice that my mother selected group photos in which she and Stacy appeared the most animated, the most center stage. It took me until I was about twenty to realize that my eyes didn't automatically shut when the camera was pointed at me, as I had once thought. My mom, it seems, liked selecting images that made me feel bad about myself.

I'm glad my mother's dead. She has been for many years. It's terrible, I know, but I hope she suffered. And yet, at the same time, I know that any forgiveness I might have offered her would have been met with the cold eyes of a rattlesnake. She didn't understand the concept of forgiveness the same way human beings do. Those who are not narcissistic and sociopathic.

The wine is gone. I put down the leather album and grab the neck of the bottle. It's cool to the touch. As it warms, I think of swinging it like a baseball bat. But I don't. Instead, I carry it into the kitchen and drop it in the recycling bin by the back door. I look out the window and wonder if Candy's bones are still out in that grave our father dug. Or if they've turned to dust.

I wish my memories would turn to dust. Maybe my father's Alzheimer's is a gift after all.

I hear Emma stirring, and I go upstairs and sit on her bed. She's pushed her covers away, as she does nearly every night. I inch up the top sheet to make her feel secure, but not overheated. I thank God for her every day. I thank God for the chance to fix all of the things that have made my family a sordid and sorry mess.

CHAPTER FOURTEEN

Friday, August 18

It's morning, and Emma stands in the kitchen looking like Stacy did at that age. I hope to God that Stacy's good looks are all that she's inherited. Emma's hair is less strawberry than it had been when she was small. Her eyes, however, are just as blue as her mother's. They flicker in that same way that Stacy's do when the light hits them just so. I find myself staring into them, wondering what else, if anything, might also be like her mother.

Before we leave for Carrie Anne's, we look at the school assignment still hanging on the refrigerator. It was the source of a great deal of effort and angst at the beginning of the summer. Her effort. My angst.

I look at the assignment, and I wonder if I've done right by Emma. She knows that her dad is dead. I couldn't lie to her about how he'd been killed in what was ruled an accidental propane-tank explosion.

I didn't tell her that her mother chose her lover, Julian, over caring for her daughter.

"She's going away on a long trip," I said three years ago when the world turned upside down. "Until she returns, I'm going to take care of you. We're going to move into Grandpa's house near the ocean."

Emma cried every night for her mother and father. I tried not to take it personally. Though I was much older, I remembered how it felt when our mother left us. I rationalized it. I thought that she was only leaving for a short time and that once she made a movie or got on TV, she'd send for Stacy, Dad, and me.

Stupid, stupid me.

In time, Emma started calling me Auntie Mommy and began to believe that her mother's long trip had in fact been to heaven. Somewhere along the way, the story morphed from a long trip to a car accident, something with more finality.

She looks up from her family tree and gives me the smile that brings me more joy than anything in my life.

"You know something?" she says, her eyes taking me in.

"What's that, honey?"

"Mommy's not in heaven."

My heart skips a beat. I wonder if she's overheard me bad-mouth Stacy one too many times. I've tried so hard to keep my anger toward my sister in check. It isn't an easy endeavor.

We gather our things and start for the door.

"What do you mean?" I ask.

"I saw her," she says.

Emma had frequent dreams about her mother the first year of her absence. Not many since. Though I know better, I ask her anyway.

"In a dream?"

"No," she says. "For reals."

I lie to myself. I tell myself that a child's imagination is powerful. I give Emma a big hug and lay a soft kiss on her cheek. As we head out into the hot blankness of the world outside for the car, I pretend to fidget with my keys and lock the dead bolt. I'm buying time. I try to hide the worry on my face by looking deep into my purse.

How to answer her?

"I know how much you miss your mom," I finally say as I start the car. "And your daddy too. I know they are watching over you, Emma." It's a lie, but it's also a kind of wish too.

As it turned out, taking a swing at a police officer was only the middle of a very bad day for Luke Tomlinson. On the morning of the fourth day of the case, charges were amended from second-degree murder to homicide. I wasn't in booking to hear how the news went down, but Nora Harper, the department's victim advocate, has excellent hearing.

I catch her eye from my desk, and she stops her loping gait. She looks perturbed about something.

"What is it?" I ask.

Nora folds her arms and takes a breath as she stands outside my office. She's closing up, centipede-like.

"I'm telling you—and you know I don't like to talk about pending cases whatsoever—this rant of his was completely over-the-top. I was outside the jail and I could hear him wailing and yelling and repeating over and over how 'you have it all wrong! You don't know me! I'm not that guy!'"

Nora stops to allow me to soak it in.

"But I think he *is* that guy," I say as she stands outside of my office.

"He probably is," Nora says. "Due process is needed, of course. But seriously, Nicole, he was all over the place, pitching the biggest fit that I've ever heard in my life. He was like a three-year-old at the checkout line wanting a Snickers bar. Such a fuss over his county-issue clothes. Like that was something to be mad about."

"I get the picture," I say.

"Get this," Nora goes on, a bit uncharacteristically. "Never once did he mention his daughter. Or his wife, for that matter. It was all about him, him, him."

"He's his own favorite person, is he?" I say, without a touch of sarcasm.

None needed.

"Yeah," Nora says, letting her arms dangle. "I don't get it. I really don't. Mia seems like a lovely young woman. What in the hell did she see in him? She's working her butt off, trying to get her nursing degree and make some real money, and she's somehow ended up with this selfish, self-absorbed moron."

Nora lingers a little in my office doorway. She's a towering figure at nearly six feet tall, but her ability to reel people in makes every conversation seem like she's at eye level. I suspect she wants to come in, but the truth is we really can't talk about the case any more than we already have. We are smile-and-wavers, people like Nora and me. The ties that bind us are solely the result of the cases that keep us awake at night. While it feels like there is a friendship, it's really not like that at all. It's more like, I imagine, the relationships that maybe stamp or butterfly collectors share. They can talk all day and night about an Abraham Lincoln stamp or an Amazonian swallowtail, but after that, they have nothing else to say to each other.

I want to ask her if Mia had said anything useful, but Nora won't go there because she's professional and she knows that divulging any information to the police will eat away and almost certainly destroy her relationship with victims.

Nora Harper needs victims more than she needs friends or allies.

I understand. Not long ago, I needed the sound and promise of the casino's slot machines more than I needed my old life. I can see more clearly now the things that have blinded me. Disaster has a way of either saving or killing you.

"Leaving your child in a hot car to die," I say to her, "is the cruelest way to kill that I can think of."

Nora nods. "Of course he says—and I mean very loudly—that he didn't do any such thing."

"Right," I say. "Just a mistake he made."

She sighs. "The biggest mistake he'll ever make, I suspect, for the rest of his life."

"I guess that's what we're here to figure out," I say. "Just where he will spend the rest of his life."

"That's up to you and the prosecutor's office," Nora says, finally turning to leave. "I can't help you there, but I think you know where my prayers are going."

I give her a slight nod.

"Same place as mine," I say, but Nora's already gone.

The news alert on my PC flashes. It's a story about Luke Tomlinson's charges being amended to homicide. His booking photo has already made it to the media. He looks at the camera dull eyed. His mouth seems to be in a smirk, but part of me wonders if it's just because I know what he did.

Just like he does.

The story recounts what happened in that parking lot and indicates that Luke researched hot-car deaths just prior to Ally's murder. Some anonymous friends of the Tomlinsons talk about how shocked they are that it happened, and they say the police have it all wrong. "The lead investigator has a lot of baggage of her own. She's botched up some cases in the past."

One slings an arrow in my direction, but I don't wince. I'm stronger than that. Of course, I can't argue against that. In fact, when Carter got me into the department for the interview, he told me that the key to my future would be to view everything as the next step in some kind of personal rehab.

"Never push back on what anyone says about your past. Pushing back will only add more fuel to a fire in which you have no control. Like an arsonist who miscalculates how much gas it will take to burn down a house—and kills himself too. Your good work over time will see you through this."

He's right and I know it.

I scroll down and read some comments below the article. They are all written in the same vein.

Luke's a creep.

Kill him.

Put him in the oven.

Stick him in a microwave.

Make him lick a cattle prod.

That last one is original, and more appropriate for a child molester, but the Internet mob takes everything to the nth degree.

The people of Grays Harbor County have been through a lot since the mills closed. While they have been smacked hard by the economy, oppressed by more cloud cover than just about anywhere in Washington, they are a people who want justice, especially among their own.

A woman from Montesano writes:

Jesus Christ! I have four kids of my own. I don't have a good job. Things are hard. But they've always been hard. I would have taken baby Ally in a minute and loved her like my own. Some people are so selfish that they can't see anything but their own reflection. That's Luke. Piece of shit, I'd say.

Luke's reptilian stare looks back at me from the computer screen.

She's right, I think to myself. *You are a piece of shit. And I'm going to make sure that you stay right behind bars for as long as we can. Ally deserves that. Mia too.*

CHAPTER FIFTEEN

Friday, August 18

"The lead investigator has a lot of baggage of her own."
    That night at home that phrase circles back to me. Pushing me.
Pulling me. *I know who you are* or some variant always reminds me of
the name of a Jennifer Love Hewitt film when I was a teenager. The dark
threat comes from nowhere but bores into one's psyche until he or she
is forced to do what they probably should have done all along. I avoid
googling myself for the very reason that I already know what's out there
about me. I know who I am and what I've done.
    The dachshund card niggles at me too, though I know I'm an idiot
to let a printed piece of paper get under my skin. I know that. Even so,
I find myself staring at my laptop, with a glass of sauvignon blanc taken
from the shelf just above WinCo's polished concrete floor. When I type
in my name, I find what anyone can find about me. The first mention of
me that pops up is in connection with the Kelsey Chase murder investigation. Before that, I was probably only listed in Classmates.com or
in the posted board minutes from my old condo in Bellevue. I'd asked

for permission to add a narrow—and I thought very tasteful—window box to my kitchen window.

Denied.

I think now that I should have said that the window box would be used to grow herbs for the disadvantaged.

Approved!

I look through the bread crumbs of my name online, just as I know someone else did before sending the dog card. As others have done since Ally Tomlinson died in her father's sweltering Subaru.

Kelsey Chase Murder Case Baffles Bellevue Police

That article suggested that we didn't know what we were doing—but that my ex-boyfriend and partner, Danny Ford, insisted that everything was under control. I know now that's because he was wrapped up in it tighter than the expensive sheets in which the little girl's body was found.

I sip and scroll through articles that highlight key points of the investigation and our focus on Alan Dawson, a registered sex offender who was married to his victim at the time. Both were teenagers at the time of his statutory rape conviction, and I know now that while there should never be a gray area in cases involving sexual abuse, that time there was.

I gulp instead of sip when the next headline jabs me.

Dawson's Widow Says "No" to Suicide Claims

Charlene Dawson's face comes to mind. I have never seen such assured fury before. She had every reason to be enraged at me, though at the time I really wasn't sure if her husband had committed suicide or not. That's a game I still play with myself, avoiding what really happened in his jail cell.

Detective on Leave from Bellevue Police Department

The beginning of my extended tour of shame began with my dismissal from Bellevue PD. While I hadn't participated in any of Danny's machinations to control the case, I had been with him every step of the way. I had been the healthy limb on the maple tree that had to be sacrificed in order to save it.

Ford Pleads No Contest on Obstruction Charge

Again a reference about me that only amounted to a single line. "Prosecutors say Nicole Foster, Ford's former partner and girlfriend, was in line to be a chief witness."

Ford Sentenced to Prison for Falsifying Records, Confession

They ran my academy photograph with this one. My father would have been so ashamed if he could remember who I was.

Detective Resigns, Seeks Treatment for Gambling Addiction

No picture this time. Just a short mention that I recall wasn't even juicy enough to be on the front page—a gift from God or the night desk editor for which I will be eternally grateful. Whoever thought any publicity was good publicity was probably a publicist. Not a human being. Not someone like me. I could never apologize enough for the mistakes I made.

Two Dead in Kirkland Gas Leak Explosion

I'm buried at the end of the story that recounts the explosion that killed Cy Sonntag, Stacy's husband, and Tomas Vargas, a nineteen-year-old gardener with no family in this country. The teen had been at the wrong place and wrong time. In the three years since it happened, the burden weighing on me has only grown heavier. I think about Tomas all the time. It weighs on me more than a pile of stones. I tried to find his family.

"That part was an accident," Stacy had insisted, as if that absolved her from a second murder.

Gas Leak That Left Two Dead Ruled an Accident

Someone at the scene took a picture of me comforting Stacy as we stood on the street just after the blast. My name appears only in the caption. I can still feel the phoniness of Stacy's embrace and the tears that she'd mimicked from watching others who have a heart that does more than circulate blood through the human body. Even now, I hear her whispers in my ear.

"You have to believe me," she tells me like I'm a moron. "I didn't want for this to happen."

I didn't answer her back. How could I? She set a trap for her husband. She cooked up a plan that got her what she wanted—rid of her husband, money beyond anything we could have imagined as kids, and a new lover. "You have to break some eggs to make an omelet" came to mind—an adage that our father frequently used when one of his schemes fell flat. Stacy was that cavalier about it. She was. She really, truly was.

And that was it. I was shamed. My sister escaped a murder charge. My new boyfriend, Julian, had been in cahoots with her all along. I was the safety net, I guess. Someone who would come to her aid if the investigation went sour. That was what I was to her. A thing to be used. Now, when I look back on it, I find something in the hideousness of

Stacyland, a place in which she's the princess and the rest of us are a herd of footmen or Cinderellas, that gives me hope and makes me want to breathe another day.

Emma.

It's always been that little girl. She's like me, I think. Not a mini-me in her looks. Not even her personality. She's brighter. She's comfortable in her own skin. She sees things to marvel at, instead of things to fear. She's like me in that I knew that something was wrong with my mother. I knew that she didn't have the capacity to really love me or Stacy. Emma didn't deserve that kind of upbringing—the kind that makes a child an accoutrement, an accessory that can be shelved, boxed up, pushed aside. I goddamn wasn't going to let that happen to her. Period.

Chapter Sixteen

Saturday, August 19

Saturday morning cartoons no longer captivate Emma, and she sits on the sofa with the family album in her lap. A planned day trip to Ocean Shores with Carrie Anne and the other kids the next day fuels more interest in my family's past when I tell her that we still own a little cabin on the coast not far from there. She wants to go, of course.

"Renters moved out a few weeks ago," I say. "I suppose we can go sometime soon and see what needs to be done."

She looks up at me and smiles while turning the cellophane-covered color and black-and-white photographs.

I wish that I'd thought to burn the family album, but I didn't.

"Is this you and my mom?" she asks, tapping on a photo.

I slide next to her and put my arm around her gently. The photograph is the one of Stacy and me standing next to Candy, Stacy's pony.

"Yes, Emma," I say. "That's your mom." I indicate Stacy. "And that's me," I say pointing to a girl I can hardly remember.

"Whose pony?"

"Your mom's," I say.

"I wish I could have a pony," she says.

I wish you could have had a decent mother, I think.

"Maybe someday," I say.

"Mom was pretty," Emma says.

"Yes," I say. "She was. She was the prettiest girl in the county. That's what Grandpa said. Grandma too. When your mom was first born, Grandma and Grandpa used to go to the Wishkah Mall to push her around in her baby carriage just to soak up all the compliments."

Emma's already-enormous eyes grow even larger.

I don't tell her that when I think of Stacy in that carriage, my mind touches on *Rosemary's Baby.*

"Do I look like Mommy?" she asks.

"You do," I say, turning her chin so she looks into my eyes. "You do. You are just as beautiful. But you're more than that, Emma. You are smart and funny and caring."

She smiles, returning to the photo.

I wonder if Stacy would have been a different person if our parents hadn't focused so much on her looks. If they'd emphasized the importance of character instead.

"What happened to the pony?" Emma asks.

"The pony got old and died," I say, lying to the little girl I love so much.

"That makes me sad," she says. "Mommy wasn't old when she died, was she?"

"No," I tell her. "She wasn't. Sometimes accidents happen and people are taken very young, like your daddy and your mommy."

She thinks a bit.

So do I. I think about how Stacy killed Cy. I think about how I lied about the car accident that I said took Stacy's life.

"I really miss my mommy and daddy," she says.

No words are more difficult to hear.

"I know," I say. "They are still with you." I touch her heart. "Right here. Always right here."

She turns a few more pages of the album, and I provide a kind of bland commentary on our growing-up years in Hoquiam. It's the kind of speech one would give a neighbor, just enough to ring true, but nothing the recipient of the stories could use against you later.

"I don't miss her as much as I used to," Emma says, going back to thoughts of her missing mother. "Is that bad?"

"No," I tell her. "Memories fade over time."

She can see the sadness in my eyes, and she backpedals a little, I think to make me feel as though the loss isn't so great and that she's doing fine. "She wasn't always nice to me," she says. "She made me play in my room all the time. By myself."

"She was very busy," I say, unsure why I continue to defend Stacy. But I do. To Emma, I always do.

"You're busy too," my niece says, closing the book. "You find time to spend with me. You never make me go to my room to watch a video. Mom did. She did that all the time."

"Let's get some ice cream," I say, ending the conversation.

She grins. It's a happy and genuine smile, and in my heart I know it has nothing to do with ice cream at all.

The rest of the day passes as all Saturdays should. Emma, Shelby, and I spend our time together. We're a family. We have been one for three years. I won't let anything get in the way of that.

Not even Stacy.

CHAPTER SEVENTEEN

Sunday, August 20

The weather changes overnight as low clouds roll off the Pacific on Sunday morning. And nearly at once a steaming mugginess is replaced with a marine layer that hugs Aberdeen and Hoquiam like an oppressive grandmother. The temperature has dropped twenty-five degrees. At least. It's a welcome change, of course. I don't have AC in the house, and the quintet of fans that I've set up to force hot air out and cool air inside have left an octopus of extension cords that I know carry a risk. The scene outside my father's house is slate and white, a kind of blankness that comes when the foggy curtain descends over the area, as it does for most of the winter. The heat wave that killed Ally Tomlinson is gone.

I think of Ally's last ride with her father as I buckle my seat belt and turn on the ignition of my car. Yesterday was an anomaly. There is no Sunday during a homicide investigation. At least there isn't in Aberdeen.

I wonder if Luke had the radio on when Ally fought for her life. If he played a Nirvana song to match the sticker on his back window. I wonder which one. "All Apologies," I think, imagining that he had some feelings for the little girl who he let bake to death. Stupid me. After I drop Emma off at Carrie Anne's for the trip to the beach, I drive the short distance along the flatness that is most of Grays Harbor County to the Clark Terrace Apartments. The spaces allotted to the Tomlinsons are empty. Mia is at work. Luke is in jail. I watch for a minute as a stoop-shouldered old man with a Smith Brothers beard swings a leaf blower over the asphalt of the parking lot. A cottonwood shed its silver-backed leaves during the heat wave, and the force of the leaf blower moves them like a cyclone to a vacant lot where they'll be someone else's problem.

I wish Ally had been discarded like that, given away to someone who'd love her. Or just left in that lot in the hope that someone would see her and scoop her up. At least abandonment would have given her a fighting chance. There were a zillion other choices that Luke could have made that morning. More than a zillion. All would have been better than what he ultimately did. Why, I wonder, was that the solution he settled on?

I start driving toward the McDonald's where Luke gave Ally her last meal. Had he thought of it that way? Was there a moment after McDonald's that he considered changing his mind? I order a cup of coffee in the drive-through speaker and pull up to pay at the cashier's window. The girl who takes my debit card wears braces and a big smile.

"Have a really super day," she says.

"You too," I say.

I ease my car toward the second window, and this time a young man with shaggy black hair and a Band-Aid over a tattoo on his neck hands me my coffee.

"Warning label, ma'am," he says. "Coffee's super hot."

As I pull away, I drive toward WinCo, tracing Luke's route to work. Traffic is light, and as I pass by a vacant grocery, an astrologer's storefront, and a tavern, I wonder if there was anyone out that morning who saw the wine-colored Subaru with the little girl in back as it made its way to WinCo.

I park and get out. River smells fill my nose. I peer up at the video cameras. I wonder how much they captured. Ally was so small. Had she drifted off to sleep after McDonald's? Or as Dr. Beakman suggested, did she awaken in a weakened state, crying out for help before succumbing?

I think of the Internet links that Luke visited. All had decent and prudent advice on avoiding the scenario. None was a how-to-kill-a-child-or-pet website like the kind terrorists and anarchists put up to guide the gullible, the stupid, the angry, into doing harm.

Leave your window open if your dog is in the car.

Never leave a child unattended.

Break the glass if you see a child or animal locked in a car.

Every second counts.

Luke Tomlinson did what he wanted to do. I get back into my car and drive to the Starbucks parking lot where Luke would have a purported epiphany that his little girl hadn't been dropped off at day care. Jordan Conway would spring into action, and Luke would stand there wringing his hands as if it were all some big human error.

All apologies.

Chapter Eighteen

Sunday, August 20

After meeting at the police department, Carter and I return to Clark Terrace and park in the visitor's space closest to the Tomlinsons' unit. A wilted bunch of daisies sits forlornly on the welcome mat in front of their apartment. It's quiet. Unbelievably sad. I wonder who brought the flowers. Some kids circle the parking lot on their bikes, and two cats hunker down in the shade under the sole landscaping near the entry, a rhododendron. The Tomlinson unit had been thoroughly searched, of course, but there is always the chance that neighbors can tell us something helpful. I lived in a place similar to this in Bellevue before I bought my now-foreclosed condo. Condo and apartment neighbors generally keep their distance, barely offering a nod or wave. Most times, neighbors pretend not to even see the person who's getting out of their car and trudging up the stairs to the unit next door to their own. Despite all of that, they listen. They watch. They have opinions and complaints about everyone.

We knock, and the door is answered by a man who gives his name as Mick Hightower. His unit is to the north of the Tomlinsons'. Mick is a large man with a barrel chest and a white plume of chest hair that pokes like a fountain out of the top of his shirt collar. I tell him why we're there, but he already knows.

"Look," he says, opening the door a little wider, but not inviting us in, "that kid cried all night. All night. Every night. I had to buy a box of earplugs to shut out the noise."

"That must have been annoying," Carter says.

"I have kids," Mick says. "They're grown and gone now. But, yeah, it was very, very annoying. Cute kid, though. I've got nothing against kids. Not like those two."

"What do you mean, Mr. Hightower?" I ask.

He rubs his big hands over his thinning hair, and in doing so, his chest-hair plume pushes toward me like a spear.

"Nothing specific," he says. "Just a feeling that they couldn't be bothered with the little girl."

"You say *they*?" Carter asks.

"Yeah," he says. "Look, who lets their kid cry like that? I thought for a while that maybe parenting rules have changed again. Like, when my boys were small, it was suddenly no longer okay to give 'em the belt. Maybe you can't do anything if your kid cries now."

I want to say, *You can comfort them,* but I don't.

"You mean both of Ally's parents, right?" Carter asks.

He nods.

"You ever see them do anything to Ally?" I ask.

Mick thinks a moment. "I don't know what you're getting at, Detective. If I'd actually seen anyone harm a child, I'd bust 'em in the snot locker so fast, they wouldn't know what hit them. So, no, I never saw anything. All I saw was a couple of young, selfish kids who didn't seem to give a crap about their little girl. Nothing specific with the exception of the constant crying."

I give Mick my card and thank him.

"World's going to hell in a handbasket," he says. "I used to think that Aberdeen escaped a lot of the bullshit that you see on the news all the time. Not anymore. What kind of piece of shit leaves their kid in a car to die? No way to make sense of that. I'm not going to try. I guess that's your job."

I take down his information. There's nothing specific here that could be used in a case against Luke, just the sick-to-my-stomach feeling that Ally never had a chance.

Carter and I knock on a few more doors, but either no one is home or the resident says he or she never even noticed the Tomlinsons.

In the car on the way back to the station, we sit in silence for a while. I feel like crying. It feels so hopeless. Not the case but the reality of what happened to Ally.

Carter sees it in me.

"I feel the same way, Nic," he says.

"Just plain sad," I say.

"Just a baby," he says.

"Yeah. A beautiful little baby girl."

"Any other family would have been overjoyed to have her," Carter says.

I know I would have. I know how blessed I feel to have Emma. Her mother really didn't want her; otherwise, she wouldn't have given her up to me. Threats or no threats. Stacy handed over Emma as if she were a white-elephant gift that she didn't mind forgoing on the off chance she'd get something better.

"In every child-abuse case that I've worked," I finally say, "there have been a handful of people who saw something that wasn't quite right but didn't report it to anyone."

"Yeah," Carter says, pulling into our lot. "No one wants to be the person who trips the trigger on an investigation like that. Not unless they saw something that couldn't be explained away. Like bruises on a kid."

"I had a case in which the grandmother saw bruises and a broken arm and believed that her grandson was accident-prone, because that's what her daughter told her."

"She didn't really believe that," Carter says.

"No, probably not. It was a lie she told herself."

"What happened to the kid?"

"Died. The little boy fell down the stairs. His mom shoved him."

As we sit there in the parking lot of the Aberdeen Police Department, the air-conditioning chills my spine. I think about all of the kids unlucky enough to be born into a family in which there was a monster. They are out there. Always trying to placate the monster so they won't be hit, beaten, locked in a closet. They start each day with the hope that something will be different. They retrace everything they've done to find a path to love. What did they do? How can they undo it? Are all kids punished like this?

Are all kids bad?

It hits me so hard that I can barely breathe. The cold air from the AC is coming at me with such force, I think that I can't pull in any oxygen. Carter looks at me with those caring eyes of his. I want to tell him more about my sister, because he is the only one that I can trust.

But I don't.

Instead, my mind races back to Emma. I will never give her up. No matter what. She is mine. My love.

And I will never fail Ally Tomlinson.

I failed one little girl already. Every day and every night, I think of Kelsey Chase. I know I always will.

The engine is off now.

"Are you all right?" Carter asks me.

I glance at him. "I'm fine," I say.

It's a lie.

I'm never fine.

CHAPTER NINETEEN

Monday, August 21

It's early the morning of the seventh day of the investigation, but I cannot miss this appointment for any reason. It's at a church, but it isn't about God exactly. Even so it has been my salvation.

The faces in the basement of the Methodist church on Sitka are more beat-up versions of the ones that confronted me when I attended Gambler's Anonymous meetings in Bellevue when my desire to win at slot machines ruled every waking hour, every relationship that I had. These people aren't doctors and lawyers or PTA moms, although they might have been if they hadn't been a millworker's son or daughter. Like any disease, gambling is classless. It sucks the rich, the poor, the smart, and the stupid into its glittery world of quick riches.

It's a disease that tells the afflicted that life-changing moments come with the pull of a lever or the push of a button.

I'm Nicole here. I'd be Nicole F. if there were another Nicole, but there isn't. Two Ambers, though. Used to be two Desirees, but one quit the group. I smile as I look around. I know that a few of those sitting on the metal folding chairs stamped with the church's initials know that I'm a police detective. I don't mention my work, but Aberdeen and Hoquiam are small towns through and through.

Amber C. is sort of a friend. Not really anyone that I see outside of the group, but someone who always gives me a friendly nod and stops fidgeting with a paper clip that she's turned into a whale, swan, house, bus, or RV. I can't tell.

Despite all that's going on, I know that I have to hit the "Pause" button on my life at least twice a week and face who and what I am.

Especially today. Today it is my turn to share.

"Hi," I say, in words that used to stick in my throat like I imagine one of Amber C.'s paper clips might if I tried to swallow it. "I'm Nicole. I'm a gambling addict."

"Hi, Nicole!" they all say.

That greeting used to feel like an assault. Now it oddly feels like an affirmation. I start talking. I tell them about some of the things I used to do. How I'd go without food and use my money on the slots. How I ended up in a women's homeless shelter in Seattle. How I slept with the most narcissistic man on the planet because I thought that I was less than nothing.

They've heard most of this before. Saying it over and over sort of takes away the shame. At least a little of it. These ten people in this church really don't know me at all, but they know more about me than Carter or anyone who I work with at the Aberdeen Police Department.

I tell them about my latest temptation while they drink coffee from mismatched church mugs that, while clean, likely haven't seen a dishwasher in years.

"A few days ago," I say, "I found a string of lotto tickets in the parking lot."

Nate brightens immediately. Lotto was his drug. *More than one ticket? Much better odds*, he's thinking.

I'm sure of it.

"It was just there, you know. By my feet. Someone dropped it when they loaded up their car."

"Was it Double Summer Sizzler?" Nate asks, though he's really not supposed to.

I answer with a nod.

"Anyway, I admit that I picked them up. You know, someone had lost them. I put them in my car on the passenger seat."

I'm sure Nate is drooling now.

"I'm not a lotto person," I say, glancing at Nate. "No offense." I take a sip of coffee. "Before I started to drive away, I noticed that one of the tickets had been scuffed up a little. I don't know why I did it, but I picked up that ticket and turned it every which way to see if I could see anything. Something that might tell me if—"

"If it was a Double Summer Sizzler winner," Nate says.

I can tell that he likes lotto better than sex now. His chair has inched closer to me. In a minute, I'm sure, he'll be on my lap.

"Yes," I say, "I guess. Anyway, here's the thing. It passed through my mind that maybe there was a million dollars behind that silvery latex covering. That if I scratched it, my life could change forever. But I wasn't tempted. I know that doesn't mean that I'm cured. I know that I'll always be a gambler. I look at it this way . . . that if I was like a heroin user with my slots, then there is no need for me to go down a path to start smoking crack cocaine. Does that make sense?"

The two Ambers nod. So does lotto-man Nate (whom Amber B. and I call Lotto Trouble).

"I folded up the tickets accordion-style and took them inside the Safeway. I told the checker that someone might have spent their last dollar to buy them and while store employees might think it would be all right to see if there were any winners, they shouldn't do it.

"'Someone might have given up an awful lot to buy these,' I said to the checker. 'Like, everything they had.'"

The group is silent. Lotto Trouble crosses his legs and looks away. It wasn't the ending he wanted, but it was the ending that made me feel as if the lure of easy money might not have been about money at all. My counselor had told me that once, and I dismissed it out of hand.

"It's almost never about the money," Melissa Tovar said, in that hippie-dippie, gauzy way she had whenever she spoke. "The gambling trigger is deep inside of you, dear. You're trying to make up for something else that's missing in your life."

Someone else shares something about an online poker tournament that sucked them in to the tune of $1,200.

I thank God that I didn't go that route. Slot machines are in casinos. An online poker game is at your desk, on your phone.

Amber C. comes up to me after the meeting. "I know you're not supposed to talk about a case that you're working on," she says.

I nod and put down the stale donut offered as a refreshment. It's one of those white powdered affairs that leave a mess and the eater feeling like crap for eating it in the first place.

"That little girl," Amber C. says. "That car."

"It's a very sad case," I say. "And I'm sorry, Amber, I can't really talk about it. Ongoing investigations are kind of tricky."

She nods and gives up on her donut too.

Amber C. is a beauty. She's in her late twenties, with thick, dark hair and blue eyes the color of those geothermal pools in Yellowstone National Park. She works the counter at a deli downtown called the Upper Crust. She's bright and fun. She might have been a good friend, but good friends two gamblers can never make. And, like mine, her gambling addiction was also tied to casinos. She was a bingo player. A good one, if there can be such a thing. One time Amber C. won more than $56,000 on a single card at the Shoalwater Bay Casino in Tokeland, less than an hour from Aberdeen. The amount of her winnings was impressive, for sure, a bigger score than anyone I'd ever actually known. The current group included. Despite her big win, she hated telling people that she was hooked on bingo.

"Does anything sound more lame?" she asked one time.

Everyone in the group said it was fine, but, yes, deep down we were kind of embarrassed for her. I mean, bingo. Honestly.

I indicate some white powdered sugar on her lips. Only a friend would do that.

She wipes it away. "Well, I don't know if it has anything to do with anything." Her words drop to a whisper. Her blue eyes look troubled.

"What is it?" I ask. "Are you feeling all right?"

"Oh, I'm fine. I don't even know why I'm telling you this."

I wait.

She doesn't speak.

"Telling me what, Amber?" I ask.

She shifts her gaze toward the rest of the group; the pull-tab guys that Amber is sure are a level below bingo give her the eye.

"I don't want anyone to hear," she tells me.

The basement doesn't have many options for privacy. "I need to use the bathroom," I say. "Come with me."

I haven't escorted another girl to the bathroom since some girl needed her ponytail held up away from the toilet because she drank too much. It flashes in my mind right then that it was Debbie Manning.

Debbie. Figures. She probably demanded I assist her.

We get inside and do a cursory check of the stalls. Empty. No feet. Suddenly we're alone facing the mirror and looking at our reflections rather than facing each other. It's weird. But I go with it.

"What is it, Amber? Something's really bothering you. Do you need me to do something for you?"

She doesn't answer.

"Are you all right?"

Her eyes glisten with tears.

"It isn't me," she says, stammering a little. "It's my sister, Rachel."

"I know Rachel," I tell her, studying her face in the mirror. She seems to be in a world of hurt, and what she has to tell me is lodged in her throat. I perform a verbal Heimlich maneuver, giving her a breath to talk. "She worked in the bakery. Now in the floral department at WinCo," I say.

The name of the store sends a charge of electricity through the air. Her eyes blink.

"Does this have something to do with Luke Tomlinson?" I ask.

Long pause. I hear a toilet flush in the men's room on the other side of the wall. It's loud, *like the unleashing of Niagara Falls*, I think. Finally the sound fades away.

"Yeah," Amber says. "Rachel would probably kill me, but I think you should know about her and Luke."

"What about her and Luke?" I ask, though I already have an idea of what she's going to say.

"They were seeing each other for a while."

"Seeing each other how?"

"You know. Dating."

"Oh," I say. "Dating. You mean before he and Mia got married."

The toilet on the other side of the cinder block wall flushes again. I remember now how one of the pull-tab guys has colitis.

"No," she says softly at the mirror. "Not before. They started seeing each other after Ally was born."

I can tell that she loves her sister. I wonder if her sister loves her. I know how half of that equation works only too well.

"That's unfortunate," I say. I can't think of anything else to say. I like Rachel. She makes wonderful spring bouquets. She has great judgment about flowers. Men, not so much.

"Yeah, I was pretty sick about it. Our folks consider Rachel the good one. You know, the bingo-free girl. It would kill my dad if it gets out."

"When did the affair end?" I ask.

She finally turns to face me. "That's just it, Nicole. I don't think it's over. She told me last night that she still loves him, and she's sure that he's not the kind of guy who would do anything like the newspaper says he's done."

"I'll need to talk to her," I say. "You know that, don't you?"

She nods. "Right. I do. I told her that I was going to tell you and that if you thought it was important—and only if you thought it was important—you would have to speak to her. Get a statement, right?"

"Yes," I say. As we stand there, it runs through my head that Luke Tomlinson might be the most despicable man on the planet. I think of a bunch of those smug jerks who kill their wives or kids or parents: Drew Peterson; Scott Peterson; the Menendez boys, Erik and Lyle. Charles Manson goes through my thoughts too.

It's a hall of shame of the worst testosterone has to offer.

And Aberdeen has one of the newest members right there in our little jail.

"Please don't tell Rachel that I'm coming to see her," I tell Amber.

"You don't want her to run off?" she asks.

I don't say it, but I think it: *Bingo.*

"That's right," I say instead.

◆ ◆ ◆

The WinCo floral department is in the center of the store. It's kind of a cheerful mecca for people needing to do something nice for someone who's sick, has a birthday, or has given birth. A bunch of helium balloons emblazoned with Disney characters adds to the overall promise that whoever visits the department will leave with a smile.

Unless, of course, they've come for a funeral wreath.

Or an I'll-never-do-that-to-you-again bouquet of roses.

Or, in this case, if they work here and they are about to be outed as having an affair with a suspected child killer.

Like the young woman behind the counter, Rachel Cromwell. She's unaware that she's about to get sucked into something that she likely has not considered in her young life. She's about nineteen, I think, taller than her older sister and not nearly as pretty. Her brown hair is pulled back and falls softly down her shoulders as she concentrates on curling some white ribbon with a pair of scissors.

"Hi, Rachel," I say.

She looks up, first with the smile everyone in retail wears when encountering a customer. This one dissolves right away.

Rachel knows who I am too.

"You're not here for flowers, are you? We have some late-summer hydrangea stems." She indicates a galvanized bucket brimming with scoops of periwinkle-blue floral clusters.

I shake my head. "They're lovely," I say. "But no. I'm not."

A woman approaches and lingers by some cactus plants that have been augmented with glued-on strawflowers.

My eyes shift back to Rachel. "Can we talk somewhere?" I ask.

She sets down her scissors. "I don't want to talk."

"There's a lot at stake here," I say. "I need your help."

"I made a mistake," she says, "but I didn't do anything illegal. And neither did he. Right now I'm feeling really pissed off at my sister. God, I hate her so much."

We could find some common ground there. I'd said those same words about Stacy more than a time or two. More than a thousand times, I'd wager. *Wager*. A gambling term. Where did that come from just now?

"This is important," I tell her. "If you think that Luke is innocent and you care about him, then you need to help." The idea of helping Luke makes me sick, but the truth can be messy and sometimes misguided. I'm all but certain he killed Ally on purpose, but the ultimate arbiter will be a jury or a judge. Rachel might play a role in the outcome of the judicial process. I just need to know how.

"We can't talk here," she says, her lips tightening over perfect teeth. So perfect that I wonder if she and Amber are actually from Grays Harbor County. "I work here and this place is gossip central."

"I'm sure," I say. "We can talk at the police station."

Her eyes widen. "Oh, no way! That would weird me out. Let's go over to the Starbucks. I'm off shift in twenty minutes."

"Fine," I say. "I'll see you there."

The cactus lady catches my eye as I leave.

"I can't tell which one," she says, pointing to a yellow- and red-flowered duo.

"Both look pretty prickly," I tell her. "I like the yellow."

She smiles and puts it into her shopping cart. "Me too."

God, how I wish every decision in life could be so simple.

I text Carter and let him know to meet Rachel and me at Starbucks.

Me: She had a relationship with Luke.

Carter: No kidding.

Me: That's your response?

Carter: OTW. Order me a mocha Frappuccino. Venti.

I shake my head. I don't tell Carter that the beginnings of his spare tire could be stamped "Frappuccino" instead of "Goodyear."

CHAPTER TWENTY

Monday, August 21

The Starbucks across the WinCo parking lot is completely dead inside, though the baristas feverishly pull espresso shots for drive-through customer beverages. I order a Frappuccino for Carter, a couple of iced lattes for me and Rachel, and wait patiently while the machine that turns coffee, ice, and chocolate syrup into Carter's drug of choice roars like a chain saw under a cloche. A hipster jazz track plays, and I find my way to a table in the back under the community bulletin board. Advertisements for car washes and rummage sales blanket the space. Community here means selling something.

Carter finds me and immediately makes a face.

"Didn't I say no whip?"

"No, you didn't."

"I'm trying to cut back a little," he says, sliding into the seat next to me.

"Really? I haven't noticed."

He sips his drink, and I fill him in on what I know about Rachel.

"Maybe I should join some self-help group to get some leads," he says. It's meant to be a joke, and I'm not offended. If I had been, I would have suggested that Overeaters Anonymous might have a space for him. But since I'm not, I don't. I just think it.

Rachel Cromwell makes her way to the table. She looks nervous. Her face is pink.

"Should I have a lawyer here?" she says, sitting down. "I've never done this before and I just don't know."

I introduce Carter, and she gives him a quick nod.

"I can't answer if you need an attorney or not," I say. "If you've committed a crime, then all right, let's not talk here."

"I told you that I didn't."

"That's right," I say. "So I'm pretty sure no need for an attorney."

I slide Rachel's drink across the table. She thanks me and forces a smile. Again her pretty teeth are revealed. Around her wrists are tattoos of Scandinavian runes. In a land of barbed wire and sea-related ink, her selection is oddly out of place. Sophisticated, even. I remind myself once more to check my biases against the people and the place that I escaped and ultimately returned to.

"I know you are upset about all of this," I say.

She removes the paper wrapper from the familiar green straw.

Carter chimes in. "We realize this can be kind of embarrassing," he says. His words are meant to support her, but she bristles instead.

"Love," she says, her eyes glued on Carter's, "is never, ever embarrassing."

More annoying smooth jazz fills the air.

"When did it start?" I ask.

Rachel Cromwell pokes the now-naked straw through the X on the top of the plastic lid sealing her cup. "It's been on and off for a while," she says. "Neither of us planned it. It happened. One time we were hanging out in the WinCo break room and the next thing I knew we became a thing. Like I said, not planned. Just happened."

"Right," I say. I feel a little uncertain about her. Rachel seems smart and capable. And yet she's done the most idiotic thing a woman can do. She fell for a loser. Of course, I did the same thing too. "It started in the break room," I finally repeat.

She gives me a look—a glare, I think—and then one to Carter. "We didn't have sex in the break room, if that's what you're getting at."

It had crossed my mind, but that's not what I was thinking, and I tell her so.

"Sorry," I say. "What was it about Luke that attracted you?"

She smiles. "You've seen him, right?" she says. "Sure, he could lose a few pounds, but he's a catch. Has an awesome personality. Called me 'Sugar.' Because of my bakery gig. Sweet. So much fun. We fell for each other plain and simple. I'd come out of a bad relationship and he was in the middle of one."

"Unhappy with Mia?" Carter asks.

She thinks before answering. "Miserable. All she cares about is her stupid nursing degree. Studying all the time. Never even considering her husband and his needs. Really kind of a selfish bitch. But you know that. You've met her."

I don't even know how to respond. Thankfully, Rachel goes on with her thoughts about Mia and Luke and what she denounces as a "marriage from hell."

"I'm actually kind of surprised they even had a baby," she says, wadding up the straw wrapper. "She never had any time for Luke. He practically had to beg her for birthday sex. That's how she got pregnant. On Luke's birthday."

I calculate nine months from Luke's birthday. The math doesn't exactly compute. Luke's birthday is in September. Ally was born in August. Only an elephant would have had a longer gestational period.

Rachel indicates things have cooled off between them in the past few weeks.

"We still catch up with each other," she says. "But not as often as we used to. He's busy. The office guys have so much more work to do than those of us on the floor. For a while I have to admit that I did feel a little bit like a booty call. That was before I found out what a bitch Mia was and how she made him do all the housework, take care of the baby, and still move up the ranks at WinCo."

"Mia wasn't nice to him?" I ask, though I'm skeptical and mostly concerned with keeping Rachel talking.

"Nice?" Rachel repeats, her voice shaking. "Luke showed me text messages that he'd get from her telling him what to do and when to do it. Treating him like he was nothing, and all he wanted was to do right by her."

She stops talking. It's abrupt. I go for it.

"You're in love with him, aren't you?" I ask.

She stiffens a little and pulls back away from the table. "It's kind of obvious, I guess. I am. I think he's awesome. He can be a little rough around the edges, but that's okay. I can handle it. Yeah, I love him."

"What did he say about Ally?" Carter asks. "Anything?"

"He loved her. He said she was his bundle of joy. He said that he was trying to get used to life with a baby and that it was really hard, but he never regretted having her. Told me over and over that he wished I'd been the one that he'd gotten pregnant instead of that bitch." She takes a moment. She's thinking about whether or not she's going to disclose more.

"Continue, please," I say, pushing her gently.

"I don't know. It sounds kind of stupid, I guess. I mean, I still love Luke."

"Go on, Rachel," I say. "I can see that."

"Well, as great a guy as Luke was, I knew that we could probably never really be together."

"He was married," Carter says.

She gives up a bona fide glare in his direction.

"Yes, I know. But marriages around here seem to be mostly temporary, right? In the beginning I did think we'd be together, but then something happened. I figured Luke was more like my dad than the man of my dreams."

"What happened?" I ask.

She sighs. "My dad was a cheater. I'm pretty sure Luke was too."

I don't get this girl. Of course he was a cheater. He cheated on Mia.

"Right," I say. "He cheated on Mia."

Rachel almost laughs, but she stops herself, proving once and for all that she has a modicum of self-control after all.

"On me, Detective Foster. Can you believe it? Luke cheated on me."

I could.

"No," I say. "Seriously?"

She nods. "I saw his car over by the river landing. It was random. I was just going by and did a U-turn. I figured he was just chilling or something."

Her voice cracks a little.

"And?"

"I couldn't park next to him because he was at the end of the lot and another car was there. I went up to the driver's window. You know, to surprise him. He was all leaned back in the seat with his eyes closed. I was about to knock to wake him, but I could see there was another girl with him."

"Wow," I say, charging my voice with a little shock and urgency. "Seriously? Who was it?"

Amber's little sister looks down at the table and picks up a napkin. She starts to shred it like a manic gerbil.

"Some girl," Rachel says, letting a little bitterness out. "All I could see was the back of her head in his lap."

"Did you confront Luke?" Carter asks.

Though this is obviously no party, her napkin is now confetti.

"Later I did," she says. "He said that I had to be mistaken. That it was someone else who had borrowed his car. He has a Nirvana decal on his back window—which I saw—but he still lied to my face. That's when things kind of ended for us. I figured that Luke cared so much about me that he didn't want to hurt my feelings. He's that kind of guy."

I want to know more about his relationship with Mia.

"We're going to need to take a statement, Rachel," I say before adding, "down at the station."

She pushes away a little. "I don't really want to be involved."

"You know that you already are."

"But he didn't kill Ally on purpose," she says.

"We really don't know that," I tell her.

Rachel's eyes look at me, pleading. "But I told you, he's a really good guy."

I'm convinced now that her taste in men is worse than mine. At least Danny didn't two-time me—that I know about, anyway.

"You can ride with me. I promise it won't be difficult, and you don't have to do anything but tell us what you told us here. You'll sign the statement and then we'll bring you home."

CHAPTER TWENTY-ONE

Monday, August 21

After taking Rachel's statement, Carter and I settle in front of my computer screen to watch the video surveillance clip from McDonald's. The image is so clear that it nearly catches me off guard. I'm used to the low-grade, grainy video that makes it nearly impossible to identify a subject. This is high-def.

"Want to get something to eat?" Carter asks.

"Didn't know you were a McDonald's fan," I say.

He shrugs. "Fries are pretty good."

I nod as Luke comes into view. He's carrying Ally. She's smiling at everyone. At one point Luke pushes his daughter toward the cashier.

"What's that all about?" Carter asks.

"Not sure," I say. "It's like he's showing her off to the McDonald's staff."

"Why?"

"Maybe to make sure that they see Ally?"

"Why?" Carter asks. "He's planning on killing her in a New York minute."

I can't argue with that. "Maybe to show what a great dad he is. I don't know. To point out later that he couldn't have done this on purpose because the video proves that he loves her. Or something along those lines."

Carter gives a little shrug. "Could be. Who knows what a sick bastard like Luke Tomlinson thinks."

The cashier takes Luke's debit card and sets up a tray for his order.

"Wow," Carter says. "Three Sausage McMuffin sandwiches. No wonder the guy has the belly of a forty-five-year-old."

Pancakes are served next. Ally reaches for them right away, and the McDonald's employee laughs. Father and daughter turn away from the camera.

I switch to the next video clip. This one shows Luke and Ally in the dining room. It's busy, but the two of them sit in the back in front of a giant rendering of Ronald McDonald. Ally is in a high chair, eating her breakfast. Luke has a Sausage McMuffin in one hand and is scrolling through his phone. A few seconds later he sets down his breakfast sandwich and texts a message to someone. After he sends it, he glances over at the counter, presumably at the young man who took his order. He smiles and nods.

"Nothing to really see here," Carter says.

"Agree," I say.

We watch until Luke and Ally's meal concludes. It takes all of ten minutes. Luke picks up his daughter, and the two of them exit the restaurant.

"I always bus my table," Carter says. "Luke's a total slob."

I nod. "Yeah. As I was watching, I was wondering about only one thing."

Carter gives me a look. "How much you hate McDonald's?"

I smile at my partner. He knows how I feel about the Golden Arches.

"No," I tell him. "I kept wondering what it was that Luke was texting. And to whom? He seemed intense. Did you notice how at one point he poured more syrup on Ally's pancakes without even looking at her?"

"Yeah," Carter says. "Surprisingly good aim. Takes some skill and decent peripheral vision too. Might be the only positive takeaway that I can come up with here."

I drink from my coffee cup. It's cold, but I don't really care.

"That too," I say. "Whatever he was texting had to be something very, very important to keep him fixed on his phone like that."

"Phone's not back from the lab," he says.

"No," I say, "but as soon as his and Mia's phones get over to us, I expect we'll find some much-needed answers."

We watch the clips a second time. Nothing else jumps out at me. Carter, however, makes an observation.

"He was playing a little pocket pool," he says.

"Huh?"

"Other than moving some syrup over to Ally's plate, the only other time Luke took a hand off his phone was to make a little adjustment to his junk."

"I had a boyfriend who did that all the time," I say, thinking of my treacherous ex, Danny Ford, but not saying his name. "A loser too."

◆ ◆ ◆

Before going to bed, I lay out my clothes for the next day. I'm a traditionalist when it comes to things like funerals. I choose a black skirt, white blouse, and black jacket. I wonder if I'll look like a waitress. I hope not. I'll be at Ally's funeral to mourn the death of a child.

And to catch her killer.

CHAPTER TWENTY-TWO

Tuesday, August 22

Fern Hill Cemetery sits on a small knoll a stone's throw from the Wishkah River. It's an old cemetery with a mix of graves that harken back to Aberdeen's founding in the 1880s. If there are any ferns on the hill, I don't see them. Perhaps they are a victim of the heat wave and have melted into the landscape. In any case, Carter and I stay back from the mourners who've come to pay their respects to a dead one-year-old girl. I don't doubt the sincerity of those who are there but who didn't know Ally or her parents. People rally around a dead child. This is the case here, for sure. Ally's death has sparked media attention locally and as far away as Seattle. The lid of gray that has descended on Aberdeen feels especially present on Fern Hill.

It fits the mood. It fits my mood too.

All eyes are on the pink casket donated by the funeral home.

Like a wedding, where it is obvious which side is the bride's and which is the groom's, people have segregated themselves into two distinct camps. The WinCo crowd in their khakis and comfortable, thick-soled retail shoes stand to the right of the tiny pink casket; nurses in skirts and doctors in suits are on Mia's side. A woman with spun gray hair and a stoop-shouldered man stand next to Mia, a kind of human pergola.

"That must be her folks," Carter says.

They look too old, but it's hard to tell these days. "Grandparents, maybe?"

Mia sees us and gives us a nod, though it is more dismissive than welcoming. She's wearing heels and a pale yellow dress with a photo button of her daughter fixed just below the neckline.

Others are wearing the same button. I'm silently amazed at how fast a tragedy becomes a thing. Not all tragedies. Just some. I'm sure that some parents try with all they have to bang the drum of attention, but to no avail.

Ally is a thing now. That's not intended to be mean. It's just the truth. Her death hit the news cycle on the right day. She's white. She's cute. Her parents are young. How far this attention will go is tough to surmise. Ally could be regional first, then national. Or she could fizzle if some other tragedy comes on with a better backstory and a more appealing victim.

I think of all the cases I've observed over the years and know that the zeitgeist of crime is fickle.

Carter offers me a stick of gum, and I decline. I don't want to be photographed like I'm the Borden cow. It doesn't matter if he's caught chewing. Women get beat up in the media for things that guys do all the time. No one ever judges a male cop's attire. A woman police officer is slammed for looking slutty. Or lesbian-like. Fat. Or out of style.

"Lot of people here," he says.

"I thought there would be," I say. "Ally's been all over the news. Have you heard of Google news alerts?"

Carter makes a face. "What's Google?"

I ignore his semijoke. He's dressed for the funeral. He's wearing the same sport coat and slacks that he wore when I interviewed at the department. The top button strains across his chest, but only a little. I don't say anything about that, but I think Carter has lost a little weight.

"You clean up pretty good," I say.

He gives me a Carter half smile. "You look all right yourself, Detective," he says.

"Mascara and a new blouse," I say.

A police cruiser, lights flashing, silently edges up the hill to a parking spot next to a masonry chapel. Right away, a *Daily World* reporter scurries over with her camera in position.

Luke Tomlinson has arrived from the jail.

It's the moment everyone has been waiting for.

I watch as Mia separates herself from her supporters to greet her husband. She speaks to the officer while Luke stays planted in the backseat. I know I'll find out later what she's telling him. Carter says something, but I'm so surprised by what happens next that I can't hear him.

Now out of the cruiser and facing his wife, Luke appears to be sobbing.

"What is he saying to her?" Carter asks.

"I wonder," I say.

Mia looks at the officer and says something. A second later she gives Luke a warm embrace and bends close to whisper in his ear.

Carter nudges me. "Officer shouldn't let them touch," he says.

"No shit," I whisper back.

The hug is quick, though. The officer is joined by a second officer, and the four of them walk across the parking area to the grave-site awning with its folding chairs set up and its mound of freshly dug dirt covered in dark green carpet.

"Let's move closer," I say.

Carter agrees, and we find ourselves next to my old high school pal Debbie Manning and her resourceful assistant, Brooklyn.

Both of them bristle a little at us. Cops are seldom welcome attendees at either weddings or funerals.

"Thank God you people let Luke out," Debbie says, sending vodka vapors over me like disinfectant spray. "Can you imagine missing your daughter's funeral?"

I don't have a daughter. I have Emma. And, yes, I hope I miss her funeral. I hope she lives to be one hundred years old and I'm long gone.

Brooklyn says nothing. She's wearing jeans and a crop top, her flat, taut stomach the envy of every woman there who's given birth. I wonder if she's off the clock or if her boss is paying her minimum wage to ensure that she's there. When the wind drags over Debbie's black dress, I catch another whiff of vodka.

Though it is one in the afternoon, I wonder if Brooklyn is Debbie's designated driver.

The minister thanks everyone for coming and at the family's request pushes the "Play" button for Eric Clapton's ode to tragedy, "Tears in Heaven." Even from where we stand, I can see Mia's and Luke's shoulders shudder with emotion. I look around, and everyone is crying.

Even Carter seems caught up in the emotion. He turns away and dabs at a tear.

Ally's death is definitely a thing.

Prayers follow. First the Lord's Prayer, then something vaguely nondenominational. Everyone is crying now. The minister talks a bit more, and then he holds a microphone up to Luke. He glances around and nods at his WinCo friends—including Rachel, his former flame from the floral department. She gives him a little wave and a smile.

I don't think they are really finished after all.

"My precious," Luke begins. His vocal cords seem tight, and he clears his throat. I can't tell if it's an affect or if he's genuinely overcome. "That's my little girl. In this box right here. This isn't right. Nobody can tell me otherwise. I made a really bad mistake that morning. There's no way of getting around that. I own that."

Mia and Rachel are sobbing in stereo as Luke kicks his mea culpa into overdrive.

"I should never have left Ally in the car and forgot about her. I try to wrap my head around the events of that morning every minute of the day. How could I, of all people, do this? I knew there were dangers in a hot car. Everyone who watches the news knows that. But what people don't know is that sometimes you can make big errors in judgment. Even when you are a really good person. My little girl's an angel now and I know it's all my fault. The only consolation I can find in this tragedy is that she's in heaven where she'll never, ever hurt again. She's not in that pink box."

His arm goes limp for a minute, and the microphone is now at his side.

"Her body is," he says, moving the mic back to his lips and looking around at the mourners, who by my count number more than two hundred. "Yes," he goes on. "But she's up there, smiling down on all of us, grateful that she's free from her earthly body."

Luke looks over at one of our officers, and the officer nods.

Ally's father moves toward the casket and caresses its velvety-smooth surface.

"Jesus," Carter whispers to me, "he's not going to open it up and drag Ally out, is he?"

I don't answer. Mostly because Luke's decidedly over-the-top performance is riveting in every way imaginable but also because I'm really not sure. Luke Tomlinson, as far as I can see, is pretty much capable of just about anything.

"Ally, baby," Luke says, "people have said terrible things about me but you know the truth. You and you alone. And that's all that matters. I'm your daddy. You are my precious, and no one with a badge is going to rewrite our story."

Mia looks over at the same officer. A second later she has her arm around Luke's beefy shoulders. The reporter from the paper moves in for a shot. I don't even need to wait for the headline the next day to know what it will be.

Grieving Mother Stands by Accused Husband

After another prayer from the minister, the casket is lowered, flowers and dirt fall, and the crowd starts to disperse. The officer who brought Luke leads him back to the waiting cruiser. Mia and her hospital friends linger by the casket. As funerals go, this one is at once tragic and bizarre.

Carter and I turn to leave, when I feel a tap on my arm.

"You know he's innocent," Brooklyn says as she and Debbie face me. "You're making matters worse for that family."

I remember how she considered Luke a good guy because he wasn't a creeper like some of the other dads who came to the day care. She's young. She's trusting.

"We're only doing our job, Brooklyn," I say.

Brooklyn shrugs off my remark.

"I'd rather work at a gas station than do something that makes innocent people feel terrible," she says. "You totally suck."

CHAPTER TWENTY-THREE

Tuesday, August 22

The sun turned up the heat again and has transformed patches of the parking lot into liquid. I've tracked tar into my office, and I know that I'll never get the stains out of the formerly pristine carpet. I guess I don't care. Not when I think of all the other things that are more important than a scolding from the department's janitor. I sit in front of my computer to reread the autopsy report for the third time—the image of the casket and the mourners fresh in my mind. Nothing on the face of the earth is more wrong than a baby's funeral. I try to make sense out of what happened. It's what I do. For a moment I allow myself the possibility that Luke had some kind of a major brain freeze and forgot his daughter. It was possible that the reminder about the canceled beach walk from Debbie Manning's Little Pal's Day Care didn't jog his memory that he'd forgotten to drop off his little girl. The tech guys are deep into the laptops and the phones, and I know whatever they find will lead the investigation where it needs to go. Can't lie with data.

I drink a warm Coke and fight the urge to Facebook-stalk friends from my old life. It's a fight I can't win. I can't not look at the life

I had and the people I once knew. I scroll through my feed. A few have blocked me, which crushes me to the core. Those that haven't still inhabit the same old lives. I see children who have grown so much in three years. Colleagues who have been promoted. One fighting cancer. I see bits and pieces of my discarded life, and I have no one to blame but myself.

Okay. Sometimes I do blame Stacy a little. I tell myself that God allows me that because no one on this earth has blazed a deeper trail of destruction than my little sister. No one has been more brazen in her quest to do whatever it was that she wanted to do. More selfish. More evil.

I hate Stacy.

And I miss her—and what I imagined she was when we were little—with all of my heart.

I refresh my computer and see that the email from Tech has arrived. I open the file and start reading. Within thirty seconds I'm running down the hall to Carter's office. He's glued to the report.

"Holy crap, Nicole," he says looking up.

"He planned this whole thing," I say.

"Yeah, more than a dozen Internet searches for 'hot-car death' and 'how long can a child survive in a hot car.'"

"And the date," I say.

He shakes his head. "Yeah. The date. He looked it all up the first day of our heat wave."

It's confirmation of what I knew, and it still hits me hard. "Luke didn't forget Ally at all," I say. "He left her in the car to die."

"Not only that. He checked on her after lunch to make sure."

"This guy has to be the most evil piece of shit of all time," I say. "Ever."

I seldom swear, and this brings a slight smile in the grimmest of moments to Carter's face.

"You can say that again," he says.

I don't.

"What do you make of Mia?"

"What about her?"

He looks down at his screen.

"You didn't get that far, did you?"

"No, I guess not. What?"

"She researched it too. Two days after Luke did."

"No," I say.

"Right. She did. They must share the laptop. The Dell was beyond life support. It's dead. The MacBook has two different sign-ons."

"I don't get it," I say. "Why would she do that?"

Carter picks up his key ring. I notice for the first time that the fob says "My Dad's #1." He sees me looking at it, and he shoves the keys into his pocket.

"We'll need to find out," he says.

◆ ◆ ◆

Having learned that Mia has already returned to work on the afternoon of her daughter's funeral, we go to the hospital. "Mia's on break," the charge nurse tells us when we arrive.

"People handle grief in their own way," I remind Carter when he gives me a look.

"I didn't say anything," he says.

"You don't have to."

I think of a case I worked in Bellevue in which a schoolgirl brought her homework to the hospital as her mother lay dying of antifreeze poisoning. She couldn't face what was really happening. Routine brought comfort.

The nurse tells us Mia is in the cafeteria.

"She's usually in the back along the windows."

The woman in her midforties has caring eyes and soft, delicate features. She's everything I wish the people taking care of my father were. She's probably never been to a tattoo parlor. Never come to work after a weekend drunk. Never wished that some old codger would just die, because taking care of someone who can't speak is so utterly boring.

"Kind of a loner," she goes on. "Breaks my heart, considering how she must be grieving. Doesn't take a hug too well. Sorry about that. Love's the only real medicine. Sweet, but a loner," she says before burying her face in her sheaf of paperwork.

As promised, Carter and I find Mia alone with her stir-fry and Greek yogurt.

"Mia," I say, "the main desk said we'd find you here."

Mia puts down her fork. "So you found me. Are you here to search me too?"

She's angry. I'm fine with that. Yes, her daughter is dead. But, seriously, she has some explaining to do.

"Luke researched hot-car deaths before Ally died," I say.

"I told you that already," she says.

Carter lets me handle her. "Yes, you did. You said it wasn't research but he was concerned about it. Don't you find that odd?"

"The weatherman said it was going to be hot. Very hot. What's so strange about Luke looking up information on that?"

I wait a beat. An intern smiles in Mia's direction. It's a sad smile. I'm sure he knows—I'm sure everyone in the hospital knows—that Mia's baby has died and that her husband appears to be guilty of a crime somewhere in the spectrum of negligence and premeditated murder.

"But he wasn't the only one who researched it, was he?"

Our eyes lock. She has suddenly shifted from grieving mom to a person of interest, and she's aware of it.

"I don't know what you mean?"

Mia's attempt at playing dumb is an epic fail. She knows it. I know it.

"Mia, please," I say, unraveling some rope.

She looks at her tray and arranges the silverware as though she's at a dinner party.

"So much has happened," she says.

"Yes," I say, "that's true. So much has happened. You know what I'm getting at, Mia. Don't you?"

A little more rope off the imaginary spool.

"I guess it seems bad," she finally says. "But I think I looked it up too. You know, after Luke started talking about it."

Carter can't contain himself. My guess is that he never could. Not when it comes to kids. He talks about his all the time.

"Does my partner look stupid?" he blurts out. "Do *I* look stupid? You're telling us that you looked up the same thing your husband did— the same thing that killed your little girl? You seriously want us to think that coincidence after coincidence is how the world works? People do shit like what you and Luke did on purpose. Things don't just happen."

For a minute I thought he was going to add *missy* to the end of the rebuke. I'm glad he didn't.

Mia sits up like someone under the table has goosed her.

"It is the truth, Detectives," she says. *Now her face is Venetian red,* I think. "God's honest truth. Luke was worried about the hot weather. So, yes, he read up. I was worried too. So I looked it up. Just because someone wants to find out how to protect their child shouldn't be reason to think the worst of them. Far from it. I'm a nurse. I see the messed-up things people do to each other. Sometimes I see them before they even get to the likes of people like you. So check your suspicions and take them elsewhere. I have a job to do. I have a husband to get out of jail."

Her voice was far louder than needed. She has suddenly become the center of attention in the hospital cafeteria. So have Carter and I.

A couple of nurses and a doctor glare in our direction.

At that moment Mia Tomlinson is Norma Rae holding up a placard for everyone to see. Instead of "Union," it reads "Persecuted."

Carter gulps. I step away, reeling in the rope.

Mia cannot be stopped. She drops the final bomb.

"And if it matters to either of you," she says, jabbing a finger at us, "I have a daughter to mourn! A daughter who was cooked alive!"

She bolts out of the cafeteria, and we slink out. Awkwardly. I turn to Carter and whisper in his ear. "That went really well."

"Tell me about it," he says as we start to walk out. "I hope to God if anything happens to me, they airlift me to Seattle. I won't stand a chance here."

Even the nice nurse glares at us when we pass by the nurses' station. Word travels at warp speed in any institution that's built on the sanctity of confidentiality. Telegraph. Telephone. Tell a medical care provider.

"Seriously," I say as we go back out into the black goo of the hospital parking lot. "Mia is either a misunderstood mom or a really good liar in as deep in this as her husband."

"She's a liar," he says. "I'm telling you, Nicole. I have a sixth sense about these things. You know that."

I can't argue with his sixth sense. I don't dare remind him of other cases in which he said the same thing and led us down a primrose path to a conclusion that couldn't have been more wrong. This time, however, I want him to be wrong. I want more than anything to believe that Mia was researching because her husband had piqued her interest.

Not because she was part of the plot. Even though I'm not a mother and I have no road map in my own life to fall back on, I know in my bones that motherhood is an elevated honor. It's clear to me every time I look in Emma's eyes.

CHAPTER TWENTY-FOUR

Tuesday, August 22

It's late at the office. Emma is staying with Carrie Anne and her brood. It's Simone's fifth birthday. I have never been the kind of mother—though I know I'm not really one—who longs for nights away from her child. Indeed, I feel skittish when Emma's beyond my reach. I don't want to be overprotective, but the pendulum swings hard sometimes. My own parents were completely disinterested in me and Stacy. Mostly me. Stacy, quite obviously, is more like our mother than I am. Sometimes I wonder if she ever even thinks about her daughter. Before the postcards came, I tried to imagine where it was that she and Julian had taken their insidious and toxic relationship.

My mind ricocheted to all the best places in the world. Stacy always liked the sun. She loved the beach because she loved having all eyes on her when she walked a stretch of sand, her teeny-tiny bikini holding on for dear life. She looked great. I'll give her that. Like Snow White's poison apple. Like an angler's new fishing lure, sparking silver in the water and calling for an unwitting salmon. Like the weather forecast for a June wedding in Seattle.

I settled on a Mexican villa pitched on a cliff above sapphire and turquoise waters, though deep down, as much as I know my sister, I doubted that would satisfy her thirst for extravagance—not when she undoubtedly had millions of dollars to spend.

When Carter pokes his head into my office and says he's off to get a bite and asks if I want to come, I do something I've seldom done before.

"Sure," I say. "Give me five minutes."

"Really?" he asks. "Wasn't expecting that."

"Me neither," I say.

"How does Red Lobster sound?"

It sounds terrible.

"Fancy," I say.

We take his car and I watch the #1 Dad key ring sparkle as it swings when we drive over a pothole that seems to go unchecked by the city. "How are they doing?" I ask.

He looks at me. "Who?"

I indicate the key ring. "Your kids. I know you miss them. I'm sure they must miss you."

Carter gives me a cursory nod as we pull into the parking lot of the Red Lobster. It's new, so it's busy for a weeknight. He finds a spot in the last row.

"Kids are all right," he says. "I talk to them about every day, though sometimes I wonder why I bother. They don't have much to tell me, except how much they want this or that."

"That's the burden of being number one dad," I say.

He grins, but it's a forced one. "Right. I guess. I wish there was a do-over for my life, because I sure screwed things up. I know all of this is on me. Now Sherry has a boyfriend. Serious too. Pretty soon all I'll be to anyone is an ATM with a serious bank balance problem."

I give our name to the hostess, and we go into the bar and find a couple of empty stools at the far end.

"This isn't a date," I say. It feels a little mean when it comes out of my lips, and it wasn't meant that way. I just wanted to be clear. I don't date partners anymore. That was one of many mistakes that I don't—I can't—revisit. And seeing how I don't meet anyone else, that pretty much seals my fate as a spinster aunt to Emma.

Carter nods. "I know. You've made that clear."

I feel bad for him. I'm not sure what mistake he made, but I'm pretty sure he wasn't a philanderer. He has zero game. Quite possibly less than zero.

"Sorry," I say. "Not that I think I'm all that. And not that you aren't a hell of a nice guy. It's just something I can't ever do."

"Because you did it once before," he says.

"Right," I say. "And we both know how that turned out."

I order a whiskey sour. Carter orders a glass of rosé. *Seriously.* My phone pings, and I look down at the text message from the DA's office. *Crap,* I think, but I set the news aside.

When the bartender working our end of the bar returns with our order, he mistakenly sets the pretty pink wine in front of me and the amber-hued cocktail by Carter. We do the switch when the server leaves.

"I didn't figure you for a whiskey drinker," he says.

I shrug. "Don't get me started, Mr. Rosé."

Carter grins, and we drink and we do what cops always do: we talk about the case.

"You believe Mia?" he asks.

The whiskey sour is good, and I'm going to savor it. No matter how long and bad my day has been.

"What part of her story?" I ask.

"I'd say all of it," he says. "Any of it. She's about as reliable as Luke is. I doubt very much that she researched hot-car death because her husband had been talking it up. Just doesn't hold water."

"That's probably why I believe her," I say. "The craziness of her looking up the same subject before it happened and then blurting out that Luke had left Ally in the car when the blues picked her up at the hospital."

His glass is now empty. "You don't think that's far-fetched?"

I do, and I tell him so. "Of course it is. It's so far-fetched that it just might be a genuine coincidence. She'd have to be seriously stupid to bring all that up if she had a hand in Ally's death. I don't think she's stupid."

Carter indicates to the bartender that he wants another glass of wine. The woman behind the bar points to me, but I shake my head.

Carter pushes back from the barstool.

"Because she's a nurse?" he asks, sipping from a second glass while I continue to nurse my whiskey sour.

"No," I tell him. "Because she is—rather, was—Ally's mother. That's a big bond."

I realize the stupidity of my remark. My own mother snapped the big bond like a twig. Stacy did too. My idea of motherhood and its importance has been completely warped by my own inexorable need to fix things in my life.

"Table's ready," says a server in a white shirt and black slacks.

So fancy, this Red Lobster.

We get up with our drinks in hand and follow the young man to a corner booth in the dining room adjacent to a mammoth aquarium holding a group of lethargic lobsters. A basket of biscuits greets us. By the time we slide into the booth, Carter has one in his mouth.

"I haven't eaten a thing all day," he says, a tiny avalanche of buttery crumbs falling to the tabletop and onto the front of his pale blue shirt.

He really has zero game. I think of flicking off the crumbs. But I don't.

"Makes me sick they let Luke go to Ally's funeral," I say.

"No shit," Carter says, the wine loosening him up a little.

"Yeah," I say, picking at the crispy edges of a biscuit. "DA says that Mia and her parents pled with them to allow it. Said that if he's exonerated, then they'll feel like crap that they kept him away."

"He won't be exonerated," Carter says, scanning the menu like he's studying a latent print.

"They said that about Casey Anthony," I say.

He lifts his eyes from the menu. "*Not guilty* isn't the same as *innocent,* you know. I wonder how the lobster is here," he says with a wry smile. "Think it's any good?"

Carter makes me smile just then. That's a good thing. I need a smile.

◆ ◆ ◆

The house is as still as the air outside when I get home. Shelby meets me in the kitchen with a tail that I'm certain could whip cream. I pick her up.

"God, girl, are you getting heavy."

She licks my face, and I do nothing to stop her. I wonder if she's getting a taste of those oversalted and -buttered biscuits that Carter— with a tiny bit of help from me—demolished before our food came.

Shelby was supposed to be a miniature dachshund, but, weighing at least fifteen pounds, she's clearly a standard. I sit in my father's chair by the front window. It's a leather chair that Stacy and Cy got him when they first got married. Shelby finds a cozy spot on my lap while I look through the mail, a few bills for the water and electricity, a notice that my father's pension is all but tapped out. A copy of *This Old House* magazine holds my interest as I turn its pages, trying to see just what it was that appealed to my father. He was the worst carpenter ever. He watched videos. He read books. He subscribed to magazines. No matter what he did, he just couldn't do anything right. Just like me, trying to win myself a new life in front of the glittering lights and sounds of the slots, maybe my father was trying to fix himself. Maybe home improvement was his personal metaphor.

I go upstairs and lie on Emma's bed and look up at the same ceiling that I gazed at when I was her age.

I was hoping that my mother would come home.

I wonder if Emma lies here missing her mom too.

◆ ◆ ◆

Ally has been dead eight days. Autopsied. Mourned. Buried. It is hard to reconcile that because to really think about what happened is completely bone-chilling. But it's my job.

I think about the time line as I settle in my father's old chair, my laptop casting a glow on my face and the wine glass on the table next to me. The answer is often found there—between point A and point B. A time line is the backbone of circumstantial cases. I know this. Every cop does. And while life is never really on schedule—at least, mine has never been—prosecutors love nothing more than a time line without the slightest bit of wiggle room. Defendants often consider the concrete points in a chronology as their best chance for an acquittal.

"I couldn't have done that," a suspect who'd killed his mother with a piece of Carrara marble tile from an installation he was doing at her home told me one time. "I was at lunch when she was killed. Twenty people can vouch for me."

"It doesn't matter that you were at lunch at twelve thirty-seven when your mom's body was discovered. She'd been dead for three hours. She was dead when you left her."

"The medical examiner's time of death is hazy," his lawyer said.

I pushed back. "Not hazy enough to get your client off."

While Shelby curls up next to me, I put together the elements that are best known to Carter and me. A few are incontrovertible: time stamps from video surveillance and charge cards. Others are less concrete but are a close approximation. Off maybe by two or three minutes.

I lean back and scrutinize the time line.

6:00 a.m. Mia goes to work.

8:30 a.m. Luke and Ally leave the house.

8:39 a.m. Luke and Ally arrive at McDonald's, order their food, and eat.

8:55 a.m. Luke and Ally leave McDonald's for the drive to WinCo.

Around 9:00 a.m. Luke arrives at work.

10:23 a.m. Luke gets beach walk email from Little Pal's.

11:45 a.m. Luke and pals leave WinCo for lunch at the nearby Jersey Mike's.

Around 12:30 p.m. Luke returns to the back parking lot to put his printer cartridge into the car.

Around 4:00 p.m. Luke departs WinCo.

4:16 p.m. Luke pulls into the Starbucks parking lot, gets out of his SUV, and screams that something is wrong with his daughter.

4:33 p.m. Ally is pronounced dead.

◆ ◆ ◆

I see Shelby by the door waiting patiently. She's fully recovered and wants out. Except when there are strangers, she's mostly a silent dog. I close my laptop and go to her. I love her so much that it hurts sometimes. People who don't have a dog can't know how it feels, just like those who don't have children can't understand that kind of love. They aren't the same, of course. But both are real. As I watch Shelby's pointed muzzle grow a little lighter with time, I can't help but panic a little inside. She's older. *Older* means an end is coming. I swing the door open, and she looks up with those soulful brown eyes, a look that is only for me.

"Go on, now," I say.

The poisoning and the rush to the vet were a jolt to my heart. A canine defibrillator. She's been with me through every terrible mistake I've made. She won't be here forever. And that kills me.

She trots out into the dark, and my thoughts go back to Luke and Ally and the time line—such a mundane little day with such horrible consequences. Luke will never be able to wriggle out of his culpability.

He was the only one in the car with Ally.

Chapter Twenty-Five

Wednesday, August 23

It's morning before work, and I go where I try to go every Wednesday. My father sits in that peculiar wheelchair with its very high, stiff metal back in his room at Ocean View. He's strapped to it. As my eyes graze over the scene, Hannibal Lecter comes to mind. The famed fictional serial killer had a similar seating arrangement when guards moved him from one prison to another. Dad's not wearing the hockey mask, but he might as well be. He's spoken barely a word during my last several visits to the care facility. Emma has asked several times to see her grandfather, but I've told her that he's not feeling well. She knows he's ill, but I don't need her to see him as a monster.

Alzheimer's is scary enough without the serial-killer-in-a-wheelchair visuals.

We sit in the TV room as an infomercial for a countertop appliance that promises to fry food without a drop of oil runs on what I'm sure is an endless loop. Chicken wings. Empanadas. Wontons. All of fried foods' greatest hits play out in glorious crispiness while my dad and another man, whose name I don't know—and my guess is that he doesn't, either—watch raptly from their respective chairs. My dad has the weird chair. The other guy, a normal one. The light from the television screen moves across my father's light blue eyes, and I wonder if anything he sees registers with him at all.

"Remember that time you ate ten thousand barbecued wings in one sitting?" I ask him.

There was no such time, but I know I can say anything I've ever wanted to say and there is only the slightest chance it would show up anywhere in the shattered essence of his subconscious.

I could say anything in the world to him right now. I could disclose my darkest secret. Instead, I ask one of the questions that has haunted me all of my adult life.

"Why did you wait all those years for Mom?" It's a subject that I've never had the heart to give voice to before, but one that framed everything about our lives after she left us for California.

He doesn't answer, and images of oil-free empanadas command the TV screen.

"I remember how much I wanted to just punch you in the gut for believing that she was ever going to return to Hoquiam. To us. Don't you know that your hope kept us all hostage? It wasn't right. Don't you know, Dad, Stacy and I stupidly believed you when you said you were sure she would come home?"

"*Cherry empanadas are piping hot now. Next, an amazing lemon curd recipe!*"

The host's assistant, a middle-aged woman with the biggest eyes I've ever seen outside of an anime character, bites into an empanada and goes into full-on orgasm. It's undoubtedly the best thing she's ever eaten in her entire life. *Or perhaps,* I think, *she's been held in some shipping container somewhere and hasn't had anything decent to eat in eons.* The man next to my father leans a little closer to the screen, and a faint smile comes to his lips while his hand slips into the waistband of his pajamas.

This guy's clearly not dead yet.

Dad, however, is fish eyed with a blank grouper gaze at the TV.

"Mom was a complete bitch and only cared about herself, Dad," I say.

No reaction.

I consider grabbing him by the shoulders and snapping him out of his perpetual twilight. But I don't. Not yet, anyway.

I keep my voice low so as not to disturb the masturbator in the wheelchair next to us. "She never wanted you and she sure as hell never wanted Stacy and me."

His eyes flutter with some recognition. "Stacy," he says in a kind of semilucid mutter.

Her. It's always her.

"I'm not Stacy," I tell him, reminding myself that he's not half as smart as one of those empanadas. He's parroting a word. That's all. Not really thinking of anyone.

Not *her*, I tell myself.

It isn't that I despise my sister, though God knows she's given me a million reasons to do so. It's that I just never understood how it was that she was so favored. Beauty can't be everything. Can it? She is a sociopath like our mom. She doesn't give a flying fuck about anyone other than herself. I tell myself that she wasn't always that way. She grew into it. A sweet baby. A cute little sister. And then the evil inside her grew. I could give my dad a litany of the evil Stacy has wrought in the world. I want to. Yet I know that even if I did, and even if he could understand, he would side with her. That *I* would be the bad person.

How could you betray your sister like that?

My sister killed her husband.

She's your blood.

Her blood is poison, by the way.

Get out of here. You're nothing but a gambler.

None of that conversation transpires. I know in my father's eyes I could never win against Stacy.

So I do what I've always done. It's supposed to be from the heart, but it always feels a little like groveling over splinters of broken glass.

"All I ever wanted was to find a way to make you happy—a way to forget about her," I say. "You have no idea now, I guess. You had no idea back then. Every mistake I've made in my life is my own, but, Dad, I want you to know that you sent me on that road. You. You really did."

Tears come to my eyes, but I don't let them fall. In some weird way this confrontation with my dad makes me feel good. I'm not yelling at him, but it feels cathartic, like I'm in primal scream therapy or something of the like.

"I could have left you in that other place in Hoquiam—the place where the rats had nicknames—and you'd be lying in your bed right now with a chapped penis and a dirty diaper. But I didn't. I got the money from Stacy and I moved you here, Dad."

He pulls his eyes away from the TV.

"Stacy," he repeats.

Her name has always been a mantra of sorts. Sometimes I wonder if it is because her abandonment of him hurt him more than my devotion made him feel better. That he'd rather wallow in missing Stacy than be happy that I'm here, sitting in the godforsaken TV room, watching hash brown potatoes fry without a drop of oil.

"It's the magic of hot air," the host says, while his excited assistant moans and those eyes of hers roll back into her head.

Hot air is right.

I notice some food—dried egg, maybe—stuck on Dad's chin, and I gently pick it off.

He looks up at me once more with his chambray-blue eyes. For a second I see—at least, I think I see—a bead of recognition.

"Dad," I say, seizing this potential moment of lucidity, "I need you to know this." I hold his bony shoulders, shoulders that once seemed like the cornerstones of some massive building but now are rubble. He is nothing if not flawed. Yet out of the family that I had, he was the closest to what I envisioned was normal. Loving. At least mostly. "I would never have wanted another father other than you." No matter what, I want him to get this and hold on to it somewhere in the part of his memory that still functions. "When I finally figured out that Mom was never coming back, I prayed that you would find a new wife. Not for me. Not a mother for me. Or even for Stacy. But someone to love you, Dad."

His eyes glimmer. I stare deeper inside, searching them to see if somehow what I said has found a spot that is making sense of it.

No real reaction. Instead, my dad turns back to the TV.

Before my frustration turns into self-pity, a nurse's aide comes into the room with a plate of still-warm chocolate chip cookies.

I smell sweet notes of vanilla mixed with the chocolate, and I think of Dad's long shift at the mill making vanillin and how I couldn't wait to breathe him in when he walked through the back door.

"Anyone want a cookie?" the nurse's aide says, in a sweet, lilting voice.

I'm afraid my dad and the horny guy watching the infomercial will choke on a cookie, but I don't say anything. I just nod.

The girl is new. In every way. She's barely twenty, with ringlets of chestnut hair that I can tell is the heart of her daily routine. Every lock is in place, but only casually so. It takes a lot of work to look as though you haven't done a thing.

She smiles in my direction.

"You must be Stacy," she says, handing cookies to the TV watchers. I take one of the silver-coated plastic trays as well. "Your father talks about you all the time. Says that you're kind of a big deal. Super proud of you."

I nod, but say nothing. Of course my dad brags about Stacy.

"I'm Sasha Clayton," she goes on. "I'm new here and I don't have to tell you, this place is kind of sad, but when I hear things about people like you, well, it kind of lifts my spirits. Your dad and a few others help me to know that these folks are still listening, still thinking, even when they don't always show it."

I don't correct Sasha and say that I'm Nicole. There's really no point in such a disclosure. I eat a cookie while the woman on the TV screen has her third food orgasm. Gambling ruined my life. Food could have brought a similar rush, and I could be four hundred pounds right now. Or dead from a heart attack. Everybody I know has something a little bit wrong with them. Sometimes you just don't see it. Pain and problems can be concealed with a smile. I know this in my bones.

Sasha smiles in my direction as she wheels out the other old man, whose erection, surprisingly, is lifting his pajama bottoms like a pitched tent.

"Bye, Stacy. Nice meeting you."

"Bye, Tasha," I say, deliberately messing up her name.

I admit it. Sometimes I'm just not very nice. But I'm working on it.

CHAPTER TWENTY-SIX

Wednesday, August 23

The Tech Department at the Aberdeen Police Department isn't the largest or most current in the world. It's a far cry from what I'd had access to in Bellevue before my fall from grace. On the plus side, we have Angelina Marco, a brilliant high-tech sleuth. Seattle PD and the Washington State Patrol have tried to recruit her, but each time she's stayed put. As smart as she is, she just isn't ambitious like that. One time she told me that she preferred computers to people and that she was used to everyone here in Aberdeen.

"I'm fine where I am," she told me one time. "I just don't want to start over and smile and suck up and act interested in new people. I'm not into people."

Angelina is barely five feet tall. Her hair is a bluish black, and she favors sweatpants over any other attire. She's trim, but her slouchy clothing suggests that she just can't be bothered with things like fashion.

"In the lab or the break room," she told me once, "I fit in just fine." When she dresses for court, she looks like a different person—a person she doesn't necessarily want to be.

Carter, looking like he is catching a cold or maybe hungover, comes with me to meet Angelina in the conference room next to her office. On the wall above the old library table is a flat-screen that displays the contents of the MacBook we picked up from the Tomlinson residence.

"The Dell really was dead," she says. "I sent it out to WSP because there's a guy there who can work miracles when they're needed."

"Can't you just reboot it?" Carter asks as he slides into the seat next to mine. "That usually fixes all tech problems."

Angelina smiles. "Actually," she says, "that does work now and then. But this one's given up the ghost. If there's anything on it that's retrievable, we'll get it. Not that you'll need it."

She seems pleased.

"You found something else," I say.

Angelina picks up the mouse. "A treasure trove," she says, "that we almost missed because it was buried in an encrypted Dropbox account. Pretty disgusting too."

Carter and I are all ears. She tells us that there had been some effort to conceal some content from prying eyes.

"People forget that there's a pathway to everything. You can delete your search history easy enough, but really all that does is make you think you've deleted it. If you know where to look, you can find just about every click that was ever made on any device. Same thing about encryption. Not all that hard to get in, when you know where to look."

"Treasure trove," I repeat.

Angelina nods. "Yeah. Let me show you." She indicates what she says is a hidden folder.

It's a series of photos that flail at us. It's a pornographic jack-in-the-box. Selfies. Nude ones. Some images are a close-up of Mr. Magnum, both flaccid and erect.

Carter shifts uncomfortably in his chair. I imagine that it's awkward sitting with two women and looking at another man's private anatomy.

"Not sure how useful all these photos will be," Angelina says, "but it might have some bearing here."

"Jesus," Carter says, "why do guys do this?"

"I was thinking the same thing," I say.

"Compulsion," Angelina says as she puts up more photos one at a time. "Can't keep it in their pants, off their phones, in the locker room. Guys are weird like that." She looks over at Carter.

"Some are," he says.

"Was Luke sending these out to people?" I ask. "Or were they just for home use?"

Angelina stares at her report. "Nope. He didn't send them by email. Not that I could find. He might have used his phone. In fact, I'm pretty sure that he took all these with his phone. Images were backed up on the cloud, which is how they ended up here on the Mac."

"He's a scumbag," Carter says, with the kind of conviction that makes the statement seem completely definitive.

"No argument from me there," I say. "What else have you got?"

Angelina turns back to the screen. "Let's finish the photos first," she says. "I like saving the best for last. Cherry on the sundae is coming up next."

Angelina really does hate people. She's stringing us along a little. *Her passive-aggressive way of having a good time,* I think. That's fine. She's good at what she does.

She shows a series of photographs of Ally next.

"There are about a dozen of these," she says.

"Weird that there are so few," I say. "Most parents take more than ten thousand photographs in the first year of their baby's life."

"And we do nothing with them," Carter says. "A lot of effort for something that never sees the light of day."

I don't say anything, just nod quickly. The pictures of Ally show her with her mother and father, mostly. A few have her posed alone. The one that touches my heart the most is the photo taken of her next to that big pink WinCo cake for her first birthday. Her smile matches the cake. She's a beautiful little girl. Everyone says that about anyone who has died under tragic circumstances. In this case it's true. Anyone would have wanted Ally. Loved her. Made sure that she got through school. First date. Danced at her wedding. All of the things that we long to do with the little ones we love.

Before we get to the cherry on the sundae, Angelina gives a quick review of the contents of both Tomlinsons' email accounts.

"These two aren't heavy emailers," she says. "Most of Luke's were spam from porn sites and women looking to hook up. I mean, probably not real women. Just the kind of Internet come-on that plagues guys who click on porn. Out of his emails there were a few from his friends and family, but nothing illuminating. I printed those out for you here."

She taps the top of a black binder.

"What about Mia?" Carter asks.

"About the same," Angelina says. "Not the porn part. She exchanged information with a nursing study friend, but nothing of importance. My guess is that they use text messaging more than email to communicate. Most younger people do now."

I look at Carter. He smiles. He knows I'm teasing him a little about his lack of texting prowess.

"What about their phones?" I ask. "Can you recover their texts?"

Angelina nods. "We can," she says. "I mean, *I* can't, but the prosecutor's office is already on it. The information we need is stored on the phone company's servers, and it will take some time to get that content. We'll likely get it, but not immediately. Phone companies are the worst. They scream 'privacy' all the time, yet cheat ratepayers whenever possible. I hate my service provider."

People.

Service provider.

Angelina hates a lot of things.

"I read the initial interviews conducted with Mia by the responding officer and the two of you. I know she indicated that Luke had done some research on hot cars and children."

"Mia did too," I say. "Said they were both worried about it."

"Right," Angelina says. "So, yes, there were several searches in the days before Ally's death."

"How many?" Carter asks.

"Too many," Angelina deadpans, "for idle curiosity, if you ask me. Anyway, you know they did that. And by the way, there were fourteen such searches to be exact." She has our attention, but she pauses anyway. "There's one that I think you should see."

"News articles?" I ask. "We've seen them."

"No," Angelina says. "A video. It was under a search string other than 'hot-car death.'"

"What was it?" Carter asks.

She looks at him and then me. "'Does a baby dying in a heated car make any noise?'"

Carter pushes back from the table. His face morphs from disgust to rage, yet he stays silent. We've both imagined the depravity of people like Luke. We see them in our jobs. We read about them in psychological case studies. Even on TV. We know the darkest acts perpetrated by another, and we are seldom surprised.

But now. Now we are.

"A YouTube video by a Plano detective recounted what he understood happened to the human body, a child's body, at those kinds of temperatures. That was watched multiple times."

She goes to the video and it plays quietly. I don't need to hear the words. Dr. Beakman told me how Ally had suffered in that Subaru.

"We can't tell which one of them accessed the video?" Carter asks.

"No," Angelina says. "Not really. I looked at the time of day and, judging by what Nicole told me about the Tomlinsons' work schedules, I'd say that Luke was likely the primary researcher. His log-on was used a lot more than Mia's. And mornings were a favorite time for what he was up to."

I think of Ally just then. She was sitting in her high chair, drinking milk from a sippy cup while her dad was hunched over his laptop, plotting to torture and kill her.

"Don't you want the cherry?" Angelina asks.

Her remark catches me off guard. "There's more?"

She nods. "Yeah. And it's a whopper." She clicks on a link in the history tab, and a bulletin board–style page comes into view.

"What's this?" Carter asks.

"It appears to be Luke's favorite Internet destination. His handle is Big Guy."

"Of course it is," I say.

The site is simple. It looks like Reddit or one of those old fan sites that used to be popular in the days before Facebook. Its threads are collapsible, the number of responses indicated with each. The newest posted on top, descending downward on the page to those topics that have cooled over time.

The site is called Kidzzz.

"What is this?" Carter asks. "Some kind of perv site?"

"Perverted, yes," Angelina says, "but not in that disgusting sexual-abuse way. This site is for parents who wish they never had any children. That having kids has ruined their lives. It's the biggest bunch of whiners and complainers that I've ever seen anywhere."

"Like wanting to hurt their kids?" he asks.

"Not that," she says. "At least, I didn't take any of the comments that way. Mostly parents just longing for the days when they didn't have to haul their bratty progeny off to soccer and stuff like that. That it was hard to deal with a kid with colic at 2:00 a.m. Or that the kid's college education had cost them their retirement. It seems to span the whole gamut of parenthood. The ugly and the mundane. I'll tell you one thing, no one on this site is bragging about their kids and how much they love them."

She scrolls down to Big Guy's most recent post on a thread called "I don't get any anymore."

"Nice title," I say.

Angelina looks at me as she clicks on his message.

Before it was born I got tons of pussy. I got it from my wife every which way I wanted it. I'm talking dirty, fun shit. I get hard just thinking about it. Now look at me. I'm chang- ing diapers. It wants to be fed. My old lady's too wrapped up in her career to give a shit about either one of us. Should have gotten her an abortion when she begged me. Stupid me. Catholicism sucks.

"He calls Ally an 'it.' What a piece of crap he is," I say.

Carter jumps in. "What a fucking dumb shit! And a big baby! Changing diapers? Like that's so hard. I loved every minute of being a dad. Maybe not the diaper part so much, but, Jesus, this guy's warped."

"More than warped," I say, though I don't think I can articulate just what more that might be. On the repellent scale of one to ten, with ten being the highest, I put Luke Tomlinson somewhere around fifteen. Maybe twenty. Now when I see his pudgy face and dull-eyed stare, it will be through eyes that have been made fully open by his callousness.

"What about Mia?" I ask. "Did she post too?"

Angelina shakes her head. "Not that I could tell."

She pushes the binder and a thumb drive in my direction.

"That's the highlight reel," she says. "Most of the details and print- outs that align with the case in any way are here. Some photos from a folder are proof the guy's an idiot too. Feel free to dig in, ask questions if you need to."

Carter and I thank her.

"No problem," she says. "Just make sure the bastard never goes free, all right? He's the crap on the bottom of anyone's shoe. The funny thing is, I think even he knows it."

"How so?" I ask.

She grins. "Maybe this is a double cherry on this shit sundae. But one of his Internet search strings was 'How to survive in prison.'"

"Seriously?" I ask.

"When was that?" Carter chimes in.

"Two days before Ally died."

"This gets better and better," Carter says.

"Or worse and worse," I say, "depending on your POV."

Angelina lays her hand on her report. "In case you're wondering, Luke learned a number of important rules that I trust would be helpful in Walla Walla. He learned never to snitch on anyone, not to get too friendly with the guards, to always take your pants off when going to the bathroom, to never argue with a guard, to cozy up with members of your own race, to never show emotion, and, let's see . . . to pray that you'll live long enough to get out one day."

"Some great tips, there," I say, with mock admiration.

"What's that thing about the pants off?" Carter asks.

Angelina nods. "Yeah, that one caught my eye too. Apparently most prisoner violence takes place while inmates are in the bathroom and you should be seated no matter if you are going number one or two. Pants should be off so you can get up and run without tripping. Seriously. That's a tip."

"And a great tip it is," I say.

"Have at it. Enjoy the photos," Angelina says. She leaves, and Carter and I sit side by side to go through the binder. He smells different today. A new shampoo, I'm guessing. Carter isn't the type to splash on cologne. He smells good. I don't remark on it. I just let it pass through my mind.

"Guy's a total perv," he says.

"No argument there," I say as we take a deeper dive into the contents of the binder. "Angelina's done a thorough job here."

"She's good," he says. "Best one we have."

I smile. "She's the *only* one we have."

Carter grins back. "Right. But say we had ten people: she'd still be pretty damn good."

I turn the pages to the section marked "Personal Photos."

And there he is. Mr. Magnum in all his glory.

"God," I say, "why do guys do this?"

"I don't," he says.

"I didn't mean all guys, Carter. But why are some guys compelled to take a photograph of their junk?"

Carter narrows his gaze in my direction. "You haven't taken a selfie?" he asks.

"Not of my vagina," I say.

"Some guys do it," he says, "because it's a turn-on, I guess."

"Taking the photo? Or sending it?"

"Sending it, of course. They think it's cool when they get a naked picture of a woman sent to them. And, I guess—because, like I told you, I don't have any personal experience here—they think a woman will like receiving one."

"Highly doubtful," I say, thinking of Danny Ford. "I'm speaking from experience, Carter. I had a boyfriend who took lots of photos of himself as though I wanted to see the images. I think he just wanted to show off. Probably sent them to others too."

Carter nods. "He probably did."

I go on. "Just so you know, no woman I know wants to get one of these. At least, none would want it as their introductory photo from a dating site. Just not cool."

I look through the photos. There are seven. Some erect. Some flaccid. All are close-ups. None show Luke's face, which I know for sure has never been his best asset.

"Nic, we don't even know if these are his dick pics," Carter says.

I give him a look. "Who else's would they be?"

Carter shifts in his chair. "All right, they are probably his, but other than telling us that he's an even bigger pervert than we thought, what's the big deal? No pun intended, by the way."

I smile. I don't mind the pun at all.

"We won't know until we find out how he used the photos," I say.

"Did he share them during one of his online chats on the Kidzzz site?" Carter asks, turning to the printout of his postings, where I'm running my finger down the list.

"No photos posted here," I say.

"Then where?" Carter says. "He took them to share them."

"We need to get his phone back from the lab," I say.

CHAPTER TWENTY-SEVEN

Wednesday, August 23

When I go to see her at the hospital, Mia Tomlinson is sitting in an empty "family" room at the hospital—not her usual haunt along the cafeteria windows. She no longer appears like she's going to blow away in a good gust of wind. She looks like she's planted her feet on the floor. She's full of resolve as I tell her about Rachel Cromwell.

"That fuck face," she tells me.

I don't respond, at least not immediately with words. I try to keep my expression somewhat flat. Interested. Empathetic. Not too encouraging. I want to see where she's going to go now that I've told her that Luke was having an affair. The conversation seems more casual, and I never lose sight that she's lost her daughter. I hate more than anything to bring such news to the mother of a dead baby, but what Mia knows about her husband's affair could be crucial in the case.

"He could never keep his dick in his pants," she says. "Makes me sick to think that he was out screwing around with some floral slut while I'm working my ass off, trying to make a life for us. Good God. He's such an idiot."

She watches me for a beat, and then her eyes focus on the window and the scene outside. Clouds lie low over Aberdeen.

"It might rain tonight," she says.

"That's what they say," I respond.

We sit in silence for a moment.

"Are you okay?" I ask.

"I'm fine," she says. "I know why you're telling me this, Detective Foster. I'm not stupid, you know."

"I'm telling you this because it might be important. It might have some relevance."

Her eyes stay on the window.

"You're here to judge Luke. I get it. You're here to make me tell you something that will help you. I've lost my daughter. Now you want to take away my husband forever. You really are something."

I hadn't expected her to push back so hard. I thought to myself that if I had been lucky enough to be a mom, a *real* mom, I'd attack whoever hurt my child. I might find forgiveness somewhere if what happened had been an accident. But, to be honest, that would take a million years.

"I know that, whatever screwing around he was doing, it had nothing to do with what happened to Ally," Mia says. "If that's what you're after. I mean, if you think that—just because a guy will stick it wherever he can—I can tell you right now that's the way things work. You're older; you might not get how things are today."

I bristle inside, but she can't see it. Yes, I am older. Not that much. Not old enough to be her mother, not even by the narrowest of Hoquiam generations. Mia just told me a lot about herself. She and Luke are a match made in heaven. The person they love more than anyone in the world is the person they see in the mirror. *Ally.* Poor little Ally. Her parents had very little use for her. They certainly had very little interest in a baby. Luke was out screwing around, and Mia was so focused on her career that she seemed glad that Luke had distractions that didn't involve her.

"Look," Mia says, "I love my husband. The reason I can say that is that I understand and accept him. He's a moron. He's a traitor. He only gives a crap about his video games and his buddies at work, but he's mine. He's the husband that I have and I love him. That doesn't mean I give him an easy pass on everything. When I see him in the jail tonight, I'll make him blubber like a baby. He'll get everything I can throw at him. He will. I promise you. And as far as the florist girl goes, fuck her. I don't care. I love Luke."

"Just so I understand," I say, because I'm really not sure that I do. "Are you saying that you didn't know about Rachel? That now that you do, it doesn't really matter?"

Mia toys with her hospital ID tag before answering. She seems irritated by my question.

"Again," she says, "this might be generational. People my age don't hold on like you do. Like my mom did. Guys cheat. They're dogs. Whatever. Move on. Get over it. It happens."

We talk a few more minutes, but if she has anything against her husband, she's holding it back. She excuses herself to get back to work.

"Look," she says, "I know you're just doing your job. I'm sorry if I was harsh to you. Sometimes a tragedy or an accident is just that. A stupid mistake isn't always something evil."

When she's gone, I call Carter to let him know how it went. It goes to his voice mail, and I leave a short message.

"She's in denial," I say. "I don't think we're going to be able to get much more out of her. Heading back to the office. See you."

A young nurse pokes his head into the family room just as I get up to leave. His ID card indicates his name is Trevor Johns. He's young, short, balding, and wears wire-and-plastic-framed glasses. He's got everything working against him but the look in his eyes. They're deep blue and full of indisputable emotion.

Worry and anguish, I think.

"I saw Mia leave," he says. "You're the detective working on her daughter's case, right?"

I introduce myself, and he lingers a little before shutting the door behind him.

"I like Mia," he says. "To a point." He stops and withdraws a little. I can see that his hands are trembling slightly, and when his eyes catch mine, he shoves his hands into the confines of his pockets.

"Trevor," I say, "I can see you're troubled. What is it? You know that this is important, right?"

He swallows. "Yeah. I know. I just don't want to cause trouble, but I haven't been able to sleep very well. In fact, not at all. Not since Ally died. I just keep wondering about something and I feel like I should tell someone. You, I guess. I don't think I would have had the guts to call you. But seeing you here. It was like God was telling me that I needed to say what I needed to say."

"That's good," I tell him in my most reassuring way as we take a seat side by side at a table. If we sat closer, I would tap him lightly on the knee to indicate our connection in a calming, nonthreatening way. "What do you want—what does God want you—to tell me?"

Invoking God might seem manipulative, but I'm a believer. Prayer went hand in hand with the recovery from my gambling addiction. A higher power was never a crutch but a scaffold. Faith kept me steady when I needed it most.

He talks about her personal habits for a minute, telling me that Mia's always the first to seek credit for something, the last to shine the light on others.

"The day Ally died, she pulled a typical Mia. She came late for staff recognition. Acted like it was a bother to be there."

I nod. "There's something bigger here, right?"

Trevor pauses and then unleashes.

"Mia didn't like being a mom," he says. "I mean, she really, really didn't like it. She told me one time that she wished that her daughter had never been born. She said that Ally was cramping her style and that she and Luke were turned off by parenthood."

I'm drinking in every word. And I suddenly feel sick.

Trevor stops. He's assessing my response, and it fuels him. It tells him that what he needs to say is important, maybe necessary.

"She told me that having Ally shifted her priorities against her will. Or it would if she let it. She said that if Luke wanted to be Mr. Mom, then that was fine, but she had her degree to attend to. And as far as downtime? They could no longer go out and party because—and these were her exact words—'the alien that I popped out cries all night long.'"

"'Alien'?" I repeat. "Ally?"

"Right," Trevor says. "She told me that. Mind you, I thought at first that it was a joke; it seemed funny. She riffed on it all break long, saying that she felt like she was the host organism and only Sigourney Weaver could save her. We laughed. We all did. Later, I don't know . . . it seemed wrong, what she did afterward."

"Like what?" I ask. "What did she do?"

Trevor crosses his arms with such vigor that it seems as if he's giving himself a reassuring hug.

"Like coming back to work after her baby died. The next day. Who does that?"

"Sometimes people need to hold on to a routine," I tell him. "A big piece of their life has shattered and the only way to stay sane is to maintain the other pieces."

"It was more than that," he says. "I went to give her a hug and to tell her that I was so sorry. Because, wow, I was."

Tears fill his eyes. They fall, and even though he surely must feel them as they roll downward, he ignores them. He makes no crying sound. Just the slow, steady stream of a deep, deep hurt.

"What did she say to you, Trevor?"

His lips move a little, but it's more of a tremble than an attempt to really speak.

"Tell me," I say. "Please."

"It seems so crazy. So wrong. Mia told me not to be sad; that everything was going to be fine. She was going to get her degree and Luke wasn't going to be forced to change diapers. She actually said that it would be okay! Ally was dead, and somehow it didn't really matter to Mia at all!"

His story is a series of poisoned darts. I knew that Mia Tomlinson was ambitious. I thought she was like a lot of us Grays Harbor County girls, looking for something just a little bigger in life than a retail job, vacations at Ocean Shores, the occasional trip to Seattle or Portland. I knew that she loved her husband. And while I couldn't really make sense of that attraction, I knew that no one who really knew me could see my attraction—other than the obvious physical attributes—to Danny Ford, my last boyfriend. Probably my last forever. If what Trevor is telling me is true, Mia wore a mask. It was a flimsy one at best. She passed herself off as someone who cared so much about others—a nurse—and wore the mask of a mom who doted on her baby girl; a wife who worked her way through nursing school so that her husband could nurture their child.

Such a giver, that Mia.

Trevor pulls himself together.

"You aren't going to tell her what I said, are you?" he asks. "I sure hope not. I have to work with her, and she has a way of making people look like dirt around her. She turned me in to the charge nurse one time for stealing from the vending machine. They wrote me up. I really didn't steal. Someone tried to get some Doritos and the package got stuck. I put in three quarters and got two packages. Big deal. Mia was mad because I didn't give her one. So she told on me."

While Trevor's story hints at a grudge between him and Ally's mother, it also suggests something more.

Mia Tomlinson is a woman who gets what she wants.

Back in my car, I take a call from Rick in Evidence.

"WinCo surveillance camera images are in and being processed. Ready in the morning," he says.

I thank him and check my speed as I drive. I don't want to be the cop who flashes a badge to get out of a ticket. My mind swerves to the scenario that I hope never comes to pass.

"But I have a murder to solve," I'd say.

"Nice try, Detective."

"But really."

"We all do."

Chapter Twenty-Eight

Wednesday, August 23

She's back. I feel it. I *know* it.

My sister is like the monster that never died. Letting her go was only delaying a reunion that I didn't ever want. I could have done things differently. *I could kill Stacy,* I think as I turn off the ignition outside of Carrie Anne's. There must be some part of me that will enable me to do the kinds of things my sister has done without hesitation. We come from the same parents. The same poisoned blood of our mother courses through our veins. The same pathetic blood of our father that allowed Mom to do whatever she wanted without him standing up to her even once. All the boxes are the same. I tick off another. We were raised in the same gloomy, weather-beaten environment, a place in which a blue sky seemed so rare that we lived most of the summer without expecting any sunshine at all. Overcast. Heavy air. The weight of Hoquiam and everything that happened when we grew up nearly suffocated us like a pillow pressed to our faces at night.

I could kill Stacy.

I really could.

If I did, I'd be rid of her forever. I'd never have to look over my shoulder. I'd never have to worry that she'd crawl like a scorpion into Emma's bed and sting her with what she would insist was merely a kiss. If Stacy were gone, I'd be able to breathe in like I've never breathed before.

Killing Stacy would set me free.

It also could send me to prison.

Life's full of tough decisions, I think.

I get out of the car to get Emma. The dog next door, an insufferable Pomeranian, yaps at me like she knows what I'm thinking at that very moment. That I'm no good. Dangerous, even. That I would snuff out the life of my sister. I love dogs. But not that one. At least, not right now. That one sees right through me. I glare at that yappy puffball.

Killing Stacy would make me a murderer. Doing so would turn me into the kind of human garbage that I have spent my life trying to put away. I think of Cy. Of Tomas. Of Kelsey. Of Julian. I think of the wreckage left behind in my sister's formidable wake. I tell myself time and again that murdering Stacy would ultimately save lives. It actually would be the humanitarian thing to do. *The compassionate thing.* Not only would Emma and I be free of her, but any other unsuspecting soul who might come in contact with Stacy in the future would also be safe.

Emma lights up when she sees me.

"Hey, kiddo," I say, reaching down to scoop her up.

"Carrie Anne says we can go to the beach tomorrow, if that's okay with you."

I hug her like it's the last time. Since Stacy arrived, every time feels a little like the last time. Or could be.

"That'll be fine," I tell her.

Carrie Anne appears behind Emma. "We're getting close to the end of the summer and I thought a day at the beach would be a great way to celebrate. You can come too if you can."

I shake my head and plant Emma's feet back on the ground. "Love to," I say, "but probably can't get the time off."

"Tomlinson case is something else," Carrie Anne says, her voice low.

"Emma knows all about it," I say, catching Carrie Anne's look of concern.

"Yeah," she says. "I guess all the kids do. Seattle TV's latched onto the story. They love portraying us like a bunch of backwater morons one level below moonshiners in the woods of Kentucky."

I smile at her. "I could use some moonshine."

She grins back. "I'll look up the recipe on the Internet. Day care receipts are going to drop when the kids skedaddle back to the classroom. I'll need a sideline for sure."

"I'll look the other way," I say.

Behind Carrie Anne, I notice her ex-husband's gun cabinet. Most of the guns are gone and a few of the vacant spots have been filled—ironically, I think—with Precious Moments figurines. The cabinet's locked, and I've never worried about it being in the living room of Emma's day care. Suddenly, however, I think of it as a source of inspiration. I could shoot Stacy while duck hunting out on the edges of the Wishkah.

If either of us were the duck-hunting type, that is.

Carrie Anne calls over to her kids to quiet down, and Emma and I tell her goodbye and start the drive home. While Emma chatters about all the things that happened that day, I continue to think of ways to kill her mother. It's like an annoying song on perpetual repeat, and I can't get it out of my head.

We pass a Safeway with cherries on sale featured on its reader board. The idea that I could bake a cherry pie—with a lattice crust, because Stacy would have no other—and lace it with cyanide pops into my head.

"Have an extra big piece," I'd tell her. "I'd join you, but I'm gluten-free now."

A car merges into traffic and slams on its brakes to let an old drunk weave across four lanes to the other side of the road.

I could run Stacy over in the car. It would be brutal and messy and I'd almost surely get caught.

"What are the odds that you'd hit your own sister?" An investigator would surely ask.

"I didn't know it was her," I'd lie.

Shooting her. Poisoning her. Hitting her with the car. Those are only the first ones that come to my mind. Drowning. Drug overdose. A rope around her neck. Those and other possibilities I'm all but certain will visit me when Emma's asleep and I'm lying in my bed, trying to come up with a way to save her from a life with her mother.

Shelby greets us at the door.

I could feed Stacy to an alligator. If I had one. But I don't.

As Emma hurries inside, I pick up my dog and hug her. God, how I wish Stacy had never come back. God, how I wish that my mind were free of the hideous thoughts that are circulating through it.

"Mac and cheese?" I say to Emma.

"The good kind?" she asks.

The good kind is the fluorescent orange pasta from the blue box. I made the mistake of making it from scratch one time—with smoked Gouda and panko on top. It was delicious to me. To Emma? Not so much.

"Yes," I say. "The good kind."

I could stuff Stacy's head into a pot of boiling water. I could put her head into the oven. I could mix broken glass into her pasta.

Killing Stacy is the only way to be rid of her forever. For Emma's sake, it is the right thing to do. It is also probably the only way to save myself.

But saving myself isn't a good enough reason to kill my sister.

The water boils, and Emma and Shelby sit in the kitchen while I open the box and pour the pasta into the pot.

"Auntie Mommy," Emma says, "I wish you could go to the beach with us tomorrow."

"Me too," I say, sprinkling some salt into the boiling pot. "But you know I can't. If I could I would."

"It's just that summer is almost over. We haven't gone hardly anywhere."

I look at her. She's sitting on the floor with Shelby's head resting in her lap. Both of them mean everything to me. Everything in the world. I set the timer and join them.

"I know," I say, putting my arm around Emma. "Not much I can do about it. I have the kind of job that takes over your life. Most people can put in for a vacation and with a little luck get it approved by their boss. I have to wait until there's a lull in whatever major investigation is going on. Haven't been too many lulls lately."

"Can't Mr. Hanson do it by himself?" she asks. "We could go to Seattle again."

I shake my head. "Not right now. I promise when things quiet down we will. We really will."

Her beautiful eyes are filled with disappointment, and they stab at my heart.

The timer goes off, and I give her a hug.

"Promise?" she asks.

"Promise," I say, getting up from the floor and reaching for the timer.

First I need to get rid of your mom, I think. It's a song. An ugly one, I know. Yet it won't leave me.

Later that night, I do just what I imagined I would when Emma is asleep and Shelby has to be let out for the umpteenth time. That song plays over and over, but it's not a song. It's an anthem that tells me that getting rid of my sister by killing her is absolutely the right thing to do. Even though it is so wrong, I go with it. I drink some wine and ponder what might happen if I did kill Stacy. In one scenario, I would get away with it. All would be fine. Emma would grow up smart, perfect, beautiful, and loved. She would never need to know the treachery of her mother and how a life with her would have starved her of true happiness. In another scenario, I'd get caught and Emma would be a ward of the state. Both of her parents would be dead. I would be tried and convicted. It is likely that she would never forgive me for what I'm thinking of doing. She doesn't know her mother the way I do. If I got caught, the only good thing would be that Stacy would be dead and— barring the possibility that she's a female version of Freddy Krueger or Jason Voorhees or Michael Myers—she would be gone forever.

That's good.

Just then I see my reflection in my wine glass. I'm smiling. It's not a happy smile but one of strange satisfaction. But I see something in my eyes too. It startles me a little, and I take the last gulp of wine and set the glass down on the ceramic coaster I made my mother in school. I wonder who that woman is. Who is that woman who would kill her own sister?

Is it you, Nicole Foster?

Do I even know who I am anymore?

CHAPTER TWENTY-NINE

Thursday, August 24

It's a drumbeat that hits me like a sledgehammer every morning. Nine days now. Nine days since Ally was killed. Nine days is not a long time for a homicide case.

If we can prove it.

Nine days.

Hammering at me.

The videotapes that WinCo assistant district manager Darren Huff brought in are not tapes at all. Someone in Aberdeen has finally gone digital. That's a good thing. Surprising too. That'll make things easier and faster. Spinning hours of analog videotape was necessary and tedious work. On the other hand, a digital asset could be manipulated by a keyboard, not a "Play" or "Fast-Forward" button.

Carter is holed up in his office, on his cell phone, dealing with a family issue. I can't tell if it's about one of his kids or if his ex-wife is dropping another bomb in her quest to annihilate him. According to him, that's what she's been up to. First the affair. Then the promise of reconciliation, followed by a process server. Then the divorce. I know that there are two sides to every story, but since I work with Carter, I'm on his side. I have to be. Partners need that kind of unconditional trust. No questions asked. At least, never asked aloud.

I put the thumb drive in my computer, and it whirls away, sucking in the video. I find the time stamp and move my cursor close to the lunch hour. The parking lot is relatively empty except for the Tomlinsons' Subaru. It's quiet. The angle isn't perfect, though. In my own sad heart, I long to see if Ally tried to fight her way out of that car, but there's no way of really seeing that. Ultimately, I think that's good. I wouldn't want Mia to sit in a courtroom and watch as her daughter's torture played out before a jury of twelve strangers. No mom should ever endure that kind of gruesome reality TV.

I let the images move across my screen a little faster than normal speed while I drink coffee and think about the case. As I sip, my eyes stay glued on the screen. Finally, I see some activity. It's Luke. While the picture is less than ideal, I'm sure of it. He cuts through some shadows from trees at the edge of the parking lot. His gait is slow, deliberate.

I freeze the image and check the time stamp.

It nearly matches what his coworkers Gavin Wilcox and Al Black said about their return from Jersey Mike's: 12:38.

I slow down the video to a frame-by-frame view.

My face is nearly pressed against the screen, I'm so close.

Luke looks left, then right, as he approaches the car. He puts a bag on the front seat. He cocks his head a little inside the driver's side. I wonder if he sees Ally. Or if he hears her. It's so fleeting that it would be hard for anyone to argue that he actually saw his daughter.

And then the unexpected.

Luke looks over at something out of the range of the camera. He puts his hand up to his mouth for a second. I can't see if he's talking or not, but it seems very, very clear that there is another person just out of camera range. Luke turns and looks at the Subaru and then back at what I'm sure is another person. He's saying something, but I can't read his lips.

My heart is pounding. I didn't expect anything like that.

Luke walks a few steps to the car and then does an about-face. His fists are clenched now. It's as if he's very angry at something.

Or someone.

Carter pokes his head into my office.

"You look like you're going to lose your cookies," he says.

"If I'd eaten some, I expect I would," I tell him. "Check this out, Carter." He sits down, and I swivel the screen in his direction. "Look. Right there." I tap the glass. "Luke Tomlinson is talking to someone."

Carter's eyes widen. "Seriously? To who?"

"I have no idea."

"Can you read his lips?" he asks.

I shake my head and turn my attention back to the screen. "No. But he's definitely talking to someone. He looks angry too. Upset, even. Hard to read."

I click on the icons indicating the content recorded by the other two cameras. The images roll by, and I see nothing but a blank parking lot and a seagull tussling with what appears to be a dead rodent.

"WinCo might have a vermin problem," Carter says.

"*We* have a vermin problem," I shoot back. "His name is Luke Tomlinson."

Carter moves from the space next to my computer to the visitor's chair across from my desk. He sits and stretches out. His long arms find their way behind his neck, and his fingers massage the tenseness from, I expect, his phone call with his ex-wife.

"It's none of my business," I say. "But whatever you were talking about with whoever it was . . ."

"Right," he says. "It's none of your business."

Carter is shutting me out right now. I know it's because he doesn't want me to see him at his worst. I know that he has an immense pride and that his failing marriage has all but chewed it away.

"I know," I tell him. "I just want you to understand that I care. You know, I've gone through some real shit in my life and I know that if I had a real advocate and not someone who substituted lead for a life vest, I'd have pulled out of the mess a whole lot faster."

I'm thinking of Stacy, of course.

"Appreciated," Carter says. "But I'm not you." His facial features have tightened, and I know that I've hit a nerve. "I'm digging my way out of all this on my own. Enough said. All right?"

"All right."

"My guess is Luke was talking to one of his buddies or maybe Rachel Cromwell," he says, putting the conversation back on the rails, where it belongs.

I'm not sure, and I tell him so.

"It's possible, Carter. I guess it is. When I think about his coworkers at WinCo and Rachel, I just don't see them leaving out a confrontation with Luke—not when there's so much at stake. Leaving it out would make them complicit. And I really don't see that."

Carter thinks for a minute. "I know what you're saying. I get it. Yet, if it wasn't one of those three people, who the hell was he talking to?"

That's the big question.

"We'll need to find that out," I say, looking down at my phone. A message from Ocean View:

Your father has been asking to see you.

I look at Carter.

"Something's up with my dad. I was already there once today."

"You better go," he says. "Could be something."

I shrug. I really have no idea.

CHAPTER THIRTY

Thursday, August 24

A young nurse's aide whose name tag proclaims *Hi, I'm Sammy-Jo* hurries over as I maneuver my way past a group of women in wheelchairs, their heads hanging as though something very intriguing were happening on their laps. Her smile is so broad that it threatens to cut her face in two.

"Stacy," she calls over to me. Her voice burbles with enthusiasm.

"I'm Nicole," I say back.

"Sorry," she tells me. "I just wanted to let you know how much your father loved the Mexican chocolate. We *all* did. It was so nice of you."

I look at her questioningly. "I'm sorry," I say. "I don't know anything about Mexican chocolate."

Now Sammy-Jo looks as confused as I feel at that moment.

"Stupid me," she says. "It was your sister. Stacy, right?"

Stacy wrong, I think.

"She's never been to see our father," I say. "She lives out of the country."

Sammy-Jo shakes her head; her blue turquoise drop earrings threaten to break orbit from her earlobes. "But she has. I'm sure of it. Your dad adores her."

"My dad has Alzheimer's and he thinks Richard Simmons is president," I say.

Sammy-Jo brightens. "Follow me. She signed in the book. I saw her. Are you twins?"

"No," I say, trailing Sammy-Jo as we proceed to the welcome center. I know that I'm supposed to sign in, but I never do. I don't see the point in it. Not really. My dad doesn't know who I am. The staff does. Except Sammy-Jo.

She opens the sign-in book and turns its pages back to the previous pages of the visitors log. She presses her finger on a signature and spins it toward me.

"There. Stacy Chase. That's your sister, right?"

The air is propelled from my lungs with such a force that I'm all but certain everyone at Ocean View can hear my gasp. But there it is. In that overconfident, swirly, girlie script that my sister thought made her look as though she were autographing a fan's photo is her name.

And Julian's too.

I didn't know it, but my sister has not only returned to Grays Harbor County, she's done so with a new last name. My sister. My adversary. My love. My hated rival.

The poisoned blood of my lineage.

When I can finally speak, my words come in a whisper.

"She's back," I say. I had felt her shadow, but now it was real.

"I don't get along with my sister very well, either," Sammy-Jo says, throwing some kindness in my direction to mitigate what is a stunningly awkward moment. "She hogs the bathroom when she knows I have to get to Ocean View. Being late is a serious offense around here. Sometimes I think my sister wants me to be late because she's so jealous of my work here."

"Sisterhood is a challenge," I say.

She closes the book. "She left a note for you," Sammy-Jo says, suddenly remembering something very important. "It's in your father's room. Pinned on the bulletin board with all of his memory reminders."

Dad's room is quiet. He is asleep. Or dead. I watch for a second for a slight rise of the sheet covering his shrinking chest. It moves. He's alive. The whiskers on his chin are tiny white spikes, and it angers me that the staff here doesn't keep him clean-shaven. Dad was particular in that way. Even when he worked those long, grimy hours at the mill, he never left for a shift without looking like he might be going somewhere special. I saw how other dads looked when they made the same trek to work. I knew that my dad took extra care because he'd married my mother. He stepped it up. He knew that she was the most beautiful woman in Hoquiam, which I know doesn't sound like much, but she *was*. He was handsome. Strong. Neat. Clean. He didn't have her charisma, but he knew that if he wanted to keep her, he'd have to provide her with the right setting. She was the diamond. He was the gold band.

The memory reminder board has done nothing to spark a memory for my father. Emma and I scoured the house for pictures, ticket stubs—the Rolling Stones in Seattle!—his old car keys, anything that we thought could trigger some kind of recollection. I put pictures of Mom, Stacy, Emma, and me in a row across the top. I selected the worst photo of my sister that I could find—a quest that wasn't easy. She was going out on a date with a boyfriend who she'd stolen from me. Dad took the shot and must have clicked the shutter before she stood, hook-armed and beaming. Her eyes are half-shut.

I love that shot.

Images of our house and yard are affixed below the family photos. I even pinned Dad's locker tag from the mill.

Every now and then I add something new to see if it sparks any kind of remembrance.

None of it does.

And there, pinned over a photograph of our house decorated for Christmas, is a present that I never expected to see. Or wanted. It is a white envelope, and it is addressed to me. The handwriting is undeniably my sister's.

I park myself on the edge of my father's bed. He stirs. I fill my lungs with air and notice that my fingers tremble as I open the envelope and remove its contents. For a second I feel like a shadow has covered me. A chill. A kind of darkness that I knew would come for me. Stacy is like the psychopath in a horror film. She'll disappear, but she'll always come back. With Stacy I doubt it will ever be safe to go down to the cellar alone.

Dear Nic,

First things first. I'm not about to make any trouble for you. I could, but you know that's not who I am. I've been away for a couple of years now and I think I'm a better person for it. I've grown. I've made some mistakes and I'm sorry about them. At least most of them. I've been living in Mexico and, well, things just didn't turn out the way I thought they would. I guess you could say that I miscalculated how my life would go after Cy died.

She's being careful with her words. When I read that line, I think, *how my life would go after I murdered Cy,* but that's just me.

Dad moves his leg and I pat his foot. A nurse walks by the open doorway, and I glance in her direction. She smiles warmly. She thinks I'm sharing a touching moment with my father when in fact it's my sister on my mind. And the wetness in my eyes is not from sadness but fear.

I read on.

Nic, I want you to know that I appreciate everything you've done for Emma and I see how she's growing up. I want to visit her. I want her to know that I still love her and that I might not have been the best mom ever but that I did the best I could. When you think about it, we didn't have the best road map for motherhood, did we?

She's right. Our mother was a narcissist. We were important to her when we were young enough to dress up and show off to her friends and admirers. The term *show dog* comes to mind. As terrible as Mom was, as far as I know, she wasn't a criminal. A person who made money from a child's death. A killer. My sister was all of those things, and I've known that deep in the marrow of my bones for a very long time. And yet as wrong as it is, I keep letting her inch into my life. I keep thinking of that beautiful little baby sister and how happy I was when she came home from the hospital.

I'm here for a couple more days. I'm staying at the Quinault Beach Resort & Casino. I really don't want to cause you any trouble. You have to believe me. I'm in room 322. Come and see me. I want you to bring Emma too. She needs to know that I'm all right. I'm sure she misses me terribly.

Emma did. The first few weeks after Stacy handed her to my care, Emma was distraught. She knew her daddy had died. She knew that her house had been destroyed. That her world had been shattered. She loved her mom. Missed her. We always love our moms no matter what. I was in the worst position then. I wondered if I'd made the right decision, taking her like I did. I had a willing participant in my sister, of course. Stacy was wrapped up in a litany of drama of her own doing. She just wanted to be free.

And now she's back. I just knew this day would come.

> *Remember, neither of us is perfect. Everyone deserves a second chance.*
> *Love,*
> *Stacy*

Love? Stacy never knew the meaning of the word.

◆ ◆ ◆

On the drive home, I feel the bile in my stomach rise. I know it isn't anything that I've eaten, because I haven't had a bite all day. It's my sister. She's doing what she always does to me. She's like the throwing knives from one of those magician acts we used to watch on TV. The assistant stands like a statue as the knives are hurled in her direction, just barely skimming her cheek as their tips dig into the backdrop. Relief comes each time there's a miss. The assistant appears to be calm, but deep down everyone watching knows that there's always a chance the magician will twitch or cough or do something to break the concentration required not to miss her. Stacy is those knives. I'm the girl who tries not to blink. I think of all the things she's done. I think of her note, a half-hearted attempt at reconciliation but with an overt dig at my greatest failure.

She booked a room at the casino. Yes, it is the nicest place in the area. And, yes, Stacy always demanded the nicest things. Never a hand-me-down. Never a used car. Never just the steak, when lobster was also on the menu. Stacy is purposeful. She's staying at the Quinault because she knows that I'll have to pass through the casino to get to her.

Seriously, Stacy?

I am stronger now. Smarter too. I can do this because I have to do it. I have to do it for Emma.

Chapter Thirty-One

Thursday, August 24

Like water balloons hurled by a mob of preteens, raindrops pelt my windshield as I pull up in front of Carrie Anne's after a brutally long day. After days of heat and sun, dips and dives in the heat, the clouds finally unzip. My wipers haven't been used in weeks, and the glass shows the stain of motor oil and dirt that has accumulated on the rubber blades. Sitting in front of Carrie Anne's house, I pump the blue-colored cleaner a couple more times. I make little attempt to dodge the raindrops when I run to the door to get Emma. My blouse and slacks are soaked.

"Auntie Mommy!" Emma chimes as she meets me at the door. "Guess what? Carrie Anne has a stalker!"

I'm startled by the word.

Just then Carrie Anne appears behind Emma and draws me inside. Carrie Anne is one of those no-nonsense unflappable types. I met her at church after a GA meeting my first week back in Hoquiam. She was there to set up for her book club. We became friends over detective fiction. She's a true friend.

"What's going on?" I ask.

"Little elephants have big ears," she says, shutting the door.

I nod and then kneel down to approximate Emma's height. She looks at me with those wide blue crystalline eyes.

"Honey," I say, "go get your backpack and I'll meet you in the TV room. *Scooby-Doo* is on."

"I'm too old for *Scooby-Doo*," she says.

"You're seven. You're not." I disarm her with a smile and a bribe. "We'll go through the TacoTime drive-through on the way home. If you're good."

"I'll be good," she says. "But I know what a stalker is too."

"Of course you do," I say.

She runs off, and I see something in Carrie Anne's eyes for the first time. She looks frightened. Carrie Anne is never scared. A person who can handle ten kids at a time is as fearless as a SWAT team leader.

She leads me into the kitchen and positions herself against a sink full of primary-colored plasticware. On the window ledge is a row of avocado pits that have been pierced with toothpicks to keep their bottoms submerged in water. A sweet-potato vine coils from a similar setup.

"I'm sorry," she says. "I shouldn't have used the word 'stalker' in front of the kids."

"It isn't a swear word," I say.

"It's an ugly one," she says. "A scary one, Nicole. I really am sorry."

"What happened today?" I ask.

Carrie Anne tugs at a tie-dyed shirt that I recognize as the first of the summer's activities. The washer has faded it somewhat, and the dryer has made it a size too small. She wears it anyway because her kids—and Emma—think it's cool.

"It wasn't just today. Yesterday too." She stops and calls over to the kids to settle down before continuing. "So I saw this car out there. A rental from Avis. I didn't think anything of it. I thought the Fergusons had out-of-town guests. But when I saw Suzanne, she told me that she didn't know what I was talking about. She and Clyde haven't had any guests all summer."

"What made you think it was a stalker?" I ask.

"Okay," she says. "That word is ridiculous. But the thing about it is that the car was only there during our outside playtime. Someone was sitting behind the wheel and watching us. It kind of unnerved me but it wasn't a man. It was a woman, so I wasn't completely unnerved. I can't be sure, but I think the car was there the day before yesterday too."

"Did you get the plates?"

Carrie Anne shakes her head. "I seriously need glasses, Nicole. I can't lie to myself about that anymore. I could barely make out the Avis sticker."

"What make was the car? What color?" I ask.

"I think it was a Lexus or some other high-end SUV. Definitely not a domestic car. Just too nice for that. The color?" She looks upward, thinking. "Somewhere between silver and taupe. I'm guessing for a car like that they call it champagne or something classy."

"Washington plates?" I ask.

"No," she says looking upward. "California. At least, I think so. Maybe North Carolina. Like I said, my eyes are complete crap."

"Did you notify the police?"

"No," she says. "I didn't think it was such a big deal. It only felt like a big deal when Emma and the other kids got all excited because I used the word 'stalker.' God, I'm so stupid."

"No," I tell her, "you're just being careful. Careful is good. Do me a favor, though."

"What's that?" Carrie Anne asks.

"If the car shows up tomorrow, can you take a photo? Get the plates in it?"

"Sure. I think so. I should have done that today."

I give her a warm smile.

"Now I'm off to TacoTime," I say. "I'm so lucky."

"We're having fish sticks and fries. Want to stay?"

I hate fish sticks. They remind me of my childhood. We ate so many boxes of Mrs. Paul's, I thought of her as a relative.

"Thanks," I say, "but tacos are calling."

Emma chatters incessantly as we pull into the fast-food drive-through and I order. When my car was new, I told myself that no one could eat in it, but having a seven-year-old and the need for a distraction now and then has made that rule vanish into the bin marked "What Seemed Like a Good Idea at the Time."

Emma crunches down hard on a taco shell, shattering it and sending lettuce and cheese every which way. We both laugh. It's funny how things that would have bothered me in the past if another passenger had done it make me smile when it's my beautiful, wise, and silly niece doing it.

"I thought that lady was you," she says to me.

"What lady?" I ask.

She lets more lettuce fall like confetti. "Carrie Anne's stalker," she says.

Carrie Anne didn't mention that detail. I wonder if it was the reaction of a seven-year-old corrupted by those *Scooby-Doo* mysteries she is all but certain she's too old to watch.

"You saw her?" I ask.

"Yeah." Crunch. Crunch. "She wanted me to come over to her car."

My heart rate quickens a little, but I keep calm. I set down the diet cola I ordered and look at Emma as we drive, taking my eyes off the road for a second. Long enough to weigh whatever she's telling me.

"Did you go over to her?"

Emma shakes her head and swallows another bite of the taco, which has become a salad on her lap.

"No," she tells me. "We have to stay in the yard. It's rule number one or maybe number two. It's a high-up rule."

I'm grateful for Carrie Anne's rules. Her eyesight is terrible, but her rules are sound.

"Did she say something to you?" I ask.

Crunch.

"No," Emma says. "She waved for me to come to her, but I didn't do that."

"You said you thought it was me."

"I thought that for a minute. But when I got a better look at her I knew it wasn't you. She just looked a little like you, Auntie Mommy."

"You'll tell me if you see her again, won't you?"

She nods. "Yeah, I will."

I take a breath and lie to myself. Wondering if it is just a funny circumstance and not the least bit nefarious. I think about what Mia said, and I know that she's right. The nature of my job is always looking for the darkest things. A stranger asking for directions is someone hell-bent on casing someone's residence. A person asking to see some kittens is a criminal waiting to pounce. A teacher taking a keen interest in a student is a pedophile.

Sometimes they are looking for kittens, asking for directions, wanting to see someone excel.

When we get home, Emma takes a bath and I lay out her pajamas. She emerges from the bathroom, a damp duckling. I towel her off, and her teeth chatter in the way that kids sometimes do—even when they are not all that cold.

"I'm glad it's raining," she says.

"It has been a while," I say as she gets dressed.

"Our grass is dead," she says. "It hurts my feet when I walk on it. Carrie Anne's grass is green because we run the sprinkler all day."

"Carrie Anne is smart that way," I say, though I think she must have an enormous water bill.

"Yeah. She's nice too."

I tuck her in, and she's out before I can turn off the light. It has been a long day for both of us.

Downstairs, I open a bottle of wine that I hope will last for three days. That's my goal. I don't want to be one of those people who drink alone every night. I know what I'm doing, yet I can't stop. Not completely. Not when my brain is a shooting range. Emma's given me the kind of purpose that I could not have imagined. It's funny how I knew that I loved her when I took her from my sister, but I had no idea how deep that love would go—that as much as it was back then, it has doubled, tripled, quadrupled over time. Moms would die for their children. I'm her protector. If anyone tries to hurt my little girl, they will have to go through me first. I will never let her down.

The wine slides down my throat. I put my feet up. I turn on the TV to catch the last of a news report from one of the Seattle stations. The faces on the screen are a jolt. I put down the glass and call Carter.

Seriously?

"Did you see the TV?" I ask after he picks up.

"Hi to you too," he says. "No, I didn't. But I heard that they interviewed Rachel and she dropped the bomb about her affair with Luke."

"Why didn't you call me?" I ask.

"Just found out. Just a little while ago. Prosecutor told me."

I'm holding the phone tighter than I need to. I loosen my grip. I don't need this kind of aggravation. I know that I'm not the number one at the Aberdeen Police Department. I should have been in Bellevue, but I screwed that up royally. Even so, I can't stop myself.

"Why didn't they call me?"

"Because I said I would." His tone suggests he knows that I'm pissed off, though I'm doing my best to hide it. I'm not great at that. I am, as I like to remind myself every day, a work in progress.

Progress is slow.

"There's a Web version of the story up now on KING 5's page. Nothing much in it. Just a tease for the reports they're running. It'll be on at eleven."

"Fine," I say. "Carter, just so you know, next time can you text me? You do know how to text, don't you?"

God, I hate that those words just came out of my mouth. I reel it back in as quickly as I can. I'm letting the stress of everything get to me. I'm picking on Carter because he's the only one I can.

"I'm sorry," I say. "I didn't mean that."

"That's okay," he says. "We both have a lot on our plates."

I tell him goodbye, and I watch TV and drink wine, realizing that by 11:00 p.m. that three-day bottle will be done. I'm not drunk. I'm close. A game show. An episode of *Chopped*. Some channel surfing. Finally it's 11:00.

Rachel Cromwell comes on camera, but she isn't alone.

A text from Carter pops up on my phone: Holy crap!

Indeed.

Next to Rachel is Mia Tomlinson.

"I'm here in support of Mia," Rachel says, looking at Ally's mother. Rachel is wearing a white eyelet top that makes her look sweetly demure. Mia is in a tailored blazer with a *Remember Ally* button affixed to the lapel. It really isn't an interview. It's more of a presser with Rachel doing all the talking and a KING 5 reporter and photographer covering as she talks. No questions. Just Rachel talking.

"I had an affair with Luke Tomlinson," she says. "I know what I did was wrong. I knew he was married. He didn't lie to me about any of that. He told me that his wife was cold to him and that she made him do all the housework and take care of their daughter, Ally. I know that is a lie now."

Her eyes dart in Mia's direction, then back at the camera.

"Luke Tomlinson told me on at least one occasion that he didn't want to be a father anymore. He didn't like all the work he had to do to take care of his daughter. He told me that he wished she'd run away or something. I said that one-year-olds don't run away and he looked at me and said, 'Well, then something. Something that makes her gone.'"

That word *gone* again.

Holy crap! Carter texts.

I text back: You said that already. But yes. Holy crap. Nobody wanted that little girl. Not Luke. Not Mia.

He's done, Carter texts.

Yeah. He is, I answer.

In the last seconds of the news report, I notice Mia's very satisfied expression. As it had been from the beginning, her affect is off. She looks intense, but not in the way that would evoke sympathy for what she's endured as a mother and as a wife. She leans into the microphone, a gold chain around her neck clacking against its surface, making scraping and static sounds.

"I don't want to say anything more than I'm just as shocked," she says. "I appreciate everything Rachel Cromwell has done. I'm not angry with her. None of this is her fault. I applaud her honesty. We need more strong women like Rachel Cromwell in this world."

The interview is over, and the bottle is empty. I crawl up the stairs to my bed. Morning, I know, will come soon enough.

Chapter Thirty-Two

Friday, August 25

I can't sleep, and daylight comes too fast. It's not that I even want to sleep. Not really. I never was much for sleeping. Slumber is a time waster. It also brings in the nightmares that have played in the darkness all of my life. I think now that some of what drew me to the casinos in the first place was that it gave me a way to escape without closing my eyes. The energy. The people glued to the kaleidoscope of colors and promises in front of them. The smell of hope and disappointment in the air. Flashing lights. Anticipation. All of those things sent a current through my body and took my mind off the things that visited me at night. At some point, a welcome distraction became an illness. That brought some relief. I'll admit to that. All I could focus on was gambling. Winning. Losing. Rinse. Repeat.

It's 6:00 a.m., and I'm showered and dressed for the day. Emma is asleep, and I sit on the edge of her bed, taking her in. I know she's been the cure for my problem, even though my counselor tells me that therapy and GA meetings are responsible. That's fine. Believe what you want. I know.

"Wake up," I say softly.

Her eyes open a little, and she looks at the Felix the Cat clock that has been in this room since Stacy and I were girls.

"Too early," she says.

"I'm taking you to McDonald's before Carrie Anne's," I say.

"I don't like McDonald's," she says, retreating into the cocoon of blankets and sheets that twisted around her during the night.

"You like pancakes," I say.

Emma stifles a sheepish grin.

She knows that I know I've hit her in a place that cannot be denied. She's a pancake girl. Forget French toast, which is my favorite ("I don't want a soggy sandwich without anything in it"). Scratch off waffles too ("dry and nasty").

"Okay," Emma says, extricating herself from her covers and landing on her feet like an Olympic gymnast on the old fir floor with the patina of decades of similar landings.

My own.

My sister's.

"I'll be ready to go in a minute," Emma says.

"Teeth brushed," I say.

"I'm not a baby," she says.

"I know."

Emma pads across the room to the bathroom down the hall. I pick up Shelby and carry her down the stairs and let her out to do her business, which she does nearly on command.

Sure enough, five minutes later Emma is ready to go.

Emma and I eat at the same table where Ally and Luke dined the morning she died in her father's car. This is intentional. I want to take in everything I can from Luke's perspective that morning.

Emma puts a forkful of maple syrup–soaked pancake in her mouth. "The pancakes are good," she says.

I don't say a word about talking with food in her mouth. Not every single moment needs to be a teaching moment.

"Yes, they are." I reach over and pick up a piece of pancake from her Styrofoam plate.

"Hey, no fair!" Emma says in bogus anger.

"Pretty good," I tell her. "I might want another bite."

She makes a face. "Okay," she says, pretending to be annoyed. "Just one more. And that's all."

When we get up to leave, I turn on the stopwatch feature on my phone. The time line is off, and I know it. I can reason away that it took extra time for Luke to get Ally into her car seat, but that can't account for all the time it took to get from McDonald's to WinCo. It might take that long for a grandmother unfamiliar with the buckles and snaps on a car seat to maneuver a squirming kid into place, but Luke was a practiced father. He'd been taking Ally to day care since she was a month old.

"We're doing a little test," I tell Emma as we pull out of the parking lot into traffic.

"What kind of test?"

"I'm just wondering how long it takes to get somewhere."

"Where?"

"From here to the grocery store."

Emma doesn't say anything. She knows what I'm doing. She's a good listener—plus Carrie Anne has the TV on all day long. Though they've moved on, the Seattle news media was all over the story in the beginning, showing the WinCo where Luke worked over and over. The

PR department at the grocery chain must have hated that kind of publicity in the worst way.

I know that Luke and Ally arrived at McDonald's at 8:39 a.m.
Sixteen minutes after that, at 8:55, Luke and Ally left the fast-food
restaurant for WinCo. He arrived and parked there, in an isolated area,
at 9:09.

I turn over my phone. I don't want to see how long it takes until I
get to the back parking lot. I want to drive like everything is normal. If I
miss a light, that's fine. Traffic is lighter this time of morning anyway. The
case is circumstantial. That means every single stone needs to be turned.

Every rock from which Luke crawled out from under, I think.

Emma talks about school and how she's heard from Carrie Anne,
of course, that her teacher is nice.

"She's really good at art," she says. "I think I'll like her."

"I like art," I say.

Emma told me earlier in the summer that she wanted to be an art-
ist. Last year she wanted to work for a home shopping channel (thanks,
Carrie Anne!). Before that, in what I hope was not a suck-up move, she
suggested that she wanted to be a police officer.

"Like you," she told me.

When we arrive at WinCo, I park and turn over my phone and
hit "Stop."

It has taken us eight minutes, twenty-two seconds, and some
change. The time between the surveillance cameras at McDonald's and
the one at WinCo was a few seconds over fourteen minutes.

"Everything okay?" Emma asks.

"Yes," I say, though I know it isn't. "I'm taking you to Carrie Anne's
now. Thanks for running this little errand with me, Emma."

She smiles. "Thanks for the pancakes."

"Next time I'll order my own," I say.

"Good idea," she says.

As I drive to Carrie Anne's, I think about the extra six minutes. Only one thing could account for that.

Luke stopped somewhere on the way to work.

Barely half a cup of McDonald's coffee in my veins, and Carter and I are back in the same little departmental conference room with Angelina Marco. I tell Carter about my experiment, and his eyebrows rise, but right now it's the Angelina show. She's hunched over her laptop and struggling to get the world's most out-of-date laptop projector working.

We need new equipment, I think.

"What have you got?" I ask.

Angelina barely looks up. "You'll see," she says, pulling a cough drop from her purse and popping it into her mouth while she fiddles with the screen input button.

Angelina has professed on several occasions that she doesn't like people much, but I know she enjoys making things into a bit of a show. I look at Carter, and I think he's thinking the same thing.

"There's a bit of bad news in the mix here," she finally says, her eyes meeting mine, then Carter's. "Mia's Samsung has been wiped clean. Set back to factory settings. Nothing on it."

"But there still is something, right?" I ask. "You can never really wipe it clean, right?"

Angelina shakes her head as a printout from Luke's phone appears on the big screen.

"Nope," she says. "Nada. All gone. It really isn't that hard to do. Go to the Web. People clean their phones before selling them to a third party all the time. No encryption. Just a blank slate and big start over."

"Well, we were more interested in Luke's phone anyway," Carter says.

"Yes, that's the good news," Angelina says. "And in this particular case I'm thinking that you're going to have all you need to get that piece of crap in prison for the rest of his life."

"Better than the laptop?" I ask.

She gives a quick nod. "Laptop was good but, yeah, there's some stuff here that'll make your hair curl. Or skin crawl. One of those things. I've pulled out a few highlights, just to walk you through some of this. Not trying to do anyone's job."

Carter looks over at me. We've talked about Angelina's aspirations before. She pleads innocence when it comes to wanting to climb the ladder, but she's got enough of the grandstander in her that we concur management might be the most logical stop on her career path.

We look at the screen as she moves her cordless mouse to open files that the state crime lab pulled from the locked iPhone that belonged to Luke.

The first entry is a text exchange between Luke and a contact named Sug.

Luke: Want to get out of here. So bored.

Sug: Me too. Work sucks.

Luke: I like sucking.

Sug: Ha.

Luke: When can you get off?

Sug: I don't know. Maybe later. Maybe never.

Luke: Don't tease me. I want to oil you up and roll around on the floor.

Sug: Sounds good.

To close out the conversation, Luke sends one of his dick pics. It makes me cringe a little that I think I could probably identify him in a lineup with his pants down around his ankles.

I look at Angelina. I'm not sure what to say, so I spit out a few words. "Pretty dull sexting exchange, if you ask me."

Carter gives me a gentle poke with his elbow. "Didn't know you had any experience with that kind of thing."

I shake my head. "I don't. Not really. Regardless, we know he's a creeper already."

Angelina speaks up. "Of course he is, but what makes this one important—and of course that's up to you guys—is the time and date of this little exchange."

"When?" Carter asks.

Angelina moves the cursor to the top of the file, where the lab techs have noted the time, date, and duration of the texting exchange. Immediately I can tell the significance Angelina is dangling over us. The realization makes me sick to my stomach.

Carter looks puzzled.

"Ally's birthday," I tell him. "That piece of shit was texting this garbage during his daughter's birthday party."

"It gets better," Angelina says.

"There's more?" I ask. "I might need some antacid."

She starts on the next file.

"Wait," I say. "Can you tell us who 'Sug' is?"

Angelina makes a face. "No. Prepaid phone. Sorry. Check this out. You'll definitely need some Tums." She takes a cylinder of the antacid from her pocket and hands them to me. I put two tablets into my mouth and wonder how something that tastes so awful could actually make anyone feel better. It's like chewing on a stick of chalk.

"This one matches your time line," she says. "Puts this series of texts during his visit to McDonald's the morning Ally died."

"I wondered what the prick was doing on his phone," Carter says.

I don't say a word. I can't. Like a minty Elmer's, the Tums have glued my mouth shut.

Luke: You look hot.

Sam: Glad you think so. I'm hot.

Gregg Olsen

Luke: Want to meet by the river later?

Sam: Sure. Been too long.

Luke: Seriously.

Sam: What time?

Luke: Going to the movies after work. Meet up after?

Sam: Cool.

My mouth can move again. "Tell me Sam doesn't have a burner phone too," I say.

Angelina fiddles with her power cord.

We need new equipment in the worst possible way. In Bellevue we had everything we needed for an investigation—and then some. Aberdeen is on a shoestring. Most small towns are. Here the mantra is "Make do." That works fine when small-time crimes are involved. Murder, not so much. In a murder case you need backup batteries for sure.

"She doesn't," Angelina says. "Again, not to tell you how to do your job, but you could just call the number or you could subpoena the phone company. Number's local. This guy didn't do much of anything other than talk about sex when he wasn't having any."

Angelina puts the next series of texts on the screen.

"This text was sent in the afternoon. According to your time line, around the time Luke was going to his car after lunch," she says. "It's also local. Nonburner. Yippee. So that's good news."

Luke: I miss you.

Mari: I'm still mad at you.

Luke: You can't stay mad at me.

Mari: I can. You really piss me off.

Luke: Don't be mad, babe. We can have some more good times.

Mari: I'm done with you.

Luke: But I'm free. Everything you wanted is going to be OK now.

Mari: Doubtful. Don't trust you.

Luke: We can play in the backseat.

Mari: God, you are stupid. I'm not trash. I'm done with putting out in your car. You're cheap. You treat me like a whore.

Luke: You know things are complicated, but that's all in the past.

Mari: You led me on.

Luke: I love you. You're so damn hot. God, I want you so bad.

Mari: Fuck you. I should never have trusted you. Don't ever call me back.

Luke: I did everything for you.

Mari: Goodbye, Luke.

◆ ◆ ◆

"Seems like Luke was having a pretty lousy day," Carter says without a single trace of irony. "He's a busy guy. I'll give him that. Seems like he'd do better with another hobby other than sex. Maybe fishing."

Angelina and I laugh, though nothing about this case is really amusing. It's sad beyond belief. Our laughter is a release. A balloon popped at a party.

"I don't know," I finally say. "He's having about as much luck as my dad did when he fished for rock cod off the Westport dock."

"Like I said," Angelina says, "there's a ream of sexts here between Luke and a bunch of women. The ones I've previewed here are pertinent to your time line. Others might be relevant to you in ways that I can't easily see. It's all here."

She hands me a thumb drive, gathers up her things, and leaves. Carter and I are alone.

"I can barely get a date," Carter says. "Okay, I can't get a date at all. This doofus has a dozen women who want to have sex with him. What's up with that?"

"You might be aiming too high," I say.

"I guess," Carter says. "That's always been my problem. Damn, my high standards."

I give him an awkward smile. "It's all right. We all have our faults."

The room suddenly feels a little awkward. I know that feeling. I *hate* that feeling. I keep us focused on the case.

"We need to find out who these three are," I say. "Sug, Mari, and Sam."

"Let's call them," Carter says. "It's faster and cheaper."

With nothing to lose, I dial the number for Sug, and after a cheerful greeting, it goes to voice mail. I recognize the voice right away. It's Rachel Cromwell, the florist from WinCo. It pops into my mind that Luke called her "Sugar" and she thought, not ironically, that it was so sweet. She didn't mention how raunchy her married lover was—or his penchant for sending photos of his anatomy. I give the girl some points, though. She didn't send any of her own—at least not that we've seen.

I run through the list of names associated with both Mia and Luke. I can't think of a single "Mari" or "Sam." "Sam" could stand for "Samantha." Is "Mari" short for "Marianne," maybe?

I dial Mari next. Like the first call to Rachel's number, this one goes to voice mail. I don't recognize the voice.

"This is Detective Nicole Foster of the Aberdeen Police Department. You are not in trouble, but I need you to get back to me as soon as possible."

I repeat my number twice and hang up.

The next call I make is to Sam. It goes to voice mail, the standard type set up by the service provider.

I leave a similar message.

"Seems like no one wants to answer a call from you," Carter says.

"A mother would late at night if her kid wasn't home. Most others probably prefer to play the message rather than answer a call ID'd as the Aberdeen Police Department."

"Our business cards tucked into a doorjamb aren't the best kind of direct marketing, either," Carter says. "Whenever I leave one and follow up with a second visit, I'm told, 'The wind must have blown it away,' or some such malarkey."

"Who says *malarkey* nowadays?" I ask.

Carter grins. "I do," he says. "That's who."

"You are from another time," I say with an exaggerated sigh, looking at the front page of the newspaper. There's a picture of Luke and Ally—one I hadn't seen. It had been printed on a T-shirt worn by a young woman.

Underneath the picture, written in block letters, are the words: JUSTICE FOR ALLY. STOP BABY KILLERS!

I wince at the photo. As much as I despise Luke Tomlinson, I know that no matter how long his sentence, his time in prison will be a short one. Men who do what he's done to his own child don't last long.

CHAPTER THIRTY-THREE

Friday, August 25

While Carter works an unrelated missing-persons case, I return to WinCo, where I find Rachel Cromwell behind the counter. The warm smile she has for the gentleman she's talking to dissolves when she sees it's me inching toward her. I wait for her to finish ringing up the man's *Get Well, Mom* bouquet.

"What now?" she asks me. "I've told you everything. You can't come here and question me again. I could lose my job. My boss found out about me and Luke and says that I could be bad for business. I just put flowers together. That's all I do. I do something that makes people happy. You want me to lose that?"

I let her finish. She needs to get it out.

"I'm not here to cause you any problems," I say.

"Are you here for flowers, then?" she asks.

I shake my head. "No, Rachel. I'm here to cross some t's and dot some i's. It will only take a minute."

"If my boss sees you," she tells me, "he'll fire me. I know he will. The publicity has been rough on him. Seeing the name of your store in connection with a dead-baby headline—wrong or right—is a customer killer."

"A minute," I say. "I promise."

She looks across the busy store. "Okay. Back room. Hurry."

I follow her as she disappears behind a big display of summer sunflowers.

She turns and faces me when the door shuts.

"What do you want now?"

"You told me that you and Luke were finished," I say.

"Right," she says. "That's what I said."

"Did you have any contact with him in the days before Ally died?"

She folds her arms. "Not really. I mean, I saw him here. We didn't talk. Why are you asking me this?"

I ignore her question. She's not primary to the case, and I don't want to be the cause of her losing her job.

"Did he send you pictures of his body?" I ask. "You know, private parts?"

She stays quiet for a beat. "Yeah. He did." Her eyes widen. "You have those photos?"

"Photographs of Luke? Yes."

"What about me?"

I shake my head. "No. I don't have any photos of you, Rachel. Did you send some to Luke?"

She looks down at the floor and then up at me. Her eyes are suddenly full of fear.

"A few," she says. "Maybe a dozen. I don't know. God, I don't want them out. They were a mistake. They were something that he insisted I do for him."

I show her the exchange between "Sug" and Luke.

"Yeah," she says, "that's me. I feel so stupid."

"I'm not here to make you feel stupid," I tell her. "I'm here to confirm that this is you."

"It's me. But this was way before anything happened with Ally. I can't be part of this case. If you make me part of it, I will lose my job."

I feel sorry for her.

"You are a part of it," I say. "You went on TV. It doesn't help the case, going to the press like that."

Rachel fidgets with her hair. "Mia asked me to," she finally says. "I've known her a long time. Before I met Luke."

"I see," I say, letting her twist in the wind a little.

Rachel fixes her eyes on mine.

"You don't have any of my photos?" she asks.

We don't. Not the kind that I'm thinking she'd sent to Luke—the kind he sent to her.

"It appears not," I say, watching the color come back to her face. "It seems that Luke bleached them right out of his phone. Didn't back them up on the cloud or anything. At least that's as far as we know."

Tears come to her eyes, and she wipes them with her floral smock.

"Thank you, Detective."

She doesn't need to thank me, but I let it sink in as though I deserve it. I need one more favor. One more piece of the Luke Tomlinson puzzle—the most important one.

"Do you know a Mari? That's with an *i*, not a *y*. Maybe pronounced 'Mah-ree.'"

"Mary who?" Rachel asks. "We have four Marys who work here. If you count a Marianne and Mary Louise."

"A girl that Luke was seeing?"

She lets out a nervous laugh. "God, no. The Marys I know are old. In their thirties. Or even older."

I was just beginning to like this girl.

"Luke never mentioned Mari? Or maybe Samantha?"

Again Rachel searches her memory. "Our relationship wasn't all that deep, Detective. It wasn't completely trash either. We didn't talk about anyone else we were seeing. I knew he was married and I assumed that I was the only thing he had going on the side. I didn't know that there was another girl."

When I'm finished questioning Rachel, I phone Carter from my car.

"Saw Rachel Cromwell," I say. "She's afraid of being outed."

"She's not gay," he says.

"No," I say. "She's scared that her naked photos are floating around the Internet somewhere and this town will be looking at her in a whole new way—a way she doesn't want them to."

Carter has no sympathy for her.

"She shouldn't have taken the photos and sent them in the first place," he says. "Doesn't anyone have a decent dad around here? I told my girls never to do anything like that. It might seem like a good idea at the time—though I don't see how—and *boom!* You're a damn Internet star for all the wrong reasons."

"Roger that," I say.

"Fine," he says. "I'll get off my soapbox now."

Good, I think. Sometimes Carter overdoes the soapbox. Now's not the time.

"No luck in finding out who Mari is. She's the one we need. Rachel has no clue who either Mari or Samantha is."

"Okay," Carter says. "I'll see what I can do here. I'll dig through the phone calls. Maybe something will jump out at me. Where are you headed?"

"Back to the impound lot. See you in a little while."

"What's up?" he asks.

"Just something I need to do," I tell him. "Something I need to be sure about."

"About the case?"

"Yes, but it isn't really anything. Just need to be sure about something that's been on my mind."

I know I sound evasive, but I don't mean to be. I just keep wondering about Ally and Luke.

Could he really have missed her in the car? Just not seen her in the backseat?

CHAPTER THIRTY-FOUR

Friday, August 25

Ally's car seat is at the forensics lab, but I borrow a Graco car seat from Carrie Anne and drive to the impound lot. It's a couple of years older than the model used by the Tomlinsons, but an online check indicates that the size and specs are the same. The only difference is the color of the upholstery. I also borrow five-year-old Simone's large Corolle baby doll, which is four inches shorter than Ally was. I can fix it by putting on a hat, which I do.

Luke claimed that he couldn't see his daughter in the car seat.

I don't invite Carter along because I know that he'd state the obvious.

"This isn't going to hold up in court," he'd say.

I know that. I also know that if we get another run at Luke, then we can tell him about the test. We're allowed to outright lie to the accused, but lying like that has never been my style. I can stretch the truth, though.

The lot attendant is a young guy with a gunmetal-gray old-school Stanley thermos of coffee that reminds me of my father's and a trigonometry book that reminds me of no one in my family. He sits in a little glass cube that serves as his office by the entrance to the lot. I show him my badge, and he motions me inside.

The Subaru sits by itself on the far end of the lot. It's been examined every which way. Inside, the smell of death still permeates everything. That acrid stench is one of those things that nothing can alleviate. I suspect that the backseat will need to be replaced.

I put the car seat into position. I take Simone's doll and set her inside, facing toward the back of the vehicle. The little white stocking cap is next. I need to give it some additional lift, and I do so with fast-food napkins that I keep in my glove box.

Once behind the wheel, I adjust the mirror and stretch myself upward. Luke is taller than me. A lot taller. And it occurs to me that his height would be an advantage in seeing Ally.

I look into the mirror, and I stretch my body, making myself as tall as I can.

This is not science. I know that.

And yet, when I look in the mirror, I see the little white hat, which catches my attention like a surrender flag.

I turn my head slightly as though I'm looking in the mirror to see traffic behind me, something that I'm sure Luke did.

The white flag again.

My phone pulses. It's Carter.

"Hey," I say.

"How's it going?" he asks.

"All right. Just trying to see if Luke was truly unable to see Ally. A little test. And before you say it, because I know you will, I know it's not admissible. Maybe some leverage later."

"Good idea," he says. "What did you find?"

I look back at the white hat on the doll's head.

"He couldn't have missed Ally, Carter. There's no way that he could have."

"Couldn't miss the smell," Carter says. "Couldn't miss the sight of her. Wonder if he heard her cry for help."

I don't say anything. The thought of what it was like for that baby in that car is nearly too much for me to take.

"You still there?" Carter asks.

"Yes. What's up? Why did you call?"

I hear the sound of traffic and the noise his lungs make when he inhales deeply on a cigarette. He's in the parking lot.

"Luke wants to talk," he says.

"No shit?" I ask, adrenaline giving me a better jolt than a double espresso.

"Yeah," he says. "Says that he's sick and tired of what everyone is saying about him and he wants to talk to us."

"With counsel?" I ask, still taking it in.

"Yeah, but that's fine. Better for us down the road when we get him into court. None of that 'I wasn't represented' bullshit that winds its way into just about every case these days."

"When?"

"This afternoon. You done at the yard? Need any help?"

"No," I say. "I'm good. I'll be there soon."

I take the doll from the car seat and hold it in my arms like a baby before gently putting it and the car seat into my trunk.

"Ally," I say to myself just before shutting the trunk, "I promise you that we'll make sure your dad pays for what he did to you. We will."

Eleven days into the case, and my resolve is stronger than ever.

CHAPTER THIRTY-FIVE

Friday, August 25

Jail attire looks good on Luke Tomlinson—better than his WinCo work attire. The flip-flops on his feet are beachworthy, and the jumpsuit fits as if it were tailor-made: no tug at the tummy like the shirt he was wearing when he was arrested. *The right outfit for the man,* I think. I hope he has a closetful of the same for the rest of his life.

Luke stays seated behind a large stainless steel–topped table as Carter and I enter the interview room. His lawyer, Thom Russo, rises immediately, jack-in-the-box style.

"I don't agree with this meeting," the lawyer says.

Too bad, I think.

Thom is in his late fifties, with a pate that looks like a flesh-toned yarmulke that has permanently been glued to his head. It's such a shiny marvel that I can't take my eyes off it as he slides into his seat next to his client.

"We're here because Luke wants us here," I say.

"We didn't ask for this meeting," Carter adds.

Thom shrugs. "I know." He looks at his client. "Say what you want to say."

Luke runs his bloodshot eyes over us. He looks like he's had trouble sleeping. I assume that killing your daughter can do that to a father. He puts his hands on the table; the chains that run from his cuffs to his belly rattle like Marley's ghost.

"I don't like what everyone is saying about me," he says.

Join the club, I think. *I've been there.*

"We can't control the media or the public," I tell him. "Is that what this is about?"

Luke looks at Carter. "How would you feel if someone said you killed your kid?"

"You did, Luke," Carter says without so much as a pause. "So you'll have to tell me how you feel."

"It was an accident," he says. "I loved Ally. I didn't mean for this to happen. You need to believe me."

"Video doesn't lie," I say.

Luke doesn't look at me. He focuses on Carter. Thom looks at his phone and reads some texts.

Luke's pudgy face goes crimson. The hue clashes with the orange of his new wardrobe. "I didn't see her," he says. "I didn't. The video can't know what I saw or didn't see."

"It shows you going to your car at lunchtime, Luke," I say. I want him to look at me. He does for only a second. I hate guys like this, looking at my male counterpart as though I didn't exist. "You opened the car door, Luke."

"Detective Hanson," he says, "have you ever made a big mistake?"

Carter doesn't answer right away. He's pausing to push Luke into spinning the wheels of whatever he's thinking.

Finally he speaks. "Look, we came here because we thought that you had something to tell us." He pushes his chair back, indicating it's time to leave. I do the same.

"Wait!" Luke says. His tone has shifted drastically. He's scared. That's good. He needs to be.

"You have to help me. It's not safe for me in here." He looks anxiously at the window to the hall that leads back down the corridor to his cell. "The guy next to me calls me Baby Killer. He's a tweaker. A lowlife. But he's a mile ahead of me on the food chain around here. I'll get shanked the first chance anyone gets."

"You should have thought about that before you killed your daughter," I say.

Luke's eyes fill with tears, and he starts to blubber.

"It was an accident. It was. It was a hot car. Those things happen. They do. You know that. You see stuff like that on the news all the time. It happened to Ally. It did. I didn't remember to drop off Ally at day care. I screwed up. I made a big mistake."

Carter and I stand to leave.

Thom Russo turns his attention to his client. His expression is stern. I can't tell if it is fatherly or if he's simply annoyed. "That's enough, now, Luke," Thom says. "You've said what you wanted to say."

He looks at us. "We're done here."

Luke tries to stand, but Thom pushes him back into his seat. "But they aren't listening," Luke says, his voice now sandpaper. "They aren't!"

"We heard you," Carter says. His tone is flat, unemotional.

"We'll see you both in court," I say, driving a sharp little spike into the conversation.

Not a great idea.

Luke is now in attack mode.

"You bitch," he says, his voice filling the space around me. "You're a fucking gambling addict. Everyone knows it. You fucked up that case of the girl in Bellevue. You walk around like you're all that, but you're nothing."

Against my better judgment, I fire back.

"Yes, I've made mistakes, Luke. But I've never killed anyone. That makes you the winner in our race to the bottom here."

As Carter and I exit the room, I can hear Luke railing about me to his lawyer. He's saying all the things that I know could come at me in court later. How I was unstable. How I was homeless. How I gambled away a promising career. I hate all the things that I did. I think about them every single day. The thing is, I know in a very real way that everything creating the downfall that brought me home has made me stronger. To think of it any other way is to admit defeat. I came home in search of a new beginning for Emma and me.

"Wow," Carter says, "that was a waste of oxygen."

I nod. "Yeah. Luke's tears were for himself, not his daughter."

"Sociopath for sure."

Carter knows that Luke's words stung a little.

"Don't let what he said get to you," Carter says.

I breathe in deeply and let out a sigh. "He's right about some of it," I say. "I did mess up. I do know that people can make mistakes, but going to the casino and gambling away every penny wasn't an irremediable mistake. I own what I did—I take the consequences to heart every day—and I live a different life now because of it."

"Yeah," Carter says, "I know you do. I saw that the minute you came here for the interview. I knew that Nicole Foster had been knocked down, but she had dusted herself off and was never going to let that happen again."

Carter not only says the right thing at the right time, he says so without a hint of pity.

I like that.

CHAPTER THIRTY-SIX

Friday, August 25

Our departmental receptionist, Chadwick Meeker, summons me to the front desk not more than twenty minutes after we finish with Luke.

"Someone here to see you, Detective. Says you left a message to come in."

I wind my way down the hall, catching Carter chatting up a records clerk.

"We got an answer to one of our messages," I tell him.

"Mari or Samantha?" he asks, stepping away from the pretty new girl.

"Don't know. At the front desk now. See you in the interview room when you're done here."

Carter looks embarrassed. The records clerk looks irritated. Suddenly I feel better.

I open the door to the reception area. A young man in a McDonald's uniform sits by a sad ficus that has dropped most of its leaves like it thinks autumn has arrived indoors.

I look at Chadwick.

"That's Sam," he says.

Sam?

Not Samantha.

I recognize him from the video. He was the one behind the counter. He's in his midtwenties, with close-cropped hair that's done that way for the style, not to cover a waning supply. Leather and silver chain bracelets adorn his wrist. He gets up and meets me halfway across the room.

"What's going on?" he asks.

I don't know, but I don't say that.

"Are you friends with Luke Tomlinson?" I ask.

He nods. "Yeah. We're friends. Not good friends, but I know him. He came to the restaurant the morning his little girl died in the car."

I see some sweat collect on his brow. He licks his lips and never quite meets my direct gaze. His hand swipes his forehead quickly as though he doesn't want me to see how nervous he is.

And he's worried about how much I know.

"We're interviewing everyone right now," I say. "People who he knows, people he's come in contact with."

"I don't know him all that well," Sam says.

I don't want him to know that I don't know his last name.

"Let's go back to our interview room, okay?" I say, indicating for him to follow.

A minute later we're sitting with Carter, who looks completely perplexed. I pull out the folder with the printout of his text exchange with Luke and place it on the table. I'm surprised. Sam isn't Samantha.

"Sam," I say, "I need you to verify the spelling of your last name."

"Underwood," he says. "Like Carrie or the deviled ham."

I write it down.

"We saw you talk with Luke," Carter says. "You know, on the tape that morning."

Sam looks downward, like he's remembering. "Oh, yeah. He and his little girl wanted extra butter for her pancakes."

"You can never have too much butter," Carter says.

"Is that all you talked about?" I ask.

Sam thinks some more. The sweat rolls from his head to the table-top. He swipes that away too. "Yeah. I think so."

I get up with my folder. "Sam, you do know that we're in the middle of a murder investigation, right?"

"I know," he says. "I watch TV. I also read the paper."

"Good," I tell him. "Now, is there anything you can tell us that will help us with our case? We need to know everything about Luke Tomlinson that we can find out. Every single thing. A little girl is dead."

Sam slides off his bracelet and squeezes it like a stress ball.

"How did you get my number?" he finally asks.

I feel sorry for him. I really do.

"We got it off Luke's phone," I say.

Sam's quiet. He's thinking. Putting it all together.

"You aren't going to tell my mom and dad, are you?"

"Tell them that you and Luke are lovers?" I ask, opening the folder and showing the printout of the text message. "No, we won't be doing that. But you need to be honest here. What was going on with you and Luke?"

Sam starts to knead his temples. He's close to breaking.

"Hookup," he says softly. "That's all. Not lovers. Just a casual thing. We met online and every once in a while we'd meet down by the river or at my house when my folks were gone. Just sex. Nothing else. No strings."

"We didn't know that Luke was bisexual," I say.

"I don't think he cared who he messed around with," Sam says. "Luke just wanted the rush of having some *hot action*—that's what he called it—and then moving on. I think he had me in kind of a rotation that included a couple of other guys. Mostly girls, though. He told me that he was an 'equal opportunity fucker.' His words. Not mine."

Sam puts on his now-mangled bracelet, takes in some air.

"Did he ever talk about his daughter?" I ask.

226

"A little," he says. "We didn't do that much talking, but from what I remember, he told me that he loved her, but she could be a pain in the ass now and then."

"Did he talk about his marriage?" Carter asks. "His wife? Any problems they might have?"

Sam shakes his head. "Not really. Said she worked a lot. Didn't seem as interested in him as she had been. Other priorities, I think. I didn't really listen. I wasn't there to hear his life story and he wasn't there to hear mine."

"You were going to meet him for sex," I say. "The day Ally died."

Sam grows quiet. He's running through the events of the day, wondering if his relationship with Luke had any bearing on what happened.

"Yeah," he says. "But we didn't. And I didn't know that was going to happen, if that's what you're getting at. He wouldn't have killed her for sex. Sometimes he brought her along after day care."

"Seriously?" Carter asks, trying to contain his overt disgust.

"It wasn't like that," Sam says. "She didn't see anything. We were careful. We put her in front of the TV and did our thing. I'm not a pervert. Neither is Luke. He's a horndog, but last time I checked, it isn't against the law to have sex with someone who wants to have sex with you."

"Were you in love with Luke?" I ask.

Sam rolls his eyes. "No. I liked him," he says. "He could be fun. Adventurous. He'd tell me about things he liked to do and some of it was pretty wild shit. I went along with it. I'm pretty vanilla when it comes to sex. But not Luke. That guy was up for anything."

Up for anything. The phrase takes me back to the Tomlinsons' apartment when I noticed the scarred bedposts.

Yes, he was.

227

After I escort Sam Underwood back to reception, he makes one final plea for me not to tell his folks about what he does when he's not manning the drive-through window at McDonald's.

"Sam," I say, "if this makes its way into court and the prosecutor needs you for his case in chief, then there'll be no negotiating the point. You'll have to testify. If you testify, then you probably should give your parents a heads-up."

"They won't understand," he says.

"Times have changed," I remind him.

"Everywhere but here they have," he says, heading out to the parking lot to his rusted-out Toyota.

I know what he's saying. Aberdeen and, by extension, Hoquiam have stayed pretty true to their conservative roots when it comes to social mores. It has nothing to do with politics; it's more because of the very nature of the work that most of the men do to support their families. Manly work. Lumber. Mill. Seafood. Fishing. My dad was of that ilk. He was for the workingman, but that man had better not be "light in the loafers."

I find Carter in his office. He looks just as taken aback as he did when Sam first disclosed his relationship with Luke.

"I don't get it," my partner says as he crunches the empty bag of chips that he purchased from the honor system box in the break room. "I really don't. Luke doesn't give a crap about where he sticks it. Just as long as he can stick it."

"That seems to be about right," I say.

He leans back in his chair. "Gay. Straight. Bi. Trans. I don't get what anyone is anymore."

I sit down across from him. It's been a long day. A confusing one too. "Seems to be a moving line, for sure," I say.

Carter tosses the bag of chips into the trash can in the corner of his office. A satisfied look takes over the confused one for just a flash. "Don't people know who they are and stay in their own lanes?"

"I'm no expert," I say—a major understatement, as I haven't had sex for years. "Could be that Luke is just a horndog. Or maybe he's pansexual."

Carter looks completely confused. "Pan what?"

"Pansexual," I say. "That's just a clinical way of saying that a man or woman could be attracted to anyone regardless of gender."

Carter shakes his head and goes for another bag of chips.

This man needs a meal, I think.

"The world is getting so mixed up," he says. "I'm not judging. I really am not. I just don't know where the regular guy fits in these days. Seems like everyone has to be something special."

"You're special," I tease just a little, "in a predictable, completely binary way. I like that about you, Carter. I never have to worry. I always know where you're coming from, and I never have to guess where we stand. That's a good thing."

He smiles, and a look of relief comes over his slightly haggard but handsome face. "Yeah," he says, "I guess it is."

CHAPTER THIRTY-SEVEN

Friday, August 25

Carter is at his desk moving papers around with those big baseball-mitt hands of his. Country music, my least favorite genre, plays softly in the background. He's switched to chai tea, and the perfume of the cinnamon and nutmeg infuses the space with spice. *The wrong aroma for that kind of music,* I think.

At the same time, it covers the smell of cigarette smoke.

"You look beat," he says.

"Seriously?" I ask. "That's what you're going to say to me?"

He looks down. "Sorry. I just meant that you look tired."

"*Tired* is no better than *beat*," I say. "But, yes, I am tired. I'm still having problems sleeping."

"You need to see someone about that," he says, clearing a spot for me to sit without having to peer over a mountain of papers.

I ignore his suggestion, well-meaning as I'm sure it is. Sleep deprivation is somewhere at the bottom of my list of problems, which are head-lined by my sister, my father, and the case. I choose to focus on the case.

"Six minutes," I say. "That's how much extra time Luke had on his drive from McDonald's to WinCo."

"Okay," he says. "Six minutes. That's not a lot of time."

"Listen to six minutes of country music and it seems like an eternity," I say.

He turns off the music.

"An extra six," he says. "What of it, Nic?"

I'm not sure, but I know that it doesn't add up.

"Something happened on the way to WinCo," I say. "Something delayed him, Carter. There are some lights, but he'd have to have missed every single one."

"They are timed on that stretch," he says, looking a little more interested now.

"That's right," I say. "He could really only miss one. That's not a six-minute delay at all."

"He stopped," Carter says. "That's what you're thinking."

I stand up. "Correct. Get your keys. You're driving."

"Where to?"

"McDonald's to WinCo."

"I could use a sausage McWhatever," he says.

Despite his greeting that I looked tired, I don't tell Carter that he's wrong about that and that he'd be better off ordering an egg-white McSomething.

"What are we looking for?" he asks.

"The likeliest places Luke Tomlinson might have hit the 'Pause' button on what he was doing—and why."

Carter eats his biscuit while he drives from McDonald's. My eyes scan every inch of the drive, looking for a place that might have been a stopping point.

"He could have pulled over to the right anywhere along here," Carter says. "Ally might have been fussing or something."

I know that's possible, but I don't think it's what happened.

"He would have said so," I say.

"Not if he wanted to make us believe that he'd forgotten her. That she'd fallen asleep."

He's right about that. Everything Luke has said was likely a lie.

I indicate the signage that lines the street.

NO PARKING ANYTIME

"He's not going to risk having one of our traffic guys writing him up when he's on his way to kill his daughter," I say.

"Makes sense," Carter says. "I mean, about as much sense as any of this case does. Sick SOB."

Carter likes to let his vitriol loose now and then. It's healthy. Healthier than that biscuit he's just demolished.

"Pull in here," I say as we approach an abandoned Red Apple Market, somewhat ironically a victim of the customers syphoned off by the new WinCo. A sign pasted inside one of the windows indicates what comes after a grocery store dies.

NIRVANA POT PALACE

"Not another," Carter says.

I want to say that the marijuana industry has grown like a weed since Washington State made recreational pot legal. But I don't. Some puns are best unuttered.

"I guess so," I say.

Carter stops next to a row of gigantic dumpsters, each overloaded with the debris of a failed business. We get out and look around—for what, I'm not sure. Finally, I look upward.

Next to the first dumpster is a sign courtesy of American Security Services with a warning that I consider wrapped up in hope:

SMILE! YOU'RE TRESPASSING AND

YOU'RE ABOUT TO BE PROSECUTED.

I do what a sign tells me to do: I smile. Carter does the same.

◆ ◆ ◆

By the time we return to the office, the unfortunately acronymed American Security Services has left a message that they have recordings from the site backed up on a server.

I call back right away.

"We'll need a subpoena," the office manager says so half-heartedly that I know I could probably push her into giving them to me right away. I don't. Process and procedure have become more important than doing the right thing.

"All right, then," I say. "We can get you that."

Carter heads out for a "walk," which I know is his code for a smoke. I pack up my things. I'm calling it a day too. I need to see my sister. Once and for all.

CHAPTER THIRTY-EIGHT

Friday, August 25

Crap. I see Mia Tomlinson standing in the parking lot of the Aberdeen Police Department. She's staring hard in my direction as I look for Carter on his smoke break. There's no smile of recognition when our eyes lock. Just the cold, hard stare of someone who is completely angry. Something tells me it isn't about her husband or her dead baby.

"Detective Foster," Mia says as she hurries at me, "I should report you for harassment. In fact, I think I'll do that."

"I don't know what you're talking about, Mia," I say.

Her teeth are clenched in anger. "I know you've been asking questions about me."

"That's my job," I say. "I'm trying to figure out what happened to Ally."

"You know what happened to her," she says, refusing to break the lock she has on my eyes. "Luke left her in the car. That's the end of it. You have no business talking to my coworkers and neighbors and God knows who else about me and my life. I'm the victim here."

"Let's talk about it inside," I say, motioning to the door.

"I don't want to talk about it," Mia says. "I want you to back out of my life. My job is very, very important to me. I won't sit still for people like you to come along and shame me for going to work after Ally died."

Trevor must have broken down and told her what he said to me.

"No one is trying to shame anyone," I tell her. "Your job is important to you. Mine is too. I'm only trying to get to the bottom of this so that we can move on with the knowledge that we did everything we could."

Mia is not buying a word I'm saying.

"Trevor is a damn liar. He's still mad at me because I turned him down at the hospital Christmas party. He asked me out. What a freak! He'd do anything to pay me back. Little creep."

"He didn't mention any of that," I say.

"Why would he? He's a dirtbag. The hospital is full of people who act like they care about others, when they only love the drama of everything going on around them. He's short, bald, and fat. He's a loser."

"That might be true," I say, "but since you're here, let's put all of the cards on the table."

"Ask me anything, but then this stops. I won't talk to you without a lawyer. Not because I have something to hide but because you annoy me."

Sorry but not sorry.

"Trevor said that you didn't like being a mom," I say.

Mia goes ballistic, an affect that seems suited to her.

"Really?" she asks, though it's more of a statement than a question. "Are you going to give that any weight? He's a jealous prick. I loved my daughter. She was everything to me. I didn't plan on getting pregnant, but when it happened, I was glad that it did. Ally was a dream come true."

"Trevor said that you called Ally an alien," I say, studying her angry face.

She puts her hand up to flick me away. "I did," she says. "She looked like an alien when she was born. It was a joke. All kids look a little funny when they come out. Look at the coneheads in the nursery in the hospital. Babies don't come out of the chute looking like an Honest Company advertisement, Detective."

"I guess not," I say, though I remember seeing Emma at the hospital in the little crib in Stacy's private room at Overlake in Bellevue. I had never seen anything more perfect, more beautiful, than that little pink peapod.

Carter arrives from his "walk" just then and joins us.

"Your partner is making trouble for me at work," Mia says as he approaches. "There's got to be a law about harassing the mother of a dead child. If there isn't, then I'm going to start a GoFundMe page to get one going."

"No one is harassing anyone," Carter says.

Mia tightens her arms around her chest. "Look," she says, "you can tell me all you want about how it is that you have to follow every stupid lead or whatever to get to the truth, but you already know the truth here. It was a goddamn accident. My husband made a huge mistake. We are suffering for it now and I suspect that we always will."

I ignore her sanctimonious diatribe. It's as phony as my sister's implants.

"Your neighbor says that you barely paid any attention to Ally and that she cried all day and night."

"Mick Hightower?" she asks.

I don't indicate either way.

"It's him," she says. "It has to be him. For your information, Mick is a child molester. Seriously. A click of your mouse would have turned that up in a second. He's angry because we told him to keep his distance and that we knew what he was. The Internet is very helpful. You should search for a few things on it now and then. Might help you solve a case, but not this one. This one's solved."

Then, just like that, a light switch is turned on, and Mia's demeanor changes. It's so abrupt, it is nearly scary.

She starts to cry. Not just a sprinkling of tears but a torrent accompanied by gale-force wailing.

"My baby's gone. My baby's gone! And no one is helping me. You are making everything worse. I'm counting on you. Really, I am. God, I'm so stupid. I should have known that no one gives a crap about my Ally. She's not rich. She's not from a privileged class of people. No one cares about us hard workers."

A woman walking her dog past the police department runs over. She's elderly but spry. Her eyes are black like a snowman's. Her hands are knotted like myrtle roots.

"What are you doing to this poor girl?" she asks, moving closer to Mia.

Her dog lifts its leg and pees on the left front wheel of Carter's car.

"Dear," she says to Mia, "I know who you are. I'm so sorry for what you are going through. I lost a baby too when I was a little older than you. One of my twins died of a heart defect."

"Thank you," Mia says, still wailing.

"Instead of beating up a grieving mother, the two of you should put your efforts into putting this tragedy to bed. We've all had enough of this persecution of a young couple who made a mistake."

"It's a pretty big mistake, ma'am," Carter says. "We're doing what the citizens of Aberdeen hired us to do."

I stay silent. My mistakes don't need to be recounted here.

"That might be all well and good," the woman says to both of us while still propping up Mia, "but at some point you have to just stop. Just stop. Let this thing rest. Let baby Ally rest."

With that, she wraps her arm around Mia and gives her a hug.

"Stay strong," she says as the two go their separate ways.

I tell Carter that I'll try to catch up with him later.

"I've got some personal business to take care of now."

He looks at me.

"Listen to that lady," he says.

"Huh?"

"Stay strong too."

I smile. I will.

Chapter Thirty-Nine

Friday, August 25

What happened with my sister has eaten at me for more than three years. I think that secrets like mine probably cause cancer. I don't want cancer. I want to be well. I want to do the right thing even when I know that I have done something so very wrong. I am responsible for my sister going free. I could have turned her in. Sometimes I think that I should have—that if I had, I'd be a happier person now.

I discount that out of hand, though. If I'd turned in Stacy for her crimes, I would not have Emma. And, even worse, Emma would eventually be raised by a convict-mother so vile that my own would seem like a Disney princess in comparison. I have told myself over and over that everything I did was because of Emma. It was because she deserved so much more than a rerun of my own childhood.

I lied to myself a little. Maybe a lot. I know that I took Emma to make things right for myself as much as making them better for her. I think now, when I look back, that by saving her, I was really saving me. Good God. It seems so selfish now. Calling Stacy at the hotel that night to make my demands was the scariest thing that I'd ever done in my life. It wasn't because my sister would do me harm or anything like that—though she was capable of anything. It was because I was consigning myself to a lifetime of hiding the truth. Keeping a secret.

And yet it continues to drip, drip, drip. Even though it was out of love for Emma that I made sure she was in my care and my sister was gone, it was also the beginning of a great deception. I had to lie to teachers. Lie to friends—though thankfully there were few of those left in my life by then. I had to tell a story about a mother who could no longer care for her child and who had given her to me as an act of self-sacrifice.

In time, when people assumed that I was Emma's mother, I let them think it. I stopped correcting them. When she started calling me Auntie Mommy, I secretly hoped that the day would come when she would drop "Auntie" from the moniker.

And now, as my dad liked to say when he could still string together his favorite sayings, the chickens have come home to roost. Like they always do. Like I knew in my bones that they would. Stacy. Stacy is back. She is here because she wants something. Not money. I don't have that. Not Emma. She really doesn't want her. She is back because Stacy loves one thing above everything else. She revels in the power to hurt. It's funny how I can see things even more clearly since she's been gone. It's as if the threat that she would someday pop up and ruin my life was fading.

God, I'm so stupid. Stacy is back. And I'm going to do everything in my power to make sure that whatever plans she has concocted are short-circuited once and for all.

There. I admit it. I want her gone for good.

◆ ◆ ◆

The drive out to the Quinault Beach Resort & Casino is only twenty miles, but it's a beautiful twenty, winding through groves of firs contorted by the weather off the Pacific. I play every possible scenario in my head. I think of what she wants. I think of telling her what I really think about her and the kind of creature she's become. I think about things getting out of hand. She and I have always had a tendency to move in that direction. She's the button pusher, but I have pushed back in a weak, passive-aggressive way. One time she made me so angry that I used her favorite hairbrush to clean the toilet. Mean, I know. Childish, yes. Somehow it made me feel better when I watched her brush out her hair and gloat over its perfection in a handheld mirror that she used like a periscope to look at me.

I never told her.

Maybe I will now.

Like she would care.

As I pull into the Quinault to park, I scan the lot for Stacy's fancy rental, but I don't see it among the rows upon rows of cars from Washington, Oregon, and British Columbia. She's probably using a valet to park her car. My sister never missed an opportunity to have someone else do something for her. My fingers stay tight on the wheel, and I sit there looking up at the casino. I have not been in one for three years. When the department had a team-building evening there, I pretended to be ill and called in my regrets. Carter knew why. Probably others did too. No one says to my face what they know about me and the turn of events that brought me back home, but I can see it in their eyes sometimes. It's a mix of pity and disdain. I pretend that I don't see it. It's the only way to move past it all.

I try to reach up and turn off the engine but find that I'm unable to move. I'm stuck. I strain a little.

You can do this. This is not about you. This isn't really about Stacy. It's about Emma. All of this is about her.

A voice in my head tells me that Stacy has summoned me to the casino to remind me that I am weak. I wonder if she's watching me from her room. My fingers finally let go, and I swing open the car door. The air from the Pacific is a hot, wet dog's breath. I start for the entrance, and the pulsing energy of the casino spills over me. I see the lights. I smell the cigarette smoke. A couple with tan legs and hard bodies wanders out with smiles so big that I can only assume they won. The man is nearly giddy. The woman is saying something about getting a new car.

Won big. I've done that. I know that rush.

The lobby hints at the coastal Indian people who own and run the Quinault. Dark fir beams support the ceiling. Stacked stone covers the feature wall. The carpets are rich and muted. It's a place that says *Northwest*, but not overly so. In a way it is nearly tastefully bland. A few historic images add an unobtrusive pop of interest. One side of the lobby leads toward a bank of room elevators. The other side is a wide-open entrance, a vacuum designed to suck people onto the casino floor. I turn my head only slightly. I tell myself not to look. But I do. The vacuum tries to pull me in the direction of all those pretty lights, those smiling faces, those people drinking free watered-down highballs and thinking that they have a chance.

A chance to pay for their trip to Hawaii.

Remodel a bathroom.

Get a face-lift.

Buy a new car.

I am not that person. I'm just not. I know it. And yet I still look at the scene beyond. Sweat drips under my arms. Bile pushes upward once more. My heart races.

Fuck casinos.

Fuck Stacy.

CHAPTER FORTY

Friday, August 25

I knock on the door of Stacy's third-floor room. Though the casino's clatters and hums are muffled, they are insidious as they burrow their way into my consciousness. Distracting me a little. Adrenaline is coursing through my bloodstream, telling me to be alert. Reminding every fiber in my being that my sister is a cobra. She will strike when I least expect it.

The door swings open. I see her pretty but characteristically cold eyes. Her hair is no longer blond, and that startles me. It's colored and cut a little like the no-nonsense bob that I've employed since becoming a detective.

"Professional," she said to me when I adopted the look, "but so not sexy."

"Cops aren't supposed to be sexy," I had told her then.

"They are on TV," she said with a grim little smile. "At least, the ones that matter are."

I study her just now. She's tanned. Thin. Glamorous even with my hair.

"Oh God," she says, lurching in my direction. "I knew you would come." She holds me, and it feels like the way a crab holds fish bait. She cranes her neck to look behind me.

"Did you bring her?" she asks.

"No," I say, bracing myself. "I didn't."

Her eyes don't change, but I can see the fine lines around her mouth tighten. "Well, why not?" she asks.

I let out a breath. I'm not going to let her push me. I hold the cards. Emma is mine.

"Because she thinks you've gone to heaven, like Cy," I say.

Stacy pushes the door shut behind me. "You told her that? Why in the hell did you do that, Nic? I wasn't dead. You know I wasn't dead."

I want to say that I thought by saying it, somehow it would become true.

"I know," I tell Stacy. "I didn't know what else to say to her. It was triage, Stacy. You know that more than anyone."

She pulls at a sweater that I know costs more than a week's salary at the Aberdeen PD. I notice a coil of gold chains around her pretty, sun-freckled neck. I always admired her neck. I guess I admired everything about her beauty. My sister is older now, but she still looks like the teenager who literally lorded her perfection over me when she found her way down the stairs and into the front room of our house in Hoquiam. She swirled around the room, reminding our father that she was the flame to which all moths flew.

To end up burned and dead, I think now.

I scan past my sister. The room is large, a suite with a grand piano. I want to remark about how I didn't know she played, but I hold my tongue. I see no evidence of Julian, but I ask her anyway.

"Are you alone?"

She leads me to the bar.

"You mean is Julian here?" she asks.

"Right. Is he?"

She retrieves a bottle of sauvignon blanc from the ice bucket. It's a good bottle. Stacy is predictable. *That might be in my favor.*

"No. I'm sorry. And this might be hard for you, because I know you had feelings for him—"

"He played me," I say, cutting her off. Julian was as much a traitor, a betrayer, as Stacy. He'd reeled me into my sister's web because he could—because she made him. "I gave up feelings for him a long time ago. Where is he?"

She positions two glasses in front of her, fills both, and hands one to me. This gesture is a little grand. I'm thinking she wants us to toast something. I take a drink right away. *Stacy's back. I can't drink to that.*

"It's pretty sad," she says, not looking sad in the least. "And I know what you are going to think."

I immediately know where this is going.

"He's dead?" I ask, my eyes locked on hers.

She turns away and walks over to the window and looks out at the churning surf of the Pacific.

"A boating accident," she tells me.

I want to laugh, but I don't. *You never laugh at a shark.*

"What happened?" I ask, though I know she'll lie.

"We were living outside of Puerto Vallarta. Oh God, you would love our place. Right on the ocean. White sand as far as you can see. Really, a dream come true." She pauses, looking out at the water again. "Funny how this is the same ocean, but it's so different here. Grim. Dark. Cold. Nothing like our home in PV."

I don't roll my eyes, though I really want to.

"What happened, Stacy?" I ask, pushing only slightly.

She sips. The old diamond from her wedding to Cy is gone, replaced by a stone even larger, surrounded by bloodred rubies. *Fitting,* I think.

"We were out sailing, and I told him that the weather report indicated a potential squall. It was a freak accident. Really. Just one of those things you never think will happen."

I can't hold it inside. "Like the freak accident that killed Cy?" I ask.

She sips her wine. It is almost like she doesn't really hear me.

"Not fair, Nic," she says. "You can be so mean when you want to be."

She's never seen me really mean. That will change if she tries to take away Emma.

"Sorry," I say, though I'm not in the least.

"It's fine," she says. "I'm okay now. That's not to say it hasn't been hard on me. I'm a survivor."

Like a cockroach after a nuclear war, I think.

"What exactly happened to Julian?"

"I didn't see it happen," she says. "I was below deck. I heard a thump. It was pretty rough. I called up to him, but he didn't answer. When I got topside, he was gone. They found his body the next day. He'd hit his head and lost consciousness and drowned."

She's acting a little emotional. Her hand is shaking, and she's rubbing at her eyes. I don't see any evidence of tears. I've seen this act before.

She changes the subject. "Should we get dinner?"

"No," I say. "This isn't a social visit."

"Why not?" she asks, planting herself on one of the love seats that face each other.

"I don't trust you, Stacy."

She swirls her wine.

"I would think you would."

"After what you've done?"

"We," she says. "After what *we* did."

I want to hit her. "*We* didn't do anything. *You* did."

"You knew what I was going to do."

I shake my head and set down my glass. If not for Emma, I'd be out the door and into my car.

"I told you not to do it," I say.

"But I did. And you knew. And you didn't tell anyone. You are just as culpable. That's how I'll play it if I have to."

She's threatening me, but I quickly dial back my emotions. Stacy is like a fire that exists only to seek more fuel. She wants to explode. She wants to burn me. I refuse to be kerosene. I don't say anything more about Julian.

"What do you want?" I ask, trying to soften my voice.

"I want to see my family. I miss my sister. My father. My little girl. Is that so impossible to understand?" she asks, once more trying to get a chorus of violins going, but failing. She's a good actress, I'll give her that. But I know the real Stacy. "You always try to insinuate that I don't have any real feelings," she goes on, "and that's super hurtful, Nic. Really."

I take a seat in the love seat facing her. It's an oxblood shade, deep and made of leather. I feel like I'm being swallowed alive. I indicate that my glass is empty, and Stacy gets up to fill it and her own.

"You saw Dad," I say as she sits back down. "You saw me. And I know that you hung around the day care to spy on Emma. How did you even know she was there?"

"The staff at Ocean View let me update Dad's contact card. So nice of them. I saw the day care address as a potential contact point in case something happened to Dad during the day."

"Nice," I say.

"You've done an amazing job with Emma," she says.

"She's an amazing girl."

"I can see that."

"You can't have her," I say, once more setting my cards on the table.

"I'm her mother," she says.

"I didn't say you weren't. That doesn't mean you can have her. Come on, Stacy, you know you don't really want her."

Stacy looks into her glass. "You really don't know me at all."

"I do. I do," I say.

Her eyelids flutter a little. "You can't know what it's like because you've never had a child of your own. You've never even had a husband. But I've missed her every second I've been away. I have. I really have. It has been even harder since Julian died."

I know she's lying. She only cares about herself. She only cares about taking away something that belongs to someone in her way. A boyfriend. A job. A husband. A child. While it wasn't apparent when she was born—and her sociopathic behavior only emerged later—I know that Stacy can't help how she is wired. She was born that way. Mom's influence only shaped what Stacy was inside. It must be horrible to make a life out of wreaking havoc on others. I don't even want to think about it, because when I do, I feel sorry for my sister.

"I told her you were dead," I remind her.

"That was a mistake," she tells me. "How did I die, by the way?"

"Car accident." It's what I told Emma. At the time, however, it passed through my thoughts that I should have said that she'd died in a house fire. Her face burned beyond recognition. Slow and painful.

"Not very original," she says.

"Not everything has to be over-the-top, Stacy," I say.

"I like over-the-top."

We sit there silently for a moment. It's our game. She's thinking of a way to hurt me. I'm thinking of a way to kill her for real.

"I have a right to see my daughter," she finally says.

"Not the way I see it."

"She's mine. I could just go get her and leave town."

"Over my dead body," I say.

She gives me a stare. "I wish you wouldn't talk like that, Nic."

Translation: *Thanks for the idea, big sister, but I already had it in mind.*

"You can't have her, Stacy. You know that, just like our pony and Cy and Julian, you'll tire of her. That's who you are and that's who you'll always be."

Stacy's glass is empty. Her lacquered nails scratch at the armrest. "That's what you think of me? Wow. That's really cruel. I thought you were the kind one. Most people who knew us growing up always saw you that way. There's a mean streak in you, Nic. I won't be bullied by you."

That's a laugh-out-loud statement, but I don't respond accordingly.

"When are you leaving?" I ask, cutting to what I really want to know.

Stacy leans in my direction. "After I see Emma. Then I'll go."

The love seat takes another bite of me. "How am I supposed to make that happen?" I ask. "She thinks you're dead."

My sister shrugs her shoulders. "That's your problem."

My sister's right. I've made things worse. My best intentions were a mistake foolishly wrapped up in hope. "You only want to see her?" I ask.

Stacy's eyes bore into my own. I almost look away, but I don't. "I've seen her. I want to talk to her. Let's not play games here, Nic."

"You aren't here to take her from me?" I ask, letting my weakness seep into my voice. A mistake, I know. She's getting to me. Like she always does.

"No," Stacy says. "I promise."

"I'll need some time," I say. "I have to undo something that could be very traumatic."

Stacy pushes. "How much time?"

"A day or two. A couple days. I don't know. I never thought you'd come back."

I never wanted you to come back, I think, but don't say it.

"That's fine. I'm going to spend some time with Dad. Nice place, Ocean View. Expensive."

"Thank you," I say. "Your gift to me was used to pay for it."

"I know," she says. "And it wasn't a gift, Nicole. You extorted the money from me."

"I needed the money," I tell her.

"And now I need to see my daughter. I'd say we are even."

We have never been even. Not one time in our entire lives. My sister was a parasite and I was the host and that's the way it always was.

"Fine," I say as I get up from the jaws of the love seat. I'm upset, but I don't show it. The wine she poured me is mixing with my already-upset stomach. "I need to go now. I work for a living."

"Been following the hot-car case," she says. "Can't imagine anyone more horrific than Luke Tomlinson. What he did to his little girl is unconscionable. Some people are outright vile."

"Yes," I say. "They are."

You are, I think.

I leave my sister in her suite and make my way down to the lobby.

The elevator doors open, and there it is, beckoning me.

The casino.

I can't turn away. It's a bloody car crash—the kind that leaves the sheen of blood on the roadway and taunts each passerby. The flashing lights of the ambulance and police cars that arrive to pick up the pieces. You know you shouldn't really look, but you just can't stop yourself. You can't. Impossible. The lights of the casino are the same thing. Disaster that sucks me in. I don't have anything to stop me from going inside. I'm reeling. It's almost as though I'm a marionette and Stacy is the puppet master. Every part of my being is tingling. It is better than any sexual encounter I've ever had in my life. I feel hot. Sexy. I'm wet. And yet what's surging through my body has nothing to do with another human being.

It is the *Double Diamonds* machine that winks and leers at me from across the casino floor.

Damn you, Stacy.

The woman at the desk takes my credit card.

"Only a hundred dollars," I say, though I know that if I lose, I will be back in front of her. She's beautiful with tan skin and shiny black hair that she wears long to look the part.

"Good luck," she tells me.

I need it, I think.

As I walk across the carpet, my feet stick a little. It's quicksand. Flypaper. No, a glue trap for rats. Something is slowing me as I work my way toward the cacophony of bells and flashing lights that defines the row of my old love, the *Double Diamonds* machines. My eyes scrape over the large room: men at card tables, pretty girls hooked to their sides. The older crowd at the penny slots, watered-down collins drinks in hand, are only there to pass the time rather than change their lives with a windfall. And the people like me, hunched over slot machines or the keno table, thinking that they are one hit away from a new car. A new house. A dream vacation. A new life. A big fat do-over for all the mistakes that can be undone with an influx of cash.

Every pore in my body is oozing sweat. My mascara runs, and I dab at it with a tissue from my purse as I settle in next to a man who is pressing the button on his machine as if he's about to ejaculate. His eyes are fixed. His mouth is agape. He looks as desperate as I feel.

I could call someone from the group. I could throw my player's card into the trash. I could get up and make my way out of here. I could. I know I can. Then I hear her.

It's Stacy.

She's in my head:

You are always so predictable, Nicole. You always did the right thing. You're even a police officer. Seriously, what did any of this get you? Nothing. Nothing at all.

I push the card into the opening. I feel a shudder run down my arm.

Being predictable is good for people like me, she says. *We like it when people are simple like you and Dad. Never any question that you'll do the right thing. And when you do the wrong thing, it's that much sweeter.*

I press the big red button, and the machine comes to life. I feel the impulse to hold my legs together to feel the vibration that pulses through me. My heart rate accelerates, and my face becomes flushed. I'm on top of a nameless lover. I'm controlling him. I'm riding him. He's not in charge of me. I'm not lying on my stomach, putting up with his assurances that this is exactly what I want. Yes, it feels good. But it's weird. It's anonymous. I can't see his face. I can only feel him heaving and pushing and his whiskey voice telling me that I want more.

You like this.

You want all of it.

This is what you're for.

You want it deeper?

Hold on.

Hold on.

I'm coming.

The machine doesn't do that. It's passive until I command it with a swipe of my card and the touch of the big red button. I don't lie there compliantly with my face pressed against a hotel room bedspread, pretending to writhe in ecstasy until a guy that I picked up on the casino floor acts like his semen is God's gift to me.

All for me? Thanks so much!

Here, in front of this machine, I'm the one in charge. I shouldn't be here. God, have I missed it. God, have I missed being in control of the uncontrollable. I'm giddy. I feel as if I could fly right up to the ceiling, do a flip, and then land like a feather on this same orange vinyl high-backed chair.

First spin, nothing.

Second spin, the same.

Third, a loser.

A man two machines down twists on his seat and looks at me.

"That's a cold one there," he says, making a disgusted face. "You really should pull out and switch to the one right here."

Pull out. I'd heard that before too.

I give him a cursory smile. He's been there awhile. Players know what chairs are hot and what are cold. "All right," I say. "Thanks. You doing all right?"

He shrugs a little. "Not really," he says. "I mean, in the end we lose anyway. We can't win. If we won every time, then the Quinaults would have to scalp us."

"They don't do that," I say as I move to the seat next to him. "You've got your indigenous people mixed up. Scalping was a construct from back east. Not that common, really. Northwest coast clans didn't do that."

He nods. He's a nice-looking guy. Early forties, I guess, though the older I get, the more generous I am about ascribing youth to people around my own age. His bushy eyebrows could use a trim. His teeth are slightly crooked, and I know by the way he lowers his jaw when he speaks to me that he's a little self-conscious about it. I also know that he's sitting there to get lucky on something other than a slot machine.

"I'm Cal," he says. "Up here from Portland. You staying here?"

Of course it's Portland. His vintage Pabst Blue Ribbon T-shirt and dark-dyed denim jeans scream Portland. His black leather sneakers look so new, I imagine they were out of the box for the first time this morning.

When I don't answer right away, he covers his nervousness up by pretending to be interested in the machine in front of him.

I'm so messed up and so lonely, but not *that* messed up and not *that* lonely. No matter how angry my sister makes me, no matter how bitter I am about the state of my life and the choices that I have made, I'm not about to make things worse. I've done that before. A stranger in a casino hotel room can never make a heart as lonely as mine feel less so.

"Yeah," I lie. "My husband and I had a fight. I left him in the room to cool off. Going to go back upstairs in a few."

Cal looks deflated right then.

"Oh," he says. "Sorry."

I nod and look back at the screen in front of me. The diamonds are begging for another spin. I deny them. I take my casino player's card and hand it to Cal.

"This is your lucky night," I say. "I'm getting out of here."

He takes the card and nods. Not a word. At least, I don't hear one. I get up and walk toward the door. The pulsing of the lights, the smell of alcohol and sweat, and the feeling of hope and disappointment that clings to everyone as I pass by them is palpable. I nod in the direction of the young woman with the long black hair. I'm so done with all of this.

From the minute Stacy reappeared in my life, I knew she had only one purpose in mind. With her it has always been the same one. Stacy is about Stacy. Stacy gets off on other people's misfortune.

I'm so done with Stacy. This time. Really, I am.

CHAPTER FORTY-ONE

Friday, August 25

I'm beyond beat. The long day isn't over. It's after eleven when Carter and I return to the Red Lobster and find a place at the bar. He's agreed to meet me because, well, he's Carter and he can hear the stress in my voice, even when I hide it. He orders a beer this time, and I get a glass of wine. I am trying my best to avoid considering this "our place" or anything like that. And as much as I like him, I have learned from my mistakes. That's the part of me that feels solid now: the knowing that I won't ever fall so low again.

Even so, after my visit with my sister, I still need a friend. Not a shoulder to cry on. I'm not really a crier. I just need someone to listen to me.

"My sister's back," I blurt out as our drinks arrive.

"Oh, really," he says, taking a drink of his beer. Foam clings to his upper lip. I ignore it.

I sip. "Yeah. She's staying up at the Quinault."

Carter has a decent read on my whole backstory. I've never mentioned all the gory details, but the information superhighway is an easy route to amplify what I've said about her.

"What does she want?" he asks.

He knows her type, I think. He doesn't ask how she's doing. If she's well. How the reunion went. He knows that someone like Stacy only makes a move when she's after something. Or someone. She's cunning like that. Pretty on the outside. Beguiling, even.

Carter has read between the lines. That's what makes him a good friend and a great investigator. He listens, observes, and then assesses.

"Emma," I say. "She wants Emma." I set my glass down. I can feel my hand tremble a little.

"I thought she wasn't the mommy type," he says.

Understatement. Big-time.

"She's not. She says she just wants to see her. Talk to her. I don't know why. She hasn't specifically said she wants to take her away from me, but my sister is a stealthy troublemaker."

"She's legally yours, right?" he asks.

"It's a little complicated," I say. "I am her guardian. It's legal. But the reality is that my sister can revoke my guardianship anytime. It was an arrangement we made after her husband died and she was completely out of sorts."

He knows that I'm not being completely honest. He knows that my sister didn't want her daughter. I've been oblique about it since returning to Aberdeen, but Carter is a good detective. He sees things even when they aren't obvious.

"So what's the problem?" he asks.

"The problem is that I lied to Emma. I told her that her mom died. I just didn't want her waiting for her because I was absolutely certain that Stacy would never come back."

"But she has," he says, signaling our server for another round.

I nod.

"She's not here to stay," I say. "She's probably here to regroup after Julian's death."

Carter knows the name, though I don't think I've ever mentioned it. I didn't want him to think that after Danny Ford I picked an even worse lover in Julian Chase.

"What happened to Julian?" he asks, studying the bar menu now.

I wait a beat. If I wore glasses, I'd take them off with a flourish before making the big reveal. But I don't. So I can't.

"He died in a boating accident in Mexico," I say, with just a little sarcasm, because a lot isn't needed.

Carter shakes his head. "Let me guess: your sister and Julian were alone when the accident happened."

"That's what she says."

"Tempura shrimp?" he asks.

"Yes," I say to the app choice. But I'm not going to have dinner.

"Sure is an unlucky woman," Carter says. "She's buried two husbands before she's thirty-five."

I want to say everything that I'm thinking. Things about our childhood. Questions that have always lingered about what my sister really was. But I don't. I've always felt embarrassed about my sister's true nature, the layer of ugliness under her stunning, perfect veneer.

I look into Carter's eyes. It's strange how there can be something so deep in someone's eyes. He actually looks into mine. I look away.

"I can't lose Emma," I say.

"You can't go against the law," he says as the server brings the shrimp.

"What if she tells me she wants Emma?" I ask.

He takes a shrimp and dips it into some honey goo. "You have to give her back. But really, Nic, you don't know what she wants."

I do.

My sister wants to hurt me.

She has never seen any person, including her own baby, as something she couldn't manipulate for her own twisted purposes.

"I won't give her back," I repeat.

256

Carter doesn't say anything for the longest time. He sits there searching the foam in the bottom of his beer glass as if there were some solution there. He eats another shrimp. I make a defensive move and take one too.

There were only four with the order.

"You could turn her in," he says.

He keeps his eyes cast downward.

"For what?" I ask.

"For killing her husband, Cy Sonntag."

"It was ruled an accident," I say, my pulse rate quickening.

"Yes, I know," he says. "But you could turn her in, Nicole. You know that she killed him. I mean, that's how you really ended up with Emma, isn't it?"

The Red Lobster bar is spinning. I've only had two glasses of wine. I keep my elbows planted on the bar top. I don't want to fall. I don't want to sink into the floor. I'm being swallowed up by the truth spoken to me by Carter Hanson.

"Yes," I say.

"Turn her in, then," he says. "That's what you need to do."

I don't say anything more, because I can't. I can't tell him that I knew of my sister's plot to kill Cy. I can't say that she showed me how she was going to do it and that when she did, I used Cy's murder to wrestle away Emma. It was wrong. I know it. I traded the sanctity of my badge for the life of a little girl. I love my job. I want to help people. I know that if I ever told the truth, I would lose everything that matters to me.

I'd lose Emma.

"Turn Stacy in," he says.

"I can't do that," I say. Then I lie. I give him a line that I know rings false. "As much as I can't stand what she's done," I tell Carter, "I love my sister in some weird way and I can't do that to her. I can't put her behind bars."

"She's a killer," he says. "You know that, right?"

I answer right away. "Yes, but she's also Emma's mom." I swallow the last of my wine in a big gulp. I feel a compulsion to do what I've always done. Lie for my sister. Make excuses.

"There are some good things about her, Carter," I tell him, though it's hard to really be convincing. I detect a trace of upspeak in my own voice, turning a statement into a question.

He leans closer to me and puts his hand on my shoulder. It's a kind gesture. Not a move. As lonely as I am, I know the difference.

"I know you, Nic," he says. "You will do the right thing."

I feel like another drink, but when the server asks if I would like another round, I decline. I need a clear head. I need to decide what the right thing to do is and, more importantly, what the cost might be for doing it.

Chapter Forty-Two

Saturday, August 26

At home the house is dark. Soundless. But my feelings are a Vitamix on full speed as I look at Julian's photograph on my laptop screen at home. He's so handsome. His eyes sparkle with an intensity that I knew so well. The look he gave me when he "found" me in the shelter and brought me home. I was so stupid. So gullible. I mistook treachery for sympathy. Who does that? And now I look at the photograph posted on the *Puerto Vallarta Daily News* website. The article is brief. The way a lot of articles are now in a world rife with two-second attention spans. It matches my sister's story with one notable exception.

Yes, they were out sailing.

Yes, he fell overboard and hit his head and drowned.

The seas, however, were calm.

Stacy said there had been a squall. I know she lied because she needed to sell me on the idea of an accident. She had to come up with something more convincing than what she needed to tell the authorities in Mexico. Who knows? She might have had help. She was always good at getting someone to do her dirty work. My mind flashes to Marilyn

Morton, Stacy's best friend in high school. Stacy had Marilyn shoplift for her all the time. Marilyn got caught at the Tacoma Nordstrom store but never implicated Stacy.

I heard my sister on the phone yelling at Marilyn.

"Nobody will ever talk to you again, Marilyn. You burn me and you're done. Do you understand? You're my friend because you're stupid and useful. I can make things really bad for you. Remember Donna Lewis?"

I'm sure Marilyn did. *I* did. Donna Lewis was my sister's best friend in middle school. She, like Marilyn, was a follower, a Stacy devotee. I doubt my sister ever had a single relationship with anyone that was on equal footing. She was the star. Everyone else was a nameless, faceless backup dancer with the sole purpose of making Stacy more beautiful, smarter, and intelligent in comparison. It's funny how all those things are so clear to me now. Back then, whenever someone said something about her callous behavior, my dad said, "Well, that's just Stacy."

I wonder if the Bundys said, "Well, that's just Ted," when he was convicted of multiple murders?

I'm not exactly certain what led up to the incident that ended Donna's life. I know that she and Stacy had a huge blowup over some boy at school. I don't really think Stacy was interested in the boy, but she was sure that Donna wouldn't have him. The day after their big row, Donna ended up eating a bottle of her mother's pills and overdosing. I remember how shocked everyone was.

Everyone but Stacy.

"I knew that girl was weak," she said at the time.

"That's really harsh," I said.

My sister shrugged it off. "You can call it that, but it's the truth. Just because someone is dead doesn't mean they get some kind of character makeover and all of a sudden are an amazing person. Donna was a dud."

Stacy never wasted a tear on her friend. That's not to say she didn't cry. She cried only when she needed to. At Donna's funeral, the floodgates opened. Grand Coulee tears, for sure. Mr. and Mrs. Lewis spent most of their time comforting my sister.

She loved attention.

Always did.

I look some more at Julian's photo. He was smart, rich, and charismatic, but he was no match for my sister. I'll play along with her and I won't ask what really happened. I already know it. She got rid of him because she was done getting what she wanted. Like Donna. Like Marilyn. Like Cy.

I imagine Stacy's performance for the Mexican authorities as they retrieved her from the emergency call. I picture her flailing around in gorgeous agony over what happened in those iconic blue waters. How she just turned away and heard a thud. How she tried to get to Julian, but the current was too strong. I imagine she's wearing a bikini with thin straps that slide down accidentally as she reaches over to find comfort in one of the investigators' arms. Even in the throes of an ugly cry, my sister knows how to reel in a man. Instead of thinking of arresting her, they'll want to take her out for dinner.

Stacy would go if she thought she had to.

I turn off my computer. I know my sister. She knows me. She knows that I've looked up the article about Julian's death. I won't mention it, though. Neither will she. So much of our relationship is unspoken. I learned long ago not to pry too deeply into her affairs. Not so much because Stacy would push back, but because she'd tell me things that I couldn't unhear. Though I can't explain it—part of me loves Stacy. Or wants to. She's my sister. I just don't want to know more because, despite all of it, I still want to love her.

As I head for bed, it dawns on me that my sister is the dark flip side of "To know me is to love me."

◆ ◆ ◆

When I wake up, I resolve that I'll live life like everything is normal this Saturday—maybe my last Saturday with Emma. I pick her up from Carrie Anne's, where she has spent the night. *Too many nights,* I think. I cuddle her. We go to the grocery store—but not WinCo. She and I watch Food Network. I offer a movie, but she declines. I tell her I need to see my father.

"He won't know if you come today or tomorrow," she says.

She's right.

"No, he won't. I can see him Sunday."

"Let's just stay home," she says, with that serious expression that I love more than anything. She's thinking. The wheels are turning.

"If you want to," I say.

"You aren't looking at your phone."

She knows me.

"No," I say. "I'm not. I'm just here for you."

Her expression changes, and she hooks her arms around me as we sit on the sofa in the front room. I breathe her in. Shelby gets jealous and tries to wedge her way between us, but I don't let her.

"I know you have to work tomorrow," Emma says. "But let's pretend like you don't."

I kiss her on the forehead.

"All right. Let's pretend."

So we do.

CHAPTER FORTY-THREE

Sunday, August 27

I can barely breathe. She's gotten to me. She scares me. I want Dad to know how rotten that apple of his eye really is.

To the core.

It's Sunday morning, and I stand next to him in his room at Ocean View. We're alone. Just us. Emma is in the TV room. I spare her. It's what moms do. I am a mom. Dad's eyes are slits open to the vacuity of the ceiling. I'm unsure of what he comprehends, if anything at all. Sometimes I see a movement of his head that indicates, at least I hope, that he's acknowledging our conversation. As I sit there now at Ocean View, he hasn't spoken for days, but that's happened before. Alzheimer's is a progressive disease, but there are fits and starts to its cruel manifestation. Some days he will utter some phrases that nearly align with what I'm saying. Other times he'll blurt out something that is nonsensical in context but coherent as a statement. Most often it is about my mother or my sister. Sometimes I wonder if I've been completely erased from his memory bank. It's ironic. I'm the one who comes to see him. I'm the one who has told him that, despite everything he's done to me, I'm still here. I understand. No parents are perfect. My father was leaps and bounds ahead of my mother, so by default he becomes the dad that I wanted.

I look toward the door. It's just me and Dad.

"Stacy killed Cy," I tell him, leaning in close, because I really don't want anyone but my father to hear what I have to say.

His eyes open a little. Or at least I think they do.

"She probably killed Julian," I say, though I know my father never knew who Julian Chase was. I tell him not because of the *who* that she harmed but because of *what* she is.

"She killed our pony, Candy. You know she did."

A flutter of the slits.

"She's never been right, Dad. She's just like Mom. She's only able to function in Stacyland."

Stacyland was a word that my father actually coined, though I don't think he saw it as dark as I did back then. As black as tar as I think now.

"She wants your granddaughter back, Dad."

I take his shoulders in my hands. I want him to listen to me. I want someone who really understands my sister to get the importance of what I'm saying.

He lets out some air, but it's not really a response.

I grip the bones of his shoulders tighter—not tight enough to bruise, but close.

"Damn it, Dad. She's dangerous. She's not right. We have to stop her. We know who and what she is."

My dad winces from the pressure of my fingertips, but those slits never betray any real cognition.

How could they?

I imagine his brain is cottage cheese. I visualize the synapses still firing but getting lost in the gunk of his mind.

"Dad, I need help," I say, keeping my grip tight and my voice low. "I need to protect Emma."

Talking to him is ludicrous, and I know it.

And then I hear her voice. It's a pretty voice, but to me it sounds like talons dragged over a chalkboard. A sonic boom. A car crash.

"How's Dad today?"

I look toward the doorway, and my heart falls. Stacy has decided to show up. Her presence makes the room feel twenty degrees colder. I turn to look at her with a phony warm smile. She's dressed in what I think is Kate Spade, a white shift. Her purse is white too. Her earrings this time are teardrop diamonds. She wears two. *One for each dead husband,* I think. I wonder how long she'd been watching me.

And what, if anything, did she hear?

My sister is glamorous and beautiful and she attracts looks wherever she goes. I notice a couple of nurses sauntering by the open door to get a look at her. In Aberdeen at this moment, she's like a zoo exhibit. A vision in white. Probably someone famous. Definitely rich. Another nurse passes by, craning her neck to take in my sister's stunning visage.

"You and Dad seemed to be deep in conversation," Stacy says, now joining me at his bedside.

I release my fingers from his shoulders and adjust the sheet to his neck. My sister would turn me in for elder abuse if she could. Not that I was abusing our father, but I concede that while trying to make him listen, I might have grabbed him with more force than I should have.

She hovers over him and then plants a kiss on his forehead.

The kiss of death, I think.

"He's not really responsive," I tell her. "Kind of surprised to see you here. I know you saw him the other day."

"You come here all the time, Nicole. He's my daddy too."

Daddy. Her word of manipulation.

"Of course he is," I say, now facing Stacy directly. Her eyes are fixed on mine like lasers. I can't break the directness of her gaze. She's drilling into me, searching for a weakness to exploit, like a tick trying to burrow deep inside. "You look beautiful today," I say, because I know her weaknesses as well as she knows mine.

"Dress is wrinkled," she says, making a face, "but I couldn't do a damn thing about it. Got the valet fired, though, so at least no one else will ever have to endure such incompetence again."

It's the Quinault, I think. *Not the Four Seasons.*

Dad gurgles, and Stacy mistakes that for approval for "standing up for herself" and getting some poor SOB fired.

"You know," Stacy says, "you were always Dad's real favorite."

I look from her face to our father's. No one but Stacy was anyone's favorite.

"Thank you," I say.

That shuts her down.

She pets Dad's gnarled hand, scarred and misshapen from a life of hard work at the mill.

"When can I see Emma?" she asks.

"I need more time. I haven't had a chance to tell her, Stacy. This is big. Even you can see that, right? It has to be done in the right way."

Her eyes are lifeless, like a shark's. "She'll hate you for lying to her," she says. "You should never have done that. Not smart. Not coplike."

"I did what I thought was right," I say. "After all, you murdered her father."

My words are a jab. Not hard enough to provoke, but the best that I can do. "You shouldn't say that." Her lips are tight, and I imagine I hear a hiss wrapped around each word.

"It's true," I counter, pushing a little more. This is me standing my ground. "It's true."

Stacy's lovely face is now concrete. "If you ever double-cross me, I'll take you down on the same ride," she says, dropping her voice a little. "Then Emma will have no one. No family. Nothing." She stops and taps a finger on our father's head. It's more of a poke. "Maybe this mush pot will be alive, but really, who could ever count on him anyway?"

"No one will believe you, Stacy."

She hooks her arm through her purse's strap and hoists it up to her shoulder.

"I'm very, very believable," she says. "Emma. I need to see Emma tomorrow."

"I have to work," I say, thinking of a way out of this. "I'm in the middle of a big case."

"Fine, then," Stacy says. "After work. At the cabin."

Stacy turns to leave. A nurse has positioned herself at the door, and my sister nearly knocks the girl out of the way. I wonder if she heard what Stacy and I said. I hope not. She'd have reason to gossip about Stacy. Everyone does.

CHAPTER FORTY-FOUR

Sunday, August 27

It's barely five and Sunday dinner is over—a somewhat sad slow cooker special—and Emma and I take turns describing the best dessert ever. She's nixed my plan gleaned from a recipe we saw on Food Network the day before—apple pie dipped in caramel and topped with ice cream.

"Gross," she says. "Too gooey."

"Gooey is good," I say.

"I want chocolate chip pancakes with whipped cream and a cherry."

"Of course you do," I say. "How about some sliced bananas on that?"

She makes a face. No words are needed, but she offers her assessment anyway. "Bananas are gross," she says. "Slippery. Yuck."

"Right," I say. "Mushy. You don't like mushy. I know."

I'm in the moment, but I'm also thinking if this will be the last time—forever for a very long time—as I contemplate what I need to do about her mother and how I will handle the meeting at our old cabin. As I smile at her and laugh, I wonder what's wrong with me. I wonder if I'm like my sister, twisted and messed up. But not as bad as Stacy, because I can rationalize everything as doing the right thing.

Stacy might have done that too.

The bell rings, and I leave Emma and Shelby in the kitchen. The table is clear, and Emma is breaking out the tin of crayons to show me just what those perfect pancakes should look like.

I open the door to find a surprise visitor.

"Sorry to bother you at home," Debbie Manning says. "I remembered your address from high school. We were friends, right?"

She's wearing shorts that are too short and a hot pink top, both of which harken back to her high school days. Her style hasn't changed.

"Mostly you and Stacy were friends," I say, not indicating that pretty much was the case with everyone in town. Didn't matter that Stacy was younger. She was the queen bee. "What's up, Debbie?"

Debbie doesn't look happy. "This one needs to talk to you," she says, turning around.

Behind her is Brooklyn, her day care helper. She looks like she'd prefer to be anywhere but on my front steps. Her arms are folded over her Halsey concert T-shirt and I have a feeling that it would take two men to pry them away. She's visibly upset.

"I had nothing to do with what happened to Ally," Brooklyn says.

I don't know what she's talking about, and the look is plain on my face.

"You called me," she says.

I'm confused. "No, I didn't," I say.

"You did," she says, holding out her phone. I see her name right away. It wasn't a Mari who Luke texted. Not Marianne or anything like that at all. The name in the text sent from Luke's phone was an abbreviation of Brooklyn's last name: Marinucci.

"Can we come in?" Debbie asks, barely waiting for a response. "She played me your message and I told her we needed to get her ass over here."

I motion them both inside, and while they get settled, I give Carter a quick call.

"Don't start without me," he tells me. "This could be the break we need. And remember, she's just a kid."

"Right," I say.

I check on Emma and tell her that I have some work to do.

"Two people are here and I need to talk to them," I say.

"That's okay," she says, working on her pancake drawing.

"Looks good enough to eat," I say.

She smiles and focuses on her work.

"Can I get you something to drink? Pop? Coffee?" I call out from the kitchen.

"A beer if you have one," Debbie answers.

Naturally.

"Nothing for me," Brooklyn says in a small, deflated voice.

A few minutes later Carter arrives dressed in jeans and what appears to be a Western-style shirt. The only thing missing are cowboy boots. So this is Carter off the clock. Interesting. Not terrible. Just interesting.

While Debbie sips her beer, Brooklyn confides that she in fact had been having an affair with Luke Tomlinson. She sits on the sofa next to Debbie, her arms folded and her legs crossed. She's human origami. Her hair is up in a messy bun. A half-coin necklace lies against her tan skin. Her eyes are smoky, and her lips are bing cherry red. She's trying to look older, but she looks her age, sixteen.

She came of her own free will, and I don't bring up that she should probably have her parents there. Debbie, I rationalize, is filling that role. Slightly drunk, but there, doing her best Emily from *Our Town*, looking concerned.

"I had nothing to do with what Luke did to Ally," Brooklyn says out of the gate.

Carter challenges her. He's going to be the bad cop. That makes me the good cop. I prefer being the bad cop and how it unleashes pent-up anger from every aspect of my life.

"That's a little hard to believe, Brooklyn," he says, barely concealing his disdain for the girl. "Your texts say otherwise. You wanted him to get Ally out of the way."

"You can't believe that," she says, looking at Debbie for moral support, I think.

Debbie, instead, is focused on her now-empty beer bottle.

"I'm not like that," Brooklyn goes on. "I'm a good person."

"A good person doesn't sleep with someone who is married," Carter says, thinking of his own situation, I'm sure. "Neither side of that equation is on the side of good. Maybe no one taught you that."

I give my partner an exaggerated glare. He needs to stop this now. Brooklyn might be stupid, but she is underage and, technically, a victim. He reads me and, rightly so, draws back a little.

"Let her talk," I say. "She came here to help. Didn't you, Brooklyn?"

The girl nods. "Yeah, because I knew you'd find out about me and Luke. Those texts were embarrassing to me."

"But you sent them, right? And he sent them to you?"

"Yeah," she says. "But I was kind of role-playing. A game."

"But you had been lovers, right?" I ask.

Brooklyn reaches up and releases her hair from the bun. She gives her head a little shake to send her locks downward. "I don't like that word," she says. "Seems stupid. Like, we just had sex. It was for fun. Something to do. It's not like we have a lot of options in this town. Anyway, Luke was into me and I wasn't really that into him. It was nothing. It isn't like we were going to get married or anything."

"Because he was already married," Carter says, unable to resist another slap at his ex-wife through words directed at a sixteen-year-old girl sitting on my living room couch.

Brooklyn touches the gold half coin on her neck. "Old people live by old rules," she says. "Haven't you heard? Love wins. Don't be a hater."

I offer Debbie a second beer to give the interview a much-needed pause. I ask Carter to help me in the kitchen.

"You need to stop working through your past out there," I whisper to him as we stand by the refrigerator. Before he responds, Emma interrupts to show me the pancake drawing. I smile approvingly.

"Good work, honey."

Carter is red-faced but silent now. I hand him the bottle of beer.

"Give this to Debbie and let's remember that this whole thing is about a dead little girl. Not about you."

When we return to the living room, Debbie has her arm around Brooklyn.

"She's right, you know," my old not-friend from high school says, taking the second beer. "Times have changed, Nicole. Relationships aren't like those we grew up with when we were young. Love is more fluid now."

It's an odd remark coming from Debbie, who complained about being trapped with the progeny resulting from her romance and marriage to the high school football star who ditched her, but I merely nod in agreement.

"Brooklyn," I say, "tell us about those texts. What was going on there?"

"Just sex," she says. "'Booty call' is what your generation calls it."

She seems a little emboldened since Carter and I left for our impromptu powwow in the kitchen.

"Your conversation talks about him being free," I say.

"Yes. So what?"

"Free of Ally?"

Brooklyn laughs. "No. Not Ally. Mia. He was going to leave Mia."

"For you?"

"For himself," she says. "He didn't like her anymore—Mia. She just didn't do it for him."

I wonder how Sam Underwood or Rachel Cromwell fits into this, but I don't mention either name.

"All right, fine," I say. "Then you are telling me that being free was about his wife, not his daughter."

Brooklyn looks at Debbie, then back at me. "That's what I said, Detective. Can I go now? I didn't do anything."

Carter speaks up in a tone and manner that sounds suspiciously like a "dad voice."

"You lied to Detective Foster when she questioned you at Debbie's day care," he said. "You said nothing was going on with you. That Luke was a good guy. Isn't that what you said?"

Brooklyn gets up, and Debbie looks for a place to set her empty.

"Right," she says, shrugging her bony shoulders. "But I'm only a kid, just barely old enough to drive. I was scared. I didn't know what to say. I didn't think you'd understand people like Luke and me. We're not like you. We aren't conventional. We're in the gray area of sexuality that you just can't get. We like sex because it's fun, not because it has any real meaning."

"Thanks for enlightening me," Carter says.

"Whatever," Brooklyn says. "I can tell that you don't get it. That's fine. You never will."

"Did you lie about where you were between nine and ten on the morning Ally died?"

Brooklyn looks at Debbie. I think I see sparks fly between them, but I'm not sure.

"I was at work," Brooklyn says, heading to the door. "Hey, what are you implying? I was fucking the guy. That's all. I have morals. I would never hurt a kid. My job is all about taking care of kids."

Debbie nods. "Yes, Brooklyn is great with kids. She was there at 8:00 a.m. sharp like she is every day. Don't try to make it out any other way."

Debbie lingers a second as Brooklyn heads for the car.

"She's mixed up," she whispers. "Cut her some slack. Her parents died in a car crash when she was six. She's got a good heart. And, yes, she's been experimenting a little with her sexuality. Like we did in college."

I didn't go to college with Debbie. I didn't experiment, either.

"I didn't know that about her folks," I say.

"Rough stuff," Debbie says. "Don't ruin her life by getting her mixed up in something she had no idea about."

Debbie finishes telling me what she thinks I need to know. I shut the door and face Carter.

"What just happened here?" I ask.

"I guess I got schooled on the new way of doing things," he tells me.

Carter is older than me, but not by that much.

"Me too," I say. "These are the times we're living in."

"I still think she's a liar. And that's not because she's what we used to call a *skank*."

I smile. *Skank*. Such a funny, stupid word.

"She's holding back something," I say.

Emma appears from the kitchen with her drawing completed.

"Wow," says Carter, who gets the first peek. "That's pretty awesome, kid."

She beams and shows me her pancake art.

"He's right," I say to my niece. "That's the most amazing stack of pancakes I've ever seen. And that cherry on top—wow! That looks so good."

"I'm going to make another one." Emma returns to the kitchen and her incredible array of crayons.

In that moment the stress of the case and the encounter with Brooklyn evaporates. The world still turns the way it should. Emma is proof of that. She's more important to me than anything. That's why I'll fight to the death for her.

If I have to.

Later, I listen as Emma takes a bath. She's splashing around in a meringue of bubbles and warm water, unaware that her world's about to be turned upside down once more.

I hear Emma get out of the old claw-foot tub. A few minutes later she's by my side, wrapped in a white towel and brandishing a hairbrush.

"Your hair smells like lavender," I say as I brush out the snarls.

"I like that shampoo," she says.

As I continue to brush her out, I am grateful that she cannot see that my eyes are wet.

"School starts soon," I say.

"Don't have to remind me," she says. "Summer is almost over."

"It's been a good one," I say. "Hasn't it?"

"I liked our trip to Seattle," she says.

"Ruby Beach was nice too," I say.

She nods her head, and I continue to work through the tangles.

I test the uncertain waters.

"Do you miss your mom and dad?" I ask.

Emma thinks for a beat. "I used to miss them every day, but they are both in heaven and I know that they are okay."

"I see," I say. The brush glides downward. Smoothly.

"Yeah," she says, "Carrie Anne told me that once we get to heaven we get to see everyone again and that we'll all be perfect."

"You're perfect now," I say.

She twists in the towel she wears like a robe. "I mean, if you died in a car crash like my mom, you wouldn't show up in heaven all hurt and stuff."

"I like that," I say.

"I miss my mom and dad," Emma finally admits, "but I know that they would both be happy that you're taking care of me. And Shelby. They'd be glad that we have Shelby too."

On cue, Shelby joins us. She's older now, but she has acute hearing. Her name could be whispered in another room, and she'd be right there.

Emma turns around and looks at me. Her eyes are wide and wise at the same time.

"You're crying," she says. "What's wrong, Auntie Mommy?"

"I'm just happy," I lie. I've done a lot of lying. Best intentions or not, each lie feels like a betrayal now.

"I cry when I'm happy," she says. "When I watch a movie too."

I put down the hairbrush. "Yes, I know."

Emma's hair is damp but snarl-free. I give her a big hug and breathe in all of her lavender sweetness. She's perfect already. She always will be. I take another deep breath and try to focus on what I need to do. Stacy has given me a terrible task. I don't see how I can tell Emma that her mother is actually alive. It would be too confusing. Too hurtful.

The house is a tomb. Carter is gone. Emma is asleep. I lie on the sofa, looking up at the water-stained ceiling. A bathtub leak. *Great*. The day plays out like a thunderstorm, and I hold a pillow like a life preserver.

My mind goes to that place that I know is wrong, but I cannot stop myself from acknowledging something so true.

Killing Stacy is the only solution to ensure that she never returns to traumatize Emma again. It would be final. It would be irrevocable. It would also leave blood on my hands, and while I've done a litany of things of which I am not proud, I have never crossed such a line. Part of me thinks that with Emma at stake I could. Part of me thinks that's the big lie I tell myself because I want Stacy gone forever.

I do.

I can't deny that. But I also can't deny that I'm stronger than I've ever been. I know that is true above everything that passes through the history of my life. I know that the chaos that my sister brings is like a plague that clings to her—a virus that she sheds on me whenever she puts her arms around me.

Killing her would be absolute.

I try to get comfortable on the sofa in the house where we grew up, where I admired everything about her until I really saw her for what she was. The old cuckoo clock my dad bought at a flea market ticks away the time as loud as a jackhammer. Emma sleeps soundly upstairs; Shelby curls up next to me. I forgo a second glass of wine because thoughts like the ones that hover over me require a clear head.

If I kill her, I will be no better than she is.

Yes, but she'll be dead.

Ding-dong.

The insipid little wooden bird pops out of the door on the top of the clock. It startles me. Snaps me out of what I'm thinking. Most of the time I hate that clock, but right now I'm grateful for its aggressively annoying mechanism. I flip the record over. I roll the dice. I change up my thoughts to something that's closer to who I am.

I could turn her in.

That thought rolls around my brain for a moment. Enveloped in it are two things that I cannot deny or change. If I bring her in, she will go down for murder. If I bring her in, I will likely go to prison as well.

"You knew she was going to do this," they'd say.

"I didn't know it," I'd say. "I didn't believe it."

"It was your duty as an officer of the court to stop her," they'd say.

"She's my sister," I'd remind them.

The scenario could play like that for a very long time, but in the end I would lose. I would deserve to lose. What happened to Cy and Tomas was my fault. I trusted Stacy. Trusting her was somewhere near the very top of all the blunders that I've made in my life. Worse than gambling. Worse than Danny Ford.

The second all-but-certain outcome of turning Stacy in to the authorities would be that Emma would not have a single family member living outside of prison walls. She'd be a ward of the state of Washington, shuttled from one foster home to the next. Everything that's perfect about Emma at this very moment would be at risk of being erased by the mix of well-meaning and greedy people who foster children.

Yes, killing Stacy would be the easiest thing to do. I might even get away with it. But for how long? Telling Emma that her mother isn't dead after all is one thing. Finding a way to tell her that I'm the one responsible for her death is something I know I could never make sound reasonable. I would live the rest of my life knowing that, as dangerous as my sister was, I was the judge, jury, and executioner.

And that, deep down, I'd done it more for myself than for the little girl I love with everything I have.

Shelby stirs and I pick her up. She stretches her body and lies limply, happily, in my lap. Her satiny belly is warm. It calms me as I pet her. The right thing to do is oftentimes the hardest thing to do. Killing Stacy would be easy. Turning her in would be nearly impossible.

I shift Shelby a little so I can get to my phone and start a list of things that I need to do to make things right. The list is short, with only four items that need my attention.

1. Say goodbye to Dad.
2. Make arrangements for Emma's future without me and her mother in the picture—because that's the worst possible outcome.
3. Merge any assets I have into a single account under Emma's name.
4. Think of a way to get Stacy back to Bellevue so that I can turn her in to the police.

That last item will be the most difficult. I have a feeling that a Nordstrom half-yearly sale no longer has the magnetic pull it used to when we were girls. Stacy's taste and budget have moved far beyond a discounted Vera Wang blouse and a latte served in a real cup, not a paper one. She's rich. She's seen the world. She's far from the climber from Hoquiam, Washington.

I think of my sister, ensconced in her less-than-luxurious room at the Quinault Beach Resort & Casino. She's glued to her phone, flipping through the images of the beautiful people and the things they are selling. She's treating the images as though it were a fashion Tinder, swiping to the left and right as she decides what would look best on her. She's a product of growing up in a town in which everything seemed out of reach. Stacy has come back for a reason. It involves Emma. It's possible that she misses her and wants to be a mother. Not likely. But possible. She might be here for another reason. A place to hide out, maybe? Who knows what she's gotten herself into since she blew up the house and ran off with Julian? I wouldn't put anything past her.

I plan my next day. Seeing Dad, telling Carrie Anne that I'll need her to watch Emma while I go to Seattle, going to the bank to make financial arrangements, and, finally, making sure that Emma has a future. Getting rid of her mother. It might be the only thing I can give her now.

I picture myself in jail, then in prison. I try to hold that feeling in my bones. I'm lonely. Foolish. But I'm also a hero. I wonder if Stacy will be nearby. If I'll see her in the cafeteria or in the prison yard. Will she offer a wave and a smile at me or conspire with another inmate to kill me? I play all of those scenarios over and over until I think I can own them—until I think that I can live with either outcome. In a very real way, I don't see that I have any other choice.

And although it sounds juvenile and takes me back to our childhood, telling on my sister is the only thing I can do.

Shelby jumps from the sofa to the scuffed living room floor, and the two of us start up the staircase to Emma's bedroom. The vintage eyelet curtains I put up when we moved in are open, and a stream of moon-light falls over her. She's beautiful. Her hair is strawberry and her skin is peaches. She's perfect, all stretched out like a starfish on her bed. *My sister's old bed.* I pull a sheet over her and sit on the edge of the bed for a moment to watch her breathe. I wonder if this is our last night together.

I don't say the words out loud, but I compose what I would say to her if I had the courage to do so just then.

I'm going away. I need to take care of something important. This will be hard for you to understand. It is even harder for me to explain. Your mommy did some bad things and I knew about them. That means that I did some bad things too. I need to try to make things right, Emma. I need you to be strong for me. I need you to understand that whatever happens is because I love you more than I love life itself. Seeing you here in the room where I grew up gives me hope, it reminds me that new beginnings are possible. This will be a new beginning for you. And maybe for me too. Sleep, my precious. You have my heart always.

I lean in and give her a soft kiss on the cheek. She stirs. I don't want her to wake just yet. I don't want her to see me crying.

◆ ◆ ◆

It's the middle of the night. I wake up with an audible gasp. I'm sweat-ing. I'm sick to my stomach. I push my hot-water bottle dog, Shelby, to the side, and I find my way to the bathroom and sit on the toilet. I'm unsteady. I'm going through something that's making me sick. I turn and flush. As I stand, I look at myself in the mirror. The light from a butterfly night-light Emma gave me for my birthday casts a bluish glow over my face. I wonder if I will ever be the same if I resort to what I know will be something that I could never really live with.

CHAPTER FORTY-FIVE

Sunday, August 27

The coffeepot sits on the counter, and I watch it like a TV. I could run away. I could. I could get Emma and Shelby and pack the car with whatever I can fit into the trunk and the backseat of my Accord. I could do that. I probably *should* do that. I can't see any upside to Emma being reunited with her mother even for a short time. For one thing, Stacy is a snake and I can't trust her alone with Emma. I'd have to be like the CPS worker that sits idly by, pretending to read a magazine while observing every movement, every utterance. Even if I could do that and if Stacy would allow it, I still have the problem of telling Emma that her mom isn't dead after all. How do I manage that without revealing myself to be the liar that I am? I made up a story that I thought I could live with. I thought it would spare Emma the pain of wondering where her mom had gone. It would keep her from knowing that her mom had chosen money and freedom over loving her. Now I realize that was impossible. Stacy was never going to fade away completely. She was going to linger like that stench in Luke's Subaru.

God, help me.

I think of Dad just then. He's gone in every sense except for his living and breathing body. He told me more than one time that "the road to hell is paved with good intentions." Truth. I see it so clearly. My lie came from a good place. I only wanted to protect Emma from the nefarious facts of her mother's life.

God, I wish for a do-over.

Later that night I put my head on my pillow. I think how much I love this little girl with all my heart, and yet my dreams take me to the dark places inhabited by my sister.

◆ ◆ ◆

In my dream, Stacy is a smoking crater and I am peering inside, looking to see if there's any sign of life in her crystalline blue eyes. She sits on a blue velveteen chair with the Pacific behind her filling the window of her suite at the Quinault. She's ordered room service. A bottle of wine with a French label that I'm certain is of the type that's under lock and key at grocery stores sits in an ice bucket. Definitely not found among the wines that occupy my go-to lower shelf. Stacy always had a knack for the finer things in life. Dungeness crab claws encircle a salad that looks like it was designed in preparation for Instagram.

Claws. Stacy. *So precisely appropriate,* I think.

"You look a little wan," she says. "I ordered your favorite."

"I'm not here to socialize," I tell her, "but thanks for the compliment."

She lets my pushback slide by. Stacy never takes the bait. You don't have to when you set the trap. Or are the trap.

"Did you poison Shelby?" I ask.

She gives me a flat stare and crosses her legs. God, how I hate her perfect ankles.

"I don't know what you're talking about," she asks.

I don't even know why I brought it up. I told myself that I wouldn't. That she'd just lie about it. I can't stop myself.

"You sent the dachshund postcard to me," I say.

She smiles faintly and turns to the wine. "Have some wine."

I shake my head. "Then you did send it. Or you had someone else do it. I don't know. But it was you, wasn't it?"

"You must really hate me," she says, deflecting as she always does.

I take the chair across from her. How could this girl that I loved so much turn out like this? *My little sister.* What happened to her after Mom left that made her into what she's become? Or, I wonder, was it our mother's blood and our father's broken heart that forged this creature that looks so lovely but has no soul?

"I know you killed Candy too," I say.

"My pony?" she asks, now acting wide-eyed and innocent. "I admit what I did to Cy, but I had no choice. Now you want to suggest that I'm a monster of some kind that has left a trail of deaths of all kinds in my path. You seriously need to cancel your Netflix account."

I remind her that it was more than just Cy.

"You killed Tomas Vargas too."

She shifts in her chair. It's subtle, but I see the annoyance in her eyes.

"You are so unfair," she says. "That really was an accident, and you damn well know it. Look, I'm trying to make amends here. I want to move on and fix things between us. For Emma."

I ignore her olive branch.

"Stacy, something is very wrong with you." I find my eyes grow wet. "I know it isn't completely your fault. I don't know why any of this happened. I don't know what happened to you that made you like this. You need help. And as far as Emma goes, you can never have her back."

"I'm rich," she says flatly. "You couldn't survive any kind of legal challenge and you know it."

"I could tell people what you did," I tell her.

She shakes her head, and the diamond earrings, the size of dimes, catch the light and send an incongruous sparkle across the suite.

"No," she says. "No. I don't think you would do that. I don't think you would want Emma to know what you think of her mother. She'll turn on you. She'll know that everything you've told her was a lie. A car wreck? So unimaginative, Nicole."

She doesn't leave it there. Stacy-the-smoking-crater always goes deep.

"Mom always thought you were average," she says, pouring two glasses of wine. "She used to say she felt sorry for people who were average. Like, what's the point of living if you're completely unremarkable?"

She hands me a glass, and I imagine snapping the stem from the bowl and ramming it into her throat. Instead, I pour the wine down my throat.

"Aren't you going to have some crab?" she asks.

I finish the entire glass, realizing that some wines, in fact, are better than others.

"You could never beat me at anything," she says.

I find my voice. "I let you win when we were little," I say. "I loved you so much, Stacy. You were my baby after Mom left."

She sits down and scissors her legs. "You shouldn't have done that, Nic. Maybe things—maybe I—would be different. Maybe you are the reason I've turned out the way I have."

"You can't keep Emma," I say.

Her eyes lock on to mine. "I can if I want to," she says as the waves beat against the sun-bleached driftwood on the shoreline behind her.

"I won't let you have her, Stacy."

"I am her mother, Nicole. You are not. Besides, I never said anything about keeping her. I'm busy and have other things to do. You pretend that you're her mommy for the moment. I really don't care. I'm here to see her. Talk to her. Let her know that my disappearance isn't like our mom's."

For a beat I think I see something human there. But it's Stacy speaking. I put it out of my mind.

"You can't," I tell her. "It will confuse her."

"Yes, Nicole," she says. "You'll have to tell her that you've lied to her. I know that will be hard for you."

"Give me until next weekend," I say.

"You've had enough time."

"Please. What does a few more days matter?"

"Says the girl who doesn't have to live in a dump like this." Stacy gestures dismissively around the suite and its luxe fabrics and wall coverings. Not exactly *Architectural Digest* or *Town & Country*, but a far cry from an HGTV do-it-yourself building project.

Compared to the home we grew up in, the one that I live in with Emma, this is the Taj Mahal.

"Are you sure that's all you want?" I ask.

Stacy strokes the stem of her glass.

"I don't lie about everything," she says with a laugh that is meant to be ironic.

CHAPTER FORTY-SIX

Monday, August 28

Carter and I huddle over my computer as I push the "Play" arrow on the video from American Security Services. It has been thirteen days since Ally died in her father's searing-hot Subaru. The picture shows the area by the dumpsters where we stopped after retracing Luke's route. I try to advance the video to the 9:00 a.m. hour.

"This could be a while," I say. "The file won't let me fast-forward."

"Maybe Angelina can get it to work," Carter suggests. "I'll get her."

Carter disappears down the hall.

I watch as I sift through papers. At this rate, it will take more than forty minutes to get to the time in which we'll scrutinize every second of the video. I'm grateful for the video for countless reasons, although there is one above all others. It takes my mind off Stacy for a moment. I can almost feel the bricks she's stacked on my chest shift enough to let me breathe.

Carter comes back with two cups of office coffee.

"Caffeine is a good idea," I say. "Thanks."

He sits down and crab walks his chair a little closer to get a better view of the video on the screen.

"Angelina is in the middle of something," he says. "She'll be down here in a few."

"Nine a.m.," I say.

"Luke and Ally left McDonald's five minutes ago for WinCo," he says.

"Right," I acknowledge. "A drive that will take him about fourteen minutes."

The image looks like a still photo.

"You sure that's recording the scene?" Carter asks. "Looks still. Nothing moving."

I set down my coffee and tap the corner.

"Except for this rat," I say. A rat is grooming itself just under the first dumpster, by one of the wheels.

Carter leans in. "Cute little guy."

It's now three minutes after nine.

"Nothing," I say, feeling disappointment set in, though I try to shake it off. "The window of time could be larger."

"If he stopped there," Carter says.

"He stopped somewhere," I say. "He had to. No one could drive that slow."

Just as Angelina comes in, Luke's Subaru comes into view.

My heart drops.

"Need some tech help?" she says.

I put my finger to my lips. "Luke stopped here."

"Holy crap," Carter says.

Angelina hovers over me.

Another car pulls in. I recognize it immediately.

"What is she doing there?" I ask.

My eyes meet Carter's.

"Holy shit," he says.

"Who is it?" Angelina asks, clearly not as immersed in the case as Carter and I.

I let out some air because I realize that I haven't breathed. "It's Mia Tomlinson's car."

"What he said," Angelina says. "Wow. This changes things, doesn't it?"

We watch as Mia, as clear as day, gets out of her car and goes to the driver's side of the Subaru. She's wearing her nurse's aide smock—the same Tweety Bird that she had on when she came to the department to defend her husband against the charges that he'd intentionally left their baby in the car to die. Her hair is up. Her fingers jab into the air as she speaks.

"God, I wish these things had audio," Carter says.

Instinctively, I look for the volume control, though the recording has no sound.

"What is she saying to him?" I ask.

"What is she doing there?" Carter asks.

We watch Mia and Luke in silence. The camera catches Mia looking in the backseat at Ally, though she's too small and we can't see the baby at all. But she's there. We know that. The conversation is animated, though again we are unable to see Luke's face, only Mia's.

"Whatever she's telling Luke," Carter says of Ally's mother, "she's not holding anything back, is she?"

"Apparently not," I say.

Mia turns to leave and looks around. By my estimation, she's been there two minutes. Just as I add that in my notes for the updated time line, I catch something surprising.

"She sees the camera," I say, looking at Carter and Angelina.

"Nice," Carter says. "I wonder if that's been percolating in her mind. I hope so."

"She's a part of this," Angelina says.

I nod. "Yeah. We're going to need to tread lightly here. She doesn't know what we know."

"How did she come and go from work undetected?" Carter asks.

"Trevor said she missed a staff celebration that morning."

"Right," Carter says. "Wouldn't take her long to get from the hospital to the dumpsters and back."

"Ten minutes," I say. "Including the two minutes here. Still, we don't know why she was there."

Angelina reaches for her phone.

"I'm going to text my sister, Elena. She's deaf and a pretty good lip-reader."

"I didn't know that Elena was deaf," I say.

"I know, right?" Angelina says. "I don't even think of her as being deaf. I've always thought of her as just being Elena. She was born that way and Mom and Dad raised her—raised all of us—to just see that as a trait, like hair color. Something that didn't define her or us."

She sends a text, and a second later she gets one back.

"She can be here in a bit," Angelina says, looking up. Elena works in a medical office on Douglas. "Keep in mind, lip-reading isn't an exact science, but she's pretty good at it. Gets more than most do. This video is pretty clear for this kind of thing."

◆　◆　◆

Elena Marco Potter looks so much like her sister Angelina that I think they are twins, which they are not. Elena is younger by three years. Her hair is black, and she wears it in a bob that accentuates just how thick her locks are. While Angelina favors sweatpants for work in the lab, her sister is dressed in a skirt and blouse for her job as a claims mediator at the medical center. She smiles at us when Angelina makes the introductions using American Sign Language.

As she translates, Angelina glances over at me, then silently shifts her eyes to her sister. It's a subtle reminder of what Angelina told us before we gathered in the conference room to watch Luke and Mia.

"Remember, even when I'm signing, it's rude not to look at my sister. Deaf people should be addressed directly. Don't ask her to speak through me. Just look at Elena. Like I said, lip-reading isn't always one hundred percent. Some get only half of what they see. That's pretty good too. When you speak to Elena, just take your time and enunciate."

Elena's eyes are fixed on my lips.

"Thank you for coming," I tell her, realizing instantly that I'm speaking too slowly and too loudly. I tone it down. "As your sister says, we're going to look at some video. It goes without saying, but I have to remind you that this is confidential. We're in the middle of the case. You can't tell anyone about what you've seen here. All right?"

Elena takes a seat and gives an affirmative nod. She signs something to her sister, and Angelina translates.

"I will not tell anyone," Angelina says. She's not saying "She won't"; she's interpreting for her sister the way she was taught.

Before Elena arrived, Angelina told us, "I'm a conduit. I'm not speaking for her, but I'm using her words."

Angelina turns on the projector, and for once it works perfectly. The video starts.

Using both sign language and her voice, Angelina tells us that she was able to get the fast-forward feature to work. She immediately goes to the first frame in which Mia appears next to her husband's car.

Elena retrieves some glasses from her purse and puts them on. She leans closer to the screen. The three of us sit there riveted until Mia gets back into her car and drives away with Luke following her.

Elena signs to her sister.

Angelina gives a nod.

"Let's watch it again," she says.

I hold my breath as Angelina cues up the video for a second viewing. I think of Mia and how she acted at the funeral. I think of the neighbors and the coworkers who said that she was more interested in her career than her baby. How I pushed back on that because—as Mia flat-out told me—it did feel like she was being judged for going back to work rather than staying home with her baby. She said she'd searched the same things on the Internet as her husband had—because they were concerned. Maybe even a little obsessed with the idea. Cases had been on the news, that much was true.

Luke Tomlinson couldn't keep it in his pants. He was loathsome in every way. Mia seemed like the proverbial better half, though complicated, conflicted, and bitter at some of the things in the way of her achieving whatever it was that she was going after. *A nursing career,* I think, *doesn't tip the scales toward murder—not in the darkest of minds.*

Up on the screen, Mia starts talking to Luke.

Elena motions for her sister to pause the video, which Angelina does immediately. Elena starts signing and Angelina translates.

"She's saying, 'Don't do this. Don't do this to me.'"

"Mia was there to stop her husband," I say, looking at Carter. He pushes away from the table and looks in my direction. He's just as horrified as I am.

Angelina replays the same segment, and now that I know the words, I too can tell that's what Mia is saying.

Angelina signs and speaks to her sister.

"On to the next part of the conversation?"

Elena nods as her sister starts up the video. Elena's gaze is intense. She shakes her head a little as she watches Mia appear to tell off her husband. Mia's face is a study in controlled rage.

Angelina stops the video when Mia stops to take a breath.

Elena signs to her sister, and Angelina proceeds to the next piece of the conversation.

"'What's the matter with you, Luke? Are you crazy? What kind of man are you? Just stop this right now.'"

"You're right. She was there to stop him," Carter says. "Didn't see that coming. Didn't have any idea that she knew what he was up to."

"If she was so worried about Luke doing this," I say to Carter, "then why didn't she call the day care to make sure Ally arrived safely?"

While we speak, Angelina signs to her sister.

Elena waves her hand at us and indicates the video on the screen.

"Does Elena think she's gotten it wrong?" I ask, recalling that lip-reading may not be exact.

"No," Angelina says. "There's more."

She pushes "Play," and the video starts up again.

Elena stands and walks closer to the screen. Her fingers are out, and she nearly touches its surface. When she turns around, she looks at all of us. Her eyes are full of tears.

Angelina stands. "What is it?"

Elena's hands wave and swoop through the air, her fingers firing on all cylinders as she conveys what she's seen.

"Are you sure?" Angelina asks.

Elena nods.

"Here Mia is saying, 'You do this. You get this done. You do it or everyone will know about you. You know you don't want that, right? Grow a pair, Luke.'"

"That bitch," Carter says. "She wasn't there to stop him."

"No," I say. "She was there to make sure he went through with it. She followed him."

We sit in astonished silence.

◆ ◆ ◆

My phone gives off a faint ping. I look at the text. It's from my sister. I know I can no longer avoid her and ignore what she's after. I know that despite the fact that her presence has turned my life into the *Titanic* on her maiden voyage, there is nothing left to do but turn her in to the police. It's hard to say what she will do. She might fight it through an expensive lawyer. And she could win. She might grab me like a crab in a pot and pull me under with her. In any case, the love of my life, Emma, will be in good hands. I look over at Carter. His good hands.

Stacy: Don't forget, I want to see her today.

Me: I know. After work. I have a big case.

Stacy: You'll be a big case. Don't even think about screwing me over. I don't fight fair.

Understatement of the new millennium, one I'm nearly certain can never be beaten.

Me: The Ocean Shores cabin. Promise. I'll be there. So will Emma.

Stacy: Fine. I'll be there.

Me: After work.

I look up at Carter, Angelina, and Elena. They have been watching me text with my sister. My face turns crimson.

"Sorry. My sister. Lots of family drama."

Carter shakes his head a little. "Yeah, I know."

I turn to Angelina. "Can we show Elena the video from WinCo?"

"Good idea," she says. She signs to her sister, and Elena nods.

This video is far less dramatic. It shows Luke walking to his car and saying something to someone out of the range of the security camera. At first we thought it might have been Rachel Cromwell, since she worked at WinCo. But she told us she'd had nothing to do with Luke since their breakup.

The video that captured Luke after lunch with his coworkers at Jersey Mike's is ready, and we watch.

Again Elena is taking her task seriously. Her face shows no emotion this time as her eyes take in the movements of Luke's lips. When the clip is over, she looks at us, then at her sister. She signs.

Angelina turns the hand gestures into words: "'God, I shouldn't have done this. God, help me.'"

I look at Carter. "He's talking to himself. There isn't anyone there."

"Yeah, and he's full of remorse," Angelina says.

My stomach roils, and I know it has nothing to do with what I've eaten. I'm sickened by the Tomlinsons.

"Not enough remorse to save his daughter," I say. "She might have still been alive when he said that, according to the M.E."

For a moment, the four of us are lost in thought, too sickened to speak.

"He might be protesting a little much here," Carter finally says. "The truth is he's the one who left Ally in the car to die."

Angelina speaks up. "He's a pig and a killer. But Mom is the button pusher. Like, I know this isn't my area, but the tape doesn't lie."

I thank Elena for her help, and I turn to Carter.

"Let's go pick her up."

"Can't think of anything better to do," he says. "In fact, it might make my entire day."

"Week," I say.

"Year," he says.

"Since it is so close by, how about a stop at the jail and a little visit with Luke?" I ask.

Carter gives me that handsome smile of his. "Now I know this is the best day ever."

My phone pings, and I look down at a text. It's Ocean View. My father fell again.

"You chat up the prosecutor's office," I say. "I have an errand that can't wait."

"Must be pretty important, Nicole. We're in the middle of turning the Tomlinson case upside down."

I start for the door.

"My father's taken a turn," I say. "I need to see him."

It's a bit of a lie. There's something I need to tell him, but I fear I'm running out of time.

CHAPTER FORTY-SEVEN

Monday, August 28

At the branch off Pacific Avenue, I ask the girl behind the counter to take me to the vault. She smiles and I follow. Madeline, as her name tag proclaims in block letters, is wearing all black with a single gold chain around her peg neck. Her voice is soft as a feather, and she walks on sapling legs. She and I make small talk as she leads me to the entrance of the safe-deposit vault and punches a code. I wonder how many people face their darkest future while chatting about a break in the weather.

Madeline thanks me for being a customer of the bank and turns to leave.

I hold up my hand. "I'll need a witness for my signature," I say.

"I've never done that," she says, "but I think I can do it."

"You'll be fine," I say.

Madeline looks a little excited. I smile in her direction. She looks like she is at the start of a marathon. So ready to help.

I turn my key and slide the box from the wall and carry it to the table in the center of the room. The lid slides off easily. What I need is right on top of things that I've kept to remind me of things that I've done. My Lucky Eagle casino card pokes out a little, but I don't touch it. It's bright red like an ambulance's warning siren. I feel something inside my stomach, but I'm unsure of what it is. Sick, maybe. My gambling-addiction counselor told me to keep a few items from my worst times.

"You might need the jolt to your memory one day. In every addiction case outside of gambling, I tell my clients to obliterate every trace of their old lives: liquor, drug paraphernalia, porn DVDs, and the like," Melissa Tovar said early in my treatment. "Those things will come at them in the course of their daily lives, but not so with a gambler whose drug of choice is a casino, where the activity is centered in a specific location. Keep a reminder so you don't ever, ever forget how in trying to be a winner you lost everything you had."

I take out the envelope that holds my last will and testament, made here in Aberdeen when I returned to care for my father with power of attorney. I had Emma to think of then. Everything I had, small as it was, would go to her. I never addressed any of my personal wishes for her. It just seemed wrong at the time when I was lying about her mother's death.

To her.

To my lawyer.

To myself, even.

From my purse I retrieve a pen and a slip of paper with the verbiage that I copied from a legal-advice website.

I can do this. It's the right thing to do.

While Madeline looks around the dark space punctuated by stalactites of halogen light, I write out the words in a space on the last page. The young bank teller starts to watch as I lean over the broad walnut table to change my will. I take in some air. This feels good. Feels right. In the final line, I write in the name of the person I wish to raise Emma Marie Sonntag in the event that something happens to me.

Carter Wilson Hanson.

I look over at Madeline, and she immediately joins me at the table. I sign my name, write the date, and then hand the pen to her. She's young and fragile, but she writes her name with a strong flourish. Somehow that emboldens me a little. I think that if this updated legal document finds its way into court, she'll be a strong advocate for the authenticity of my signature.

I look at my phone. It's 12:30. Carter's back from lunch by now. He's dependable like that. Dependable is what Emma will need. I head to his office.

CHAPTER FORTY-EIGHT

Monday, August 28

I watch Carter as he pores over the Tomlinson case file sprawled out on his desk like the aftermath of a tornado—shards of the case everywhere. Photos, interview notes, and a time line appear to converge randomly but in fact are carefully ordered. Carter is a deep thinker. He processes each piece of evidence and looks for the places that can be linked to reveal what actually happened to Ally Tomlinson. Not just what people say happened but the truth of it all. He doesn't see me at first, and I almost use that as an excuse to just leave without telling him what I've done.

Or what I might have to do.

He looks up and sees the concern on my face. He reads me so well, and that, I would admit to no one, scares me a little.

"You okay?" he asks. "Case is okay, right?"

I step inside, close his office door, and take a seat. The pictures of his children flank him like a Sears portrait studio backdrop, a kind of realism that isn't really all that real. I know that he loves them. I know that if he could have any kind of a do-over, it would be to keep his marriage intact, his family together.

My heart beats a little softer.

"Is your dad okay?" he asks.

I shake my head. "No, it's not that. Dad's fine. Case is fine."

He neatens up some of the paperwork that held his rapt attention before I came into his office. Everything about that moment tells me that I'm doing the right thing. That I'm making the right choice to speak to him now. He asked about *me*. About my father. About the case too, but it wasn't only about the case. He cares about me. I know that.

"I changed my will."

His eyes sear into mine. He's looking deep inside.

"I don't follow," he finally says.

"Carter," I continue, "I named you as Emma's guardian if something happens to me."

He gets up from his chair.

"What are you talking about? Are you sick?"

I shake my head. "No, I'm not sick."

"Well, then you're crazy," he says.

"Not crazy," I say. "Just being practical."

I don't say anything for a beat and neither does Carter.

"You barely know me," he says, though I know he doesn't really mean it.

"That's a lie, Carter. I know you better than anyone. I trust you more than I trust anyone."

He walks around the desk and sits on its edge, knocking a pencil holder to the floor.

"You need to tell me what's going on, Nic," he says. "Wills? Guardianship? That's big."

"Nothing is more important to me than Emma," I tell him. "And I have no idea what Stacy really wants. If she's here to push my buttons and then be gone, fine. But I don't know. I really don't."

"Emma is her daughter," he says.

"Biologically, yes. But just because she gave birth to her doesn't mean that she can come in and out of her life anytime she wants."

"Actually, it kind of does," Carter says.

"She's a monster," I say, a tit for tat that I immediately know sounds juvenile.

He leans closer. I can feel tears come, but I don't let them fall.

"That's probably entirely true," he says, putting his hand on my knee. It's a gesture of compassion, but it feels strange. "But so what? The worst people on the planet can raise their children because they are the kids' parents. That carries more weight in our society than just about anything. You know that, right?"

My mind flashes on Sabrina Travis, a four-year-old girl from Bellevue who was abused by her stepfather in the worst ways one could possibly imagine; even now, years later, I cannot fathom how these impulses coalesced in his dark mind. I told the DA that Sabrina's mother was culpable because she was in the house when these things were happening to her daughter: she saw things, I was sure, and she'd chosen to ignore them all. I lost that battle. The DA insisted he needed the mother for the case against the stepfather.

"She's bad," he told me while I stood there getting angrier and angrier, "but not that bad."

After the stepfather was incarcerated for a laundry list of crimes against Sabrina, the girl with the saddest eyes I'd ever seen was returned to her mother. Turned out that Sabrina's mom was no better than her stepdad.

But she was the mom.

That's the trump card that any cretin can play.

Sabrina's mother was arrested for child abuse and sent to prison. She claimed that everything was a big misunderstanding.

"She's my daughter," she repeated over and over. "I would never, ever hurt my own little girl."

Carter leans back a little. He's opened the door to let me tell him what's really going on.

"I know all of that, Carter. I also know that Stacy is the kind of person who would stop at nothing to get what she wants. If I tell her that she can't have Emma as long as I'm alive, she'll look for a way to remedy that."

"Has she threatened you?" he asks.

I shake my head. "Not in the way that you'd understand. Or anyone, for that matter. Stacy doesn't have to say the words to convey a message. In fact, she's too smart for threats. She's a doer. She just makes up her mind and goes for whatever it is she wants. Money. Her husband's fortune. Anything at all."

Carter changes the subject.

"I'm honored, really I am," he says, "that you'd want me to take care of Emma. But I don't have much of a track record. I'm not even much of a father to my own kids. I see them twice a month."

He's treading water.

"I know that, Carter," I say, this time letting my eyes do the searing. "I also know that you would move mountains for your kids. Look at me. I don't have a lot of choices here. And even if I did, I'd still pick you. I need to make sure that Emma has an advocate—one who won't let me down. Won't let *her* down."

"You can't really think that your sister would try to kill you," he says.

"I'm sure she would if that's what it came down to. I'm just trying to plan for a very uncertain future. It gives me a little shred of peace of mind that you will make sure that Emma is safe and cared for, because I know the kind of man that you are. You'll make sure she's loved."

Carter laces his big hands behind his neck and brings his forearms together as he bends downward. I see the hint of a tattoo on his upper arm for the first time. It looks like an eagle's talons. He's never mentioned it.

"I don't know, Nicole," he says. "I don't think this is a very good idea."

I wait for his gaze to return to mine. This time I touch his knee.

"It's the only idea that I have right now," I say.

He nods. "All right," he says. "You need someone to trust. I'm here."

"Yes, that someone is you."

"Right." He mutters the word to the point of it being so soft, it is nearly unintelligible.

"Trust is everything," I say.

"You're telling me everything, right?"

"Yes," I lie.

I can't tell him everything, of course. I just can't. To say much more will bring tears, and I don't want to cry. I need to be strong for Emma. I want to hold her and to tell her goodbye, but in a way that doesn't seem permanent.

Though it could be.

I am strong. I really am. But I know that I don't have it in me to tell her goodbye.

CHAPTER FORTY-NINE

Monday, August 28

It's late afternoon, and the sky is slate. My hands shake as I sit in my car. I foolishly grip the steering wheel harder to steady myself. My knuckles pop. I can't let this feel like a goodbye, but that's how it does feel right now. I look up at Carrie Anne's house. I teased her the first year that I brought Emma here because she still had her Christmas lights up. She flicked my comment aside good-naturedly, as I'd meant it to be harmless ribbing.

"Look," she told me at the time, "when you have as many kids as I do, you cut corners wherever you can. Every December I feel like I'm ahead of the game because those silly lights are already up."

I breathe in deeply and head up toward the front door.

Carrie Anne answers.

"You're early," she says, looking at her omnipresent phone. "Emma's in back playing badminton. She's getting the hang of it."

"I'm here to see you about something," I say.

Carrie Anne sees the worry in my face, and I love her for that. She can be brassy and silly and pushy—sometimes all at once—but she is the kindest person I know.

"This seems serious, honey," she says. "Let's go inside."

I don't move. "I can't say much. I want you to do something for me. It's very important. I've made arrangements to have my partner, Carter Hanson, take care of Emma if anything should happen to me."

Carrie Anne takes me by the shoulders. "Arrangements? If something should happen to you? Are you okay?"

I shake my head. "No. I'm fine. But I'm working a very dangerous case and there's no telling what might happen."

I stop myself from telling her about Stacy and the kind of person she is—about turning her in for the murder of her husband, Cy, and her gardener, Tomas Vargas. I don't say that I knew of it ahead of time and tried to stop her. That was the biggest joke of all. Stop Stacy? Nothing stops her.

Nothing but me.

Right now.

This moment.

"You're scaring me," Carrie Anne says. "Really, you are."

I know she means it.

"Police work is dangerous," I tell her.

Being a sister, even more so.

"You need to keep Emma overnight," I tell her, my words getting stuck in my throat. "You need to see that Carter has her in the morning. I've done all the legal work. Don't worry. It might never come to that."

"None of this makes sense," she says.

"I know," I say. "I just need you to do this for me. I need help here, Carrie Anne. Please."

"Of course," she says. "I will help. That goes without saying. But you are scaring me."

Just then I hear Emma's laugh coming from the backyard. I could pick it out anywhere. It starts deep in her belly and then spills out like molten chocolate cake. Bursts of energy. Sweet. That's her laugh.

"I need to go now," I say, feeling my eyes puddle.

"What do I tell Emma?" she asks.

I hug Carrie Anne and give her my house key. "That I love her. That I haven't abandoned her. Make sure she knows that. That I have to do something so important that I can't put it off another day. That sometimes we have to do things that feel wrong to others when we know inside they are right."

"What's with the key?" she asks.

"Shelby," I tell her, turning away so that I don't get any more emotional than I am. "You need to go get Shelby tonight."

With that, I turn and go back to my car for the drive to the jail, where Carter and I are going to meet Luke Tomlinson one more time.

CHAPTER FIFTY

Monday, August 28

My stomach is still in knots from my conversation with Carrie Anne when I find Carter and Luke's lawyer, Thom Russo, waiting for me at the entrance to the jail. I suck in some oxygen, thinking that it will make me feel better. It doesn't.

Carter informs me that a pair of uniformed officers has picked up Mia from the hospital. He can see that I'm upset, but he cares enough about me to give me a little room. I need room. A lot of it.

"She's claiming harassment," he says.

"Too bad," I say, pulling myself back into detective mode.

Thom looks like the cat that swallowed the canary. I know that Carter has briefed him and dangled the "cooperation" carrot in front of his face.

"It doesn't change the facts of the case," I tell Thom, before he has a chance to say anything. "Your client left his daughter in the car."

The lawyer's face falls a little. He's been in the game for a long time, and as far as I know, he hasn't had a win lately. Being a public defender, especially in Grays Harbor County, tends to go that way.

"He wants to talk," Thom says. "I couldn't stop him if I tried."

With that, we sign in and go down the hall to the jail interview room. Through the observation window, I watch Luke as he sits on the other side of a table. A guard without a trace of expression on his face stands just outside the door. We go inside.

Thom talks first. He repeats what he told Carter and me at our last interview with Luke.

"This interview is against my advice," he says.

Thom isn't grandstanding. He's saying what he needs to say if Luke turns on him later and calls him ineffective counsel. I doubt that will happen. Luke's into this so deep that complaining about his lawyer, a favorite move of many defendants, wouldn't move the coldest, most jaded heart. Even one belonging to another lawyer.

"Luke," I say, "we saw the video of you and Mia at the old Red Apple grocery."

He looks down, his eyes refusing to meet ours.

"That was right after you left McDonald's," Carter says.

Still nothing.

Luke is hunched over the table, and I see a tear fall onto its surface. His shoulders quake. He makes no sound.

"Look," I go on, "we know Mia goaded you into this. We know that she had something over you. Was it Sam Underwood? Were you afraid that she was going to tell everyone about you and Sam?"

Thom urges his client to answer.

"Luke, you told me you wanted to do this. You wanted to come clean. This is why we're here. If you've changed your mind, we can stop. Detectives Foster and Hanson can leave you alone," he says.

"No," Luke says.

"No?" I ask. "No, what?"

Finally he looks up. His eyes are red, and his face is streaked with those silent tears. He's a wreck. I don't feel one bit of sympathy for him. He left Ally in the car. He and his wife planned it together.

"No," he says. "It wasn't about Sam. He wasn't anything to me. And, really, I don't care what the guys at work think about me when it comes to having a good time. I liked Sam for fun. Just like Rachel."

He doesn't mention Brooklyn. I make a note of that.

"I loved Ally," he says. "I did. Mia made me do it. She did. She wouldn't stop. She kept saying that she should have had an abortion and that it was my fault that she got knocked up."

I wish she'd had an abortion. I wish Mia's mom had had one too.

"What do you mean she made you do it?" Carter asks.

"She kept talking about it," Luke says, a trail of mucus dropping down from his nose, his eyes raining tears all over the table's pitted surface. "She kept pushing. Saying that we were too tied down and that being a mom was killing the authentic her. Something like that. At first I didn't pay attention to her. She can be kind of a bitch about stuff. I thought it would just go away."

"But it didn't, Luke. Did it?" I ask. I try to keep my tone even, professional. I loathe Luke Tomlinson, but I intend to bring down his wife. I need him for that right now.

He knows it.

"If it wasn't your affair with Sam," Carter interjects, "then what?"

"It wasn't an affair," he says, some defensiveness creeping into his blubbery confession. "It was sex. Don't make a big deal out of it."

Brooklyn shared a similar point of view when she and Debbie Manning showed up at my house, but I don't bring it up. Maybe I *am* old-fashioned.

"What did Mia have on you?" I ask, pulling Luke back to the motivation for an unspeakable crime.

He looks at Thom, and the lawyer nods.

"I'd been stealing stuff from work," Luke says. "Selling it. Mia was going to blab to my boss. I like my job. I like where I work. Lots of flexibility to come and go."

And to sext and send penis pics to guys and girls, I think.

"What kind of stuff?" Carter asks.

Luke sniffles and wipes his running nose on his county jail jumpsuit. "Cigarettes, mostly," he says. "That's my focus area at work. I handle the tobacco accounts. I'd go into the system, change the quantity on the invoice. Stupid tobacco companies got notification that they'd shorted our buy. Fell for it too."

"Then you'd sell the cigarettes?" Carter asks.

"Of course," Luke, much more composed, says to us. "I'm not that stupid. I'm not a smoker."

"Whose idea was it to copycat the hot-car case you saw on TV?" I ask.

"Mia's," he says. "She was the first to look it up. She told me that it would be painless. That Ally would just fall asleep." He starts to break down again.

"But she didn't," I say.

"No. She didn't," Luke tells us, crumpling his hands on the table. "When I went back to my car after lunch, Ally was alive. She was crying. She looked right at me. I panicked. I thought maybe I should get her out of there, but all I kept thinking was that if I did, Mia would tell. I'd lose my job. I was really good at it."

I think of that row of employee-of-the-month award photos outside of the conference room where we interviewed Luke's coworkers. Luke had won the award three times. I wonder if WinCo will want him to give those plaques back. Something tells me they will.

CHAPTER FIFTY-ONE

Monday, August 28

I study Mia. When people find out what I do for a living, they often ask me for insider stuff on what makes a criminal. There's no easy answer for that. It's a mix of nature and nurture. I've seen it in my own family. Stacy and I were raised in the same environment. She turned out to be a killer. I, a cop.

Ally's mother is slumped in a chair in a room that will approximate the size of the cell that I'm certain will be her home. If I hadn't seen her on the video, I would have doubted a mother could be so indifferent, so depraved, when it came to her child. Stacy and Mia are alike. Stacy never would have killed Emma; there would be nothing to gain. But she'd kill Cy, Emma's father, a hurt to a child that could never be erased.

If Emma knew what her mother did.

"She doesn't want to talk," Carter says. "Lawyered up already."

My eyes turn from Mia to my partner.

"That's all right," I say. "I'm going to do the talking."

"You should leave it be," he says, putting his hand on my shoulder. It's a light touch. A gentle one. It's meant to remind me that I can go too far. It tells me that he cares about me. He'll be good with Emma. If it comes to that.

"I'm going in," I say, opening the door and shutting it behind me. I know Carter is watching through the window.

Mia gives me a sideways glance.

"I told the officers I am not going to talk. I have a lawyer."

"I know," I say. "I'm not here to listen. I'm here to talk to you."

"Then talk and leave," she says.

I sit down. She's wearing a fragrance. It smells sweet, like honeysuckle. It's a pretty scent for such a monster.

Mia props her chin up with her arm planted on the table. It's as if she's in class, barely able to stay awake. So bored. So annoyed that she's in trouble. There is a brittleness that I see in her cold stare. I know that look well. I've seen it in my sister's eyes a thousand times.

"Mia, you are going away for a long time," I say. "You understand that, right?"

"Look, Detective, I'm not going to engage with you. You don't have anything on me. Everyone knows that my husband killed our daughter. The public is on my side. Enough said."

With that she takes her elbow off the table and pushes back in her metal chair. The feet scrape the floor as she pushes away from me. Around her neck is a necklace that is at once familiar. It's half of a gold coin suspended by a thick serpentine chain. It's the other half of the necklace that Brooklyn was wearing. I think about what Debbie said to me at the door.

"She's mixed up. Cut her some slack. Her parents died in a car crash when she was six. She's got a good heart."

"What is your relationship with Brooklyn?"

"She was the day care provider," she says. "She worked for Debbie. That's it."

She notices my eyes fixed on the necklace.

"So we were friends. We all were. Me. Brooklyn. Luke. I can't expect you to understand."

I've heard that song before.

"Try me," I say.

"We're poly," she says.

My confused expression invites her to tell me more.

"Polyamorous," she says, clearly enjoying the disclosure. I must look like a disapproving harpy to her at that moment. "You might think of it as group sex," she says with a know-it-all cadence, "but it's not. It's deeper than that. We enjoy each other. Brooklyn's my girl."

"Brooklyn is underage," I say. It's all I can come up with.

"So? She knows what she's doing."

"Like you," I say.

Now she looks puzzled.

"When you pushed your weak-ass husband into killing your baby, you knew exactly what you were doing."

"Whatever," she says.

I leave the interview room and the creature that birthed a beautiful baby but decided that she valued her freedom over the life of her child.

"What did she say?" Carter asks me.

"I don't even know this town anymore," I say.

"Huh?"

"Never mind," I tell him. "I have another monster to fight right now."

"Stacy," he says.

I put my arms around Carter and hold him for a minute. He hugs me back. It's gentle. It's kind. It's the kind of hug that I need at that moment.

"Thank you," I whisper in his ear, my lips so close that it's almost a kiss. "Carrie Anne is keeping Emma overnight. I'll be back tomorrow. I hope."

He doesn't say anything. Only a quick nod to indicate that he understands and he's there to support me.

And then I leave. I know that Ally's murder will be avenged. It gives me but a beat of comfort.

Right now I'm going to deal with my sister.

CHAPTER FIFTY-TWO

Monday, August 28

Ocean Shores, ironically, especially to me, was supposed to be a gambling mecca. My parents bought property there and put up a two-bedroom cabin that we used on and off before Mom left us. Dad was sure that he was going to make a killing in real estate, but it never happened. Hollywood people came. I remember how excited my mom was when singer Pat Boone encouraged her dreams of stardom at a celebrity golf tournament meet and greet. Developers promised so much. Like they always do. And then, like a losing slot machine after midnight, every bit of hope about what Ocean Shores could be was gone.

The Washington coast is no Pismo Beach.

I text Stacy to meet me there at seven.

Me: Emma is excited to see you. I told her the truth.

Stacy: Surprised.

Me: I know.

Stacy: I don't like to wait. Don't make me.

I want to send back something about how no one makes her wait because they are afraid of her, but I don't.

As I drive, a thought also rolls around in my agitated brain.

Am I doing this for me? Or for Emma?

My gun is resting on the passenger seat, mocking me. Challenging me.

Emma is undoubtedly watching Home Shopping Network now, Carrie Anne's favorite, which runs most of the day in her stuffed-to-the-gills-with-kids-and-toys-and-games living room. There may be no place in the world better for her to be right now. I imagine the happy look on her face. *A sleepover!* She's had a good dinner. She's surrounded by people who love her. That's what I want. I want her to grow up that way.

As I drive down our street, I hear the drumbeat of the Pacific. It too seems to be urging me on, reminding me with each wave: *If you kill Stacy, and are lucky enough to get away with it, you will be free. Emma will be free. The world will be a safer place.*

Lucky. That word reverberates in my mind. I can't shake it. I'm a gambler in a group program that teaches that luck isn't real. There's no anointing of one person over another with a gift of luck.

Stacy's rental car is parked outside our cabin, which looks to me like a pale blue shack picked up by a hurricane and plopped among driftwood and mops of sea grass. Her car looks so out of place. I park behind her and put my gun in my purse.

I'm a cop. I know how to do this. Get rid of the body. Clean up the mess. Never tell anyone what I've done. Not Carter. Especially not Carter. I'll just tell everyone that my sister has gone away. Like she always does. While there is no such thing as a perfect murder, some murders are better than others. Depending on whether you are the victim or the perpetrator, of course.

The door swings open, and my sister stands there with a big smile that melts into her angry face upon seeing that Emma is nowhere to be found.

"Where is my Emma?" she asks.

"She didn't feel well," I mutter, unable to really find my voice. "She doesn't want to see you."

Stacy gives me a hard stare, so I breeze past her and survey the living room. Memories flood in instantly. There were some good times here. The best times of our childhood. It is as if the space is haunted by our memories, the echoes of our voices as girls. The renters who just moved out took good care of the place, leaving our old table and chairs. We sat at that very table as a family. That was a long, long time ago.

"You never told her, Nic," Stacy says. "God, you are so weak. I should have never given you the option. Stupid me. Remember, fool me once . . ."

I nod. "Shame on you."

"Fool me twice," she says.

"Shame on me," I say.

Stacy is a master at blame. She always has been. She always had the power in our relationship. I'd let her win when we were kids because I adored my little sister. As an adult, I let her win because I knew that winning was more important to her than it was to me. I was so stupid to look the other way. I wonder if I had stood up to her when she was a young girl or an adult, if things might be different.

If she might be different.

I pull out the gun and point it at her.

Her eyes bulge. "Oh God," she says. "Get real. Put that away."

"I can't keep thinking that you'll come back and take her, Stacy. I'm sorry. I'm really sorry. But no matter what comes out of your mouth, I can never believe you. You don't know how to tell the truth."

I see fear in her eyes. I like that look on her. She wears it better than that J.Crew getup she's wearing now.

"You poisoned my dog. You killed two husbands. You killed a stranger, a kid no less. He was just there to cut the lawn."

"We've gone over that," she says. "That was an accident."

"God, Stacy, you have to be stopped. Something's wrong with you."

She backs away as I twist the dead bolt lock on the door.

"What are you going to do?" she asks, looking less fearful and sizing me up the way that she always did. "Shoot me then burn down this place? They'll find me. You know they will."

She's right.

"Too obvious," I say. "The cabin is in Dad's name. They'll come to me. I'm not as good of a liar as you are. Come to think of it, I don't think anyone could be."

"You are jealous of everything about me, Nicole," Stacy says. "Even my ability to tell a lie."

I reach for the handcuffs in my pocket. While holding the gun on my sister, I throw the cuffs on the table.

"Put those on," I say.

She gives me her coldest, most defiant look. "I won't," she says.

I fire the gun into the floor, leaving a sizable bullet hole.

Stacy's startled. So am I.

"Put those on now," I tell her. My voice is hard, commanding.

She fidgets and looks at me. "Look," she says, "I'll just leave town. I promise."

I'm not giving you an inch, I think. *I'm not that stupid.*

"On," I say. "Now."

She picks up the cuffs and snaps them onto each wrist. That look of fear is back on her face. I really don't like how any of this feels. I imagine telling the GA group about this and having them all applaud and tell me that I'm getting better.

"Facing the demons," one would invariably say.

Stacy is a demon. Yet, in that moment, in our family's old beach cabin, I must be too. I haven't thought this out, because deep down I never believed it would get this far. I never considered for one second that Stacy *wanted* Emma. Not really. Not the way I do. I thought she'd leave town. That she'd come to Hoquiam just to play with me like a cat does with a nearly dead sparrow, making me feel less than her and reminding me of where we came from.

And how I'm still here.

"You're right, Stacy. We can't do this here."

"They'll find my car," she says.

I nod. "I know."

I think of that scene in *The Wizard of Oz* when Dorothy and the munchkins are gathered around as the Wicked Witch of the West sinks into the beginnings of the yellow brick road. If you look closely, you can see the trapdoor rise up in a perfect square before the witch descends. I'm sinking now. I'm the witch. The trapdoor is open.

"I can't kill you," I finally say.

Stacy's fear dissolves instantly. Suddenly she's sugar in water. I'm the spoon.

"I didn't think you could. Take these off," she says, holding up her hands and rattling the chain between the two handcuffs.

I shake my head. "No, Stacy," I say, "you're right. I'm too weak to do what needs to be done. I can't kill you."

"I know that," she says. "Now let me go. Take me to Emma."

"That's not going to happen," I say. "Let's go to the car. My car."

"What are you going to do?" she asks as I keep the barrel of my gun between her shoulder blades, inching her forward to the passenger side of the car. The Pacific glows pink from the sunset. The hue washes over both of us, making me think of something beautiful in the middle of all this ugliness enveloping my sister and me.

I unlock the door. The sky is darkening.

"I'm turning us in," I tell her as I fasten the seat belt over her and go around to the driver's side and get in my car.

She looks confused. Not afraid. Surprised, even. "What do you mean you're turning us in?"

"You're responsible for Cy's death," I say.

"So what? He was a pornographer."

"Was he?" I say as I put the car into gear.

"He and that boyfriend of yours were up to their necks in that little girl's murder."

"Her name was Kelsey Chase," I say.

"You said *us*," she says. "What do you mean *us*?"

I glance at her. How is it that she can pick and choose what bothers her? The rest of us can't shake it off.

"Tomas Vargas," I say. "That's on me as much as it's on you. Maybe I can live with Cy's death. Julian's too. Not an innocent teenager's."

Stacy turns to look out the passenger window. "How many times do I have to tell you that was an accident?"

"It was," I say. "A terrible accident. One that never would have happened if I hadn't trusted you. You played me. Like always."

"Calm down," she says.

The funny thing is, I *am* calm.

"I was going to kill you, Stacy. Really. I was. I thought that was the best course, because that meant I'd be able to live my life, take care of your daughter. Break the chains of weirdness that made both of us who we are."

From the corner of my eye, I notice how my sister is struggling silently with the cuffs.

"You're an idiot, Nicole," she says. "If you confess to what you knew about the propane explosion, you'll go to prison too."

I nod. "Probably. Though not as long as you. But, yes, probably."

"I am not going to prison."

I hear her voice as a girl just then: *I am not going to school!*

The two-lane highway winds along the Pacific, and as I look out over the water, I wonder when I will see it again. Or Emma. When will I see *her* again? Will Carter be able to explain to her that I was trying to do the right thing for her?

A logging truck comes at us, and I blink away its headlights.

Stacy is quiet now. I don't like it when she's silent. It means she's thinking.

"I'm sure you'll come up with a defense," I tell her. "You'll say that you were in fear for your life. He beat you. Something. That you knew too much of what he was doing. You could say that. Convincingly. And that he'd found out."

Stacy's eyes are on the road.

"Something like that," she says.

I drive on. It will take us a couple of hours to get to Bellevue.

"Don't do this," she says, her voice now pleading. "It will ruin both of our lives. I promise never to do anything like what I've done again."

Once more I hear her voice as a girl: *Candy likes Nicole better than me. I only poked her with the weed puller once.*

"Did you arrest me?" she asks, looking at the handcuffs.

"No," I say. "Not really. Remember, I was going to kill you."

Just then, Stacy reaches over and grabs the wheel.

"What are you doing?" I scream at her.

"You bitch!" she screams back. "I'm not going to go to prison. I'm going to take my chances right now."

Chances. Gambling. That would have been my line. It plays in my head as my car careens into the shoulder and starts to roll over. One time. Two. Maybe three. I don't know which way is up. Glass shatters. Blood sprays over me. Stacy is screaming. I scream too.

Finally we stop.

The car's engine is still going, but we are no longer moving.

We are hanging upside down in my silver Honda Accord. I think of Carlsbad Caverns. I think of our parents. Of Shelby. But mostly of Emma.

I manage to unhook myself from the seat belt that suspends me from the ceiling, and I fall downward. I climb outside and crawl to the passenger side of the car. My hands are bloody. Dipped in red. Diamonds everywhere. Glass everywhere.

When I get to her, Stacy is panting like Shelby after a lazy hour in the sun.

"Are you all right?" I ask.

She looks at me, and I see a gash in her neck. A cut, I think from the edge of the shoulder harness.

I start to cry.

"I'm not going to make it," she says. "Am I?"

I don't lie to her. I shake my head.

"Tell Emma that I wasn't all bad," she says.

I look up as headlights stab through the darkness from down the highway. I find the keys to the handcuffs and undo the lock, releasing her wrists. I throw the bloody cuffs toward the ocean.

A second later a man gets out of his camper and runs over to me.

"Are you all right?" he asks.

I tell him I am.

"Anyone else in the car?"

"My sister," I say, my voice weak. "I think my sister's dead."

"Stacy?" I call out to her. By now her eyes stare upward. They are blank. Devoid of life. I know that she's gone, and as horrified as I am, another feeling washes over me. A sense of relief. It is so overwhelming. I'm falling down the witch's trapdoor. I'm in the smoke right now. I know that when it's clear, Emma and I will be free.

The man is calling for an ambulance.

"A terrible accident," he says. "Mile marker one hundred thirty-four. Driver says her sister's in the vehicle. Pretty sure the girl's dead."

He holds the phone away from his ear as he kneels next to me.

"Honey, what happened?" he asks.

"A deer jumped out," I lie.

He gives me a reassuring look and speaks back into his phone. "Says a deer jumped in the road. Dammit, that happens all the time around here. Should post a sign or something."

My eyes sweep back over to Stacy. She's still. Quiet. She's so very over. I take a deep breath. Emma is safe. I think that of my mother and my sister, maybe I'm the only one who knows that being a mother means doing anything you can to protect your child.

No matter what.

I am not a liar. Stacy died in a car accident. I didn't kill her. That's not to say I couldn't save her. It is very Stacy of me not to. It might be the only part of me that's like my sister. And I'm okay with that.

ACKNOWLEDGMENTS

The end of the publishing process (the part where you are waiting for the book to find its way into readers' hands) is a great opportunity to look back with appreciation for those who've helped launch it on its journey. I'm grateful to my wonderful editor, Liz Pearsons, for her incredible support and always spot-on advice. Liz's secret weapon is the equally talented developmental editor Charlotte Herscher, who did such a phenomenal job ensuring that the manuscript flowed smoothly and in logical order—not an easy task, for sure. Many thanks to Gracie Doyle, Sarah Shaw, Brittany Dowdle, and Heidi Ward for their help too. I'd also like to take a moment to acknowledge my awesome readers and Street Team for their enthusiastic support. Special shout-outs to Chris Renfro and Tish Holmes for their great ideas and enduring friendship.

ABOUT THE AUTHOR

#1 *New York Times* bestselling author Gregg Olsen has written more than twenty books, including the first book in the Nicole Foster series, *The Sound of Rain*. Known for his ability to create vivid and fascinating narratives, he's appeared on multiple television and radio shows and news networks, such as *Good Morning America*, *Dateline*, *Entertainment Tonight*, CNN, and MSNBC. In addition, Olsen has been featured in *Redbook*, *People*, and *Salon* magazine, as well as in the *Seattle Times*, *Los Angeles Times*, and *New York Post*.

Both his fiction and nonfiction works have received critical acclaim and numerous awards, including prominence on the *USA Today* and *Wall Street Journal* bestseller lists. Washington State officially selected his young adult novel *Envy* for the National Book Festival, and *The Deep Dark* was named Idaho Book of the Year.

A Seattle native who lives with his wife in rural Washington State, Olsen's already at work on his next thriller. Visit him at www.greggolsen. com, or follow him on Twitter @Gregg_Olsen.